THE CHILLI BEAN
PASTE CLAN

Balestier Press
71-75 Shelton Street, London WC2H 9JQ
www.balestier.com

The Chilli Bean Paste Clan
Original title: 我们家
Copyright © Yan Ge, 2013
English translation copyright © Nicky Harman, 2018

First published by Balestier Press in 2018

This book has been selected to receive financial assistance from EnglishPEN's
PEN Translates programme, supported by Arts Council England.
English PEN exists to promote literature and our understanding of it,
to uphold writers' freedoms around the world, to campaign against
the persecution and imprisonment of writers for stating their views, and
to promote the friendly co-operation of writers and the free exchange of ideas.
www.englishpen.org

Supported using public funding by
ARTS COUNCIL
ENGLAND

FREEDOM
TO WRITE
FREEDOM
TO READ

A CIP catalogue record for this book is available from the British Library.

ISBN 978 1 911221 22 7

Cover design by Sarah and Schooling

YAN GE was born in 1984 in Sichuan in China, and currently lives in Dublin. She is a PhD candidate in Comparative Literature and was visiting scholar at Duke University from 2011 to 2012, as well as writer in residence at Crossing Border Festival in the Netherlands in November 2012.

Yan Ge writes realist, witty fiction, strongly Sichuan-based, focusing on squabbling families and small-town life. She has been named by People's Literature magazine as one of China's 20 future literary masters. Her writings have been translated into German, French and other languages. Her fiction translated in English includes the novella *White Horse*.

NICKY HARMAN lives in the UK. She taught translation at Imperial College London before becoming a full-time translator of Chinese literary works. She has won several awards, including the Mao Tai Cup People's Literature Chinese-English translation prize 2015 and the 2013 China International Translation Contest, Chinese-to-English section. When not translating, she promotes contemporary Chinese fiction to the general English-language reader through literary events, blogs, talks, a short story project on Paper-Republic. org, and with the Writing Chinese project at Leeds University. She also mentors new translators, teaches summer schools, and judges translation competitions. She tweets as the China Fiction Bookclub @cfbcuk.

FOREWORD

LOOKING BACK, the days when I worked on *The Chilli Bean Paste Clan* were as quiet as the snowfall. It was in Durham, North Carolina. I was a newcomer who had barely settled in. There was no furniture in my one-bed rental so I put my laptop on the kitchen counter by the sink and drank tap water vigorously while I wrote. I remember when, in the middle of the night, I went to the fridge to get ice, the ice cubes dropping into my glass like thunder.

I remember how sweet it felt when I typed through pages and how cozy when I sank into perpetual melancholy. It was just myself, the manuscript, the desire to dive into nothingness and the profundity of the unknown.

Except that it's probably not true. I know for a fact that I had no idea what I was doing and that I hated every word I typed and called myself a fraud. For a while I thought I was never going to finish this novel and so I just gave up. I was binge-eating strawberry ice cream and quaffing four to five pots of coffee on a daily basis until I got sick. I cried a lot and eventually took a course on French literary criticism. This was all in the spring of 2012.

In the summer I came back and finished the first draft before August. And after that, all the pain and self-loathing disappeared, replaced instead by serene and euphoric days in which I just worked like the first bee in the hive.

And this is it. The reason I became a writer, and stayed one, is because I am forgetful. I've taken the habit of weaving everything into a narrative so it can be stored in order and remembered, except that I simply cannot and will not take everything in. The nature of narrative is that it's always partial. In order to tell a story, some parts have to be bent and some need to be thrown away. The strawberry ice cream was in fact zero-fat strawberry yoghurt; and I certainly did other things in Durham which could not fit into any narrative and have since perished.

When I capture an image, the rest of the scene is deleted. When I tell a story, the rest of reality is forgotten.

When I left my hometown and could relive it only through my fiction, I was saturated with nostalgia and tenderness. In the story of *The Chilli Bean Paste Clan*, there was a man who cheated on both his wife and his mistress; a mother who manipulated her children so much that they became oblivious to their own wills; there was a boy who abandoned his pregnant girlfriend to escape his tedious hometown; all the small-minded and self-absorbed characters, exhibiting their cruelty in a nearly comic way; however, I loved all of them hopelessly. I loved all of them and I was one of them. In telling the story, the pain and anger had faded, leaving only faint images of kindness and joy.

I wouldn't have been able to finish this novel if I had written it in China. The town in the story was virtually the town where I grew up. Through the faces and voices of the characters I could see my family, friends, old neighbours and acquaintances. Confined in this four-street-town, we had become extremely dependent and intimate. We cheered over our good fortune and fed on each other's misery. It was just impossible to write about this place because I was part of it and it was part of me.

So I really struggled. I had to swallow tons of ice cream (zero-fat yoghurt) and stay up all night drinking iced water; I attempted to understand Jacques Rancière and Paul Ricœur and took endless disorientating notes; ultimately, I needed to move to the other side of the world to write about my hometown. A place I lived in, loved, but could never return to.

I could never go back because it was in the past. Somehow, I could only live a life when that life had already been lost. And it was only with insurmountable distance I could write about the past. As I said, it was just the nature of narrative, the story of my life.

YAN GE, Dublin, 2018

THE FAMILY AND OTHER PEOPLE
Surnames in capitals

Dad (full name **XUE Shengqiang**), the owner of the local chilli bean paste factory

Mum (full name **CHEN Anqin**), Dad's wife

Xingxing (full name **DUAN Yixing**), their daughter, the narrator

Gran (full name **May XUE**), owner of the chilli bean paste factory

Granddad (full name **DUAN Xianjun**), now deceased

Uncle (full name **DUAN Zhiming**), Dad's older brother

Aunt Coral (full name **Coral XUE**), Dad's sister

Uncle Liu (full name **LIU Qukang**), Coral's husband

LIU Xingchen, their son; **ZHAO**, his wife; **Diandian**, their baby son

Jasmine ZHONG, Dad's young lover

ZHU Cheng, Dad's driver

ZHONG Shizhong, Dad's oldest friend (no relation to Jasmine)

GAO Tao, another bro, and Zhong's brother-in-law

Qin (full name **ZHOU Xiaoqin**), Uncle's childhood sweetheart

Old Chen (full name **CHEN Xiuliang**), the foreman (*shifu*) of the fermentation yard

And finally:
The Mayflower Chilli Bean Paste Factory

1

IN DAD'S CELL PHONE, Gran was listed as 'Mother.' From time to time, 'Mother' popped up on screen at peculiarly inappropriate moments.

Sometimes it would be during a meeting at the factory when Dad was trying to call the laughing, chattering salesgirls to order. Or he was out drinking with his bros, knocking back the *maotai*, the air thick with smoke. Or, worse still, Dad would be in bed, either with Mum or else some young woman of his acquaintance and, just when things were getting lively, *A Pretty Sprig of Jasmine* would ring out. Dad would feel himself going soft and, when his cell phone proved incontrovertibly that it was Gran, all the fight would go out of him. Floating gently to earth like a hen's feather, he'd pick up the phone, walk out into the corridor, clear his throat and respond: 'Yes, Mother'.

At the other end of the line, Gran would start to tug on Dad's heartstrings. 'Hello, Shengqiang!' 'Yes, Mother, what's up?' He'd stand, propping himself against the wall, just four or five streets from Gran. 'Mother, I know about that. Don't you worry. I'll deal with it.'

Then he'd hang up and go back into the room. But those few minutes had wrong-footed him. If he was with the salesgirls, they'd be gossiping away amongst themselves, if it was a get-together with his bros, they'd be texting or lighting up another cigarette. Or if he was with a woman, she'd be bent over scraping a callus off her heel. Still, Dad would give a cough, shut the door behind him and they'd get back down to where they'd left off.

The only exception to this rule was if the woman in the bed happened to be Mum. In that case, he had to answer a few questions about Gran first. 'What's up with that mother of yours now?' Mum would ask. Dad would come across the room, take off his slippers, and dive under the bedcovers. 'Oh, just forget it!' And they'd get back down to where they'd left off.

Dad put on a maroon striped shirt over his trousers and went out into the passageway. He called Zhu Cheng. 'Where are you? ... Right, come and get me then.'

He started down the stairs. He had only got halfway down to the next floor when he paused, then gave voice to a stream of poetic obscenities. 'You're vermin, the lot of you! Son-of-a-bitch, I'm gonna murder you all one of these days!' When he reached the ground floor, he lit up a cigarette and smoked it until, far in the distance, he saw the shiny black Audi approaching. Then he hurled his cigarette down, ground out the sparks under his foot, pulled open the car door and jumped in. 'Cornucopia Court,' he ordered.

Zhu Cheng turned the steering wheel and the car bowled along West Street towards the outskirts of town. As they crossed the intersection, Dad looked out of the window. The two streets were hideously thronged with people. No one paid attention to traffic regulations any more, not since the Tianmei Department Store had opened up here. One young couple, their arms draped around each other's waists, made a reckless dash across the road in front of the car. A young mother had her hands so full of shopping bags she wasn't holding her kid's hand and he charged out and nearly pasted himself onto the car's side-mirror. Zhu Cheng slammed on the brakes, just avoiding hitting them, then stuck his head out of the car window and shouted lengthy picturesque references to their ancestors.

'Calm down, Zhu Cheng,' said Dad from the back seat.

'These people need a telling-off, boss. They think I won't dare hit them!' Zhu Cheng steered the car through the crowds.

'Nothing's the same any more,' Dad said. 'People with shoes are scared of people without, and car-drivers are scared of pedestrians.'

'Absolutely! Chinese people are a bunch of idiots!' Zhu Cheng agreed.

They crossed Celestials Bridge on West Street. Just three years ago, a new park had been built there and the original smelly ditch filled in and covered over. Dad could see a bunch of old people gathered in the park, some chatting, some just sitting. Gran wouldn't be there though. He pulled out his cell phone and checked the time.

At the entrance to Cornucopia Court, Dad said: 'Don't bother to drive in, Zhu Cheng, just leave me here and you can be off. I won't need the car this evening, I'll walk home.'

'I'll wait for you, you can't go home on foot,' said Zhu Cheng solicitously.

'It's no distance. I can walk. And don't take the car back to the factory, come straight to the house and pick me up at eight o'clock tomorrow morning,' Dad instructed him. Then he got out.

Granddad had died two years previously and last spring their housekeeper announced her son wanted her back in the village to look after the grandchild, whereupon she upped sticks and left. Gran said she'd never find anyone else to suit and wasn't going to try, so now she lived alone in the family's old apartment, with its three bedrooms and two reception rooms, without even an hourly-paid helper. She just wanted the peace and quiet, she said.

Gran had lost weight since last year, and was getting shorter inch by inch, Dad reflected, as he walked up three floors, took out his key and opened the door. As usual, he couldn't see Gran at first. The apartment was piled high with books, magazines and newspapers, and it looked as if no one had lived there for months. 'Mother!' he shouted. Then again, 'Mother!' Had Gran lost her voice?

'Coming, coming!' Gran called back, emerging from somewhere at the back. 'Shengqiang ... it's you!'

'Yes, it's me,' said Dad, going out to the balcony to retrieve the ashtray which Gran had put beside the potted orchid. He took it back into the sitting-room and put it down on the coffee table, lit a cigarette and sat down on the sofa.

'Smoking again!' Gran exclaimed from her rattan chair, shaking her head.

'Ai-ya! Don't go on at me!'

'Well if I don't, who's going to?'

'All right, all right,' Dad said, with a puff on his cigarette.

'There's something I want to talk to you about,' said Gran.

Dad scrutinized his mother as she talked. Her hair had been completely white for a while now but she still had it neatly permed so that the waves undulated over her head. She wore a pale-green silk padded jacket over a knee-length grey silk skirt with white flowers on it. Her calves were bare below the skirt and, above her flesh-coloured socks, the skin was pallid and drooped as if half-a-dozen weights were pulling it down.

Dad let his thoughts drift back to the exact moment when he realized that Gran was old.

It was 1996, or maybe 1995, in March or April, and Gran suddenly got it into her head that she wanted Dad to take her to Chongning County see the pear blossom in Pear Blossom Gully. When they got there, the gully and all around it was crammed full of people. Gran sat in the car frowning at them.

Zhu Cheng, who had just started as their driver and hadn't quite got the hang of things, sat woodenly in the driver's seat and Dad had to help Gran out of the car. He took her left hand, and put his other hand on her shoulder to guide her out.

That was the moment it struck him Gran was old. Through her clothes, Dad could feel the skin on her shoulders hanging in slack folds which actually quivered as she moved. He froze, appalled. Then Gran said: 'Get out of my way, Shengqiang. If you stand in my way, how can I walk?'

Dad took a step back and watched as she made her way to Pear Blossom Gully. 'Mother,' he called.

Gran stopped and looked back. She looked just as normal, no different from a few minutes before, but Dad had to steel himself to look her in the face.

'Come on!' She said.

On their way back to Pingle Town, Gran had said: 'Don't you go divorcing Anqin, there's too much at stake. She did wrong, but now she's got down on her knees and grovelled to you, just let it go. The pair of you should stop bickering and just muddle along together.'

Dad gave a non-committal grunt. His right hand still tingled.

'Are you listening to me, Shengqiang?' demanded Gran now, after waiting in vain for his response.

'Yes, right,' Dad said again, putting out his cigarette, lifting his eyes from her calves and nodding.

'Off you go then. I'm going to read for a bit and then go to bed.'

'Yes, you get an early night, Mother,' said Dad stolidly.

Outside Gran's apartment, Dad paused for a moment, then went up to the fifth floor. Here, the staircase ended and two lonely doors faced each other. Dad took out his cell phone and made a call. It rang just once, then someone answered.

'Open up,' said Dad.

In a second, the door had opened. Pretty Jasmine Zhong stood there, her hair hanging in a gleaming black curtain around her dainty face.

Dad's face finally cracked a smile. He went in, shutting the door behind him.

In Dad's cell phone, Jasmine Zhong had gone under a variety of guises, all masculine. A few months ago, she'd been listed as Zhong Zhong, then for a couple of weeks, it changed to Zhong Jun; recently Dad had decided to keep life simple, and he listed her as just Zhong. Once, Dad had been at home eating dinner with his phone beside him on the table and it rang. Dad didn't pick it up straightaway and Mum leaned over and took a look. 'It's your friend Zhong,' she said.

'Oh,' said Dad. 'Hey, bro,' he said into the phone. 'I'm at home having dinner. A game of *mahjong*, eh?'

There was a gasp of surprise from Jasmine at the other end.

'When I've finished eating,' he went on with a smile, 'I've got to do the washing-up too.'

He put the phone down and Mum said: 'It's been a long time since Zhong asked you over for a game of *mahjong*, isn't it?'

'Yes,' said Dad, selecting some pepper and aubergine with his chopsticks then raking some rice into his mouth. 'When I've washed up, I'll go round and see him.'

'You go as soon as you've finished dinner,' said Mum, looking sidelong at him. 'Any mention of *mahjong* drives you crazy, I know. I'll wash the dishes.'

And Dad went off happily, congratulating himself on having cleverly listed both the girl and his old friend under 'Zhong'. It had been an inspired choice.

A little later that evening, Jasmine asked him: 'So I'm your bro now, am I?'

'Uh–huh,' said Dad, who was engrossed in caressing her breasts. They were not big breasts, but, under his caress, they were cool and weighed in his hand like antique jade.

'Then call me that!' Jasmine ordered him with a giggle.

'Hey, bro!' he said.

'Oh, what a good little boy!' she responded with delight, sticking her bottom in the air then grinding herself against him.

To be perfectly honest, it was this foolishness that Dad really liked about Jasmine. When they were having sex, he liked to yell: 'Stupid cow!' at her. Jasmine never got angry at being called names, in fact she acted up to it.

She and Dad had been an item for nearly two years now and, it has to be said, Granddad could take some of the credit for the affair.

Just three months before Granddad died, a fortnight into the New Year—Granddad was then eighty-four, coming up eighty-five, and Gran had just turned seventy-eight—Dad's phone rang early one morning.

The shrill ring startled him and Mum awake.

Dad fumbled for the phone and saw Gran's name on the screen. He stifled his irritation and said: 'Yes, Mother.'

Gran was weeping down the line. Dad rolled over and sat upright. 'What's the matter, Mother?'

'I want to divorce your Dad! I want to divorce your Dad!' she wailed.

Mum and Dad got dressed and Mum drove Dad there in her car. 'Are you sure you weren't mistaken, she really wants a divorce?' she asked as she drove.

But there was no mistake. They got to Cornucopia Court, and Mum went to park the car while Dad took the stairs two at a time and let himself into the apartment. Gran was in the sitting room, her tear-streaked face hidden in her hands.

'Mother, don't cry,' said Dad going over to Gran. 'Just tell me what's happened.'

'Ask your father!' said Gran, with a jab of her finger in the direction of the balcony.

Granddad was sitting out there in the cold, in a rattan chair, wearing a leather overcoat over his vest and long-johns, puffing away at a cigarette and dropping cigarette ash all over his fur collar.

'What's up?' Dad asked, going out onto the balcony.

Granddad shook his head but said nothing.

'Your father's got a mistress!' Gran's voice came from the sitting room.

Dad didn't know whether to laugh or cry. He exchanged complicit glances with his father and said: 'You're quite a one, Dad! Still up to it at your age!'

Granddad gave a dry laugh. Mum arrived at that point, and Gran set up a wail as if someone was trampling her underfoot.

'Mother!' Mum cried, hesitating in the doorway and looking through to Dad on the balcony.

He gave a careless wave. Mum gathered nothing terrible had happened. She approached Gran, crouched down, and put a comforting hand on her shoulder. Softly she said: 'Mother, don't cry. Tell me all about it.'

'I can't go on like this,' said Gran. 'I told him, I've had enough of house-keeping for him. Let him go off with whoever he wants, I just want peace and quiet.'

The housekeeper had gone back home for the New Year a few days before. So Mum heated up the previous day's chicken soup, and prepared noodles and pickled vegetables, so that at least they could have some breakfast.

'Shengqiang, after breakfast you can phone your sister and get her back here. I'm going to divorce your Dad today. I've always been a decent, honest woman and I won't force him to stay with me, he can go off and have his fun, it wouldn't be right for me to stand in his way.'

Granddad buried his face in his bowl and said nothing. Dad was about to speak but Mum tugged at his sleeve.

Gran never did talk to Aunt Coral and Dad thought that it had all blown over.

But three months later, Granddad's blood pressure shot up and he was admitted to Pingle Hospital. And right up until the day he died, Gran refused to step outside the door of their apartment. Everyone had a go at persuading her—Mum, Dad, Aunt Coral, Uncle Liu too—but she wouldn't go and see Granddad.

'No!' she said. 'Get that cow to go and see him instead.'

After much thought, Dad felt he should broach the subject with the old man. He sat down at his bedside and asked him: 'Is there anything you'd like me to take care of? I can do it for you.'

Granddad looked at Dad, took a last breath, shook his head and, gripping Dad's hand, passed away.

It was the end of the road for a hero and sadness welled up in Dad. He suppressed the tears, but he couldn't suppress his anger. Hell! Less than two months later, Dad took up with Jasmine Zhong, a salesgirl at Longteng Telecoms City, and installed her upstairs from Gran's apartment. Son-of-a-bitch, these stupid cows. 'I'll murder you all one of these days!' Dad used to say.

That's right. Dad used to pepper his love-making with a lot of swearing.

Truth be told, Dad was not a bad man. Just two months after his seventeenth birthday, Gran got him his first job in the chilli bean paste factory, where Chen Xiuliang became his *shifu* and taught him his trade. Chen Xiuliang was also not a bad sort, just a bit lazy and fond of his tobacco. Every day when Dad left his home to walk to work, he had to stop off and buy him a packet of Peony cigarettes. Chen would accept them with a beaming smile and put Dad to work. Without the cigarettes, no doubt he would have indulged in a bit of bad language—and still put Dad to work.

Thinking back, it must have been 1983, or perhaps 84, and the way Mum told it, it was Dad's job was to keep watch on the fermentation vats. It was the end of May, nearly June. The sap was rising, the air was full of flies and sparrows and the ground crawled with *jiuxiang* bugs and mole crickets. But this was also the time when the townsfolk had to get busy fermenting the bean paste in the sunshine. Gran pointed with her slender white hand and Dad was taken off by Chen and left to kick his heels all day in the fermentation yard.

Fermenting the bean paste in Pingle Town was an esoteric art; few outsiders had seen it, while Dad had seen enough to make him sick of it. Serried ranks of earthenware vats, three or four feet tall and with a girth as big as two arm spans, held a bubbling mixture of broad beans which had been left to go mouldy, to which were added crushed chilli peppers and seasonings like star anise, bay leaves, and great handfuls of salt. As the days went by in the hot sunshine, the chilli peppers fermented, releasing their oil and a smell which was at first fragrant, then sour. Sometimes the sun was so strong that the brick–red paste in the vats boiled up and started to bubble. Then Dad had to take a stout length of wood as tall as he was and, vat by vat, stir the contents. It was vital to stir the mixture and Chen spent a lot of time instructing Dad and clipping him around the head to get the message across. 'Slowly, slowly,' he would shout, standing to one side, cigarette between his lips, making pressing-down motions with his hands. So Dad slowed down, manipulating the stirring pole as if it was a spoon, but Chen was annoyed again. 'Quicker!' he shouted. 'Get some speed up!'

As the pole went around, the chilli oil vapour rushed up Dad's nostrils. It was so pungent it seemed to reach right down his guts and turn them bright red. Finally Dad had had enough and, flinging the pole into the vat, shouted: 'You want it slow or quick? Stop messing with me!'

'Your Dad thought he'd get a beating for that!' Mum told me.

But he didn't. Instead, Chen pensively finished his cigarette, threw the butt to the ground and ground it under his heel then, all smiles, he went and picked up the pole and demonstrated to Dad how to do it.

'Xue Shengqiang, you watch carefully. Hold the pole tight but relax your wrist, and move the pole from side to side. And remember something else, I'm only going to tell you once: you stir the beans the way you fuck a woman, you get me? Think of the vat as a woman's cunt, if you make her happy, then you're stirring properly.' Dad hadn't fucked any woman yet, in fact he still hadn't figured out what those bits of a woman even looked like, and he watched his *shifu*, agog.

Chen rhythmically stirred the beans as if this was a witches' brew: slow, slow, quicker, a couple of flicks of the wrist, slowing down again, until the sludge gave off liquid moans and exuded flaming red chilli oil. A strong musky odour rose into the air and Dad, as he stood staring in the fermentation yard, got an erection.

Needless to say, in the fullness of time, Dad became a pretty good stirrer. He reckoned he was pretty good at fucking women too.

I haven't said just how Dad was a good man. It wasn't nearly as glorious as the way he learnt to stir the beans, and Mum didn't tell me about it either, but in Pingle Town everything leaked out sooner or later.

Dad never spoke about it but he can't have forgotten how that summer he nearly drove himself mad thinking about women.

It was all the fault of that fucking Chen. Dad lay drenched in sweat on his bamboo sleeping mat, cursing the man as he jerked off and fantasized about the prettiest girls in town, wondering what they looked like naked and so on and so forth.

But Dad kept his wits about him. The way he figured it, he was very unlikely to get a girl to fool around with, at least without the other townsfolk or Gran finding out. So after he'd spent a week wanking he decided to go off to Fifteen Yuan Street, and pay a reasonable price to get a woman naked.

Fifteen Yuan Street doesn't exist anymore, or rather it appears no longer to be there. But if you know the password, you can find the way in. The bums and petty criminals of Pingle Town all know exactly where it is, in other words, all the townsfolk are only pretending not to know. In actual fact, if you head out of town on South Street, as you get near to Factory 372, there is an inconspicuous little road with osmanthus bushes dotted along it and ropes strung from the branches on which towels and wet clothes sometimes hang. This is the famous Fifteen Yuan Street. It wasn't called that when Dad was young, in fact, it wasn't even a street, it was where Baby Girl lived and did a bit of business in her home. Dad had heard she charged five *yuan*, or four *yuan* 50 if you were lucky. It took ten years for this to turn into the famous Fifteen Yuan Street—that became the going rate after a whole bunch of other women moved in as Baby Girl's neighbours. Business boomed, with some vermin even catching the one *yuan* 50 minibus from Yong'An City, to get themselves a woman. But when Dad paid another visit, in 2000, or perhaps it was 2002, the woman put out her hand: '150 *yuan*.' And that was when Dad felt that the good times really were gone for good.

In the year 2000, or 2002, coughing up 150 *yuan* was nothing to Dad. But a dozen or so years before, things had been very different. He spent a long time racking his brains over how to get hold of five *yuan*.

Every day, Dad ate breakfast at home, then went to work at the chilli bean paste factory, where he had his lunch and dinner. Apart from the money he bought Chen's cigarettes with, he had no other pocket money. So he devised a plan based on Chen's cigarette money. A pack of Peony brand cost 53 cents, but a pack of Jiaxiu cost 24 cents, so he could save 29 cents a day and in 18 days he'd have enough to go and see Baby Girl. There was another, even bolder, plan: a pack of Peony brand cost 53 cents, but a pack of Silver Fir was only 13 cents. That way, he could save 40 cents a day and could make it in thirteen days' time.

Dad did the sums on a scrap of paper three times and pondered that five days' difference as he stood in front of the tobacconists eyeing the cigarette packets on display, his head full of those women. Finally, he steeled himself and said to the shop-owner: 'A packet of Silver Fir.'

Chen didn't say anything, just took the packet, squinted at it and grunted. After all, a smoke was a smoke. It was the height of summer, and he sat under the big eucalyptus in his sleeveless vest, half a Silver Fir dangling from his lips. The sun was so dazzling, Dad could not see anything, so he stopped looking at Chen Xiuliang and went off, head bowed, to give his beans a stir.

The sound of the bubbling beans nearly fucking finished Dad off when he was a young man. Even now when Dad passes the fermentation yard, he can't help sneaking glances at those perfectly aligned rows of bean-paste vats where he had had his sexual awakening.

To cut a long story short, Dad bought Chen Xiuliang Silver Fir for thirteen days, and finally scraped together five *yuan* 20. That day he marched proudly off to Fifteen Yuan Street, head held high, to lose his virginity. His memories of that day are a bit hazy, whether because Baby Girl was so professional or he was just a natural, he's not too sure. He's never forgotten her ecstatic cries however. They were something else. When he'd finished, he gave her every cent he had.

'You've given me 20 cents too much, kid,' she said kindly.

'That's for you,' Dad said, modestly playing down his generosity.

So in the end, the earnest maxims that Gran had drummed into him from boyhood had had an effect; they had turned Dad into a young philanthropist.

One evening, Dad was at the Floating Fragrance Restaurant with his bros Gao Tao and Zhong Shizhong and somehow the conversation turned to Baby Girl from Fifteen Yuan Street. Gao Tao took a last puff on his cigarette and stubbed it out on the tail of the duck in the dish. He shook his finger at Dad and said in a slurred voice: 'You remember Baby Girl, Zhong? That was Shengqiang's first love!' '"First love", be buggered!' Dad spat out angrily. There was no way he was going to admit that Baby Girl had been the one to take his virginity. Zhong carried on regardless: 'As I remember, you were forever running off to Fifteen Yuan Street as a young lad. You even stole a rabbit from the Huangs and sold it to pay for Baby Girl, do you remember?' Dad and his friends had somehow arrived at an age when, with a drop of drink in them, they'd start reminiscing about the good old days. 'I remember it like it was yesterday!' Zhong was getting into his stride. 'His mother was so angry with him, the wee prawn had to come and stay two nights with me!'

'You two old farts! That was a lifetime ago! Can't you think of anything else to talk about?' Dad grabbed a half-empty pack of cigarettes from the table and threw it at Zhong's head; Zhong gaily caught the pack, shook a cigarette out of it and lit it. Their waitress giggled behind her hand.

'Anyway,' Zhong took a couple of puffs and pulled himself together, 'how is the old lady, your mother?'

'She's very lively!' said Dad. 'She had me over the day before yesterday to talk about her eightieth birthday celebrations.'

'Ai-ya!' Gao Tao exclaimed, clapping his hands together. 'It's a big deal, an eightieth birthday! You'd better do a good job of organizing it!'

'Of course I will!' Dad picked up a piece of duck with his chopsticks and crunched it up, bone and all. 'The old lady says she wants the whole family to be there, my big sister, my big brother, everyone. Then there are relatives who live in the Pingle Town, and friends, it's going to be a big occasion. And me, I'm the one who has to sort it all out, while my revered siblings, who normally we don't see hide nor hair of, just float along when it suits them!' he complained.

'Ai-ya!' Gao Tao could tell Dad was annoyed. 'But Shengqiang, you're so capable, besides you live close to the old lady. You're the right person to take it on.'

'Capable!' That somehow made Dad furious. 'Sodding "capable"! It's not as if I had any choice in the matter. The country forces me to do things, society forces me to do things.' He lifted his cup and the three of them clinked and swallowed their *maotai*. 'Mother forces me to do things!'

This wasn't just mouthing off, it was actually true. When Dad was honest with himself, he had to admit that the reason he hadn't ended up fucking his brains out with the girls of Fifteen Yuan Street, that he was doing well for himself now, that he was a man of some importance in Pingle Town, was all down to Gran forcing him to do things.

'Good people come from gold rods,' Gran always said. 'Spare the rod and spoil the child.' Dad remembered Gran saying this every time she picked up the cane to beat his bottom with. He remembered perfectly well, though of course he wasn't going to admit it, that right up until he was in his early twenties and was going out with Mum, when Gran caught him playing *mahjong* she was quite capable of having his trousers off him and making him lean over the table in his long-johns for a beating.

Gran had always insisted on the proprieties, and if a thing was worth doing, it was worth doing well. All Dad's life, she had been a refined figure at his side, landing blow upon blow on his long-john-clad buttocks, repeating in level tones: 'Look, Shengqiang, you must obey me. The whole Xue family depends on you. Don't blame me for beating you. Spare the rod and spoil the child.'

Nonsense! Dad had spent his whole life muttering angrily to himself. *How come you never beat my older brother or sister then?*

For over twenty years, Dad had never dared say this out loud but he was pretty clear in his own mind that ever since he'd emerged after nine months in Gran's womb, he'd been the family whipping boy.

'Open another for us, Miss!' Dad bellowed, pointing at the *maotai* liquor. What was money anyway? Just so much paper! And once it was gone, it was gone. It made Dad very happy to spend the factory's money.

In Dad's phone Contacts, his elder brother 'Duan Zhiming' came right at the top. This was annoying because, when he looked up a name, 'Duan Zhiming' always seemed to catch his eye. Sometimes he just ignored it, other times it filled him with an obscure fury. Once he nearly deleted the surname, so that he could fucking move it from D for Duan to Z for Zhiming. Out of sight, out of mind. But then he didn't. Having only his brother's given name in his address book gave the impression they were close. No, he'd bloody well put up with the annoyance of seeing that creep's name a few more times.

Dad was more respectful about Aunt Coral. He very properly saved her name under 'Sis'. Every time he called Aunt Coral, he also very properly went somewhere quiet, like the corridor or the balcony, before pressing her number.

The morning of the dinner with Zhong and Gao Tao, he had called her. She answered after a couple of rings with a light: 'Hello, Shengqiang.'

For as long as Dad could remember, Aunt Coral had always spoken mandarin rather than the dialect of Pingle Town, and for that reason alone, Dad made an effort to speak nicely to Aunt Coral. Her voice came over the phone line, sounding just like she sounded on TV: 'Has anything happened at home, Shengqiang?'

And Dad moderated his usual bad language and pronounced, in the way he might have reported to the Production Team head: 'Nothing's happened. It's just that Mum's eightieth birthday's coming up next month and she'd like everyone to come and celebrate it with her.'

'Is it really?' Aunt Coral sounded a bit surprised. 'I almost forgot! Well, I should come back for that. You set the date and I'll be there.'

'Right,' Dad assented. It was Aunt Coral he was talking to. If it had been his brother, he would have muttered *sotto voce: So, Duan Zhiming, you want me to fix the date, book the restaurant, and you just come back to eat and drink once I've got everything ready for you!*

'Is everybody well?' Aunt Coral asked. 'How is Anqin? And how's Xingxing been lately?'

'Everyone's fine,' Dad responded, disingenuously.

'That's good, then,' said Aunt Coral.

Aunt Coral's question effectively stopped up the words on the tip of Dad's tongue. No one else knew, probably not even Gran, but Dad knew very well, that if it wasn't for Aunt Coral, he and Mum wouldn't be together any more. It was Aunt Coral who had dissuaded him from getting a divorce, not Gran.

That was the first time ever that she had given Dad a call of her own volition: 'Shengqiang, are you really set on divorcing Anqin?'

Dad said nothing. The day before, he had made repeated promises to Gran, but he was still seething with anger.

Aunt Coral understood perfectly well what his silence meant. She sighed, and went on: 'Shengqiang, I know once this kind of thing happens and you want a divorce, it's difficult for anyone to dissuade you, but I introduced you to each other and I want to say a couple of things. Will you listen to what your sister says and take it in?'

'Go ahead, Sis,' said Dad earnestly and sat down on the sofa, his eyes fixed on the front door at the end of the entrance lobby.

'For good or ill, Anqin and I worked together for two years and I know she's a good woman, otherwise I wouldn't have introduced you. And now that I've seen you together I really hate to see you split up. So today I'm going to beg you on her behalf, will you listen to me?'

'I'm listening, Sis,' Dad said, his eyes still fixed on the front door.

'I'm not saying that Anqin's right or Anqin's wrong. I'm just saying that if you divorce her, what will you do? What will Xingxing do? Every family's got to have a home-maker. At your age and with your abilities, it'll be easy for you to find someone else for yourself, but where will you find another mother for Xingxing? If you find someone your own age, then she'll come with a past, and that'll mean all sorts of problems. If you get someone much younger than you, it'll be quite improper. I'm your sister, I know you, and I know the factory's doing well and you're a popular man, so the girls are always after you, but they're just for fun, you can't take them home. With a family like ours, how will you find one to take home, Shengqiang?' Her manner of speaking reminded Dad of seeing his sister on TV. She might as well have been reciting her lines from the autocue.

Dad stared at the apartment door as he listened to his sister. Her words certainly had an impact—after all, she made her living from speaking. Her questions beat on his chest, and he had no answers to them: 'Where will you find another mother for Xingxing? What will happen to the family?'

However badly his wife had behaved, she really did love the kid.

'All right, Sis,' he said finally.

They talked a bit more and, just as Dad finished the call, Mum put the key in the lock and pushed the front door open. She was carrying some vegetables in one hand and, hesitantly, her head bowed and avoiding looking at Dad, she went into the kitchen.

'Anqin,' Dad called her back.

'Huh?' said Mum, quivering like a frightened rabbit. She turned to look at Dad. Dad had to admit that, even as a middle-aged woman, she had kept her looks, with her pale, oval face adorned with a delicate nose and bright eyes.

'What are we having for dinner?' asked Dad, leaning back into the sofa and picking up the TV remote to turn on the TV, just as if this was any old evening.

Years later, Mum finally rallied, stood tall and assumed her rightful place in the family again. Then, finally, home was home, bright and clean, the family was the family, and all was peace and harmony. Dad knew that this was thanks to Aunt Coral's intervention all those years ago, and he almost didn't say the words that came to his lips.

'Mother wants Liu, Xingchen and all of them to come too.' He'd said it now. There was no taking it back.

'Is that what she said?' came Aunt Coral's voice, down the line.

'Yes, the old lady wants us all there, with no one missing,' Dad said. 'She says she's going to be eighty and she wants a really lively party.'

'I understand. So you fix the date as soon as possible.' And she informed him: 'A weekend is best. Xingchen and Zhao are busy during the week, and Diandian's at kindergarten.'

'Fine, I'll let you know tomorrow or the next day,' said Dad quickly. Then: 'Sis, if this is going to make life difficult for you, I can have a word with Mother.'

'Forget it,' said Auntie, cutting him short. 'Don't worry about it, Shengqiang. Family is family, no matter what.'

He'd grown up with his sister for nearly twenty years before she married and left home, and Dad was well aware that Aunt Coral was a tough cookie. So he said nothing more and was about to hang up when Aunt Coral suddenly mentioned their brother. 'And Zhiming? Have you called him?'

'I know I need to phone him,' said Dad. 'Sis, you don't need to worry about anything.'

He cut the call, then opened his Contacts list again and saw Duan Zhiming at the top of the list. Dad stared at the name for a few seconds. He was on the point of calling when he changed his mind.

Now's not the right time, he thought to himself. *I'll call tomorrow.*

Instead, he scrolled through the Contacts until he came to Zhong's number. Once he got him on the line, he said: 'Hey, bro, what about going out to eat?' … 'You're eating right now? Then chuck your chopsticks down and get out of the house!' … 'Nonsense! At the Floating Fragrance! It's on me, I'll get Zhu Cheng to go and get us three bottles of *maotai*, let's have a real booze-up tonight!' He knew his friend; a drinker like him would never be able to resist the invitation. Zhong did agree, but suggested calling Gao Tao too.

'All right, all right!' Dad knew quite well what Zhong was up to; Gao Tao was counting on his advertising company getting the contract from the chilli bean paste factory next year, and was constantly on the phone and sending gifts. This had been going on for two weeks. Zhong and Gao Tao were in-laws, and

Zhong was keen to give Gao a helping hand by getting him and Dad together.

'The three of us haven't seen each other for ages, let's have a good night out!' Dad said into the phone, though what he was really thinking was: *Gao Tao's business is chicken feed. He's got a nerve to call it an advertising company and want to do business with me!*

'I'll be back drunk as a skunk! Drunk as a skunk!" said Dad, as he walked out of the front door of the apartment.

That evening, as Dad, Gao and Zhong were on the third bottle of *maotai*, and Dad sat at the table, breathing heavily and imagining their waitress turning into a fairy before his very eyes, his phone suddenly rang.

It was nearly 11 o'clock at night. 'Is that your old lady wanting you home?' asked Zhong, startled.

'Her?!' Dad grunted, but he picked up the phone anyway.

He could see the name 'Zhong' clearly on the screen. Jasmine. Dad sneaked a look at his friend and went out into the corridor, then took the call. 'It's the middle of the night,' he slurred. 'Has someone died?'

He was startled at his own words. Perhaps something had happened to Gran? He leaned against the wall, so scared at the thought that he stopped listening to Jasmine. Once Gran died, the family would fall apart at the seams. How would he ever manage to pick up the pieces? He was filled with gut-wrenching fear.

He pulled himself together and gathered that nothing major had happened. Jasmine had just got some foolish fancy into her head and was tearfully begging him to go over.

'I'm out drinking, how can I?' Dad attempted to placate his 'stupid cow' but recently she'd been seized by strange fancies and was getting a bit uppity.

'I don't care! You've got to come now!' came her voice down

the phone.

'Really, I can't. I'll come tomorrow first thing, OK?' Dad carried on talking gently into the phone. Jasmine really was too childish, he thought to himself. Using all these words like 'got to' and 'don't care'? Who'd been getting her into bad habits?

'No! I want you here now!' Jasmine surprised him by sounding distinctly unfriendly.

Dad leant against the wall and scrutinized a piece of the wallpaper which was curling up at one corner on the wall opposite. This was a scene he was extraordinarily familiar with. It was just like every time Gran phoned him up.

The thought made him furious. A young girl like Jasmine making a scene and harassing him like this! And to think that when he first saw her, she was a maroon-uniformed slip of a girl in Longteng Telecoms City, bowing demurely and saying Yes Sir, No Sir to the customers.

Choked by anger and phlegm, Dad was about to spit both out when he heard Jasmine say: 'If you don't come now, I'm going downstairs to your mother's apartment and I'm going to knock on her door. Just you see if I don't! I'm going to get her out of bed and tell her everything about you and me. We'll see what she says then!'

Dad sagged, as if the hand brake had been slammed on when he was about to have sex. He was getting older, it wasn't surprising that sometimes all the fire went out of him.

He went back into the side-room to face the inevitable ribbing from Gao and Zhong: 'His fire alarm's gone off. He's got to go and douse the flames!'

All Dad could do was to grab their waitress around the waist and bellow: 'Take me to pay the bill!'

The girl made a token effort to push his arm away: 'Mr Gao's already paid it, Sir!'

Even though he'd expected this, Dad gave a polite exclamation of surprise. While he was at it, he gave the waitress's waist a pinch or two and discovered she was wearing tights, above which a roll of fat protruded. He kneaded it between his fingers, and a sudden rush of affection for her.

Now he was in the mood, Dad decided to make it a long night and rushed off to Cornucopia Court to indulge in amorous activities with Jasmine. He had to. Otherwise, he'd wake up furious in the middle of the night and wonder how he was ever going to get out of this mess.

He was keenly aware that he wasn't giving his best performance because he was so drunk. All the same, Jasmine moaned and groaned happily until Dad hushed her: 'Keep your voice down. It's the middle of the night.' From underneath, Jasmine looked up at him: 'What's up? Who are you afraid will hear?'

Dad gave her a couple of savage thrusts. He felt extremely aggrieved. It was hard just being human, let alone being a man. It was ever thus. He was one of the workhorses of this life, always needed to do the hard graft. He was fated to be the doormat, working himself to the bone to satisfy his mistress, and so give his old mother a good night's sleep. Saints and sages were always lonely and misunderstood, always put upon, always working.

Tomorrow morning ... Dad thought to himself as he made love to Jasmine Zhong for the last time. Tomorrow morning I'll get things sorted out, I'll give my brother a call, and settle down to arranging Mum's eightieth birthday party. Let's get it sorted ...

2

When did it begin? Dad wondered. He sat in the Director's office behind a palatial desk, smoking a cigarette. He stubbed it out in an ashtray as big as a bum cheek, and lit another. *When?*

'It' was thoughts of Gran dying. It must have been in 1997 or 1998, certainly no later than 2000. The daydreams would come if he'd had a lot to drink, or for some reason couldn't get to sleep and was having a late-night smoke. It was all very puzzling.

For some reason, Dad was convinced that Gran's demise was imminent. His fancies focussed on how they would find out. There were various scenarios: his cell phone would ring, and the word 'Mother' would pop up on the screen, but it wouldn't be Gran at the other end. Dad would know straightaway that that it was bad news. The person at the other end, the neighbour perhaps, or one of Gran's old friends, would say: 'Shengqiang! It's your mother!' Or maybe there would be a knock in the middle of the night, or early in the morning. Dad imagined himself mumbling to Anqin: 'There's someone at the door.' Mum would get up and answer it while Dad lay there half-asleep. He heard her voice rise, and start quavering. Then he knew it was all over. Mum came back and stood at the bedroom door, hiding her face in the shadows, and said: 'Shengqiang, something's up with your mother.'

Once he got together with Jasmine, the scenario changed. In this version, his mobile rang at some very inappropriate moment, and Jasmine's voice said: 'Shengqiang, come quick! Something's happened!'

The 'something' would be that Gran had died. Dad lit another cigarette and pursued his imaginings. He would have to organize the funeral. The coffin would have to lie in Marshalls Hall at the Martyrs Memorial Garden. He would get Zhu Cheng to go and buy at least twelve wreaths, one for each branch of the clan: starting with himself, then Aunt Coral and her family, her son Liu Xingchen, and all the other relatives (even that brother of his, Duan Zhiming). He'd have to write all the condolence messages himself, because half the family were out of town. It would be a magnificent occasion, with rows of wreaths and two funeral wailers kneeling at the entrance of the funeral parlour, keening as if their hearts were breaking. That way, anyone who came to pay their respects would be suitably impressed at the grand send-off they were giving to the old lady from the Xue family.

Dad ran over and over the details until he had it all carefully worked out. He even decided that the parlour should be filled with lilies piled around a gilded coffin. Spectacular!

OK, so Gran didn't die. Granddad did though, and before his time. Dad was very distressed, but still had to bury him. It was 2005. Well, why not give Granddad just the same funeral—flowers, paper offerings and all—as he had planned for his mother? But Gran was dead against such an ostentatious send-off. 'It's all so vulgar. When someone's dead, they're dead. They turn to ashes, and that's that. Why go to all this fuss with a funeral? You just need a gravestone for the family to go to on Tomb-Sweeping Day, somewhere for them to remember their loved ones. There's no need for more than that.'

'If you lay him out in a viewing parlour, you'll have the whole town in there,' she went on. 'And everyone has to give money. If you think that's a good way of screwing money out of them, you're wrong. You have to give all that money back when their turn comes. You're a wealthy factory owner, Shengqiang, don't be so petty.'

Dad sat opposite Gran, smoking and saying nothing. His mind was a blank.

Luckily, Gran came around to his way of thinking. 'Of course, he is your father. When my turn comes, you can just sprinkle my ashes in Clearwater Creek, no need to get all weepy. Just forget about your old mum.'

Dad, still silent, stubbed out his cigarette. He was thinking, *That's easier said than done, Mother!*

In the end, Gran herself realized it wasn't that simple. One night, there was a thunderous knocking on her door. It was four or five in the morning, certainly before six o'clock. It had to be serious. She got up, put on the trousers that had been hanging over the back of the chair, and took a maroon cardigan from behind the door. Then she tidied her hair in the mirror, and went to open the door.

Jasmine Zhong stood there. The stairwell light shone harshly down on her, draining the colour from her cheeks. She jumped, as if she hadn't expected the door to be answered so quickly. Her eyes fixed on Gran, she opened her mouth to speak but no sound came out.

'What's happened to Shengqiang?' said Gran.

At this, Jasmine really did jump out of her skin. Stricken, she pointed upstairs, then finally got out: 'He ... he ...'

Gran pushed Jasmine out of the way and hobbled up the stairs, pulling on the bannisters at each step. When Jasmine came alongside and reached out to support Gran's other arm, she found herself flung off. Gran was so focussed on getting to the fifth floor, she was not aware of rejecting Jasmine's hand. Memories of past humiliations trickled over her like dirty water from a foot-washing bowl, and a sultry songstress sang in her head: 'I may die under a skirt, But a ghost can still flirt.'

And now Shengqiang had gone to be a flirty ghost. She

got to the fourth floor and looked up at the half-open door of Jasmine's apartment. As she climbed the remaining twelve stairs, she wondered what to do. It wouldn't be right to get Coral to come and sort it out. She'd have to phone Duan Zhiming. They'd have to have a viewing parlour at the Martyrs Memorial Garden. The more scandalous the death, the more dignified the funeral had to be.

Of course, there was Anqin to think of. She'd better get Coral home to calm her down, she thought as she pushed the door open. The apartment was laid out exactly like hers and she headed straight for the bedroom.

But Dad wasn't dead. He was lying in bed, looking very sorry for himself. His head was turned towards the door, and he stared at Gran as she came in. Tears poured down his cheeks, whether from fear or from relief, Gran did not know. He opened his mouth and, after a pause, managed hoarsely: 'Mother!'

The sound of his voice galvanized and steadied Gran. After all, she was nearly eighty and there had been plenty of upsets in the family during her lifetime. Disgraced or not, her beloved son was still with her.

Now she was sure Dad would live, she bustled around doing what had to be done. First, she called the hospital for an ambulance. Then she told Jasmine to go downstairs and keep out of the way. She ignored Dad, did not even look at him. He was lying in bed, chewing on a facecloth covered in white spittle. Of course she had no idea that the reason he had ended up like this tonight was because, out of the goodness of his heart, he had been trying to spare his old mother from having her rest disturbed.

Anyway, that was how it happened, or so Mum told me.

Dad was going to pull through, and that should have been good news. But that was not the way Dad himself saw it. Whether or not it caused his mother grief, he wanted to quit this rotten world and let Gran, Mum and everyone else sort things out for themselves. *Let that bastard Duan Zhiming pick up the pieces!* he thought vengefully, as he lay curled up under the covers of his hospital bed watching 'Golden Wedding' on the TV. He knew this was the series that Mum watched every day. In fact, maybe it was what made her behave so oddly.

The thought had scarcely entered his head when the door of his room was pushed open. Mum came in, with a huge lunchbox in one hand and a thermos under the other arm. When she saw Dad sitting up in bed, she hurried over and put the things down on the bedside cabinet. With her dainty hands, she pushed him back onto his pillows. 'Shengqiang, what are you doing sitting up!' she exclaimed. 'You need to rest!'

Before Dad could open his mouth to speak, she had pulled the bedclothes up to his chin and tucked him in so tight that all he could do was watch as she straightened the corner of the quilt. *Have you come to pay your last respects?* Was what he wanted to ask, but did not.

'Are you hungry, Shengqiang? I've brought you a fish soup. It's carp. I asked Doctor Song and he said that chicken soup was too oily for you just now. Have some, it's nourishing and light.' Mum chattered on without pausing for breath. She deftly unlidded layer after layer of the lunchbox containers. Dad glanced sideways and saw a colourful array of tripe. Just looking at it made him feel full.

But Mum was not interested in whether he was hungry. She laid the containers out in a square, as neatly as if she was performing an operation, poured Dad a bowl of milky white carp soup, and held it firmly to his lips. Dad managed to get his hands out from under the cover and took the bowl from her. 'I can drink it by myself,' he said. His voice sounded odd, even to himself, maybe because he hadn't heard himself speak for such a long time. 'I can drink it by myself,' he repeated, and this time he sounded normal.

'Yes, right!' Mum slapped his hand away, turned her back for a moment and produced a drinking straw. 'Drink it with a straw. You'll spill it if you drink straight from the bowl.'

'I've been drinking straight from the bowl for forty-odd years!' protested Dad in a whisper. 'And I haven't spilled a drop yet.'

'Ai-ya!' Mum took it all in her stride. After all, they had been together for twenty years and she knew his moods better than anyone. She put the straw in his hand and turned to serve out the rest of the food.

Dad obediently sank the drinking straw in his soup and drank some. The soup was lukewarm and uniformly pale in colour, because the fish had been sautéed. It was also bland, seasoned with just a pinch of salt and a hint of fresh ginger, and was not going to make a blind bit of difference to him. No one could persuade Dad of that.

He watched Mum placing morsels of food over the rice, as precisely as if she was brick-laying—two thin slices of steamed belly pork, spare ribs with potato, ground pork and peas, and stewed pig's tripe. Doom stared him in the face. Mum finished placing the last morsel of sautéed leeks in the lunch box with her chopsticks. She was about to turn around. There was no escape for him now.

At that moment, as if by telepathy, the door was pushed open. Dad looked up eagerly, hoping it was his driver, Zhu Cheng, or Dr Song come to check up on him or, at worst, the nurse bringing his medication. It wasn't any of them.

It was the delightful Jasmine Zhong. She came in with a carrier bag full of fruit, saying: 'Just as I was leaving the hospital, I remembered you hadn't had your fruit. You should always eat a bit of fruit after your meal, so I bought you some.' At that moment, she saw Mum, and froze. The door swung to behind her.

'Hello, Mrs Chen,' she finally managed a polite greeting.

'Ah,' said Mum. 'I see you've already fed him.'

Jasmine could see that the bedside cabinet was covered with dishes, so she put her bags down on the chair under the TV screen on the other side of the room. 'That's right,' she said in a small voice.

Mum looked round at Dad, who was bent over the bowl of soup, sucking it through a straw like a little boy, ever so careful not to let even a drop roll down his chin.

'Shengqiang,' said Mum sternly. 'This is not funny. If you'd already eaten, you should have told me. You're not a child anymore. If you go and stuff yourself when you're already full up, you'll get indigestion.'

Dad heard these words without the trace of a smile. Mum and Jasmine didn't smile either.

But the atmosphere in the room was not as chilly as it might have been. Quite the opposite, in fact. Just the afternoon before, an elderly relative of Dad's from a village near Pingle Town, had dropped in for a visit. He supplied the factory with the baskets in which the chilli bean paste was packed, and was grateful to Dad for the work, so when he heard the news, he hurried over laden with supplies of rice and meat and eggs. He pushed open the door, and there was Dad lying back against the pillows, with Mum on one side kneading his shoulder muscles, and Jasmine standing on the other, doing acupressure on his temples. Dad looked over at the door: 'What are you doing here, Uncle?' he exclaimed in surprise.

Mum and Jasmine stopped their massage and looked around too. Of course, Mum recognized him, and pulled up a chair for him with a smile. Jasmine nodded politely, then washed a cup and poured him some tea.

The old man hadn't seen our family for a while, and had not heard the scandal of my admission to the psychiatric hospital. He looked Jasmine up and down as he held his hands out for the tea, and said: 'Hasn't your daughter grown up quickly? She's such a big girl now! Quite a young lady!' A snort escaped Mum. She buried her face in her hands and her shoulders shook, although whether she was laughing or crying, it was hard to tell. Jasmine handed over the cup with steady hands, then stepped back, expressionless. Not a flicker of a smile crossed her face.

Dad looked at Jasmine. 'Say hello to Uncle,' he said.

'Good afternoon, Uncle,' said Jasmine.

'Uncle' was a guileless old man. 'Have you gone soft in the head, Shengqiang?' he remonstrated. 'I'm her great-uncle not her uncle!'

Mum's shoulders shook for a long time. Finally she came up with: 'Ai-ya, Uncle! This isn't our daughter, this is a friend of Shengqiang's!'

The poor old man went scarlet with embarrassment. He kept apologizing, getting up to speak, then sitting back down, and very soon said goodbye.

Left to their own devices, Dad, Mum and Jasmine had carried on being surprisingly polite to each other. Now it was Jasmine's turn to apologize: 'Mrs Chen, I'm so sorry, I just thought I should pick something up for Mr Xue to eat on the way, I really had no idea you'd made him all this.'

'Don't worry about it,' said Mum as she tidied up the food containers. 'I just made a few bits and pieces, nowhere near as good as restaurant food. I'm just glad he's eating something. Did you enjoy your meal, Shengqiang?'

Jasmine and Mum both looked sternly at Dad and waited for his answer. Had he enjoyed his meal? Dad was aware he hadn't done it justice. Those two swords hanging over him, if only he could have taken one, stuck it in his belly and made a big hole. Then he could have scooped out his first meal and made another attempt on Mum's food.

Finally he said: 'Yes, the food was good. And the soup was

good, too.'

All smiles, the two women got down to their tasks. Mum went to the bathroom to wash up the soup bowl, and Jasmine used the lunchbox lid as a plate to slice the fruit on. 'Would you like an apple or a pear, Mrs Chen?' she called out.

'Apple, please, I don't like pears,' said Mum.

'We'll have apples, then,' said Jasmine. 'Pears are too cooling.' And she set to, cheerfully. She sliced one, then another, peeled and cored them and arranged them in a star formation on the lunchbox lid, each segment skewered with a toothpick.

Were his two 'stupid cows' really stupid or just pretending to be? Dad mulled it over from his hospital bed but, for the first time in his life, he was truly flummoxed. Wife and concubine, it was just like Imperial times. He must have mad cow disease.

He lay back in bed, closed his eyes and pretended to be asleep. Through half-closed lids, he could see them pottering around the sickroom. Anqin was saying nothing about a divorce, but he had no idea whether Jasmine would steer clear of her either. Dad just wanted to die. If only he'd died that night. At least that way, he'd have popped his clogs having good sex. Right now he was caught between a rock and a hard place. Being in hospital was like being in prison, but as soon as he got better, he'd be out. Then he'd be faced with his wife and his lover. *Son-of-a-bitch, which one do I sleep with first?* He asked himself. *Well, I'll just wait and see.* And he took advantage of his two women clearing up to take a nap.

Admittedly, it was only a dream. But it was a bit more than that, because he remembered every detail afterwards, which was very strange for him. The whole family was there in his dream: Gran and Granddad, his brother and his sister—and he was there too.

He and Granddad had gone to buy a whole soy-stewed duck, something to do with celebrating his sister coming home on a visit. Granddad made a big show of putting a ten-*yuan* note in his breast pocket and took Dad with him. The butcher took a fine big duck off the shelf and put it on the counter and flattened it so it looked like a small airplane. Then he raised his knife and, with a few neat chops, chopped it into pieces and tipped them into a plastic bag. Dad, on the other side of the window, watched intently. His sister was at college, so that meant he must still have been in junior high. Just a squitty little kid who was always hungry. The sight of the duck made him drool. 'Do you want the tail?' asked the butcher. 'Yes!' said Dad.

Granddad glanced at Dad with a smile. 'You can give it to him,' he told the butcher. The butcher pushed the window open and poked his greasy hand through. Dad stuffed the piece of meat in his mouth. The fat spurted out and ran down his chin. He felt as if he had twenty people all kissing him inside his mouth.

'Mr Duan, your son's grown tall!' commented the butcher to Granddad. 'He must be all of five foot seven inches!'

'He still behaves like a kid, though. Just a big kid,' said Granddad. Then he said to Dad: 'Wipe your mouth, Shengqiang.' In his dream, they went back home and although it was only a short way, they seemed to be walking for hours. Granddad was very tired and disappeared. Dad got home, carrying the duck. They were still living in the old house behind the chilli bean paste factory then. Dad pushed the gate open and went into the small courtyard, where his brother Duan Zhiming was playing chess with some school friends. They had just finished a game and were setting the pieces out again.

'Want to play chess, Shengqiang?'

Dad was itching for a game, so he said: 'Let me go and put this down first.'

'You have a go, Shengqiang,' said his brother. 'I'll take the duck in.'

Dad gave him the bag and sat down to play. After one game, or maybe two, it was time for dinner. The table was covered with dishes. There was Gran, his sister and his brother but, for some reason, Granddad still wasn't home.

'We won't wait for your dad, we'll start without him,' declared Gran.

They all started to eat. There were plenty of other dishes but everyone was tucking into the duck. His brother pulled off a thigh with his chopsticks, his sister took a wing, Gran chose the neck and Dad plucked off a bit of breast.

It was Gran who spotted it first. 'There's something funny with this duck!' she said to Dad. 'It's only got one wing and one thigh!'

'That can't be right!' Dad was scared. It was the sort of exaggerated terror you had in dreams, as if his heart was going to leap out of his chest. They all sat there counting the bones on the table and the duck pieces in the bowl. One thigh and one wing really were missing.

'I don't understand,' said Dad. 'The butcher put the whole duck into the bag, I saw him.'

Gran was silent and everyone carried on eating. Suddenly she said: 'Shengqiang, don't think you can play the fool with me. If you don't want to be found out, don't do it in the first place.' Dad looked up from his bowl but could not catch her eye. She was eating a morsel of stewed duck breast, a benign expression on her face. Before he had a chance to reply, she continued: 'I'm not going to make a fuss about it. I've said enough.'

Dad woke up, enraged. The sense of injustice still rankled bitterly. He needed to vent his fury on someone but the two women had left the sickroom and there was no one there. So he raged silently: *You douchebag, Duan Zhiming! You've always been a son-of-a-bitch!*

Dad had to admit that, after all these years, it had taken a dream for him to solve the mystery of the missing half-duck.

Dad was always taking out his fury on any poor jerk who happened to be around, whether it was his brother or the factory staff. But it goes without saying that he never, ever, lost his temper with Gran.

After three days shut up in hospital, he regained his freedom and left laden with bags of pills. Zhu Cheng was there to meet him, and drove him to Cornucopia Court.

'You're a good son to the old lady,' said Zhu Cheng, glancing over his shoulder. 'You go and see her the minute you get out of hospital, even before you go home.'

Dad said nothing. Zhu Cheng had no idea what fate awaited Dad at home, and the worst of it was, neither did Dad.

'What did you say to Anqin?' he asked Gran once he was sitting on her sofa. He groped through his pockets in a fruitless search for a cigarette and had to be content with pulling apart a bit of toilet paper and rolling it back and forth between his fingers.

'You're asking me that now? Why did you never ask me when you moved that woman into the apartment above me?' was Gran's response. She was reading the newspaper, her glasses perched on her nose.

Son-of-a-bitch, thought Dad, his heart sinking. There was nowhere to hide.

After a pause, he pulled himself together and went over with Gran what he was going to say to Anqin. He was going to be very, very sorry. He kept his head down as he talked, and twisted the shredded toilet paper until he had a long, thin pencil shape, then pulled it apart and rolled it up once again. Halfway through his speech, he was almost overwhelmed with emotion and groped again for a cigarette, but his pocket was as empty as before. Why on earth had he come here without cigarettes? He felt utterly despondent. He had to put up with a telling-off from Gran and an admonition to behave better in future. It wasn't going to be easy but he had to put an end to his little 'sideshow', they both agreed on that.

'I'll do whatever you say, Mother,' Dad concluded hastily, putting a brave face on it.

As for everything else, they would carry on pretty much as he had originally planned. The eightieth birthday was to go ahead, no matter what, so Uncle would be called back home, and Aunt Coral's entire family had to come too, no exceptions allowed. 'And Xingxing?' Dad asked, ever so tentatively. My grandmother scowled. 'Wait till she's right in the head and gets out of the mental hospital, then we'll see.' Gran and Dad could sort out Dad's affair between themselves, since Mum was not going to make trouble. Some things would have to change. Jasmine would have to move out, for starters. Was the apartment upstairs rented or bought? asked Gran. Rented, said Dad. In that case, he could get rid of it. And he should drink and smoke less and look after himself better. 'And no blabbing,' said Gran quietly. 'Be discreet.' And she took her glasses off and began to massage her temples.

Listening to Gran made Dad crave a cigarette so badly he was almost apoplectic. But he got to his feet without a flicker of emotion. 'Mother, I'm off home now. Anqin knows I'm out of hospital today. She said she'd get off work early so she could have dinner ready.'

Gran nodded. 'You know, you should really give Anqin a hand around the house. All you do is sit there like a corpse and eat your head off. You don't make life easy for her.'

'Right,' said Dad meekly and opened the door to leave.

'Oh, and something else,' came Gran's voice from behind him. 'Shengqiang, you're old enough to know what to do. Don't go making a fuss.'

If Dad had arrived at Gran's apartment feeling gloomy, he left it utterly drained. He reached the bottom of the stairs and, without daring to glance up at the fifth floor, rushed to the kiosk at the entrance gate to buy some cigarettes. Once he had the packet in his hands, he relaxed. He dragged on the cigarette like a man starved of oxygen, and walked home taking puff after puff. He wondered what Gran had spiked Mum's drink with. Why was Mum being so forgiving? It was almost as if she was prepared to accept Jasmine. But he couldn't live like that. The girl would have to go. *Tough tittie*, thought Dad, *She's just a girl.*

By the time Dad finally arrived, the dinner table was covered in dishes all ready to serve. Mum put her head out of the kitchen and said: 'You're just in time, Shengqiang. Dinner's ready.'

Dad dropped his bag of magic pills by the shoe cupboard and put on a pair of slippers. 'What's for dinner?' he asked, sniffing appreciatively.

'Oh, so you've finally got your appetite back?' said Mum with a smile. She ripped open a plastic bag and tipped the contents into a bowl. Dad could tell at a glance that it was soy-stewed duck from the shop in West Gate.

'I went out specially at lunchtime to get it. You know, he's doing so well, he shuts up shop in the afternoon!' Mum reached into the bowl for the duck's tail, and popped it into Dad's mouth.

The spurt of oil in his mouth did not fail him. It was as if he was being kissed by twenty Jasmines.

Mum carried the bowl in both hands to the table, followed by Dad with two bowls of rice and the chopsticks. 'You're a funny man,' she said. 'The bits that other people throw away are just the bits that you like best.'

They sat down and Mum deftly picked up a fine fat piece of thigh with her chopsticks and placed it on top of the rice in Dad's bowl.

'Have some nice thigh meat,' she urged him. 'It's much

better than the tail.'

Dad looked at the gleaming duck thigh reposing on a bed of snowy white rice and made up his mind. 'Let's not watch TV tonight. Let's get an early night,' he said to Mum.

And that was how Dad solved the problem of who to have sex with first after he got out of hospital.

Dad was a loyal man at heart. Now he'd had sex with Mum, he was embarrassed to do it with Jasmine for the time being. So when they met soon afterwards, he just sat with her on the sofa and they chatted politely.

'Are you feeling better?' Jasmine asked. 'I hope you're remembering to take your medicine.' She had the fruit bowl balanced on her knee and was cutting up a pear. She didn't arrange it star-shaped, the way she cut the apple in the hospital, but peeled it first and, holding it in her hand, sliced pieces onto a plate. It made for a more uneven result, of course, but Dad didn't care about that. He speared a bit with a toothpick and put it in his mouth.

'Ai-ya!' he exclaimed, as the clear sweet juice slid down his throat and he relaxed back into the sofa. 'You shouldn't make a mountain out of a molehill, either of you. I'm fine.'

Jasmine stared unwaveringly at Dad. The rims of her eyes turned as red as a rabbit's. She was only young, after all.

'Now don't make such a fuss!' Dad repeated, helping himself to another slice of pear. 'Don't worry! Nothing's going to change. We'll go on just the same as before. The only thing is, you'll have to move out of here for a bit, now that the old lady knows about you.'

Jasmine nodded meekly. 'I know. I'll get my stuff together and go back to my place.'

Dad had only been there once. She shared a rented two-roomed apartment where she had the back bedroom. He had taken her out one evening, and they had eaten and gone shopping. Then he drove her back, along with all her bags.

Outside the apartment block, he could not help saying: 'Let me come up with you. That's too much for you to carry.' But Jasmine said: 'No, don't bother. I'll manage. My roommate will be there and I don't want her to see you.' 'Ai-ya, Jasmine!' Dad protested, his voice rising. 'I'll just carry them up the stairs for you. I won't sit down even if you drag me to a chair!'

Jasmine could hardly refuse, and up they went. Dad was in luck. The other door was firmly shut and it was obvious the girl was fast asleep. 'I'll just drop everything in your bedroom,' he said sweetly.

Once they were through the door, however, he seized his chance. Shutting it behind him, he threw his arms around Jasmine and pushed her onto the bed. Her almond eyes were round and startled as she looked up at him, but she didn't dare make a sound. He felt her hands pushing on his shoulders like the paws of a kitten. Dad couldn't remember the last time he had wanted a woman this much. He didn't bother taking any clothes off, just unzipped himself and got on with it.

Thinking about that occasion, Dad couldn't help feeling a bit sad. 'If you need anything, you know you can tell me and I'll get it for you,' he said in a softened tone.

'I've got everything. You've bought me so much,' Jasmine said quietly.

Dad badly wanted to fondle her, but he remembered Gran, ensconced in her armchair a couple of floors below. So he got out a cigarette instead, lit up and dragged on it.

'You should drink and smoke less, and look after yourself better, you know,' said Jasmine.

Dad carried on: 'For the next few weeks, I'm going to be busy arranging the old lady's birthday celebrations and I've got a lot of work on at the factory too. Besides, things are a bit difficult with Anqin so we won't be able to meet, but don't worry, we'll get back to how we were before in no time at all. If you need anything, just give me a ring, or you can give Zhu

Cheng a ring if you like,' he finished, stubbing out his cigarette.

He left Jasmine's apartment and passed Gran's on his way down. Her door was firmly shut and all was quiet inside. He didn't know what she was up to but couldn't be bothered to go in and see. As he went down the stairs, he felt as desolate as if he had just had an abortion.

What the hell, he said to himself. *She's just a girl. And it was her fault anyway for getting me over here so late at night, and leading me on. She brought it on herself.*

Dad found Zhu Cheng waiting for him as he left Cornucopia Court. Zhu Cheng was on the phone, but cut the call when Dad got into the car. 'Where to, boss?' he asked. 'Back to the factory?'

'Yes,' said Dad. He needed to vent his pent-up fury on a few employees, give them good telling-off and let off steam. 'Zhu Cheng, if Jasmine calls you,' he went on, 'just tell her I'm up to my eyes in work.'

Zhu Cheng was a lot sharper than he used to be, and caught on straightaway. 'Right, boss,' he said. 'I get it.'

Dad sighed. 'I know it's not easy for a country girl like Jasmine to make a living in the city. I'd like to do what I can for her, it's just that I really am up to my eyes in work. I haven't even started preparing for the old lady's birthday, and that's only a few days off now.'

'Shall I book the Floating Fragrance?' asked Zhu Cheng, following Dad's train of thought, and mentally consigning Jasmine to history.

'Well, the Floating Fragrance is OK, but what about the Prince's Mansion? The Prince's Mansion has more space, and classier décor too. The old lady's only going to be eighty once. We've got to do this properly. Book their luxury private room and two singers, and buy balloons and flowers to decorate the doorway. We want to make a bit of a fuss of her.'

'Right, right,' said Zhu Cheng, 'We'll make a fuss of her.'

When did it begin? Dad asked himself again as he leaned back in his seat. He went over it in his mind. She had somehow got to the age of eighty in spite of the fact that she always used to complain about her health. This wasn't right, or that bit hurt. Dad remembered how, when Granddad was still alive, she used to lean back on the sofa with one hand pressed to her back and grumble: 'You really like getting on my nerves, don't you? All of you! You'll be the death of me! And when I'm dead, you can just get on with your own lives. You,' (pointing at Granddad) 'you can bring that woman back here then, and you' (pointing at Dad), 'you can have all the fun you want, every day. And Zhiming, and Coral, they won't need to come home ever again. Once I'm dead, you'll all have a much better time, you'll get on so much better, and that's fine. When I die, you'll all be just fine.'

But the years went by, and Gran hadn't died. In fact, in spite of her moans and groans, she grew more hale and hearty by the day.

Of course, Mum often quoted the old saying: 'An old person is the family's treasure.' And she was right. The very fact that Gran had lived to a ripe old age was a great good fortune for the whole family.

Dad stretched out at his ease in the back of the Audi. Such good fortune made him feel quite emotional. 'Zhu Cheng,' he said, 'When we get back, call the retail department staff together for a meeting.'

'Yes, boss,' said Zhu Cheng, gripping the steering wheel firmly as they made steady progress towards the factory. All the employees knew Dad's temper. And they knew what it meant when he called a meeting of the retail department: he wanted to curse and swear at them.

Dad himself may have forgotten all about it but there was still someone who no doubt remembered: he first heard someone curse, 'Fuck your mother!' from Granddad, when he was a boy. One afternoon, classes had finished early, something to do with a visit the next day from the education department director. The pupils were told to give the school a good clean. Uncle wasn't about to do a thankless job like that, so he collected Dad and the two boys set off for home. They were still friends back then. As they walked along, Uncle said: 'Shengqiang, do you fancy a baked sweet potato?' Uncle's words made Dad start to drool. 'Yes!' he said.

'When we get back, why don't you go and ask Mum for some money?' Uncle suggested.

And the two boys put on a spurt. They pushed open the gate into the courtyard and were just about to go into the house when they heard Granddad swearing at someone inside.

'Fuck your mother!' shouted Granddad. 'Fuck your mother!' What's more, Dad could hear that Gran was in there too. He could hear murmurs, as if she was speaking some foreign language.

'What are they doing, Zhiming?' Dad asked his brother anxiously. He was about to open the door, but luckily Uncle grabbed him in time. 'Don't be an idiot, Shengqiang!' he said.

They stood in the courtyard listening for a while as Granddad shouted lots more swearwords. Uncle was smiling, and his face was as cherry-red as if he'd already eaten his baked sweet potato.

That evening after dinner as Dad did the washing-up, clattering the dishes and splashing water over them, he kept thinking about that 'fuck your mother' stuff. It seemed to stick in his throat like phlegm. Finally, he had to spit it out. He opened his mouth and heard himself say: 'Fuck your mother!' As soon as the words were out, he felt better. He stood over the sink, repeating obsessively: 'Fuck your mother, I fuck your mother, I fuck your mother, I fuck your whole family!' Strangely, it gave him a pleasurable tingling feeling down there, almost as if he wanted to pee, but different.

Finally Gran overheard him. She dragged Dad away from the sink and yelled at Granddad: 'Duan Xianjun! Come and listen to your son swearing!'

Granddad came in and was forced to give Dad a thrashing. After all, he'd said an awful lot of 'Fuck your mothers'.

Of course Dad knew now that Granddad and Gran had been in their room having sex that day, and that Granddad liked to swear when he had sex. Like father, like son, Dad did the same. Actually, the older he got, the weirder and more wonderful the swearwords he thought up in bed, but from time to time, he still came back to 'Fuck your mother'.

Of course, swearwords like that wouldn't do in the factory. Dad was careful of his image. The worst he'd call anyone, male or female, was 'dumb idiot'. When he gave the retail staff a telling-off, he kept Scarlet for last. Scarlet had only been in the factory a year. She was young and pretty and had caught Dad's eye immediately. So she got an especially long telling-off, in fact sometimes he reduced her to tears. When that happened, he would try to calm her down, but he never overstepped the mark. The closest he would get was to give her a couple of pats on the shoulder, as he said something like: 'Now, now, don't cry, you're a big girl now.' Gran had drilled into him his whole life that rumours could spread like wildfire. There were plenty of fish in the sea, he didn't need to catch one so close to home.

Today was no different from other days. He had a good go at Scarlet, she hung her head and her eyes reddened. Suddenly, his phone rang.

A Pretty Sprig of Jasmine. The ringtone gave Dad goose pimples. He pulled out his phone, and there it was on the screen: 'Mother'. His ears buzzed and his heart thumped. He left Scarlet on her own in the boardroom and went into the corridor to take the call.

'Hello!' he said tentatively. But there was no sound at the other end.

'Hello!' he repeated.

Finally someone spoke, but it wasn't Gran at all. An unfamiliar baritone voice at the other end of the line said: 'Hello!'

'Who is it?' Dad was at a loss. If this wasn't Gran, who was it? He wanted to ask, *What's happened to my mother? Is something up?* But, being a devoted son, he could not bring himself to say the words.

There was a lengthy silence at the other end of the phone. It might have lasted as long as five seconds. In those five seconds, Dad marshalled his thoughts. Gran's entire life passed before his eyes. He made up his mind to get Mr Zheng, a retired Chinese language teacher from Pingle Town, to write the funeral eulogy. Zheng had graduated with flying colours from the Central University (China's most prestigious institution in those days), and Gran admired him greatly.

'Shengqiang,' the voice at other end spoke again.

Dad suddenly realized that Gran wasn't dead. Worse still, that brother of his, Duan Zhiming, was back. *You bastard!* He thought. *What do you mean by turning up out of the blue and going to Mother's house first?*

Dad felt as betrayed as if he'd discovered his woman had been with another man. He stood in the corridor, examining the wall intently. His mind was a blank, but plenty of expletives rushed up from his gut and stuck in his throat.

'I reckon we should organize a celebration for Mother's eightieth,' said his brother. 'When you have a spare moment, drop by her apartment and we can discuss it.'

Who the hell asked you to get involved? The way you talk, you sound like you've been looking after her all along! You douchebag, Duan Zhiming, you've always been a son-of-a-bitch and you haven't changed! Dad thought. And those were just the repeatable bits.

'OK,' he said.

3

DAD DID NOT CALL Zhu Cheng to bring the car. Instead he left the factory and pottered along West Street on foot. He did not give Uncle a second thought. His head was full of bean paste and Sichuan peppers. Chilli bean paste was big business, had been for Gran's family for four or five generations. Sichuan peppers, on the other hand, were the sort of thing any small trader could sell. All they needed was a place to set up their stall. But, humble though the trade was, the Sichuan pepper was as essential as chilli bean paste at all Pingle Town dinner tables. The thing is, the townsfolk grew up with a hole in their tongues. In fact, they were almost born eating Sichuan pepper powder. Even rice porridge needed *ma-la*: the numbing, tingling *ma* of Sichuan pepper and the hot, spicy *la* of the chilli. They could not imagine life without that numbing-hot duo.

Dad had kicked around the chilli bean paste factory for over twenty years learning the ins and outs of his trade under the tutelage of his *shifu*, Chen, and if it had taught him one thing, it was that people were born to sweat. You ate chilli bean paste, and Sichuan peppers, and *ma-la* spicy hotpot, to work up a good sweat, and screwing a girl made you sweat even more. The more you sweated, the happier you felt, Dad reckoned. He remembered the fiery heat that the sweat-soaked bed-sheets in Baby Girl's house gave off.

It all made him rather melancholy. But Dad pulled himself together and turned into Caos' Alley on West Street. Just as you went into the alley there was a Sichuan pepper shop which had been in the same family for two generations. As he stepped inside, who should sitting there but Pingle's beauteous Sichuan pepper seller, Qin. She jumped to her feet and hurriedly dropped her book onto the counter. 'Shengqiang! I haven't seen you in ages! What brings you here?' 'That's no way to greet an old friend, Qin!' he said. 'What's wrong with me popping by to see you? Has this year's crop of peppers from Han Yuan County got here yet?' As they talked, he sneaked a look at the book she had dropped on the counter. It was a Readers' Digest. *Why were you in such a hurry to hide it? It's not porn, is it?* he wondered as she weighed him out two bags of Sichuan peppers. Dad paid her, asked after the family, bent to pick up the bags, then strode out of the shop.

It was on his way to Gran's that he began to have serious thoughts about his brother. *What did I do to deserve this? I hadn't even got around to phoning him and he turns up like a bad penny. I suppose Sis might have called him, or Mother?* As soon as he got to Cornucopia Court, he spotted a Honda SUV, right in front of the door to Unit 3 next to an old VW that had been parked there for months. Dad ignored it and strode right on by.

He took his key out to open Gran's door and heard his brother say: 'Anytime you'd like an outing, just let me know. If Shengqiang's too busy, it doesn't matter, I'll drive you.'

'Who says I'm too busy?' Dad said with a little laugh, before he had even got through the door.

'Shengqiang, it's you!' Uncle greeted him, getting up from the sofa. His mother stood up too, just as if Shengqiang hardly ever honoured her with his presence.

'Shengqiang, look at all the presents Zhiming's brought for me and you, and Anqin too!' Gran pointed to the dining table which was heaped with packages of all sizes.

'You're too kind, brother,' said Dad with a smile. 'And, look, on my way over, I picked up something for you.' He airily handed over the two bags of Sichuan peppers.

'Ai-ya! You didn't need to buy me anything! What is it?' Uncle came over and took them with his right hand. He was dressed in beige slacks and a white shirt, topped with a grey-blue linen jacket, which gave him an air of casual elegance. He put the bags on the table and sat down again. 'What kind of tea would you like?' asked Gran from the kitchen. 'Hua Mao Peak,' he said. Less politely, he thought: *Now what bee have you got in your bonnet?! When did you ever in a million years ask me what tea I wanted?* 'Mother,' said his brother, 'give Shengqiang some of that Pu'er. It's good one, especially for someone who drinks so much alcohol. He should drink more Pu'er tea.'

'No, no, no!' said Dad with a protesting wave. 'I've got a ton of Pu'er tea at home, my friends are always giving it to me, I can't get through it all, it smells mouldy! Just give me the Hua Mao Peak.' But Gran said: 'Ai-ya! You just listen to your brother. I've done you some Pu'er.' *Why are you so quick off the mark today!* thought Dad, as Gran emerged from the kitchen with a cup of Pu'er tea in her hands.

'Shengquang, listen to what your brother has to say. He's just come back from a trip to Europe.' 'Only to a conference, Mother, nothing worth talking about,' said Uncle with a smile, taking a sip from his teacup. 'Anyway, why should Shengqiang be interested? It's not as if he's never been abroad.'

Dad said nothing. Uncle didn't know, though Gran knew perfectly well, that the furthest Dad had ever been was a single trip to Hong Kong. In four days there, he had only been able to enjoy a bit of sightseeing on the first day. He had eaten seafood, bought a leather belt and a pair of shoes, and then killed time in the hotel, going up and down between the fifth floor and the ninth floor to have his hair washed and his feet massaged, while Mum went out shopping. The worst of it was there was no Sichuan pepper or chilli peppers. 'The food was so bland I might as well have been in hospital!' he grumbled when, thankfully, he was back in Pingle Town and went out for a hotpot with Zhong and a bunch of their bros. 'I'm not going there again. Why spend money on punishing yourself?'

'That's what travel's all about,' Zhong had told him. 'Spending money on punishing yourself ... and taking pictures. You did take some pictures?'

'No I didn't!' Dad had waved dismissively. 'I just took a bunch of Anqin.'

'Well, that's taking photos!' Zhong had been friends with Dad for so many years, he knew just how to humour him. With his chopsticks, he had extracted a large morsel of eel from the hotpot, and placed it in Dad's saucer.

Dad stared blankly at Gran, as she put the cup of tea down in front of him, waiting to see if she would rat on him. But there's flesh on both side of the hand, as they say. She simply went back to her chair without speaking and regarded the brothers with a beaming smile.

'Ai-ya! Did anyone have such a fine pair of sons, so successful!' she exclaimed.

'I can't hold a candle to Shengqiang,' said Uncle. 'He's a big businessman nowadays, I'm just an impoverished teacher.'

Creep! You talk more baloney than a bargirl! Dad only managed to suppress the urge to swear by digging his hands in his trouser pockets and bringing out a pack of cigarettes. He stood up, laughed and addressed his brother as 'Prof!' and went out on the balcony to fetch the ashtray reposing by the potted orchid. That had been Granddad's orchid, and was many years old. Granddad had always kept his ashtray there because Gran wouldn't let him smoke indoors. So Granddad would eat his dinner, then go and sit on the balcony, look at his orchid, light up a Tianxiaxiu, and puff away.

'Dad, have one of my cigarettes,' Dad used to say. He always wanted Granddad to accept one from him. He had started on Hong Ta Shan, then went on to Yunyan brand and then, in 2000, when the chilli bean paste factory opened a shop in Yong'An City, Dad progressed to China brand, the sort that came in soft packs.

But Granddad always refused: 'I'm sticking to Tianxiaxiu. I know what I like, and that's that!' Sometimes Dad smoked Tianxiaxiu too, and the two of them would puff away together on the balcony. Gran would call from inside: 'You're a pair of junkies! You're polluting the atmosphere!'

'Just this one!' Granddad would protest, turning his back on her so he could puff the smoke out over the railings.

'Shengqiang!' Dad heard Gran's shout from inside. 'Can't you stop smoking for a minute? Your brother's come to see us!'

'I'll be back as soon as I've finished this cigarette,' said Dad. He had just lit up and nothing was going to make him abandon it now. He sat outside in Granddad's chair, the old man's ashtray in his hand, and watched his mother sipping her Pu'er tea and chatting happily away to Uncle. *Son-of-a-bitch*, he thought, and took another puff.

Dad decided to smoke his cigarette right down until the stub burned his fingers before he went back inside.

Even though he wasn't a university professor like Uncle, Dad was no fool. He knew exactly what he was doing when he bought those two packets of Sichuan pepper and gave them to his brother.

To explain what this was all about, we have to say a bit about Uncle's hand. There was something else: Dad was convinced his current position as the family's doormat had a lot to do with Uncle's hand.

Of course, only Gran could confirm that, and trying to get her to spill the beans was extremely difficult. Dad, however, had plenty to say on the topic. Ever since he could remember, his mother was always on at him: 'Shengqiang, give some of that food to your brother,' or 'Shengqiang, can't you see how

heavy that is? Carry it for your brother.' Or it would be the
neighbours: 'Come here, kid. How's your brother's withered
hand getting on?' Dad was two years younger than Uncle and
ever since he could remember, Uncle's withered hand had
been the subject of gossip in our small town. At first, Gran
was distraught, then she burned joss sticks at all the temples
in town, and took him around all the doctors. Finally, she sat
down with Uncle, took his left hand in hers and looked at it:
'It's not too bad to look at, just very small. It's perfectly nifty,
and it doesn't matter that it's a bit weak. Lucky it's the left hand
and not the right.'

Of course, Dad did not know all the ins and outs of it, but
Uncle's hand had not only made him into the family doormat,
it also nearly made his parents divorce. Gran sometimes beat
her chest and lamented what a fool she had been not to grab
her chance! She was fed up to the back teeth with living with
Granddad ... and she'd missed that one opportunity. Anyway,
Gran took the line that Granddad had caused the injury to
Uncle's hand (and now that Granddad was dead there was no
one to contradict her). The three children used to hear her
shout at him: 'He was just a little baby, and you wrenched
his hand so hard, all I asked you to do was change his nappy.
You had no reason to be so angry with him.' Every argument
between Gran and Granddad always ended up being about
Uncle's hand. He and Uncle and Aunt Coral would sit silently
in the courtyard while this was going on. Uncle played with
the abacus which Gran had bought him so he could exercise
his hand, sometimes messing around and playing it as if it was
a pipa. Aunt Coral was in fifth or sixth grade of primary, or
maybe first year of middle school, and that allowed her to take
over the chess table to do her homework on. Only Dad had
nothing to do and no toys to play with. But he wasn't giving up.
He invented a new game, sitting in the flowerbeds, carefully
clawing through the black dirt with his fingers so that every

fingernail was packed underneath with black dirt.

Dad would never forget one particular day as long as he lived. *I've always known that Zhiming was a devious creep! That was the day I found out!* Gran and Granddad fought themselves into a corner while, in the courtyard, the three children gazed up at the darkening sky. Aunt Coral had long since finished her homework and was sharpening her pencil to a sharp point. Uncle had had enough of his abacus, and Dad had made each one of his fingernails evenly black. He looked at his sister, then at his brother, and said: 'I'm hungry! When are we going to eat?'

But no one could answer that question. Uncle thought for a while, then got to his feet and went into the house. Dad, and perhaps Aunt Coral too, stared after him in alarm. But to their surprise, they heard Uncle's quiet voice: 'Mother, don't blame Dad. There's nothing the matter with me, I've just got one big and one small hand. You never know, maybe that makes me lucky.' *My fucking brother was only five or six years old! And he was that mealy-mouthed even then!*

That night, thanks to Uncle's good luck, the family finally got something to eat, under the stars. Gran was still weepy. 'Dong Zhiming's such a mature child,' she sighed. 'He's had such a hard time and he never complains.' She kept picking out food with her chopsticks to fill Uncle's bowl. They were lucky enough to have two slices of meat that night for dinner, and he got both of those too. Dad didn't know how Aunt Coral felt, but personally he would have done anything to have a withered hand, a tiny eye, a bit less flesh, even one leg less. He couldn't have cared less ... He just wanted not to be starving hungry every day. He would have given an arm and a leg to get one fucking mouthful of meat!

In any case, all that was back in the 1960s, either 68 or 69. But Uncle's hand brought him good luck again much later, though it took Dad a very long time to figure it all out. It happened in 1990, Dad was very sure of the date this time because he remembered the Asian Games were being held in Beijing. China came out top and in every snooker hall in town, they were singing the Games' anthem, including the girl who wanted to screw him, who had pouty lips like Wei Wei, the singer. Dad had only been married to Mum for a bit over two years so as far as other women were concerned, he'd gone back to being a virgin again. But Dad still remembered perfectly clearly Zhong sitting by the snooker table in the South Gate snooker hall, and digging him in the ribs with his elbow. 'Shengqiang, look at that! That girl's making eyes at us!' Was Zhong married then? No, he didn't get married till the end of the year.

She was too. Miss Pouty Lips definitely smiled at them, before she turned away to the boys and girls at her own table. 'She looks a bit like Wei Wei,' Zhong whispered into Dad's ear, 'So what?' Dad shot him a scornful look.

'So nothing, just now.... Let's wait and see!' Zhong's eyes were glued to the next table and he kept missing the ball.

'And what about Gao Yang?' Dad tut-tutted. Zhong and Gao had been going out for nearly two years, and said they were getting married at the end of the year.

'What about her?' said Zhong dismissively. And that evening, whether it was because Dad had put down six shots of liquor, or there was too much singing of the Games anthem, but one thing led to another, and what Dad remembered quite clearly (though he didn't remember much else) was that his bros from both snooker tables all went off together for a hot and spicy *ma-la* hot pot, washed down with two bottles of *baijiu* liquor, and, wait a second, yes, now he remembered, just he and Pouty Lips were left in the guest-house. Dad still remembered where she came from, she worked in 372 Factory, and spoke standard mandarin too, like Aunt Coral. They had spent so long kissing that Dad got a numb tongue. (*This girl has an engine in her mouth!* he thought to himself.) But the truth was (though of course he would not admit it) that Dad was starting to get the shakes. If you added the time he'd been going out with Mum to the years they'd been married, that made three years since he last slept with another woman. He was well out of practice, and his pecker was a bit leery.

But that girl was something else. She grabbed Dad's hand and pushed it under her skirt. Dad's fingers were freezing cold and slippery with sweat as he felt her ... suddenly an image of the bubbling vats of chilli bean paste came into his mind. After three or four hours under the fierce glare of the sun, it gave off a moan as you stirred it and the chilli was so strong you couldn't open your eyes. Dad gulped, and in an instant made up his mind. One way or another, he was going to screw this girl today, and not only that, he was going to screw many, many more women in his lifetime.

In that instant, Dad felt a jolt as if someone had touched his funny bone: he saw in a flash how the rest of his life was going to pan out, and he also understood Duan Zhiming's secret.

Nothing had been said, but he knew in his heart, all the same. He traced it back to one day sometime in 1983, when Duan Ziming, dressed in an enviably fashionable matelot T-shirt, took Dad off to meet the girls and his bros in Pingle Town. There were nods and winks, and comments about Duan Zhiming's 'hand skills' ('out of this world!') that he couldn't make head or tail of. And he, Xue Shengqiang, was so fucking stupid, it had taken him till he was twenty-five or twenty-six before the penny finally dropped!

So it was true what Uncle had said: that withered hand of his really did bring him life-long luck.

But Dad never had that kind of luck. When he was a kid, he never got any meat to eat, and he was seventeen before he ever caught a glimpse of a girl's arse. All he could do was tag along after Uncle. Even with Baby Girl, he remembered hearing:

'That fucking Duan Zhiming certainly has a nifty hand! Baby Girl only took four *yuan* 50 off him!' The youths and bums of Pingle Town took this kind of thing seriously. That fifty cents he'd saved made Duan Zhiming legendary.

In 1983, Duan Zhiming was in the third year of upper middle school. He got good marks, he could play snooker and he could pull the girls, even the likes of Zhou Xiaoqin and Liu Yufen, who hung around with the lads. They were as close as Pingle Town got to stars like Teresa Teng and Barbara Yung. Uncle was coolest dude in Pingle Town. Dad had to admit that being able to hang around with the West Street crowd and having Duan Zhiming as his older brother made him pretty big-headed. *I was such an arsehole back then!* was how he explained it to himself afterwards.

Qin started to show her bump in May. Her dad went off to the chilli bean paste factory, his carrying pole over his shoulder, to sort them out. In a situation like this, Gran was probably the only person in town capable of keeping the lid on it. In any case, no one quite knew how it happened but, very strangely, the Zhou family took the money and shut up and, even more strangely, Gran whipped Dad's bum until she drew blood and, stranger still, Dad found himself learning the ropes with old Chen in the fermentation yard and—hey presto!— that creep Duan Zhiming suddenly flitted off to university!

Dad, even now, had still not worked out what really happened but, as he said to himself: *What the hell, I never did like studying.* In any case, here he was twenty or so years later, happy as larry: he was running his own chilli bean paste factory in Pingle Town, screwing the women he wanted, playing the *mahjong* he wanted, eating the *ma-la* hot pots he wanted. He was living *la dolce vita.* As for Qin, she married a man who sold Sichuan pepper. Sichuan pepper and chilli bean paste were kith and kin and although the business was small, it gave the couple a decent livelihood.

In all seriousness, Dad had given careful consideration to those two bags of Sichuan pepper.

Anyway, there was Dad, sitting smoking his cigarette on Gran's balcony.

He sat in Granddad's chair, watching Gran and Uncle chatting away indoors. He had no idea what Uncle was saying to Gran but she laughed, leaned forward and nodded, resting both hands on her knees, and nodded again. He looked at Uncle, sprawling comfortably on the sofa, one hand in his jacket pocket, the other hand tapping his thigh, as he always did. It was two years since they had last met and Dad finally could not repress his curiosity, and stared intently at Uncle's face, trying to work out whether he looked older. But he was still as weird as ever, with his ashen pallor, prominent nose and those hazy, always speculative eyes ... *All those people who say I look like my brother must be stupid,* said Dad to himself.

He stared abstractly at mother and son, heedless of whether he had taken one, or two, or possibly even three cigarettes, out of the packet to light, until finally they stopped their endless chat and seemed to remember he was there too. Uncle turned and looked at him through the French window, then looked again, and Gran looked at him too.

'Damn, they're talking about me smoking again!' Dad stubbed out his cigarette, jumped to his feet, pushed open the door, and came into the sitting room.

Dad had not even had time to sit down on the sofa before he heard Uncle say: 'Shengqiang, I just told mother that I'll take charge of her birthday celebrations, you don't need to bother.'

'What do you mean? I've done everything, I even got my driver to go and book the room! It's the Prince's Mansion Hotel, it's a really classy place and the food's good too,' said Dad, looking from Uncle to Gran.

Gran ignored Dad. She was looking at Uncle.

He's like the prodigal son who can't put a foot wrong. I've never missed my weekly visits in all this time. Dad couldn't help feeling aggrieved. Uncle was still babbling on: 'Ai-ya, Shengqiang! Mother's not like any old eighty-year-old, and this birthday is a bit special. The Duan-Xue family's not like the neighbours either. We've got to do this really well, it's got to be out of the ordinary, really special. You get on with your own work, you've got the factory to run, and you haven't been well recently either. This trip back, I'm going to stay around for a few days and organize Mother's eightieth birthday. Besides, you and I haven't seen each other in a long time either, we ought to get together, go out for a few drinks.'

Dad wanted another smoke. He felt a surge of anger. But he finally sat where he was, thinking to himself: *Duan Zhiming, you creep, you think you can keep up with me? I can drink you under the table or my name's not Xue!*

Gran must have seen his expression. She hurriedly intervened: 'No drinking, no drinking! You can have your meals at home, drinking's bad for you!'

'Right, right! No drinking then!' Uncle hurriedly agreed.

'So, what do you think, brother, how shall we do Mother's birthday? Are you going to get singers? You just say what you want and I'll pay. I'll pay for everything!' Dad gave an expansive wave of the hand.

'Ai-ya, Shengqiang! You're too much of a businessman. Don't be so vulgar! Not everything's about money! You listen to your brother!' Gran intervened again. *These two really have got it sewn up!* Dad fell silent. All he could do was stare at Uncle and wait for him to talk.

Uncle went rat-a-tat on his knee, then said: 'This is not going to be just an ordinary birthday celebration, because we're the Duan-Xue family. It's got to be grand, and really classy, but it mustn't be tacky. The Prince's Mansion Hotel or whatever, that's fine, but getting singers along is just a way of throwing money around! The Duan-Xue family's not like other families. Pingle townsfolk are really uneducated, right? They're all humble folk, every one of them, and they do things just so-so. But we Duan-Xues aren't tacky, so we're going to make this a very grand occasion indeed.' Gran was nodding her head. *Right, you just keep nodding away!* thought Dad. 'We're not going to hold this party in a restaurant or a hotel, we're going to hold it at our factory, in the old fermentation yard behind the main building. It's big, quite big enough, and the weather will be good in April. We can dress it up a bit. Make the link between the Xue family factory with all its years of history and Mother's birthday. It will be an appropriate way to celebrate how much culture is bound up with our factory. We can ask Mr Zheng from Central University or some professor from Yong'An University literature department, after all, they're friends of mine. I can talk to them about it, offer them a bit of money, and get them to write a eulogy especially for the occasion, celebrating the Mayflower Factory and Mother's years of building it up into the magnificent business it is today. Then we can have the calligraphy mounted on a board, and have an unveiling ceremony, and invite all the locals, and reporters, and officials, and the TV station, we'll invite them all along. Nowadays, that's the way new products are always launched, Shengqiang, maybe you didn't realize that because you're stuck here in Pingle Town. Whatever you're selling, you're selling culture too, and the same goes for chilli bean paste. So, doing it that way, Mother gets her birthday and the factory gets its birthday too, two happy events together. And it won't be a bit tacky! It will be really special! The townsfolk will never have seen anything like it. It'll be beyond their wildest dreams!'

Gran was still nodding her head. 'Shengqiang, don't you think your brother's put it well?' She asked Dad.

Son-of-a-bitch, Dad wanted to say, *No, he hasn't put it at all well*. But then something else struck him. *OK,* he thought, *You just do it, Duan Zhiming. And let's see how you get on!*

So he nodded and said: 'Extraordinary, Zhiming, I could never have thought of anything like that. Very sophisticated!'

Uncle carried on tapping on his thigh with his left hand. Dad looked at him. *It's like he's afraid people won't realize just what a good hand he's got there,* he thought.

'So, Duan Zhiming,' Dad summed up, 'You'll take charge of everything. 'But if you need me to help, you just let me know. I'll make the arrangements for the venue at the factory and, remember, I'm paying the bills!' Dad added with stubborn insistence.

But Uncle skilfully brushed him off. 'Ai-ya, Shengqiang, stop talking about money. Brothers shouldn't haggle over money. Why are you bringing money up when we're giving Mother a birthday party? It's not as if any of us are short of it!'

'Yes, indeed!' said Gran. 'All this talk about money! So tacky.'

Yeah, that's me, tacky as they come! But Dad swallowed the words back. Three foot of ice takes more than a day to form, and he was big enough to take it all on the chin. He was made of sterner stuff. After all, he still had a factoryful of employees waiting for him, the retail department, the factory floor, the marketing department, his driver Zhu Cheng. And since there were so many of them, he wouldn't have any trouble in finding someone to vent his bad temper on.

And if the worst came to the worst, he could always have a go at Mum instead. He was so furious he could hardly think straight.

Poor Dad was just looking forward to letting off steam once he'd taken Uncle and his packages to a hotel, and checked him in, when Gran cut in: 'You can stay here, Zhiming. Your father's room's empty, and it's all nice and clean.' But Uncle said: 'No thanks, Mother. It's not like the old days. There's all this talk of privacy now, we have to respect people's personal space. I've come back to see you, but I'd rather stay in a hotel. I'm so often at conferences, I'm used to staying in hotels, it suits me.' *Son-of-a-bitch! Mother's taking it like a lamb. What's Duan Zhiming got that I haven't,* Dad wondered? *It's like even his farts smell sweet!*

So that was that. Gran waited by the door as the brothers picked up the things to take downstairs, all the while exhorting Dad to make quite sure to find a nice clean safe guest-house for Uncle to stay at. It was only when she had finished, that Dad remembered his domestic problems. That is, he remembered Jasmine.

Heaven knows, he would rather have forgotten all about it but, as luck would have it, just as he and Uncle got out of the door, they bumped into Jasmine. She was coming down from the fifth floor, carrying a bag of things, some clothes, perhaps, or some make-up. Her face was like bedewed pear blossom, as delicately pretty as Xishi, the legendary Chinese beauty. The three of them almost collided on the stairs. Jasmine gasped, not quite managing a greeting. Dad wavered, unsure whether to go or stay. He remembered that he had told Jasmine she had to be out of the apartment by that afternoon. Luckily, at that moment, Uncle stepped in, with a jovial: 'Who's your friend, Shengqiang?'

'Uh,' said Dad pointing upstairs. 'Our upstairs neighbour, Jasmine.'

'Good afternoon, Mr Xue,' Jasmine finally managed to get the words out.

She uttered the words so charmingly that Dad, standing outside Gran's door, was surprised to feel a rush of ice-cold sweetness.

'This is my brother,' he said, looking at Jasmine's red-rimmed eyes and feeling his heart lurch again. 'Good afternoon, Mr

Xue.' Uncle smiled. 'My surname's Duan,' he said kindly, and offered his right hand for her to shake. Jasmine hurriedly offered hers in return: 'Nice to meet you, Mr Duan.'

How many years has Duan Zhiming been away? And on his first trip back, he has to bump into Jasmine! thought Dad, grumpily as he sat in Uncle's car and directed Uncle to the Golden Leaves Hotel. 'Shengqiang, are you all right now? Mother said you'd been in hospital.' Uncle, still jovial, spoke up first. 'I'm fine!' said Dad. 'You know Mother. She's always making a mountain out of a molehill. It was nothing!' But Uncle wasn't satisfied. 'I'm your elder brother and I haven't lived forty-odd years without learning a thing or two. I know you have to do business dinners, but you should really look after yourself. You could do with smoking and drinking a bit less!' But Dad had heard this all before. It was exactly what he heard from Gran, hundreds of times over. Now, as then, it fell on deaf ears. Water off a duck's back.

'Yes, yes, yes,' he said impatiently. 'But, tell me, what have you been up these last two years?' Having finally extricated himself from Gran's clutches, Dad was eager to put his questions.

'When do I have time to be up to anything? The college keeps me so busy. I was given six PhD students this year! The teaching system nowadays is in trouble. We're treated worse than animals! There's a constant stream of national projects, as well as meetings, so we're run off our feet!' 'Ai-ya, Zhiming! That's not what I want to talk about! I want to know if you've met someone suitable!' Dad cut short the work report. Uncle sighed. He almost looked at Dad then turned back and stared fixedly at the road ahead, as if he was worried a demon might jump out in front of him. 'Oh, that,' he said reluctantly. 'Well, I can't really say.'

'Hey, I'm your brother! What can't you say to me? Don't push me out!' protested Dad.

'It's difficult,' said Uncle with a sigh gusty enough to whip up half the dust on West Street.

'What's so difficult about it?' Dad turned to face him. 'Zhiming, you've got everything going for you! You only have to look at a girl and she'll come running!'

Uncle did at least glance at Dad. Then he grimaced: ' Shengqiang, you are being ridiculous. I'm in my forties, I'm old! All my friends have kids at university. It's not like I have so many girls to choose from!'

'Hey, brother!' Dad slapped his thigh. 'You're not thinking straight! You're too much of an academic! The town's full of girls in their twenties. And then there are loads of cute-looking thirty-year-olds too. What do you mean, there's no one to choose from?'

'Shengqiang,' Uncle was still swinging his head from side to side, and the steering wheel too. 'What are you talking about? What it boils down to, what a man looks for in a mate, is someone he can talk to, be close to. What would I want with those young girls? Like that girl you just introduced me to, Jasmine, what would someone of our generation ever find to talk about with her?'

Son-of-a-bitch, Duan Zhiming! You don't miss a thing, do you? Dad felt like he had been shafted. He forced himself to smile and said nothing. But he couldn't reflecting, *What on earth do Jasmine and I chat about? Fuck it, I can't think of a single thing!*

Luckily, Dad was a born optimist. It immediately occurred to him that he got plenty of chat with Gran, more than enough in fact. He and Duan Zhiming sat in the car heading towards North Gate. Now that they were out of Gran's hearing, there was no need for discretion. Uncle took the opportunity to needle Dad. 'Shengqiang,' he asked innocently, 'how's Xingxing these days? Has she made any improvement? The last I heard, she was able to read a bit now.'

The question annoyed Dad. *My family affairs are nothing to do with you!* He pretended to study the telegraph poles flashing by, then said casually: 'Yes, she can read now. She's getting better slowly, she's got a good teacher and she's in good hands.'

'That's good,' said Uncle. 'That girl's had a hard time. You should take more care of her.'

Luckily he couldn't hear Dad's silent retort, and they arrived safely at the Golden Leaves Hotel at North Gate. Dad got Uncle checked in and signed the tab. Then he solemnly proffered the two bags of Sichuan pepper. 'This is this year's harvest,' he said. 'I bought it specially for you.'

So Uncle reached out his right hand, and accepted the bags of fragrant, fresh, green Sichuan pepper with a smile.

Finally, Dad asked him: 'Shall we go out for dinner tonight? I'll get some old friends together, and we'll give you a welcome-home dinner.'

To his surprise, Uncle said: 'Actually, I'm tired today, I'll think I'll have a rest. I'm around for a few days, after all, so we still have time to catch up. Besides, you know what Mother said, 'You should drink less!"

Dad didn't press him. He felt he had done his bit, done what had to be done and said what had to be said, and could wash his hands of it and go home.

He gave Zhu Cheng a call, but he didn't pick up. Fine, he'd walk. It was close enough. He still felt a bit down, so he called Aunt Coral, but she didn't pick up either. In a fit of pique, he decided to call Jasmine—but her phone was switched off.

Dad scrolled through his Contacts as he crossed the intersection. It was the evening rush hour and the streets were packed with people and cars. It used to be the time when the market was full of people shopping for their dinner but nothing was as it should be any more. Nowadays, they preferred to do their shopping in the supermarket, it was the same food but somehow they felt that more expensive food was cleaner.

Of course, Dad knew perfectly well that it was because everyone had more cash to spend and nothing to spend it on. They lived in this piddling little town, where walking from East Street to West Street only took fifteen minutes, yet every family insisted on getting a car, then spent their time weaving in and out of traffic jams in the clogged-up streets. The streets hadn't caught up with the changing times. They used to be a couple of inches wide and they were still a couple of inches wide. It was unbearable. *The streets are more like parking lots,* Dad grumbled to himself as he squeezed between the cars to cross the road. *Don't people have legs? Everything's walking distance, but they take the car to go and buy a bag of salt! Even if they have a grocery outside their front door, they go and queue up in the supermarket! Twenty minutes to get to the till! They're mad!*

He was getting crosser and crosser as he forced his way through the heaving crowds. Car horns blared in his ears, and drivers slammed on the brakes if they saw someone they knew, so they could pass the time of day.

'Savages!' he raged.

'Bunch of ignorant savages!' he spat a gob of spittle which landed on the pavement under a roadside tree.

Just when Dad thought things couldn't get any worse, who should he run into but Bai Yongjun. Bai was walking along with his son, now a young man grown half a head taller than his father.

'Hey, Mr Xue!' Bai greeted him. He could hardly pretend he hadn't seen Dad since they had slammed right into each other.

But Dad wasn't going to 'Mister' him. 'Well, hasn't your boy grown tall?' he said.

'He's starting lower middle school next term,' said Bai eagerly. 'Say hello to Mr Xue, son!'

'Hello, Mr Xue!' said the boy.

'OK then, I'm off home,' said Dad.

'So are we,' said Bai.

And they went their separate ways. Dad had behaved with perfect self-restraint over the last couple of years. He wouldn't even have exchanged a 'hello' with the man just a few years ago. Back in those days, he made it known that if Bai knew what was good for him, he should not show himself anywhere on the streets of Pingle Town.

Dad was in the prime of life back then, (that was in 1995 or 1996) and Bai had had the effrontery to cuckold him! Dad was going to take a bloody revenge but Mum had wept, fallen on her knees, and even tried to brain herself against the wall. She swore solemnly that it would never, ever happen again and finally managed to convince Dad not to go after Bai with a knife. The years passed, and more years, and gradually Dad began to see things from Mum's point of view. After all, how many years had he been screwing other women? He was a man with a sense of justice, after all. In all fairness, he should let bygones be bygones, just this once, there was no point in bearing a grudge. Mum should be forgiven.

But you can't fill a belly without belching, and the volcano had to blow. At dinner that evening, Mum and Dad were talking about Uncle's visit home, when Dad suddenly asked: 'Where did you buy these cold pigs' ears?'

'The supermarket,' said Mum.

Dad erupted. 'No wonder they don't taste right!' he raged. 'You try them! These pigs' ears are off! You're all the same, you people. What's wrong with pigs' ears from the market? Why do you insist on going to the supermarket? God knows how long they've been sitting around?'

Mum tasted a bite, and considered it, her head on one side. 'They're not off,' she said. 'They're fine.'

'They're off! Off!' Dad raged, and pushed the bowl of pigs' ears to one side. 'I refuse to eat them! And don't you go buying them in the supermarket, ever again!'

'Your Dad's always been like that, flying off the handle for no reason at all. He can't stand your uncle, never could. He's got the worst temper in the family, but you can't hold it against him, we all have our faults.' So Mum told me later.

Of course, she said nothing of the sort that evening. She knew better. She had been married to Dad a long time. She picked out a bit of stir-fried chicken and bamboo shoots with her chopsticks, put it in his bowl, and simply said: 'Have some of this chicken. I made it myself.'

So Dad ate it. It was an old favourite, Mum used the factory's own chilli bean paste in it. Dad could not find any other excuse to pick a quarrel, so he put his phone on the table and waited for someone to call. It didn't matter who, Zhong, Jasmine, whoever. Any excuse to go out drinking or screwing.

But no one called him today. Dad suspected that everyone in town had heard the news: withered-hand Duan Zhiming was back in town. Now that brother of his had fucking stolen his thunder. His big brother always had been the bigger draw.

Back in 1984, he'd done whatever it took to screw Baby Girl, even stealing the Huangs' rabbit or sneaking eggs to sell on market day. With five *yuan*, he was Baby Girl's client and Baby Girl was nice to him.

Then one day when they'd finished having sex, and were lying there chatting, Baby Girl suddenly asked: 'Have you got an elder brother? His surname's Duan?'

Dad was in a post-orgasmic haze and just grunted. 'Uh-huh.'

'Ai-ya!' she raised herself on her elbows and looked down at Dad. 'The first time I saw you, I reckoned you were his spitting image! An absolutely identical nose!'

'So he's at university, is he?' she asked again. 'I heard he came top of the county in the college science entrance exams!'

Dad would have loved to deny it but he was riding a tiger he couldn't get off. Finally he gave a reluctant nod.

Baby Girl was thrilled, and babbled on and on about Uncle. When he left that day, Dad pulled out the usual five *yuan*.

'Ai-ya! You're Duan Zhiming's brother! I'll give you a discount!' Baby Girl said with a merry laugh, and scrabbled around for fifty cents change.

Dad took the fifty cents and left. As he picked his way down the street, he felt mortified. He was only seventeen. That son-of-a-bitch brother of his. He'd never be able to go and screw Baby Girl again.

This evening, just as he was about to go to bed, Dad's phone finally rang. It was Aunt Coral, asking why he had called her that afternoon.

Dad brought her up to date on the last two days' family news without, of course, telling her about his stay in hospital.

'So, Zhiming's back,' said Aunt Coral quietly.

'Uh-huh,' said Dad, equally quietly. 'Mother wants him to organize the birthday celebrations so I don't need to bother.'

'That's good,' said Aunt Coral. 'She won't fuss so much if he does it. I'll give Zhiming a ring in a bit, and ask if he wants any help.'

'What about my brother-in-law and the rest of them?' asked Dad 'Did you tell them? It's looking like the party will be next Sunday.'

'I told him,' said Aunt Coral. 'Xingchen and his wife will come too. I've told them.'

'Sis, how have you two been getting along lately?' said Dad, finally asked, after a long pause for thought.

'We're fine,' said Aunt Coral with a sigh. 'Listen Shengqiang, don't you worry about my affairs. We're in our fifties. Nothing's going to happen. That's what things are like nowadays. What man doesn't have a bit on the side?'

'Sis ...' Dad started, then stopped. There was so much he wanted to say but none of it seemed right. He finally went on: 'If there's anything I can help with, just give me a call.'

'Right,' said Aunt Coral, 'I'll hang up then. You get to bed. Give my best to Anqin.' Dad cut the call and went back indoors, where Mum was still watching *Golden Wedding* and reading a book at the same time. Dad always teased her about this: 'Comrade Chen Anqin, make up your mind! Are you watching TV or reading a book?' Mum paid no attention, just reached out and slapped him. 'What rubbish you talk! What's it got to do with you?' Dad glanced at the book in her hand. It had a bright red cover and was called: *Rage against Death*.

'Whatever's that you're reading? What a scary title!' He tried to grab it off her but she wasn't letting go. The fifteen-minute adverts came up on the screen, and she buried herself in its pages, reading furiously and muttering: 'Ai-ya! You don't know what you're talking about!'

He felt suddenly uneasy, and Mum seemed to feel a slight change in the atmosphere too. She raised her head from her book and asked: 'Who was that on the phone?'

'Sis. She sent you her best wishes,' said Dad, glossing over his awkwardness. 'How is she?' 'Fine.' Dad took off his slippers and got into bed. 'Have you washed your feet?' demanded Mum, who had a keen sense of smell. 'They stink to high heaven! Go and wash them!' Dad supposed he had walked a good long way that day, and obeyed. Only he couldn't be bothered to get the enamel foot-basin out, just stood in front of the sink and lifted one foot up and washed it, then the other.

When he thought back on it not long after, he reckoned he must have been missing one of his women just then, one of the ones he'd screwed. He couldn't remember which one in particular, probably Jasmine, or maybe Baby Girl, or even Miss Pouty Lips. If not them, it must have been Bai's old lady. She wasn't bad-looking, a bit too much fat on the belly, but a nice light skin.

He dried his feet and went back to bed. Mum was still watching the soap on TV, clutching her bright-red *Rage against Death* in her hands. Dad stretched out in bed. *At least I can finally go to fucking sleep,* was his last thought before he dropped off.

4

THE LAST TIME the family was all together must have been at Chinese New Year in 2005. Gran wanted them all to have a New Year's Eve dinner together but Liu Xingchen wanted to go to his in-laws. He and Zhao were just married that year. Dad worked on Gran, saying that if the young folk weren't happy then no one would enjoy it, and Gran nodded and moved the dinner to the 29th of the first month. It was to start at half past twelve, midday, and would held in the Cuckoo Garden private room at the Floating Fragrance Restaurant.

It was to be the last New Year's dinner with Grandpa, but since no one knew that at the time, everyone came looking very casual. There was Aunt Coral and Uncle Liu Qukang, Liu Xingchen and his new wife Zhao, who was pregnant with Diandian, Dad, Mum, Grandpa and Gran. The only one missing was Uncle. 'Zhiming's gone to Japan,' announced Gran, looking pleased, 'so he can't come back for a New Year's dinner.'

And I don't want to see him either! Dad cheerfully opened the bottles, and the men of the family started drinking.

'This is our New Year dinner,' pronounced Gran, 'so I'm not going to stop you. Having a drink livens the party up, but in moderation please, no getting drunk.' 'Shengqiang,' added Aunt Coral, 'Don't keep re-filling Qukang's glass, and you should go easy too.' Mum was next: 'Xue Shengqiang, I'm warning you, do stop showing off. And if you drink yourself paralytic, don't think I'm going to look after you!' 'I'm driving, so I'm not drinking a drop,' said Liu Xingchen. His new wife sat there saying nothing at all.

So the three men, Dad, Grandpa and Uncle Liu, lined their glasses up in the middle of the table and poured out the Five Grain *baijiu* liquor. 'Half a glass down in one!' cried Grandpa. 'Let's start on half a glass!' 'That's enough for me!' said Uncle Liu. 'Enough! You have a bit more, Shengqiang, I'm going easy tonight.'

Dad was fed up. These men were pussy-whipped. 'Now you listen to me! Drink up! None of you are going home till you're properly pissed!' And he filled their glasses until they brimmed over.

Suffice it to say, that evening the men got pissed as newts. The womenfolk sat there, clucking away at their husbands, sons and brothers: 'Ai-ya! Go easy on the *baijiu*!'

The first to concede defeat was Grandpa. He only got as far as the second round when Gran signalled to Liu Xingchen to take his glass away, and share the two digits of liquor left in it between Dad and Uncle Liu. Grandpa said nothing, just raised his glass one last time and drained it to the last drop.

After a while, Aunt Coral told Uncle Liu to stop too. 'Ai-ya! Sis!' protested Dad, trying to fill Uncle's glass again. 'Let the old man have a bit more! New Year only comes once a year! We're bros, we want to celebrate!'

'Xue Shengqiang,' said Gran. 'You should look after yourself.'

'I've had enough,' said Uncle Liu. 'I can't drink anymore.'

So Dad poured the remaining six shots into his own glass, covered his glass with the palm of his hand and said: 'Fine! If you're not drinking it, I will! And don't any of you try stopping me!'

No one else at the table could do anything about it. 'If you want to drink, then you go right ahead,' said Mum. 'If your mother's not bothered, why should anyone else be?'

The meal went well on the whole, however, and Dad didn't get terribly drunk. Once he had finished his glass of *baijiu*, he tried to persuade Uncle Liu to split a bottle of beer with him. 'Have a drop of beer, Dad,' he offered Granddad. But Gran said: 'Your father can't drink beer. He has gout.'

It was nearly three in the afternoon when the party broke up. At the restaurant door, Aunt Coral and her family got into Liu Xingchen's car and set off for Yong'An City. Mum was going to drive Granddad and Gran back home. Dad said he would walk, they were practically on the doorstep. 'Fine,' said Gran, 'I don't want to have to breathe in your fumes anyway.'

Dad waved them away and swayed off down the road to his home. The street was full of kids letting off firecrackers. He felt chilled to the bone and there was a buzzing in his ears. Suddenly he thought of Zhao and Xingchen's baby. It's got to be a boy! There are far too many bossy women in this family!

In August that year, Liu Xingchen and Zhao had a little boy, Diandian. The senior Mr Liu, his grandfather, was delighted and conferred on him the formal name, Liu Shangqiang. Dad was gloomy. Yes, it was one more male in the family, he reflected as he puffed on his cigarette, but Grandpa had passed on by then, so it made no damned difference at all to the numbers.

They did not go to Diandian's one-month party—Gran was not in the mood for celebration. Then, a couple of months later, Uncle Liu phoned Dad.

'Shengqiang,' he whispered. 'There's something I need your help with.'

'Of course, Qukang, what is it?' Dad said cheerfully. Of all the men in the family, it always came down to him to fix problems.

He wondered what it could be about. His brother-in-law was the son of officials and, after the regulation few years working on a farm, had landed a job in the Provincial Secretariat Complaints Department where he worked for the next few decades. Maybe his cosseted upbringing had addled his brain: it turned out he was calling Dad to ask him to look out for an apartment on the new development area at the edge of Pingle Town 'for a friend to live in.'

It was absurd. They were men of the world, and Dad did not need to be told that the 'friend' had to be a woman.

As Uncle Liu stammered down the phone, Dad didn't know whether to laugh or have a go at him. *Liu Qukang, you dumb bastard! You've been lucky to have Sis as a wife all these years, you don't earn much, but she pays for your nice clothes and a nice car for you. And now you think you'll take a mistress just like everyone else?*

It occurred to him that his brother-in-law had form in this department. Dad sat in the study, stubbing a half-finished cigarette out in his ashtray and thought back to 1996.

It was just before Chinese New Year, and Dad was busy at the factory all evening hosting a dinner for the staff, their clients and local government officials, and giving out gifts. It was all a huge headache. Then, late that night, his phone rang. Where was Mum? Ah, he remembered, they still hadn't got back to sharing a bedroom again.

He did not recognize the voice at the other end: 'Mr Xue, your friend Mr Liu is in police detention. Would you stand bail for him?'

Dad hadn't been able to think, for a moment, who 'Mr Liu' was. 'Son-of-a-bitch! What dumb ass is that?' he said. 'Why's he messing me around in the middle of the night?'

There was a shuffling at the other end of the line and then Dad heard Uncle Liu's voice. 'Shengqiang, it's me, your brother-in-law,' he said, almost inaudibly. 'I'm, er, at the South Street Police Station, um, there's been a bit of trouble, um, me and my bros, I'm sorry to bother you but could you lend me

3,000. I, um, I'll pay you back tomorrow.'

Dad had put two and two together. Zhong had warned him a few days before: 'Shengqiang, you better stay away from Fifteen Yuan Street for a bit. The coppers are out to make a bit of money over New Year. I've been told by some of my friends in the police that they'll be doing a sweep of the red-light district!'

Dad had said. 'We're living in the 1990s! You don't get your head chopped off for going to a brothel! I don't believe any copper in Pingle Town would dare bang me up!'

'All the same, don't go there. I mean it,' Zhong said earnestly.

Dad was pretty pissed off at that. He gave his friend a punch: 'You're really out of order! You don't think of me when it's anything else, only when they're going to raid the brothels!'

And now this unholy mess. Dad had to get dressed and drive to the police station in Mum's car, to get Uncle Liu out. There were two officers on duty. Uncle and his friends were sitting on sofas in the inner office, clutching paper cups of tea which the police had made them. Dad was well known about town, and when he arrived, he was greeted politely, handed over the money and they were released. Dad then spent the rest of the night driving them home to Yong'An City.

On the way, his friends were as subdued as a bunch of capons, but Uncle Liu sat in the passenger seat gabbling away, effusive with thanks, and giving Dad a blow-by-blow account of the evening's events. They had been on a New Year's office outing and, on the way back to the city, some of them had got it into their heads that they wanted to go to Pingle Town's red-light district. Uncle Liu knew all about Fifteen Yuan Street, after all, he'd married into a Pingle Town family. So he was happy to take them along. And they'd landed right in the shit.

'Shengqiang, please don't tell your sister,' Uncle Liu finally stammered.

'Ai-ya, brother!' Dad exclaimed, turning the headlights on

full beam and looking at the road ahead. 'Of course I won't! We're all men, we understand each other. There's no need to tell the womenfolk! Don't worry, it's not a big deal after all! Just bad luck!'

And that was when Uncle Liu realized that the lad he had watched grow up had turned into a man. He pushed his glasses up his nose and said: 'Shengqiang, I'm sorry we've caused you all this trouble. You certainly know how to look after your family.'

As Dad smoked, he thought back to that night. He had fucking made a rod for his own back. He had been totally taken in by Uncle, and had responded, in all sincerity: 'Qukang! How many years have we known each other? You don't need to go all polite on me! Anything you need, you just tell me. And so long as I can do it, I will!'

Dad had given his word, he decided, and when Uncle Liu came to him about the apartment, well, it wasn't him who was taking a mistress, and there was absolutely no advantage in telling Aunt Coral, and if Qukang hadn't asked him, he would go and ask someone else so, right, there it was. Better not wash the family dirty linen in public, it was only a girl after all.

So he gritted his teeth and rented a brand-new, furnished, two-bedroom apartment in the new residential area. It was smart and cosy. When Uncle Liu came and got the keys, he told Dad all about his 'friend' who, he said, was from out of town and didn't known anyone here and just needed a place to live for a while, and so on and so forth.

Dad looked at him. Uncle was in his fifties. His hair was dyed jet-black, and he was still a fine figure of a man, with his gold-rimmed glasses and his air of culture. But he talked as much baloney as a bargirl.

It was all Gran's fault. In 1980, or maybe 1981, Aunt Coral had been going out with a young man at the Grain Bureau. They were getting on really well, but Gran was trying to match her daughter up with Uncle Liu. 'Mr Liu senior is in the provincial military. They're a highly-educated and cultured family. If you marry into a city family, it will do you great credit, Coral. You listen to your mother, my girl. I made a bad marriage, and look at the hardships I've had to put up with. If you marry a boy from Pingle Town, things will never be any better for you. I'm not going to say any more, but you know very well that it won't do you any good to stay around Pingle Town any longer. Of course, I'm not forcing you, I'm just advising you. It's up to you to make up your mind.' Dad overheard Gran talking and he also overheard Aunt Coral crying all night in her room. He was only fifteen back then, so Aunt Coral must have been twenty-three or twenty-four. But time flew by and now here were Aunt Coral and Uncle Liu, middle-aged and with their first grandchild a few months old. The fact that Uncle Liu was taking on a mistress in her twenties—yes, that was all Gran's doing!

That was the first time Dad felt the burden of being in charge, and the first time he felt his family was completely dysfunctional. There he was, setting up Jasmine in her apartment. There Uncle Liu was, getting himself a mistress on the quiet. That day, like a proper head of the family, he got out the keys and gave them to Uncle Liu. 'I've paid six months' rent in advance,' he told him. 'Now it's down to you.'

'Now it's down to you' was something Dad had heard Gran say but he knew it was nonsense. Of course, Aunt Coral had found out about Uncle Liu's little frolic, Dad never dared ask how. He reckoned Uncle Liu wouldn't have dared rat on him, so Aunt Coral probably never knew it was her own brother who rented the apartment for her husband.

Dad felt that this was the worst thing he had done to a woman in his whole life.

But, well, what was said was said, and what was done was done. The next day, on the way to the factory, Dad pulled out his phone and, just like that, gave Jasmine another call. The phone rang a dozen times but no one answered. He leaned back against the soft upholstery of the Audi back seat, feeling uneasy. Eventually, he asked Zhu Cheng: 'Has Jasmine phoned?'

'Uh?' Zhu Cheng, glancing at Dad in the rear-view mirror, was evasive.

'Jasmine,' repeated Dad. 'Has she called you?'

'Oh!' Zhu Cheng swung the car round the bend. 'No, she hasn't.'

'Let me know if she does?' Dad instructed him.

'Sure.'

At the intersection, there was the usual traffic jam outside the Tian Mei Department Store. It didn't seem to matter whether it was Monday or the weekend, whether it was blowing a gale or raining, there were always pedestrians overflowing onto the road here. But this time Zhu Cheng kept his temper and just sat quietly in the driving seat, drumming on the steering wheel with his right hand. Suddenly, Dad remembered something: 'Zhu Cheng, how old's your little one now?'

'She's going to be two,' said Zhu Cheng.

'Time flies!' Dad said, looking out of the window, watching the crowds, some familiar faces among them, flocking across the road like ducks. 'I don't know how it happens! Your baby's nearly two years old! It seems like yesterday that you were only twenty-two or twenty-three yourself!'

'Ai-ya!' responded Zhu Cheng. 'Time does fly. I'm past thirty now! I'm an old man!'

'You're in your prime,' Dad laughed. 'Don't try and tell me that thirty-something is old! I'm the one who's old.'

'Mr Xue, you're not old!' protested his driver. 'In the eyes of the world, you're still a kid!' Zhu Cheng finally managed to squeeze the car through a gap in the crowds and drove on towards the bean paste factory.

So when did Dad himself feel old for the first time? It must have been last year, yes, definitely last year. It was his fortieth birthday and Zhong and some other friends insisted on taking him out to celebrate. In fact, they did the same as usual—drinking, smoking, eating, girls—and there was shouting and yelling, and swearing and telling off-colour jokes about each other's misspent youth. It was going on nine o'clock and Zhong, who was pretty pissed, grabbed hold of a waitress and would not let her go. (Gao Tao wasn't there that day, or he would not have gone so far.)

'Come here, girlie! Drink a glass with me!' he shouted, his arm tight around the girl's waist and trying to bury his face in her breasts.

'Ai-ya! Zhong!' Dad protested, and extracted the girl from his embrace. 'Just mind what you're doing!'

'Me, mind what I'm doing? Now who's talking? I'm not the one who needs to mind what they're doing!' Zhong, his eyes bloodshot, looked up from the table. 'You've got a nerve, Xue Shengqiang! You're such a weasel! You're got your wife in one house and your mistress in another place, and did I ever tell you to mind what you're doing? I've got nothing to mind!' he raged drunkenly, spattering saliva in Dad's face.

Everyone around the table was embarrassed. No one said anything. Zhong had lost his wife, Gao Yang, to pancreatic cancer just the year before. She was much lamented by all her childhood friends in Pingle Town. Not even forty! 'Gao Yang was four months younger than me!' said Mum. In fact, she said it many times, to anyone who would listen. Well anyway, that was how it was. The rest of them took it in turns to get Zhong out on a regular basis, for a drink and a meal.

Dad didn't want to admit it but he was so plastered, he'd forgotten Gao Yang was dead. He couldn't think how he was going to wriggle out of this one. He didn't know how the hell Zhong had heard about Jasmine, but pushed that thought to the back of his mind. He pushed the waitress back to Zhong, jumped to his feet, filled Zhong's glass and his own, and held it up.

'Zhong!' he roared. 'Don't say stuff like that! Me and my big mouth, I'm such a young nincompoop. I'm going to make it up to you! I'm going to drink three glasses as a penalty!'

He drank one glass, then another, then a third. They tried to stop him: 'Shengqiang, Zhong's drunk too, don't be like that, you can't drink *baijiu* like that. You're drinking too fast!' But Dad flung them off and shoved the glass at his lips. Only it wasn't a *baijiu* glass, it was a beer glass and held at least five shots and he was pouring it down, glug glug glug ...

That was the moment when Dad knew he was old. He got halfway down the glass, and realized he was a goner. It felt like he was swallowing his own life. His eyes blurred, his nose was blocked and he could hardly breathe. He scrunched up his big toes and, as the brimming contents of the glass surged down into his belly, he collapsed back into his chair.

There was general consternation. Zhong told him afterwards that his face had been the colour of candle wax. 'As yellow as funeral money!' he exclaimed. Everyone crowded around, pinching the acupressure point under his nose, opening doors to let some air in, pouring him some water, patting him on the back.

They were all calling his name, making such a squawking, you'd think something terrible had happened. *Ai-ya, keep your voices down!* He grumbled to himself, but could not get the words out.

The words seemed to be stuck in his throat, and all he could do was stare helplessly at the shadowy figures of the people dancing around in front of him. He felt very ill. Then Zhong leaned in to pinch his acupressure point, and pinched it so hard that Dad thought he was going to wet himself.

Then he did. It was one of the waitresses who saw. 'Ai-ya!

There's pee on the floor!'

The crotch of Dad's trousers was wet. Urine dripped onto the beige carpet and there was a pong in the air.

Dad was behaving as if nothing at all was the matter, but the rest of them were in a complete panic. 'Call an ambulance!' someone shouted.

Ai-ya! Keep your voices down! Dad was working himself into a rage. He wanted to give them a thorough bollocking but the words would not come out. He reached out to grab Zhong's arm, the arm he was using to pinch Dad viciously under his nose.

'Shengqiang! Shengqiang!' Zhong shouted, grabbing his hand and failing to stop the tears that welled in his eyes from running down his cheeks.

Do stop that bawling, you dickhead! I'm not your woman, and I'm not dying either!

Well anyway, after about five minutes, certainly less than ten, Dad revived. He gripped Zhong's hand and finally got the words out: 'Ai-ya! Can't you sons-of-bitches keep your voices down?'

Only a few of them knew about the day when Dad wet himself after drinking three glasses of *baijiu* and they kept it to themselves. It wouldn't do for the news to get out. Dad pulled himself up in his chair and said to his bros: 'Not a word about this! Anyone who breathes a word about this will get cancer of the pecker.'

Of course he didn't drink any more that day, in fact he didn't touch a drop for a whole week afterwards. 'Ai-ya! I'm really going easy on the booze, I am!' he vowed, as he sipped his glass of hot orange juice.

Zhu Cheng came to fetch him, signed the chit and brought him some new trousers. Dad put them on and felt like a new man. 'Cornucopia Court!' he ordered his driver.

He wasn't going to see Gran, but Jasmine. He had a shower,

then they went to bed. Jasmine rummaged around inside his trousers but Dad mumbled: 'Ai-ya! I've had too much to drink. Gotta sleep now, sleep,' and pulled her hand out.

Jasmine might have been dissatisfied, but she didn't show it. She leaned her head meekly against Dad's shoulder and said: 'Yes, let's go to sleep.'

Dad caught a whiff of her shampoo and suddenly thought of something. 'Which year were you born?' he asked her.

When she told him, he exclaimed: 'Ai-ya, you're so little! When I was hanging around on the street, you were still in nappies!'

That made Jasmine giggle. 'Shengqiang, what ridiculous things you say! I'm not "so little", I'm a big girl!'

'Ai-ya! I really am old!' And Dad patted her on the shoulder.

'You're not old! In the eyes of the world, you're still a kid!' Jasmine said cheerfully. Her thigh, cool and satiny soft, lay across Dad's.

Talk like this made Dad realize that things had changed. He'd been to the gates of hell and back and of course he'd changed. The days when he callously screwed anything that moved had gone for good. It was just like the advice Zhong had given him: 'I'm only going to say this once,' he'd said, 'but you're an intelligent man, it's down to you now.'

From that day on, Dad decided to get his life in order, whether it was screwing Jasmine, or Mum, or any other woman. He made up his mind there'd be no more acting stupid, no more FFM! In 2006, once he was past his fortieth birthday, Dad knew he was old.

But, of course, in spite of all his good intentions, every now and then, just once in a blue moon, if he was with some especially enthusiastic client or a hostess who insisted on a threesome in a hotel room, then Dad couldn't very well disappoint them, could he? So, a quick takeaway then?

An arm around each of them, he would sway unsteadily into

the room, have a couple of befuddled pokes, then get up at the crack of dawn and go off to the bathroom and stand holding his pecker over the toilet and pee some meagre dribbles, vowing: *This really is the last time, you son-of-a-bitch!* Still, the occasional lapse was unavoidable, because he was the only one amongst all the milling hordes of workers in the factory who could schmooze the clients. Finding and entertaining them, closing deals, getting his products onto supermarket shelves, it was all down to him. The others were all so dopy. Only Zhu Cheng had any spark to him. Sometimes, when Dad was out at a restaurant with clients, the unpleasant truth stared him in the face: hostesses were just that, no matter how much sex you had with them. But with men, it was different. You were bros forever once you'd shared a couple of bottles of spirits and paid a couple of visits to a brothel. And that was the road to ruin. He raised his glass to the buyer from the Yong'An Cheng Hui Supermarket opposite and drained it, looked down at his crotch, and felt sadness welling up inside him. Just at that moment, he glanced sideways, to see a hostess: 'What's up, sir? You look miserable!' 'Ay!' Dad threw his arms around her and pushed his face into her soft, white breasts, breathing deeply. Revived, he exclaimed: 'Don't call me "sir"! You and me, we're both escorts. Let's escort each other today!'

All the girls laughed and applauded. And that evening, he was the star of the show. The girls all clung to him, competing to serve him drinks, and pinching his thighs, while the men in the room were amazed at the magical powers he had suddenly acquired. Obviously there was no getting out of this evening's business, so Dad cheered up. He sat up straight, feeling there was still life in the old dog yet, so why not have a quick takeaway?

Fine wine and coffee, I'll drink old loves away. He sang the Teresa Teng song in his head, washed off her scent, told himself this was just a one-off and all water under the bridge. But when he walked into the two-story bean paste factory office building, and Zeng, the office manager popped his head out and said that 'Professor Duan' was waiting in his office, his heart sank. He strode into the Director's Office, to see that boring old fart of a brother of his sitting behind the enormous director's desk, flipping through his personal desk diary. Fury erupted in him. *I spent years of my life stirring those vats, I sweated my fucking guts out, till I finally got to sit behind that desk, and you just come and plonk your arse onto my chair!*

'Ah, you're here, Shengqiang!' his brother greeted him with enthusiasm

'You're early, Zhiming!' Dad beamed a welcoming smile. 'Have you had lunch?'

'Yes, I went to Seven Immortals Bridge this morning, and had a bowl of spicy tripe noodles. As good as it ever was!' Uncle sighed with satisfaction, and sat back down in the chair.

There was nothing for it. Dad had to take the visitor's chair on the other side of the desk. The pair of them faced off on either side of the huge square desk. It was not what he was used to. Normally, he sat in the chair Uncle was occupying, issuing orders to some unlucky person opposite him.

'Ai-ya!' Dad slapped the table in front of him. 'What's so special about tripe noodles? This evening, I'll take you out for a really good meal. Wait till you taste the fresh oysters at the Floating Fragrance Restaurant!'

'But Shengqiang,' said Uncle with a smile, 'You eat the local specialities every day, you don't appreciate them. I'm off here and there from one end of the year to the next, and all I can think of is Seven Immortals Bridge and their spicy tripe noodles. Don't you remember market days, how we used to go there, first thing, for a bowl of spicy tripe noodles, with a steaming layered pancake dunked in it? There was nothing to beat it!'

Nothing indeed! Dad gritted his teeth. He turned away and called the office manager. 'Bring us two cups of tea, will you, Zeng?'

'Hua Mao Peak,' he added.

At least they could start on the business in hand while they waited. Then, when Zeng came in and poured the teas, Dad made the introductions and explained the plans to hold Gran's eightieth birthday celebrations at the factory. He instructed Zeng to work with Uncle on the arrangements—there was no need for Dad to burn his fingers on that particular hot potato, his manager could handle it.

The scalding tea did burn his mouth, true, but Dad was used to that. The grey-green tealeaves and the yellow-tinged chrysanthemum flowers, floated in the steaming glass cups. It was a sight to gladden the heart. There was something about this three *yuan* a packet, Blue-and-white Brand Hua Mao Peak tea, drunk by Grandpa and now by Dad, and served to all comers without discrimination. It was a bit like the whores of Fifteen Yuan Street, where customers came in search of a bit of a wind-down, and got what they came for. Dad blew away the tealeaves floating on the surface. He sipped, and relaxed.

Uncle said nothing. The office manager's obsequious manners clung to his face like chicken feathers.

'Zhiming,' Dad broke the silence. He had had enough of grumbling away to himself, and made an effort to be polite. 'It's putting you to a lot of trouble, all this organizing Mother's birthday party. I know you're busy.'

'She's going to be eighty,' said Uncle. 'She's not had an easy life. It's the least we can do, we owe it to her as her children.'

'Time flies,' said Dad. 'Suddenly she's got to eighty years old.'

'Right,' Uncle gave a sigh. 'If our father was still here, wouldn't he be eighty-six, or eighty-seven?'

'Eighty-six,' Dad said. 'Eighty-seven after the Mid-Autumn

festival.'

So Granddad would have been eighty-seven after the Mid-Autumn festival. Dad was suddenly overwhelmed with sadness at the thought. Here was Gran, still alive at eighty, and Granddad would never make it to eighty-seven.

The last time he had seen Uncle was at Granddad's funeral. Out of the whole clan, only Dad, Uncle and Liu Xingchen went. Aunt Coral did come back to Pingle Town, but she was with Gran at Cornucopia Court, as was Mum. Uncle Liu said he would come but, at the last moment, had something else to do. Zhao was pregnant, so of course could not run the risk of getting upset. It was all very simple, as Gran had instructed. The three men were the only mourners. Uncle, as the eldest, carried the urn, and the undertakers herded them, like a flock of ducks, to Clearwater Creek where Granddad was interred. Was it raining? It must have been. Dad had a clear memory of squelching through the mud in his leather shoes. The cemetery looked like a chessboard. They made their way to the plot, which was the size of a table, scarcely a metre square, where a gravestone stood propped at a crazy angle. Dad frowned. 'Why's the grave so small?' he asked Uncle. When Granddad died suddenly, the brothers had taken charge of different things: Dad sorted out the shambles at the hospital and the crematorium, Uncle volunteered to make arrangements for the grave, and got Zhong to drive him around.

'Shengqiang,' said Uncle, sounding just like Gran. 'When someone's dead, they're just ashes. Nowadays, in the city, you just buy a niche to put the funerary urn in. It's only in a place like Pingle Town that there are big graves still. Father wasn't an ostentatious man, when he was alive. When an old man dies, the funeral's a happy occasion. The old man's gone to rest, isn't that right?'

Liu Xingchen chimed in: 'Uncle, it's nice and clean here, and everyone can come and pay their respects at the grave.'

It certainly was nice and clean. Three slabs, a small cavity the size of a bum cheek chiselled in the marble to hold the casket with Grandad's ashes, and another slab to cover it up. Before Dad had had time even to check that the slabs were level, the undertakers had puddled on the cement with a few flicks of the shovel, as if they were frying pot-sticker dumplings. Uncle thanked the workmen effusively and handed out cigarettes by way of a tip.

They lit firecrackers, tearing off the packaging, then lit the candles and joss sticks.

The first to make his kow-tow was Uncle. It really was a miserable day. The ground was muddy and littered with grey ash and red firecracker papers. Uncle asked the undertaker: 'Have you got a mat or something? I'm going to get my trousers dirty.' The man had come prepared, and produced a plastic sheet; Uncle knelt on that to knock his head three times on the ground in the proper way.

Then it was Dad's turn. He marched up to the plastic sheet, kicked it to one side, fell to his knees and thwacked his head hard three times in the mud. 'That's enough! Shengqiang!' protested Uncle. 'You're ruining your clothes!'

Dad got to his feet without a word, took a step back and found his bum wedged against the guy whose tombstone was next door. Then he bent down to retrieve the plastic and laid it out again. 'Come on, Xingchen,' he said, 'kowtow to your granddad.'

So Liu Xingchen kowtowed, and that was that. All over. At that point, the cemetery staff approached and asked for their management fee.

'Fee?' Uncle frowned. 'What on earth do you mean? A state-run business can't just levy any fees it likes! I was told quite clearly when I bought the plot and the gravestone that there was nothing more to pay!'

'That's the way we do it here, Mr Duan,' explained the

undertaker. 'We always charge a management fee. It's on an annual basis, everyone has to pay.'

'Well, you have a funny way of doing things here!' said Uncle indignantly. 'I know how these things work, and I've never heard of a cemetery charging a management fee. Why didn't you explain this when I came and settled up. Mind you, if you had, we might not have chosen your cemetery!'

'But, sir,' this was the undertaker again, 'every cemetery does the same.'

'So what's the damage then?' Dad was belligerent.

'Fifty *yuan* a year. If you pay ten years up front, you save one year's fee,' said the cemetery worker, taking out a price list with an official-looking stamp at the top.

'What's all this about?' said Liu Xingchen, taking the paper and looking at it. 'How long do we have to pay for?'

'We'll pay up!' Dad grabbed the paper off him. 'A hundred years, is that enough? Ten thousand years! We'll pay a hundred years up front, and if that's not enough, come and ask me for more! You know where to find me, Mr Xue Shengqiang, at the West Street Mayflower Chilli Bean Paste Factory!'

'Shengqiang!' Uncle reached out his left hand and rested it on Dad's arm. What a lily-white, satin-smooth hand it was. 'This is not a question of money, it's a matter of principle!'

'Damn principles!' Dad shouted at Uncle for the first time ever. 'I'll pay up! I like spending money! Money's just paper! Come on, I'll pay a hundred years upfront!'

He really did pay hundred years upfront, or rather ninety years, with ten years thrown for free. It was fifty *yuan* per year, making a total of 4,500 *yuan*. The manager of Clearwater Creek Cemetery had never seen anything like it.   'Are you paying by card, Sir?' he enquired.

'No, I'm paying cash,' said Dad, pulling a wallet crammed bullet-hard with notes, from his pocket. He counted out forty-five 100-*yuan* notes and slapped them down on the table. 'And now I've paid up, just mind you look after our grave properly!'

'Oh, for sure, Sir, for sure!' the manager counted the money and got an assistant to make out a receipt.

Dad came out of the gate, holding the scrap of paper in his hand. Uncle and Liu Xingchen were waiting for him by the Audi. Zhu Cheng was not there, so Dad was driving.

'Shengqiang! Whatever were you doing? Even if you're loaded with money, you shouldn't splash it around like this!' Uncle sighed.

Dad said nothing. He got into the driving seat and started the engine. Then he drove them back to Cornucopia Court.

Back at Gran's house, there was, of course, no mention of the hundred-year management fee. Everyone was busy consoling the newly-widowed Gran. Mrs Tang had prepared the funeral meal, and the tables groaned under plates of fish, chicken, duck and other meat and vegetables. They should have had a cheerful wake and then gone their separate ways. Except that Gran—perhaps she had dosed herself with some medicine that disagreed with her—spent the whole time criticizing everything from the duck stew (tough) to the chopsticks (dirty) to Aunt Coral, who wasn't trying hard enough to better herself. She might have been sacked as presenter to her TV show, but she hadn't put up enough of a fight. Well, so be it, but 'Coral, what do you mean by being so high-minded?' demanded Gran. Then it was Uncle's turn: Why was he still not married after all these years, how long was he going to go on shilly-shallying about? 'Don't you think you owe it to me, to your father, to get yourself a wife, Zhiming? The whole family worked so hard to put you through university, and you did all that studying!' And she quoted the old saw from Mencius: 'There are three ways to be undutiful, and having no sons is the worst! Well? Don't tell me you don't understand that!' Clearly, Dad was going to be next in line, but Uncle flew into a temper. He went first white, then red. He threw his chopsticks down and raised his voice: 'Mother, I know you're upset because Father has passed on, but don't you start on me and my sister! We've been working away from home for years, and life's not been easy. We're all sad to lose Father but you've no reason to go taking it out on us! You've always had a temper. Father had to put up with you accusing and nagging at him for years and years. Don't you do the same to us!'

Mum looked as if she was going to try and smooth things over, Dad just looked down at his bowl and carried on munching. Gran must never have imagined that anyone would dare speak to her like that. She was so startled her chopsticks froze in mid-air, and she stared bug-eyed and trembling at Uncle. 'You're crazy! The whole family's crazy! The whole lot of you!' And she burst out crying.

This sent everyone into a flap. Some got hand towels, others told each other off, or paced back and forth between sitting-room and dining-room.

Dad just carried on eating, listening to Gran weeping and scolding. They all got scolded: Granddad, Uncle, Aunt Coral, and Dad too (but it was water off a duck's back to him. He'd been beaten through his childhood till his bottom was black and blue. What difference did a bit of verbal abuse make?)

And that was how the wake ended. Mum stayed on to keep Gran company, Dad went downstairs to see off his brother and sister. Liu Xingchen was driving them, Aunt Coral sat in the passenger seat, leaving Uncle in splendid isolation in the back. He hung his head and stuck his hands in his pockets.

Dad thought for a moment, then got out his wallet. He pulled out all the remaining money and held it out to Uncle. 'Zhiming, I had a word with Zhong and he says that the plot and the gravestone came to 20,000 *yuan*. I've just paid them 4,500, and I don't have all that cash on me, but there's 18,000 in here. You take it now and I'll give you the remaining 2,000 next time I come to the city, or on your next visit.'

Uncle looked up and Dad realized his eyes were red-rimmed. 'Shengqiang, you may take me for a poor prof with not a bean to his name, not a rich businessman like you, but I can afford this!'

Aunt Coral looked round, whether at Uncle or at Dad he could not tell. Liu Xingchen was gripping the steering wheel firmly, as if he was afraid that the car might refuse to start if he let go.

'Ai-ya, Zhiming, take it!' Dad insistently thrust the wad of notes through the car window. They dropped on the seat, and scattered. 'That's not what I meant. My money, your money, it doesn't matter, it all belongs to the family. Take it, and I'll give you the 2,000 later!'

They drove off. That was over two years ago. Aunt Coral had paid a couple of visits home in those two years, but Uncle dug his heels in and refused to come. He phoned, on occasion, to say he was off to the TV station to give a lecture today, or going to a conference in Java tomorrow. He was full of this and that, but he never put in an appearance.

Gran no doubt realized that she had mortally offended Uncle that day. A few times she said to Dad: 'Shengqiang, isn't there any way you can persuade Zhiming to come home and see me?

'He's my big brother,' said Dad. 'He won't listen to me.

You stupid son-of-a-bitch, Duan Zhiming! He thought to himself. *Why did you fly into such a temper with me? And as for falling out like that with the old lady!*

That really was two years ago. Dad shilly-shallied, and could not make up his mind to phone Uncle. He was half-afraid that all the rude things he had been silently saying would come popping out of his mouth. Then, quite unexpectedly, Uncle came back, driving a fancy 4x4, his arms full of gifts, looking like he really had gone up in the world.

Who made that call and told you? What are you going to do now you're home? This was what Dad really wanted to know. He was not interested in talking about how his brother had been getting along, their filial duties towards their mother, and so on.

But neither of them mentioned that. The 2,000 *yuan* debt had been written off too. They sipped their tea, smoked their cigarettes and chatted, watching the clock go round until it was noon and time to go and eat lunch.

Perhaps Gran was right. All those well-worn mantras she had been reciting down the years, had finally struck home.

'Keep your cards to your chest at the first meeting,' was one.

After lunch, Dad felt like going back to the office for a nap. Uncle said he wasn't sleepy, and asked the office manager to take him to see the old fermentation yard. At last Dad could get some peace and quiet.

He took out his mobile and gave Jasmine a couple of calls but there was no answer. He thought for a moment, then shrugged, turned on the office computer and started a game of on-screen *mahjong*.

At around five o'clock, Zhong called, asking if Uncle was back. Someone thought they had seen him at the Seven Immortals Bridge this morning.

'Zhiming's a famous prof now! He's on TV all the time! We've got to celebrate his return!' Zhong burst out in excitement. 'Let's go out tonight! Have a decent dinner with plenty to drink. It's on me!'

'Are you really going to fork out? In all these years we've eaten together, I've never once seen you touch your wallet,' said Dad, bluntly.

'Ai-ya!' Zhong burst out laughing. 'Any brother of yours is a brother of mine!'

Dad said he'd do his best to drag Uncle along. He didn't know where Zhong's windfall had come from but he was taking them to the Prince's Mansion Restaurant, a very swish place decorated with dazzling ceiling mirrors and dangling chandeliers which cast flattering reflections over the diners.

They filled their bellies with exotic dishes, washed down with plenty to drink. After all, they hadn't seen Zhiming for years. They talked of how cool Uncle had been as a young man. 'You had short sides and a slicked-up top!' said 'Zhong. 'It had the skinheads running for their lives! There was no one to beat you!' They made such a fuss of him that Uncle stopped acting shy and began to behave like the Pingle Town's number one cool dude that he once was.

With dinner over, Zhong said there was still something else on the menu. He took them up to the third floor, where Dad had never been before but thought there were nightclubs. This was a nightclub, but a very classy one, complete with delectable, elegantly turned-out hostesses. When they lined up on display, they looked like a row of university students. Uncle was put in charge, and he ordered five. Two bottles of wine were opened, the air was wreathed in cigarette smoke and the party really took off.

Dad lay back on the sofa, playing finger-guessing games with Zhong with his left hand, and with his right, casually fondling the girl sitting next to him. Uncle sat opposite them, teasing the girl on each knee, until they were in fits of giggles. Dad's mind was not really on the job though. He could not help thinking back to 1981 and 1982 when, as a drooling adolescent, he used to follow Uncle around town. One day he had screwed up his courage and asked his brother: 'Is it true you've been with Baby Girl in Fifteen Yuan Street. She's a prostitute, isn't she?'

With a smile at the memory, Dad gave the girl next to him a sly pinch, and she gave a cute-sounding little squeal.

Son-of-a-bitch, I've really got old, thought Dad.

Just then, the alarm sounded, Zhong's phone. He answered. It was his wife, Yao. She was the matron at the Pingle Town Hospital, divorced a couple of years back and nearly forty, but still attractive. As soon as she and Zhong were introduced, they took a liking to each other and after going out for just two or three months, had decided to do the paperwork. She was a good woman, but she did insist on keeping Zhong on a tight rein.

'Hi!' shouted Zhong down the phone, gesturing to the others to 'Keep the noise down! Quiet please!' then he said: 'Yes, I'm out for dinner tonight, with Shengqiang and his brother. I told you! We're still drinking!'

'No, we haven't gone somewhere else,' he went on, giving Dad and the others an embarrassed look, and patting the girl beside him. 'We're still in the restaurant, we're not going anywhere else. Ai-ya! Why don't you believe me? OK, I'll get Shengqiang to tell you.' And he handed the phone to Dad. Dad was reaching out to take it, all ready to smile down the line and say: 'Hello, Yao!' Then he heard: 'What? You don't want to talk to Shengqiang? Who do you want to talk to, then?' And Zhong took the phone back. 'Professor Duan? Why? Do you know Professor Duan? Have you ever met him? Just because you've seen him on TV doesn't mean you've met him!'

But Uncle just smiled and reached out for the phone. 'Hello, Yao!' he said politely.

'Ai-ya, don't worry, Yao. We're having dinner. We haven't seen each other for so long, that why we're making an evening of it. I do apologize! Don't worry, we'll get Zhong back to you safe and sound. We'll make sure not a hair of his head is harmed!' Uncle spoke in clear, reasonable tones.

Well, after all, he was used to appearing on TV. In a few words, he managed to pacify Yao and cut the call. Zhong took the phone back, saying gratefully: 'Ai-ya! Zhiming, a top prof like you shouldn't have to cover up for me, and you did! Thank you so much!'

'Hey, Zhong! Stop going on about me being a prof! You're my bros!' And Uncle plonked himself down with Dad and Zhong, and they allowed the bevy of luscious girls on either side to attend to them.

For the first time in many years, Dad felt Uncle was one of them. He filled his glass, held it up, and said: 'Get that down you!'

Uncle filled his own glass to the brim and the pair of them drank them dry. Then they did the same again, several more times. Dad had done this many times before. He knew quite well that if you went to a night club, the wine bottles were drunk dry and the female mozzies jumped on the male mozzies, and all sorts of things were said, in the room, under the tables, under the bedclothes, no holds barred.

What he didn't foresee, however, was that he would end up telling his brother Duan Zhiming about Jasmine.

5

The turning point came after the year 2000, thought Dad. Pingle Town before then bore no relation to how it was now. Two years went by, then 2003, 2004 and 2005 swept in like a storm. West Street changed out of all recognition, and South Street too, with the Tian Mei Department Store rising, like a great fortress, at the intersection. East Street, too, all changed, and North Street. It occurred to Dad that he hadn't walked down North Street for years.

In the old days, when Deng still served his cold dressed rabbit, he and Zhong and the gang used to wander up North Street sometimes. The alleyway by the first telegraph pole at North Gate, that was where old man Deng had his stall. He always wore a red army cap and sold the best cold dressed rabbit in the whole of Pingle Town. When his stall went, Dad was convinced he'd never get such good rabbit anywhere, ever again. Whenever they suddenly got a craving for cold rabbit, they'd make a beeline for old Deng's stall. It had to be a morning. By the afternoon, he'd have sold out. The old man always had a cigarette dangling from the corner of his mouth, a couple of inches of ash balanced precariously from the end. Getting slowly to his feet to serve them, he ladled out the peanuts, chopped turnip and celery, and added sesame and chilli oil, ground Sichuan pepper, sugar and vinegar and, finally, the heart-stoppingly delicious cubes of rabbit meat. Dad and his friends stood transfixed. The ladle clattered and rattled, then Deng mixed everything together with chopsticks, pulled a plastic bag from the roll with two fingers, filled it, tied the top and passed it to Dad, taking the money and giving back the change. Only then did he take the cigarette from between his lips and unhurriedly flick the ash onto the dirt.

There were no dirt roads left in Pingle Town, and you didn't see many telegraph poles either. In 2000, or 2001, the powers-that-be got some mad idea into their heads that the town needed a facelift. Up went the stepladders, and the buckets of paint, and all the buildings on, and off, the four main roads were covered in white paint. They looked like they'd been plastered with stage make-up. After that, the stalls and push-carts were driven out: the purveyors of cold dressed rabbit, chilli turnips and spring rolls, Sichuan eggy pancakes, rice-flour shortbread and griddled buns filled with brown sugar, even the scissor-menders and knife-grinders, were all swept ruthlessly from the face of the town. All those old faces so familiar from his childhood just vanished. The few souls that remained retreated into their shells like tortoises and made do with shopfronts as narrow as the gap between your front teeth. There they sat behind glass windows, white masks over their mouths, handing out a few bits and bobs with their surgical-gloved hands. *Crap food!* Dad swore silently.

It wasn't just that the food tasted different, the town atmosphere changed too, though Dad didn't realize it until one day when he came out of the chilli bean paste factory at noon to get himself a bowl of *zhazha* noodles and discovered the noodle stall had gone. He was enraged. He walked down South Street, over the crossroads, and was about to go back up West Street, when he realized that the whole of Pingle Town had changed. The cypresses and camphor trees of his childhood had been chopped down, the squeezed-in streets had been wrenched wider (but only by a tad), and bright blue railings kept motorized and non-motorized traffic apart. The result was that neither cars nor bicycles could get through, and motorbikes scattered into neighbouring side streets. And as if that wasn't enough, the edges of the streets were ostentatiously 'greened' with saplings brought in from god knows where. They were sickly specimens, not a pretty sight. The steel mill closed its doors for good and the tailor's shop was moved to the peddlers' market. Doctor Zhao who removed moles lost her brightly-coloured banner, and all the remaining stores adopted a uniform fascia of white lettering on a blue background, so you couldn't tell them apart. Worst of all, the passers-by changed. It dawned on Dad that, without him being aware of it happening, the people walking up and down the street had become strangers. Where were Skanky Zhu and Limping Chen from South Street, Zhong the Third and Liu the Stump from West Street? These strangers passed Dad blank-faced, without even an attempt at a greeting or a smile.

That was when Dad stopped walking. Of course, there was another reason too. Dad had officially become the boss of the Mayflower Chilli Bean Paste Factory. Now he had a chauffeur and was driven to and from work in his shiny black Audi. He saw the people of Pingle Town through the car window, their faces (from a distance), and their buttocks (up close). He smoked China brand soft-pack cigarettes and drank branded *maotai* liquor. He ate meals at the Prince's Mansion, screwed any number of gorgeous girls and was content with life. Middle age crept up on him and his belly grew pudgy.

It all started in 2000. That was the turning point. And when Dad next took a look around him, nothing was the same!

Later, when Dad got a really pudgy belly, he walked to or from work sometimes, at Mum's insistence. 'It'll do you good to get a bit fitter,' she said. 'Look at that belly of yours! You look pregnant.' 'Hah!' said Dad grabbed Mum's hand and rubbed it up and down his belly. 'You have a feel. How many months gone am I, then?' Xue Shengqiang! You're impossible,' said Mum, giving him a scornful look. She pulled her hand away and turned another page in her book.

Be that as it may, Dad got up the next morning and walked to work. He'd spent two days drinking with his bros and he felt bloated and top-heavy. As he lurched along, he decided he might as well pop by the South Gate market and get himself a bowl of buckwheat noodles in the shop opposite.

There was hardly anyone he knew in the street and even if he did recognize them, no one bothered to greet him. He got to the market without incident, and suddenly spied a tall lanky figure in the distance. The man had his back to him. He was wearing a khaki jacket and cut a handsome figure, holding himself ramrod straight, just like a PLA soldier! Then he took a closer look. He suddenly realized it was the bane of his life, his brother Duan Zhiming. With an exclamation of surprise, he headed towards him.

Up close, he said: 'Hi, Zhiming!'

Uncle turned in astonishment. 'Shengqiang! What are you doing here?'

'Hey!' Dad laughed, and pulled out a pack of cigarettes and offered them. 'Just because you're here, does that mean I can't show up? I was just popping by for a bowl of buckwheat noodles. What about you?'

It wasn't as if Dad had never imagined this scenario. Down the years, whenever he pottered around Pingle Town on his own, Uncle often came to mind. Whenever he remembered how he and his big brother had shared one pair of trousers, a bowl of tripe noodles or a bun between them, even the same hooker, it occurred to him that Uncle hadn't been in touch for ages. In a place this size, if Duan Zhiming ever did come to town, it might still be possible to bump into him even among the jostling crowds. He imagined greeting him, giving him a cigarette, and lighting it for him, saw them puffing away together, having a chat, and fixing a time to play *mahjong.*

So anyway, Dad gave Uncle a cigarette, and lit it for him. Uncle pointed to a nearby advertising hoarding and said: 'I've come to see these people about doing the advertising banners for Mother's birthday celebrations.'

Dad looked up and saw it was one of Gao Tao's adverts. He just smiled: 'How did you find that company?'

'Ai-ya!' said Uncle. 'It was your friend Zhong who gave me their name card. He said he knew them and I should get a discount.'

That fucking Zhong! thought Dad. Well, that was how they did things in Pingle Town. He considered the fact that Uncle hadn't been back home for a long time. He wasn't used to their way of doing things, that was all. And Dad couldn't be bothered to explain. If Zhong wanted to take Zhiming for a ride, then let him. He wasn't taking him, Xue Shengqiang, for a ride. If Zhong was going to swindle them, it would be the factory's not his own personal money.

'Off you go then, I'm going to get my noodles,' said Dad and turned to go.

'Hey, Shengqiang,' said Uncle, tentatively. 'I'll come with you. I haven't had breakfast either and I'm famished. I'll come back here afterwards. The shop's not going anywhere.'

Dad shot Uncle a surprised look. *Right, we'll go and eat, and let's see what you're up to.*

Side by side, they walked to South Street, and through the old city gate to the food market. Uncle was the first to break the silence: 'Didn't there used to be a shop selling tapes here?'

'Demolished, ages ago,' said Dad. 'No one wants to buy tapes nowadays.' 'And where did Skanky Zhu go? He was always here, day in, day out, with his cigarette stall,' Uncle pursued. 'I heard he's gone to Yong'An City to look after his grandson. He certainly had bad luck. He was putting aside the cigarette business money to give his son a good start in life. The son got himself a job in Yong'An and then, just like that, his wife upped and left, leaving the child behind and so Zhu's gone to look after it. He must be seventy if he's a day.' 'Well, it was always going to happen,' said Uncle. 'That's why they say, never trust a pretty woman. And Liu Yufen certainly was pretty, one of the prettiest in town back then. Skanky Zhu's son was practically foaming at the mouth, he was so frantic to get her. And it was all money down the drain!' Uncle followed Dad into the noodle shop. The boss was just cooking up some noodles in a huge wok, and Dad ordered: 'Two bowls, with extra minced pork!'

They sat down. Dad took two pairs of disposable chopsticks from the pot, pulled one pair apart and handed them to Uncle. But Uncle shook his head. 'I don't use those, Shengqiang, they're bad for the environment, and they're not hygienic either.' He fished around in the pot for a grimy pair of bamboo chopsticks instead. *Have it your own way...*Dad dropped the still-unwrapped pair back in the pot and tapped his chopsticks on the table. 'Zhiming, that Yufen you were talking about, weren't you in the same class at school? Now she's working in Anqin's office. They're good friends. Why don't I get everyone together for a meal, now you're back?'

'No, don't do that,' said Uncle. 'Everyone's living their own lives now. The ones I wanted to see, I've been in touch with. Everyone else, forget it. There's no point.'

You supercilious little git! Dad glared at the bottle of vinegar on the table.

'How about Anqin? I haven't seen her yet,' Uncle went on, 'How is she these days?'

This was a particularly unwelcome question. Dad had a guilty conscience about Anqin, especially when he remembered telling Uncle about Jasmine.

'She's fine!' he snapped. 'Why would she not be? She's got

her salary, she's got a job for life, she goes to work and reads the newspapers, she clocks off and goes and plays *mahjong*, she couldn't have life any better!'

'And her father?'

If Uncle had not asked, it could have slipped Dad's mind that he had a father-in-law. 'He's been growing pot plants, and the last I heard, he's gone mad about photography and bought himself a camera for nearly 20,000 *yuan*. I'd never splash out that much on a camera!

'Shengqiang!' Uncle began, and Dad knew instantly that this mention of Mum's father was not accidental. 'The old man's calligraphy is famously good. Why don't we get him to write the couplets for Mother's birthday?'

Dad glanced at his brother. He saw through his machinations straightaway. It wasn't Chen Xiuxiao's calligraphy Uncle was interested in, it was his political connections. The old man had been the chairman of the Yong Feng County branch of the Democratic League, and a member of the County Party Committee Standing Committee, in other words, he was highly respected locally.

'If you want him to write the couplets, you'll have to go and ask him yourself,' said Dad. Dad's father-in-law had always made it plain that he despised Dad as an uneducated businessman. He always steered well clear of him except on the occasion when, in 1996, Dad wanted to divorce Mum. Then he was incandescent with rage, and nearly beat Dad over the head with a carrying pole. 'You want a divorce!! What makes you think you can afford to divorce my daughter?' Dad never dared tell Gran what had happened, but after that, there were no more visits to his father-in-law.

'I thought I'd go and see the old man myself,' said Uncle. 'I just thought I'd better run it by you first.' The stall-holder put down two steaming bowls of noodles in front of them. Uncle thanked him politely and began to mix the noodles and the meat with his chopsticks, his face flushing red with the heat.

Dad got stuck into his noodles too. Then it suddenly struck him as ominous that Uncle was digging up old contacts, family and friends, that he had not been in touch with for years, just to please Gran. He had a bad feeling about it. He drank his hot and spicy soup, but a cold shiver ran down his spine.

That devious creep's always got some scheme up his sleeve!

Dad didn't know what his brother was on, but now that he was in charge of Gran's birthday, there was no stopping him. He boasted that he was going give their mother the biggest birthday bash Pingle Town had ever seen. And he suited the action to the words. Before Dad's very eyes, the old fermentation yard at the factory, which had not seen use for years, was spruced up, the vats were dragged away, and in came the cleaners, and hosed the yard down, squirting away the detritus of bean paste, dog shit and what not, and leaving the ground smooth and clean. But even that wasn't enough for Uncle, who set the most exacting standards. The cleaners had to get down on their hands and knees and sweep every inch of the ground with a brush. All those bottoms stuck in the air—a sight for sore eyes. It took them all day and certainly looked smarter when they'd finished, but an unpleasant smell still lingered, as Dad discovered the afternoon before when he wandered by. It smelt as if someone had eaten too many chilli peppers and then pooped and left the crap laying there overnight. Dad held his nose. For some reason, he felt sad.

'And there's something else I need talk to you about, Shengqiang.' Uncle smacked his lips and added a drop more vinegar to his soup. Dad kept down and didn't look at him. *I thought so! Duan Zhiming couldn't just have a bowl of noodles with me for the sake of it. He's such a weirdo. What a song and dance he's making over it. He's only been back a few days and he's putting on the big brother act!*

'What is it, Zhiming?' Dad swallowed his mouthful of

noodles and waited.

'That business about your mistress, you need to sort it out,' said Uncle earnestly.

Dad felt a spurt of anger. He could have tipped the table over in Uncle's face. *Mind your own damned business! Go and find your own woman to screw!*

'Ai-ya! I know,' he said.

'That day we bumped into her, I had a sense there was something not quite right. I felt that Jasmine was out to cause trouble with Mother. Shengqiang, you just be careful. You and Anqin have weathered a lot of storms together. You need to settle down.' Uncle seemed oblivious of the effect his words were having on Dad, who was seething.

'Settle down? Don't you worry, I'm well settled.' Dad drank another mouthful of soup.

'It's not that simple, Shengqiang. Look, I'm your brother, I know you. I've had a lot of good friends get into trouble because of a woman. I haven't done anything for you for years, but now I'm back, and if there's anything I can do, you just let me know, don't be shy of asking. And that includes the business with Jasmine. If you can't sort it out, then let me do it for you. I'll do it. I've got ways.'

Dad was momentarily stumped for words. *Just how are you going to sort it out?* He wondered, but it seemed inappropriate to ask that, so he didn't.

'Did you hear me, Shengqiang? Don't be shy of asking if you want me to help,' said Uncle, once again.

'Ai-ya! I'm not a little boy anymore, I know what I'm doing. Don't worry!' Dad finally said. It was true. He was a mature man now, and he could walk the streets of Pingle Town and if he wanted to walk to the left, then no one would dare to make him walk to the right. Besides, he'd only taken a mistress. What business was it of anyone else's? *Keep your nose out of this! You want to give her a poke yourself?* thought Dad.

His brother Duan Zhiming really was fucking weird. One bowl of noodles and he had so many things to fret over. He seemed to be ticking them off on his fingers, one thing after another. When he finished with Jasmine, he started on Gran, and Aunt Coral, and finally Zhong. 'Zhong wants me to go around some of the businesses in Pingle Town, and schools too, and do a series of lectures. Do you think I ought to?'

Son-of-a-bitch, what do I say to that? Dad gulped down more soup. *It's understandable Zhong taking him for a meal or a booze-up, but treating him to a night out with girls is something else again…. That man's not doing it for nothing. He's wheeling and dealing, hoping he'll get a kickback!* He did not, of course, queer Zhong's pitch in so many words. 'Of course, do it!' he urged. 'Why ever not? You're too unassuming. Don't hide your light under a bushel. You're a Pingle man like the rest of us. You go along and say a few words to them!'

Uncle accepted the compliment, and the task before him. He'd finished eating and said what he had come to say, and now he insisted on picking up the tab, all of seven *yuan*, and left, saying he was going to see about the birthday banners.

Dad stood in the doorway of the buckwheat noodle café and lit another cigarette. He hadn't given a lot of thought to the business about Jasmine, but now that Uncle had brought it up, it began to bug him, a bit like a chronic itch. He took out his phone and decided to give her a ring. It was some days since he'd obeyed Gran's orders and made Jasmine move back to her old apartment, and she seemed distant. Some of the time, she didn't even answer the phone and Dad knew she was miffed. Women! The stupid cows were so moody. But he reckoned it would soon pass. She was just a young girl after all, and once Gran's birthday was over, he'd find her a decent place to live. It was important. A man always needed girls to screw. Having got that clear in his head, he felt better. He squinted at his Contacts, and pressed her number.

Today Jasmine answered straightaway. There was something odd about her voice though, it sounded fuzzy, as if she had been taking a nap.

'He ... hello, Shengqiang, she said. Dad wondered why she was stuttering.

'How have you been?' he asked.

'Fine ... Shengqiang, are you busy today?'

'Not too busy. My brother's come back and taken over organizing the birthday party, so I can take a break,' Dad said.

'Can you come over when you leave the office, then? There's something I need to talk to you about,' said Jasmine.

Fine, thought Dad. *Time for a quickie!* The thought cheered him as he cut the call.

Still in a good mood, he strolled back to the factory. He still had to put in a day's work. Because he was in a good mood, he made another call on the way, to Zhong. He felt bad, again, for putting Jasmine Zhong's number under 'Zhong' in the Contacts list, instead of his old friend. Luckily, Zhong had not spotted this but Dad still had a pang of conscience every time he called him.

'Hey, Zhong!' Dad greeted him cheerfully. 'You're a slippery character, aren't you!'

'Ai-ya, Shengqiang, what have I done this time? You're always picking on me!' Zhong said jovially at the other end of the line.

'You introduced your 'friend' to my brother, to get the advertising banners made for our mother's birthday!' Dad teased him..

'Ai-ya! Ai-ya!' Zhong groaned. 'Gao Tao's always on at me to bring him business!'

'That's nothing to do with me!' retorted Dad. 'You do things the way you want, just make sure you do them properly!'

'Of course! Don't you worry!'

They were about to hang up when Zhong thought of

something else: 'Hey, Shengqiang, has Yao called you about the doctor? She's found someone, so you will go, won't you? You shouldn't let it drag on ... "

'Ai-ya! Ai-ya!' now it was Dad's turn. Zhong had good intentions but he was exasperating, all the same. 'I'm not a baby. Don't make such a fuss. I hear what you're saying but I've got such a pile on my plate at the moment. Let me deal with things, then I'll see.'

'Shengqiang ...' Zhong persisted.

'OK, OK. I can't talk about it now, I'm at the factory. You fix it up. We'll have a drink at the end of the day!' Having dodged that one, Dad hung up and skipped into the building.

But if Dad was hoping for a peaceful day, he was out of luck. The gods were against him. Either he'd forgotten to light the incense sticks that morning, or he'd lit the wrong kind of incense. His office manager, Zeng, was lying in wait for him, hopping anxiously from one foot to the other. As soon as he caught sight of Dad, he made a beeline for him: 'Mr Xue! Mr Xue! You're here! Old Mr Chen has been waiting for you in your office for ages!'

Who on earth was 'Old Mr Chen'? Dad figured it must be that long-lost father-in-law of his, and cursed. *That man's a complete pain!*

'He's been here since first thing this morning!' went on the office manager. 'He's been waiting ever since. He's hopping mad!'

The thought sent chills down his spine. *This town's such a piddling little place! People's mouths are bigger than their faces. Has someone told Anqin's father about me being taken to hospital?*

'What does he want?' He asked, aloud.

'Ai-ya! He's been going on and on about the cleaning-up Prof Duan ordered for the fermentation yard these last couple of days. The old man's not all happy!' The office manager was still hopping nervously from one foot to the other.

So it was not Mr Chen his father-in-law, but Chen Xiuliang, his old *shifu* in the fermentation yard, now retired.   His alarm evaporated. Whatever it was, however major, there was nothing that he couldn't sort out with the old boy.

He pushed open his office door, to find old Chen seated on the leather sofa sipping a cup of tea. In front of him, cigarette butts stuck up in the ashtray like rows of machine guns.

'*Shifu!*' Dad greeted him cheerfully as he stepped through the door.

Using the fermentation yard for the 80th birthday celebrations was bound to throw Chen into a rage, everyone knew that, in fact they had factored it in. The trouble was that too many things had happened, starting with Dad being taken ill in Jasmine's bed and waking up in hospital, and he had not had the energy to deal with it. By now, Chen Xiulang was incandescent with fury, ready to leap to his feet and stab Dad in the chest with his lighted cigarette. There was no time to waste, Dad had some explaining to do.

Ai-ya! *Shifu!* Don't get so upset. Listen to me!' he said soothingly and pushed Chen Xiuliang back down onto the sofa.

'There's nothing more to say, Shengqiang! Don't you know that the most important thing for the company is the flavour from the fermentation? And where does that flavour come from? From the vats! And the vats absorb that essence from the yard itself. And you've scraped every ounce of essence from the yard! You'll ruin the factory, and you'll be the death of me!' Chen stubbed out his half-smoked cigarette in the ashtray with trembling fingers.

This was not the first time Dad had heard Chen say this. He had been saying it since the first day Dad set foot in the factory. If he'd heard it once, he'd heard it a thousand times.

Surely Dad hadn't forgotten the first time he saw Chen, when he became his *shifu* and began to teach him the arts of chilli bean paste fermentation. The weather had been pleasantly warm but not too hot. Chen was wearing a sweatshirt, sitting at a desk in the Technical Department, a cigarette between his lips, and reading a newspaper. It must have been 1983 or 1984, and Dad remembered the bright-red banner headline over the editorial: 'Build the four modernisations!' Gran had taken Dad into the office herself, and greeted Chen Xiuliang politely: '*Shifu*, I've brought the kid.' Chen acted as if he had not heard, and finished reading the article. Then he casually folded the newspaper, stubbed out his cigarette and got to his feet. 'Ai-ya! So this is the young man! And how are you today, Sir?'

'You're such a joker, *shifu,* don't call him "Sir", protested Gran. 'We're living in the modern age, aren't we? From today, I'm consigning my son to your care. He's just a kid, so you train him properly. Tell him off all you want, and don't spare the rod.'

'No beatings and no tellings-off,' said Chen, as if he was reciting the *sutras.*

'Oh, please do! Don't spare the rod, or the tellings-off!' urged Gran.

They sounded as if they were singing an opera duet, but Dad paid little attention, apart from sneaking a glance at his future *shifu.* After all, he had just spent more than six months tagging along behind his brother in Pingle Town and, in his estimation, this Chen was a nobody. He waited as Chen wittered on at Gran and showed her to the door. Then Chen turned to Dad: 'Right, kid, now you go and fill the thermos and make me some tea.'

The thermos for boiling water sat in the corner, and Dad went and picked it up. It was heavy. He unscrewed the cap and pulled out the cork. Inside, it was full of steaming hot water. 'It's still got hot water in,' he said to Chen.

Chen sat down and lit another cigarette. Taking a puff, he

said: 'From now on, kid, if I ask you to get me hot water, you get it, understood?'

Dad clenched his buttocks and did as he was told. Granddad had drilled tea-making into him, and he recited to himself: *A scoop of Hua Mao Peak tea leaves, half a pot of freshly boiled water, don't be in a hurry to put the lid on, the steam is an Immortal's breath. When the tealeaves float, the Immortals get the jitters. When the tealeaves sink, the Lady Immortal can't run away.*

Chen Xiuliang took a sip and frowned. 'This tea pongs, kid,' he said.

Dad was beginning to get annoyed. Mum used to tell me what a fiery temper he had then. 'His face is wreathed in Buddha smiles now, but in the old days, if anything wasn't right, he'd start throwing bottles!' 'What do you mean, "pongs"?' he said.

Chen thought a moment: 'The same pong as tripe noodles from the North Street Seven Immortals Bridge shop ...'

Dad started in surprise. It was true, he had been there for tripe noodles that lunchtime.

'Didn't you wash your hands before you put the tealeaves in?' said Chen, looking at him. 'Go and wash them, and make me some more tea!'

Dad had to do as he was told. He stood beside the desk and watched Chen drink it. Chen pointed to a cane chair opposite, and said: 'Sit down.'

But Dad said: 'I'll stand, *shifu*.'

Chen had no idea that Gran had beaten Dad black and blue, until every movement radiated pain and he didn't dare sit down. He laughed kindly, and said: 'Listen, kid, you shouldn't feel you've been hard done by because you've been sent to work under me. Let me tell you something. The most important thing in this factory is the flavour of the bean paste! And here's another thing, if there's one thing I understand better than anyone else, it's how to develop that flavour! When your mother sent me to you, it was for your own good. Once you understand flavour, you'll always know how to run the factory.'

'What's the chilli bean paste factory got to do with me?' Dad muttered.

'Don't be so daft, boy! The chilli bean paste factory's got everything to do with you! You young people nowadays are so ambitious. You think a business like this is beneath you. You reckon your mother has done the dirty on you, don't you? But let me tell you, your mother's protecting you. You just learn everything you can from me about flavour, and once the business is on a sound footing, it will all be yours. Do you understand me?'

In Dad's memory, that was the first time that anyone had spoken to him with such passionate sincerity.

And so Dad learned his trade from his *shifu*, Chen, from choosing the chilli peppers, to checking the hairs growing on the mouldy beans, to mixing the paste, stirring it as it fermented in the sunshine. These tasks were all secondary, however, to his duties of boiling water and making Chen's tea and listening to him spout off, and being bawled out until a pulse throbbed at his temple, oh yes, and there was going to buy his cigarettes for him. One day, Chen actually offered Dad a cigarette.

As far as smoking went, Dad really felt he didn't need anyone to teach him. He went over and took it, holding it between two fingers, lit up and took a puff. And never looked back.

The evening drew in as they smoked, and they packed up for the day. Chen looked at Dad and smiled.

'What are you smiling at, *shifu*?' Dad was puzzled.

'You've really got the hang of stirring the bean paste!' said Chen.

'I'm only so-so,' protested Dad in embarrassment.

Chen said nothing, just took another leisurely puff. Then a mighty snort issued from his nostrils. 'Shengqiang, you can be really dumb sometimes, but you don't argue, you just get on with it, I'll give you that,' he said.

'What are you talking about, *shifu*?' Dad asked, snorting out smoke through his nostrils too. This cigarette made him feel like a fucking new man.

'You're so wet behind the ears, you can't even stir the chilli bean paste without me teaching you. How are you going to manage to give a girl a belly bump, eh? Tell me that.'

Dad was silent. Gran had drilled into him, over and over, that you did not 'talk about stuff like that outside the family!'

'Have you ever seen a woman butt-naked?' asked Chen with a smile.

Of course I have! I screwed one just a few days ago!

'Ai, Shengqiang,' Chen said, holding his cigarette between two fingers and pointing at Dad. 'In a few days' time, I'll take you with me to Fifteen Yuan Street for a bit of fun, right?'

Dad suddenly understood what he'd done and, for the first time in his life, felt real pangs of conscience. He'd ripped his *shifu* off for nearly two weeks by buying him Silver Fir brand cigarettes. What a dick-head.

Of course, Dad never had the nerve to let Chen treat him to a hooker in Fifteen Yuan Street. He remembered what Granddad used to say: 'Never borrow money in a temple, and never run up debts in a brothel.' Was that what he meant? It must have been! The very next morning, Dad bought a packet of the best Peony cigarettes and presented them to Chen. Ever after that, he kept his *shifu* in cigarettes. Even now, the cigarettes Chen Xiuliang was stubbing out in Dad's ashtray now were Hong Ta Shan brand, given him by Dad.

But the truth was that Chen really did not care whose cigarettes he was smoking, he was intent on working up a good head of steam. He was going to have his say, come what may. His cigarette dancing in his hand, he effed and blinded and spattered spittle and phlegm all over Dad's face.

'*Shifu! Shifu!*' Dad sighed and patted Chen on the shoulder. 'Just hear me out! Just listen a moment! We haven't used the fermentation yard in donkeys' years! We've got specially-built mouldering and fermenting sheds now, you know that! We've got workers and machines and it's all hygienic, we don't use the fermentation yard, so why can't we sweep it out and use it for the old lady's birthday celebrations! She's going to be eighty!'

'Who says the fermentation yard's no use any more? I use it!' Chen Xiuliang coughed. That was true. Every year, come what may, the old man rolled up his sleeves and personally made a few vats of chilli bean paste. When Dad thought of all those years that Chen had been a bachelor, he felt that stirring the bean paste was what kept the old man alive, so he let him get on with it.

'Yes, all right,' said Dad, 'but the old lady's birthday is just next week and it's only April. I guarantee that by May we'll have cleared up the yard and you can have it back. Right?'

'You've taken away the foundations! What are you giving me back?' Chen shouted.

No one had shouted at him like this for a good many of years, thought Dad as the spittle landed on his face, probably since the year 2000, when the then-factory head, Mr Zhu, was persuaded by Gran to retire and Dad finally got his feet under the Director's desk properly. After that, no one ever dared cross swords with him again, still less tell him off and call him wet behind the ears. Gran still kept a sharp eye on him of course, but at least she discussed things with him, and was very polite about it. 'We always mind our manners in our family,' she used to say. 'It takes less effort to talk quietly. If everyone listens to reason, there's no need for temper tantrums.' She said this so often that no one dared be rude to him no matter what he did, whether it was sleeping around, lying to Gran and Mum, quietly bribing anyone who mattered, even when he was telling off someone else so badly that they clenched their bum cheeks and didn't dare let off the tiniest fart.

'Ai-ya, *shifu*! Don't get so angry! I'll sort it out!'

As the old man roundly abused him, somehow those fucking feelings of guilt that had been weighing on Dad began to lift. It took all afternoon to appease Chen and send him on his way, and it stands to reason that Dad should have felt completely drained. But he didn't. Surprisingly, he felt reinvigorated. It took him back to when he was seventeen or eighteen and was forever being shouted out till his head felt like it was going to explode, and his bum was always black and blue. He hadn't given a damn. He just used to smoke a couple of cigarettes, swallow a couple of bowls of food, knock off work, leave the factory, and strut off full of bravado, all ready to shoot his load, to Fifteen Yuan Street outside South Gate.

Dad had a happy thought. *Why don't I go and make it up with Jasmine, and give her a poke?* Zhu Cheng was still out on business and Dad didn't wait until he got back to be driven there, but walked out of the factory gate and jumped in a taxi. He gave Uncle a call on the way, and arranged to go out for a meal that evening, so they could carry on talking about the birthday celebrations.

'Fine, seven o'clock then,' said Dad. 'Seven.'

But he changed his mind before he cut the call: 'I'll be there 7:30 to 8, give or take. You all go on ahead of me, right? I may be a few minutes late.'

It was actually ten to eight when Dad pushed open the door to the restaurant side-room, to see the table packed with people. There was Uncle, Zhong, and Gao Tao too. Gao Tao's two squitty little brothers were shuffling their bums on stools by the door. There were some girls too, very pretty ones, all sleek and shiny. Normally, Dad would have ogled them but today he just wasn't in the mood for it.

Zhong was the first to notice Dad had arrived. 'Shengqiang!' he shouted. 'Late again! Where have you been? Sneaking off after some woman?'

'Ai-ya! Leave me alone!' Dad waved him away. He went to the chair opposite the door and sat down. 'Bring me a Coca Cola, girl!' he ordered. 'A cold one!'

At this, even Gao Tao was moved to protest. 'Xue Shengqiang, you're out of order! You get here late, and then you refuse to have a drink!'

'Shengqiang, what's wrong? Has something happened?' Uncle asked, with concern.

'I'm jinxed!' Dad said, as he watched the waitress bending over to pour his glass of Coca Cola. It fizzed up and a few drops splashed out, wetting the girl's lily-white cleavage. But he just took his glass and tipped the drink down his throat.

Poor Dad, he was physically in the room but his mind was somewhere else entirely. The gorgeous vision of young Jasmine floated before his eyes. She had wept on his chest till her face was purply-red like a Peking opera singer. *You never imagined you were going to cry, did you Jasmine? Or you wouldn't have put that makeup on,* thought Dad but did not dare say it aloud. He patted her on the shoulder, and sneaked a glance at her rounded bottom, snugly clad in a pair of jeans. *Not a cat's chance in hell of a screw today.*

'I've been twice to the doctor,' Jasmine wept, 'but I didn't dare tell you. I know you're so busy. I didn't want to make things more difficult for you, I just never expected...'

'Ai-ya! It doesn't matter,' said Dad, 'I'll think of something.' He seemed to have been saying the same thing over and over again, all afternoon.

'I'll think of something,' he repeated. Tired of looking at Jasmine's bottom, he raised his eyes to the ceiling of her rented room from which the light fitting dangled forlornly. One bulb was blown, leaving just two bright globes. For no reason at all, Dad thought of the two between his own legs. *You sons-of-bitches have caused me a bellyful of trouble,* he thought.

His mind had gone a complete blank, just when he most needed to be decisive. All he could think of was the time when Granddad had taken Uncle and him to see *Lenin in 1918*. The bare ground was crammed with people all standing, blocking the brightly-lit screen in front. Dad had been quite little, and all he remembered was hearing someone say: 'Look at me! Look into my eyes!'

Dad really wanted to look, but all he could see was a row of dark-clad behinds.

Dad often found himself remembering that scene when he was having sex. It was Baby Girl who'd taught him that trick. One day, when they'd finished, Baby Girl had laid a cool finger on Dad's sweat-soaked back and said to him: 'Now listen to me, young man. Your little fellow can be a bit quick off the mark, if you see what I mean, and that's not a criticism ... you're still young, and it doesn't matter. But I'm going to teach you a sure-fire way of slowing down. What you do is you make yourself think of something else, anything ... going to work, eating, riding a bicycle, anything will do. If you fix your mind on something else, you won't come so quickly.'

Dad may have been no good in school but he was a bright lad and cottoned on straightaway. Once he learned the knack, he never spilt a drop along the way. In any moment of crisis, when he was having sex, or being told off by Gran, or out with friends and on their third or fourth bottle of spirits, or getting dizzy because he had his nose buried in the vat as he checked the mould on the beans, he liked to switch his mind to something completely different for a moment, before carrying on as before, delivering the goods with the girl, nodding obediently to Gran, clinking glasses with friends, or signing the order for beans.

It's just a question of marking time, he concluded.

So today, Dad did not tell Uncle and Zhong and the others

until right at the end of the meal. They ate their food, clinked glasses and opened another bottle. Each man put his arm round a hostess, had a good fondle, gave her a good kiss, toasted their undying love, and drank some more. Then suddenly Dad opened his mouth and said it: 'I'm in trouble.'

'What's up?' asked Zhong, flustered. 'If something's happened, just tell us. However bad it is, we're all bros here.'

Uncle said nothing, just looked at Dad. Gao Tao was looking at him too.

Everyone looked at Dad, almost with the critical eye with which Gran used to look at his exam results when he was a boy. Suddenly Dad felt as if he had got straight As. He might be about to get a bollocking for his bad behaviour from the rest of them, but he couldn't help swelling with pride.

He reached out for the cup and drank down the wine in it, to give himself some liquid courage.

'OK, here's the thing,' he announced. 'I've given the girl a belly bump.'

6

IT WAS JUST an ordinary April morning in Pingle Town. Dad had been around for at least forty springtimes and could describe it with his eyes shut. The trees suddenly so green they made your eyes sore, the birds and the bees going at it hammer and tongs, the lurid yellow rapeseed blossom, the blazing scarlet azaleas, even the air smelled fertile, he thought sourly. It certainly brought out the crowds, and the streets heaved with day-trippers, songsters, card-players, people out to make a quick buck, and more besides. And of course there were the couples, making out, and breaking up. Though today's youngsters did it differently from in his day. Dad stood at the factory gate, puffing on a cigarette, watching a couple standing in a tight clinch in the flowerbeds laid out down the middle of the road. Their hands were all over each other, breasts, bottoms, back. Fucking hell, it looks like they're going to be at it all morning! You never saw a sight like this in days gone by. Back then, if you shouted at the East Gate you could be heard outside the West Gate. Everyone kept a sharp lookout for scandal, passers-by, people squatting on pavements or sitting in shops. All spies, the lot of them. In 1987, or 1988 at the latest, he remembered meeting Mum for a meal at the Fatty Joe's Yong Hui restaurant by the West Gate. Then Dad had said: 'I'll see you home.' They walked, one behind the other, a short distance and, when they got to the County Party Committee residential compound, Dad said goodbye and turned back. At the crossroads, he bumped into Zhong. His friend came up and clapped him one on the shoulder, so hard that Dad grimaced with pain.

'No need to be so heavy-handed!' he yelped.

'Xue Shengqiang! You're a disgrace! You've got Xi Hongzhen dangling and now you've started giving Anqin ideas! Think you can keep two of them on the go, do you?

The news had spread like wildfire. Xi Hongzhen was Dad's girlfriend back then. That day, she was sitting at her desk in the retail department of the North Gate Local Products Company waiting for Dad to collect her and take her to eat in the night market. But even before it got dark, she'd heard the news that she'd been dumped. And the day Dad wanted it to be known that he had his heart set on Mum, well, it was all very simple: they walked a few steps down West Street hand in hand. They might as well have been preceded by a street crier. Everyone in town who wasn't deaf, blind or completely dim-witted, knew that 'Xue Shengqiang from the chilli bean paste factory is going out with Chen Anqing from the Cereals Bureau.'

Dad took another puff and watched the young couple starting another round of groping. He did not feel jealous but it did cross his mind that he had been born before his time. Then he dropped the cigarette butt and ground it under his heel to put it out.

He glanced at his watch. It was nearly twelve o'clock. He was about to call Zhu Cheng to ask where he'd got to when the shiny black Audi turned up. Dad adjusted his shirt collar and straightened his back, totted up the numbers on a couple of car number plates, then stood waiting in the breezy sunshine as the car nosed its way towards him and pulled up. He strode over and pulled the heavy car door open.

Aunt Coral sat there. At nearly fifty, she'd lost her youthful prettiness, but she was still a pleasant-looking woman.

'Sis!' he beamed a smile. 'How was the journey? Tiring?'

'Ai-ya!' replied Aunt Coral, getting out of the car. 'Not for me! Young Zhu's the one who's tired. He had to get up at crack of dawn to come and get me.'

'No big deal! It's what I'm here for!' Zhu Cheng put in brightly.

'That's what we're here for, of course it is!' echoed Dad. 'Zhiming insisted you should come back. The least we could do was spare you the drive!'

Aunt Coral smiled and patted Dad's hand. 'What nonsense you talk! We're family.'

It was only a light pat but it was enough to make all Dad's grievances bubble to the surface. Normally, and luckily for him, he was a tough character, the kind that met troubles head-on, gobbled them down into his belly, and shat and pissed them out of his system in a day or two. Dad didn't give a damn about any problems, it did not matter whether they related to the factory, life outside, his home life, even Uncle. (Though of course, Aunt Coral's return absolutely did not fall into that category.)

He took his sister into the factory. As they walked, he told her how the factory had developed in the last few years, as well as what they were organizing for Gran's birthday, what he and Uncle had done since Uncle got back, and so on and so forth.

They arrived at the factory offices and Dad paused for breath. 'You go and wait upstairs, Sis, Zhiming will be back soon, and we'll call Mother, and go and have lunch altogether. We can talk after that.'

The words came tumbling out, but he was in such a good mood that he'd forgotten someone. Luckily, Aunt Coral had not. 'What about Anqin? Is she coming?'

Indeed. On the West Street was a house and in it was his wife. He slapped his thigh. 'Of course, of course! She's coming. You're back so she'll definitely turn up! I'll give her a ring.'

It was true that the only person who could get Mum, Dad and Gran around the table enjoying a cheerful meal together, was Aunt Coral.

It was Uncle who insisted on Aunt Coral coming home. Dad was dead against it to start with.

'You do let your ideas run away with you, Zhiming,' Dad had said disapprovingly. 'Sis hasn't done a broadcast for years. What makes you think you can get her to come and host the show? She'll be exhausted.'

'Well, maybe a bit. But Sis hasn't anything to do nowadays, and after all, this is Mother's eightieth. You said you wanted an MC and she's the best possible person for it,' argued Uncle, sitting down opposite Dad and lighting a cigarette.

'I don't agree! It'll be too much for her.' Dad was still shaking his head.

'Shengqiang, I know you love your big sister to bits, and so do I, but it's not a big deal. Anyway, I've talked to her and she said yes straightaway. It so happens that she doesn't need to baby-sit this weekend, so she'll come back and take a look. She's got years of experience running shows, so she'll have lots of useful suggestions to make. Don't you think?' Uncle could be very persuasive when he chose.

Uncle of course prevailed. He made the call, arranged the time, and there was nothing Dad could say. He cursed Gran. *She's got a bee in her bonnet about this birthday thing,* he grumbled silently. *It's turning everyone's lives upside down.*

Then he got over his annoyance. Oh well, she's only eighty once, he told himself.

'All right, I'll get Zhu Cheng to drive over and fetch her,' said Dad.

'I thought that too,' said Uncle.

Dad was silent. He lit up and inhaled savagely.

They sat together smoking. Neither spoke. The main business was dealt with but they didn't get up to go. Uncle was staring at Dad in a way that gave him the creeps and was beginning to put him in a temper. Since Dad's announcement about Jasmine two days before, Uncle had often stared at him, as if he was examining him inside and out, and from every angle.

It was, of course, Dad who snapped first: 'Spit it out, Zhiming!'

Uncle stubbed out his cigarette and sighed. Dad felt a pang of anxiety and tried to forestall him. 'It's all right, Zhiming,' he said. 'I can handle the business on my own.'

'I know that,' said Uncle. 'And I know you. You're a grown man and you run the whole factory. It's just that this is a bad business. Just think about it, will you? And if you want to discuss it with me, just say the word. If you can't sort it out, I'll do it for you!'

Dad rebelled. Sort it out? Sort a baby out? Sort Jasmine out? Or maybe he was going to sort him, Shengqiang, out! Government policy stipulated one child per couple, so he hadn't broken the rules. He could have another one, what was wrong with that? It wasn't as if he couldn't afford to bring it up! Damn it, ever since Uncle had come home, there was one more person, in addition to Gran, in Pingle Town who was busy adding to his troubles. Gran used to be easy to handle, because she never went out of doors from morning till night. He would drop in and listen to her burbling on, a couple of times a month, but the rest of the time, it was 'out of sight, out of mind'. But now, Uncle was forever coming and going, and every time they met, Dad had to put up with being lectured. He was sodding jinxed!.

As for the business with Jasmine, it was basically going fine. Zhong and Gao Tao and all the rest of the gang, even Zhu Cheng, congratulated him. 'Well done, Shengqiang! Is it a boy or a girl? Lucky devil!' 'Hey, bro, don't you worry about the hospital, I'll fix it for you that she gets the best treatment! Will you need a nanny? I know a good, careful one who could live in for the first month and look after the baby, I can introduce you!' 'You should be spending more time with your mistress. You never know what can happen with a mother-to-be! Anqin won't be a problem. You can book her onto a package tour to Singapore, Malaysia and Thailand over the May Day holiday, with my wife and maybe a couple of friends, and they'll be fine!' 'Anqin's a reasonable woman, she'll comes to terms with it once the baby's born, who can resist a sweet little baby, she'll get on with it like a house on fire! It's no big deal!' 'Can't wait to wet the baby's head, boss!'

Amid all the good cheer, the only dissenting voice, and a very cold one it was too, came from his brother Zhiming. It was disconcerting the way he stared at Dad. Then he said cuttingly: 'Shengqiang! You fool! How on earth did you get yourself into this mess?'

Dad was not an unreasonable man. He was quite sure that his brother had bad memories of something that had happened in his youth, so he was prepared to let him say his piece. He had been landed with such a peculiar brother he could not do much else. But Zhiming would surely understand. They were both middle-aged, they had been around, they'd done plenty of drinking and messing with girls together in their time. In other words, they were both men and this was no big deal! As his friend Zhong put it: 'Little tadpoles will always find their way home!'

Even so, Dad did not feel like sitting with Uncle this afternoon. Every time they did, the atmosphere turned sour. He did not know what he had done to deserve it, but having someone like Uncle staring at him and saying his bit would make even a strong man feel the sky was about to cave in on him. He felt waves of panic and prickles in his bum. It was all going to end in tears. That was enough, he was getting the hell out of here. He put one foot in front of the other and made his escape. He'd go out drinking with his bros.

And that was how things were before Aunt Coral arrived

back in Pingle Town.

Anyway, as I was saying.... Dad was so angry with Uncle that he strode out of the factory gate, then stopped and made a call to Zhong. Spring was coming to the town. After all, it was April, and there was an April sky and an April earth, and that earth burgeoned, bloomed and crawled with all kinds of April creatures. As Dad stood looking, stirred by all this fecundity, Zhong answered the phone.

'Come on! Let's go and get a drink!' said Dad.

It was right in the middle of the day. Zhong said helplessly: 'Dammit, Shengqiang, not everyone's boss of their own company like you are! I've got an office job. Look at the time! It's too early to leave.'

'Are you coming or not?' Dad cut to the chase.

'I'm coming! What about Old Chen's?'

'Right.' Dad cut the call.

As Dad strolled tranquilly along to Old Chen's Bar, he thought about his friend. They went back so many years, and got on extraordinarily well. They didn't talk much but they drank together and the more they saw of each other, the better they got on, and the more they drank, the thirstier they got. While women—it was the oddest thing, but the longer you knew the stupid cows, the less appealing they were.

As he sipped his wolfberry wine, he couldn't help saying to Zhong: 'You know, Anqin, when she was young, she was so pretty, not as pretty as her colleague Yufen, of course, but still very pretty, and easy to get on with. It wasn't that many years ago, I don't understand how she's changed so much.'

Zhong crossed his legs, lit a cigarette and raised his eyebrows: ' You're hard to please, Shengqiang! You've got so picky over women, you don't know how to value what you've got! Let me tell you something: your bit on the side is just that, a bit on the side. She's just having a baby, that's all. Don't you go divorcing our Anqin! If you treat her badly, you'll have me to answer to!'

Dad was taken aback. He first thought Uncle must have been getting at Zhong. Then he thought about it for a bit and conceded there was some truth in Zhong's harsh words. So he said: 'You're right, why would I demolish the family home for a bed somewhere else?'

Zhong blew out a puff of smoke and nodded. Then he clinked glasses with Dad.

The pair of them spent a leisurely afternoon drinking wolfberry wine, crunching on dry-fried peanuts and enjoying their Zhonghua cigarettes. They'd known each other more than twenty years, Dad reflected. Actually, it was all because of Aunt Coral.

It was 1981, or maybe 1982. Dad and Uncle were still at school but Zhong was already working in the state-owned paper mill, taking home a government paycheck every month, and talking proper mandarin Chinese. Of course, Pingle Town then only consisted of four streets, north, south, east and west, and anything that flew through the air or crawled on the earth, one way or another, had to pass along those streets. Underneath the electricity poles at West Street's Celestials Bridge, someone had built three table-tennis tables from cheap local bricks, and every afternoon, or evening after dinner, the youth of the town piled along.

Surprisingly, Dad remembered the day he met Zhong with absolute clarity. They had finished their dinner, and Aunt Coral said she wanted to go and play table tennis. Uncle said he wanted to go too and Dad tagged along behind. Of course they were late and there were no tables left when they arrived. They stood to one side, watching the girls and boys, in their khaki or blue jackets with stand-up collars, slamming the balls back and forth. 'Let's go,' said Aunt Coral. 'It doesn't look like we'll get a table today.' Dad wished he could muscle in and grab a table for his sister but he was too young, just out of junior middle school and Uncle was only in upper middle school. Only Aunt Coral had just got herself a job. Too bad she was a girl. They were about to leave when they suddenly heard a shout: 'Come and play here! We need a change of partners.'

It was Zhong. And that was the day that launched Uncle and Dad on the path that made them into Pingle Town's coolest dudes.

After they became friends, Zhong finally screwed up his courage one day to ask Uncle: 'Zhiming, does your sister have a boyfriend?'

Uncle gave him a scornful look. 'Yup, and she's about to marry him!' he said.

Dad was a kind man and he never mentioned this to Zhong again. And Zhong pretended he had forgotten it. He did not go after Aunt Coral and, when Uncle went off to university, lost touch with him. Only that simple soul, young Dad, was left behind in Pingle Town, and the two were thrown together. And that was how Dad and Zhong became bros: invincible, inseparable drinking, gambling and womanising partners.

When they talked about the past, they mostly joked about Dad's great love affair with Baby Girl, or contemplated their bellies with a sigh: 'We were a lot skinnier when we were young!'

Actually, they did talk about Aunt Coral once. It must have been 1993, when the paper mill closed down and Zhong lost his job. He spent his days wandering each of Pingle Town's four streets like a lost soul. Whenever he went home to Gao Yang, she threw the empty ladle at him. One day he was drinking with Dad and burst out: 'Shengqiang! My life's not worth living anymore!'

That worried the hell out of Dad. 'Don't talk crap! The world's your oyster! The streets are full of women. Are you mad?'

'Ai-ya, Shengqiang, you don't understand. I haven't got a cent to my name, and I can't handle it!' said Zhong with a sigh.

'I've got dosh! What are you worrying about?' Dad slapped his chest. 'Your wife and kids, I'll look after them like my own!'

But Zhong did not seem grateful. He slapped Dad across the head, painfully hard. 'Xue Shengqiang! You might own everything else in this world, but you certainly don't own my wife and child. You understand?'

Dad realized he had put his foot in it. He apologised and laughed. Zhong laughed too, and then they cracked up, laughing until they were out of breath.

That was the day Dad and Zhong had a serious heart-to-heart. They went over everything they'd lived through in Pingle Town, year by year, 1981, 1982, 1983, 1984.

And, you know what? That son-of-a-bitch Zhong broke down. Tears poured down his face, Dad told me. Actually Dad cried too. His eyes reddened, and before he knew it, tears were streaming down his face like horse piss.

They cried a bit, then started to laugh, then drank some more, then commiserated, and cried some more.

Of course, that was the end of it. No way would they ever fucking mention it again.

But now Dad thought he'd better tell Zhong about Coral. When they had drunk enough and the right moment came, he said: 'Tomorrow, Sis is coming back. This was Zhiming's idea. He wants her to host the old lady's birthday celebrations.'

'Really? That's setting the bar high!' said Zhong.

'There's something I want to ask you,' Dad said, after a long pause.

'Eh?'

'The business about the baby. Do you think I should tell Sis? I mean, my brother knows.'

'Are you dumb? Why tell her? Do you want it to be all over the newspapers?' Zhong was startled.

'Listen.' Dad, calmer now, had an idea he wanted to run by Zhong. 'You can't hide a baby when it's born, it'll be a big thing. Anqin's in the dark for now, but sooner or later people will talk and she'll get to know. Then the shit will hit the fan. The only person in the family that she'll listen to is Sis. That's why I think I should tell Sis now, so she's prepared.'

That was when Zhong finally twigged that Dad was really serious about this baby. And Zhong knew his old friend better than anyone else in the whole wide world. If he wanted this baby, everything else could go to hell.

Zhong nodded. 'Then tell her,' he said. 'Your sister's the most reliable one in your whole family.'

In 1980 and 1981, when the townsfolk talked of the Xue family who ran the Mayflower Chilli Bean Paste Factory on West Street, they used to shake their heads and say: 'You don't mess with that family! May Xue was one iron lady! After the Cultural Revolution, she'd hauled herself back into the driving seat and became the factory Director. This was after ten years of hell for the Xues. Everything they owned was confiscated, and Gran's father, still director at nearly eighty, was dragged out and had his head shaved in a *yin-yang* pattern. His son-in-law, Granddad, was sent to work in a brick kiln. That just left May Xue, who was summarily demoted to factory labourer. Day after day, it was she who swept the fermentation yard, cleaned out the toilets, fed the pigs. She had to work harder than any man! But she gritted her teeth and just got on with it. Finally, with the support of the head of the County Party Committee, she got her feet back under the Director's desk. 'She must have had to do some wheeling and dealing!' they said. 'She certainly knows the right people and how to use them. You shouldn't get on the wrong side of her!' The second one in the family not to get on the wrong side of, was the eldest son, Duan Zhiming. Stories were told about how, when he was a little lad, he was a terrible cry-baby. If anyone tried messing with his withered hand, he'd burst into tears. But the next thing you know, he was a big lad of seventeen or eighteen years old. He was still the apple of his mother's eye, everyone knew that. She would have done anything for him! As a kid, he didn't disappoint her. He did well in his studies, he was quick with his fists, and grew into a good-looking young man, a good all-rounder. The girls were always after him, and he had the respect of all his bros. One New Year, at the snooker tables, some youth without eyes in his head tried to take a girl off him, and before the New Year holiday was over, he got badly beaten up by the South Gate. As for his little brother Xue Shengqiang, who was always tagging along behind him, he might have looked dumb, but you didn't mess with him either. He certainly knew how to throw a punch, Duan Zhiming just had to say the word and he was in there fists flying. They had a sister, Coral Xue, who worked in the Grain Bureau and then there was Xue Xianjun, who worked at the county annals office. These last two were quiet and unassuming enough but this was a well-respected family and you didn't want to get on the wrong side of them.

And guess what? When it came time to marry the daughter off, the bridegroom had an office job in the provincial government! Their wedding was very grand! Obviously it was going to be, given the kind of person Iron Lady Xue was. Even minor events in the Duan-Xue family always got a drum roll to announce it far and wide, and a wedding was obviously a big deal. They took over the Friends Garden Restaurant, off the ring road at the West Gate—the most luxurious in town in the 1980s—and filled all eighty tables and paid at least eighty or ninety *yuan* per table of food! There were packs of Hong Ta Shan cigarettes and bottles of Five Grain Liquor on every table. As for the basics the young couple needed to set up home, bicycle, wrist watch, sewing machine and radio, Mrs Director Xue made it quite clear: 'We're not having Chinese products, everything's got to be Japanese!' All the townsfolk flocked there to stuff their faces and marvel at the extravagance. Aunt Coral had always been a pretty girl and looked ravishing when she was dolled-up a bit. The bridegroom was the son of a high-up family in the provincial military, or so they said, and was very handsome. He looked just like the hero in the film *Lu Mountain Love*. Even years later, Pingle Town still felt Uncle Liu had film star looks.

Maybe the only one who was not happy about this wedding was Dad. He remembered quite clearly that his sister got married on Labour Day, thus putting paid to a perfectly good day's holiday! He was busy from morning till night, meeting and greeting, running around in a muck sweat, until he felt like he really had done a hard day's labour. On top of all that, Gran got a bee in her bonnet and insisted that he and Uncle should wear red flowers, like the bride and groom. The flower stalk felt more like a knife stabbing him in the chest! He was the brother of the bride, certainly every single person in his middle school knew him, and there he was, greeting guests at the door with a flower on his chest, it was mortifying. What stuck in his memory, looking back on that day, however, was how angry he'd felt. Everything had been wrong. Gran and Granddad were behaving weirdly. The delicacies on the table looked quite unpleasant. The bridegroom getting out of his Jeep looked like a Kuomintang spy. Zhiming had come with his girlfriend, Qin, and though they behaved themselves in company, they kept going off in a huddle and squeaking and whispering, like a couple of mice digging a hole in the ground. Everything was wrong, from the guests (an appalling crowd), to the damned firecrackers which managed only a few pops and crackles.

Dad looked at his sister, in her scarlet *qipao* gown, a white cape slung over her shoulders, her face flaming and dimpled with smiles as she followed her new husband from table to table toasting the guests. Dad's job was to follow behind them and refill the newly-weds' glasses. They got to a table full of Pingle townsfolk, Mrs Zhang Yao and her son and daughter-in-law, Skanky Zhu and his wife, and old Chen Xiuliang, on his own. This was the older generation. On a half-leaf table next door sat the younger ones, Zhu's son, Zhong and his friends. With one accord, they all got to their feet and Uncle Liu raised his glass and toasted them all. 'Thank you all! Thank you!' Then he emptied his glass. He thought he was so clever, but he didn't deceive the Pingle Town bums. Zhong, ever sharp-eyed, called out: 'Hey, Liu, your glass hasn't any wine in it! Shengqiang, you're neglecting your brother-in-law! Fill him up! Fill him up!' Uncle Liu had to admit defeat and allow Dad to fill his glass to the brim for the toast. Still the guests were not satisfied. 'Coral has to drink too!' And Coral had to drink, no matter how many tables she'd already drunk toasts at. So she obediently clinked glasses with every 'uncle' and 'auntie', then with the young folk, and thanked everyone. And then she tipped her head back and poured the drink down.

After all these years, Dad was still haunted by the image of Aunt Coral knocking back that glass of liquor at her wedding. She drank as if her life depended on it, tipping her head back, lifting her wrist, and drinking the entire glassful. Dad could see in his mind's eye her neck, pale as a lotus root, and those two petal-like ears that flushed pink, then flamed an angry red. He felt so sorry for his sister. So every time he had to refill their glasses, he made sure to fill his brother-in-law's to the brim but only poured his sister's half-full. Eighty tables' worth of half-glasses was still a lot of drink. Many of those tables were occupied by military bigwigs from the provincial capital, bandits, the lot of them! Whenever the bride and groom reached a table like that, Uncle Liu patted them on the shoulder and smiled, and drank their health. Of course, there would be rowdy calls for the bride to drink too, and Aunt Coral obediently did so. The city folk must have been so impressed by her beauty they felt she hadn't drunk enough. One stupid oaf yelled: 'Hey, Liu! Give your bride a kiss on the mouth!' This was greeted with loud shouts from the rest of the table. The good folk of Pingle Town at the other tables pricked up their ears and looked appalled. They were a conservative lot, and had only ever seen this kind of thing in foreign films. Aunt Coral went scarlet and said nothing. Dad had the uneasy impression she was on the verge of tears. *How dare you persecute someone from our family, I don't care how fucking high and mighty you city folk are,* he thought. He was only a kid, and the blood rushed to his head. He pushed his way to the table: 'You're being very offensive! Leave my sister alone! The Communist Party expects good manners!'

Nowadays, Dad would never admit to having spouted such nonsense. If anyone ever mentioned that episode, he would give a dismissive wave and exclaim: 'Ai-ya! Son-of-a-bitch, you're just making it up! Leave it out!' So had he actually spoken the words or just thought them? Heaven knows. Anyway, that was the wedding banquet. It lasted as long as three ordinary banquets, and the dishes kept coming. There was gingko-stewed chicken, duck in brine sauce, and steamed sweet pork. 'Any more steamed pork?' 'No, all gone!' Then dishes of pickled cabbage arrived. 'Pickled cabbage makes the rice go down! Let's have another bowl!' They stuffed themselves with rice as if they were starving, then washed it all down with more liquor. There was card-playing and *mahjong* games, you'd never heard such a din. On and on the feast went. It was the talk of the town for a long time afterwards: 'We stuffed ourselves that day! Stuffed ourselves till we could hardly move!'

Aunt Coral ended up really drunk. Scarlet in the face, she sat down and took a couple of mouthfuls of leftovers. Uncle Liu was still drinking with his friends so Dad sat with Aunt Coral. He managed to find a few bits of meat for her on the empty dishes. 'Shengqiang, you have some,' she said. 'I'm not hungry, Sis,' said Dad. 'Where's Zhiming?' asked Aunt Coral, as she ate.

Dad looked around the room. There was no one left in here, not even Uncle.

'Maybe he's with Mother and the others,' said Dad.

'Uh-huh,' said Sis, and carried on tucking in. Dad ladled out a bowl of chicken soup and put it in front of her.

Aunt Coral's eyes suddenly reddened. As she held the bowl and drank, the tears began to fall.

'Don't cry, Sis, please don't cry!' Dad said in alarm. 'This is your big day!'

'OK, OK,' Aunt Coral said.

Dad did not know what to say. After a pause, he began: 'Sis, don't worry. Me and Zhiming, we'll always be here to back you up if my brother-in-law tries anything on. Just tell us and the pair of us will sort him out!'

That made Aunt Coral laugh. For years after, she used to re-tell this story. 'That Shengqiang, he's always been like that, ever since he was small. Always the family man.'

Dad never dared protest. Whenever she said this, he just scratched his head and smiled. He was just a boy back then! Boys were always full of baloney!

Aunt Coral was seven or eight years older than Dad. She knew the score. So she simply said: 'Shengqiang, don't think like that. That's my husband you're talking about. We're going to be happy together. Strictly speaking, I never did really belong to the Duan-Xue family. In a few years' time, Shengqiang, when you and Zhiming have your own families, you'll understand. Everyone sweeps the snow off their own doorstep.'

When Aunt Coral spoke those words, Dad thought how like Gran she sounded. That had never happened before.

Engrossed in his memories of Aunt Coral's wedding day, Dad could not help feeling distressed. Quite why, he was not willing to probe. Instead, he had another drink. A couple of drinks could really make you do idiotic things. In fact, when he looked back on it, the drink was why that day ended in disaster.

Most times when he and Zhong went out drinking, they never finished before midnight. This time was no exception. They drank wolfberry liquor, then each ordered a couple of glasses of millet liquor, followed by pig's brawn and Sichuan pepper. Dad closed his eyes, rested his feet on the table and took a couple more swigs, and another slice of brawn. The Almighty himself could not shift him from this cosy spot, he thought.

And, to nobody's surprise, Dad and Zhong ended up completely plastered in Old Chen's Bar. Looking back on it after, Dad felt he must have had an intuition that disaster was going to strike, and that was why he couldn't stop drinking. He had another half-pint of millet liquor, and then Gao Tao drove up with his bros, to take them for dinner. Scarlet in the face, Dad greeted him: 'Hey, young Gao! I'm going to be a father again! I'm celebrating! Come and have a glass with us!' A glass did not seem to be enough however, and Dad emptied several glasses in quick succession.

Fuck it! However did I get so drunk? Dad thought bitterly when he woke up next morning. *You stupid fool, he accused himself. You have a few drinks and you think there's nothing you can't do!* 'Your dad has always been like that,' Mum told me. 'A couple of swigs and he reckons he can fly! Next thing, he's turned into an Immortal! Then no one can handle him.'

From what he remembered, the sequence of crazy things he did, starting that afternoon, went something like this:

First, he tried to match-make for Uncle. Zhong casually commented that, in the few days he had been back, Zhiming had made quite an impression in Pingle Town. It was about time too, according to him: 'He's got such a reputation elsewhere, your professor brother, but he never honours his hometown with his presence. It's not good, not good at all. He shouldn't keep such a low profile. We must do something to hype him up. A bit of promotion, that's what he needs. I've been doing my bit for him. He's already given talks at the three middle schools, and he's about to do one for the Culture Department and one for the Education Department, and there are some companies that want to invite him to come and talk to them. See what I've done? He's a popular man!' Zhong happily ticked them off on his fingers, his face flushed with satisfaction. 'So you've got yourself well in with him then,' Dad snorted, in spite of himself.

'Hey!' Zhong laughed. 'That's nothing! How about this: my mum was asking only yesterday how come your brother was still not married. She's got someone in mind for him!'

Dad sat on the bed with a pounding hangover next morning, mulling it over. His drunken reaction had been, *That would be doing the decent thing.* Zhiming had been such a virile young man. Why had he turned so peculiar? It must have something to do with the fact that he had no wife. Of course, he could have had anyone he wanted. It was something the family had always been good at. But when push came to shove, it just wasn't right, not to have a woman waiting for you at home. Dad began to tot up Uncle's age ... he must be all of forty-three or forty-four! The thought made him break out in a cold sweat. The years passed so damned quickly! If Zhiming went on like this, he'd have to face the ugly truth that he wouldn't even have a companion to see him into the grave!

Zhong knew he had struck home when he saw the look on Dad's face. He went on: 'What do you think? Would you like to raise it with him? The thing is, I'm not one of the family and I don't know him too well. He's a big prof now, and I don't know what kind of partner would measure up. But my mum's thought of a couple, and they're not at all bad! Should we get them together?'

Dad said nothing. *So that's what it's all about,* he thought. Then it suddenly struck him that this was his own brother they were talking about, a member of his own family. *He must find it hard to accept that his kid brother has a wife and child at home and a mistress and another baby on the way! I can imagine him heaving a sigh every time he has to face me!* Dad slapped his thigh. He heaved a sigh himself, alarming Zhong until Dad said: 'You're so right, bro! What a good thing you thought of it! It never occurred to me! My brother's got a real problem but we're going to sort it out for him!'

That was the first crazy thing he did.

The second crazy thing he did was to call up Jasmine. They were halfway through their meal and Dad had already been sick once. He must have been because he remembered his mouth had a sour taste, and then Gao Tao said: 'Shengqiang, that girl of yours, when are you going to bring her along to introduce her? If we don't know what she looks like, we might pass her in the street without saying hello, and that wouldn't be right!' 'You talk just like a woman, Gao Tao!' Zhong said. 'Forget it! That girl's a real minger!'

This was the drink talking but Dad thumped the table so hard that the chewed and spat-out bones nearly jumped into Zhong's lap. 'Not good-looking? You just say that again, Zhong! A woman of mine a minger?! When did I ever screw a girl who isn't stunning? Just tell me that!'

Zhong exploded. 'You dickhead, you're so great, aren't you? You've screwed every good-looking girl in town,'

Dad pressed both hands to his temples as he remembered the fight he'd got into with Zhong. The two went at it like hammer and tongs, effing and blinding. 'Xue Shengqiang, I have no respect for you at all!' shouted Zhong. 'You think you're so great but you're such a prick. You put on this big act, but to me, you're still a squitty little kid! Just because you've got a bit of stinking money! If you weren't loaded, what girl would ever want to screw you? In your dreams!'

Dad was so enraged he couldn't think straight. He can't have been thinking straight, because right there and then, he gave Jasmine a call.

He must have woken Jasmine up. 'Hello, Shengqiang?' She sounded dazed.

'Jasmine! I've got something to ask you! Something to ask you ... and I want an honest answer!' Dad bellowed down the phone.

'Shengqiang, what's up? What's happened?' Now she sounded scared, and wide-awake.

'Jasmine! Jasmine! I'm pissed! I just want to ... to ask you ... and I want you to tell me honestly!' Dad sprayed spittle all over his phone.

'Tell me, Shengqiang! Just tell me, what is it you want to know?' Jasmine's voice quavered.

'We've been together a long time, Jasmine, now tell me, have I ever treated you badly?' Dad asked.

'What are you talking about, Shengqiang? Of course you haven't. Don't listen to the rubbish people talk!' Jasmine stammered.

Dad was completely drunk. In front of all his bros and the restaurant hostesses, he yelled (or maybe he didn't, he did not want to examine his memories too closely): 'Jasmine, tell me! Do you love me? I want you to tell me straight, right now!'

This was as idiotic as him saying 'the Communist Party expects good manners'. Dad decided he could not possibly have said this.

By now Jasmine had realized that she was off the hook. 'Yes, Shengqiang,' she said more calmly.

'So you do!' Dad yelled down the phone. 'I love you too!

You wait now, while I give the phone to Zhong and I want you to tell him straight, that you love me! He says any woman of mine only screws me for my money! What mother-fucking shit! You tell him straight that you love me!'

He passed the phone to Zhong but it fell on the table en route, just as Dad fell off his stool.

That's the second crazy thing I did, Dad thought, rubbing his bum.

The third was the craziest of all. Dad sat up in bed remembering. He looked around at the empty bedroom and sighed. His head was swimming.

This time I've really screwed up!

It did not start out as much. Gao Tao took him home. By that time, he was at least half-sober. He and his bros all knew the score. First you ate something to soak up the alcohol, then you went for a stroll and breathed some cold night air, and you'd be half-sober before you got home. Then you could sleep it off.

Once home, Dad aimed his key at the front door. He sighed. He was having a hard job aiming straight. He was just about to poke it into the keyhole when the door flew open. Mum stood there. She stared icily at him, her face like thunder. She certainly was getting old, in fact you could almost say she was old, as she stood there, in the middle of the night, in her dressing gown, her hair straggly, her eyes narrowed, looking like a red-faced demon.

Dad's terror helped to sober him up a bit more. He managed a smile: 'Anqin!' and with a happy giggle, fell on her, aiming his lips at her face.

'Xue Shengqiang! You're off your head with drink!' Mum scowled, pulled him inside and pushed him down on the sofa. Dad dropped like a sack, and lay half on his side, grunting with pain.

'If you don't want ghosts to haunt you, then don't do anything to be ashamed of.' It was Gran who taught Dad that. And she added: 'Shengqiang, I know you think I talk too much but everything I say makes sense. There's no such thing as a wall without draughts. You need to be behave honourably with everyone.'

But by the time Gran had given him that injunction, it was too late. *What the hell's the use of saying that now?* Dad had thought. It was the year 2000, and he and Mum had been married for twelve years. He had just become director of the Mayflower Chilli Bean Paste factory, now back in the family's hands. Of course, he did not have a mistress yet, but he screwed around with one woman or another, more or less often. To be perfectly fair, it was not all Dad's fault. His wife had been sleeping with someone else and he did not like that at all. Screwing other women evened things up. Mum knew all about it but she wanted to keep the peace and turned a blind eye.

Later she told me: 'But this time he'd gone too far. It was a matter of principle.'

Son-of-a-bitch, Duan Zhiming's put a curse on me!

Somehow, Mum had heard about Jasmine's pregnancy. It was the final straw. She flung in Dad's drunken face all the accumulated resentments of years.

Things went from bad to worse. 'Xue Shengqiang, do you still want your family or not?' Mum ranted. 'Well, do you?'

She went on: 'I should have listened to my father all along, shouldn't I? But I insisted on marrying you. I never thought you would turn out like this! I've put up with you all these years. Well, that bitch can have you for all I care! Don't let me hold you back!'

Tears poured down her face. 'I've made mistakes all my life by not listening to my dad. Your whole family's impossible. Take your mother, how many years has she had a down on me, just for one mistake? She's even taken it out on Xingxing because of me. I've put up with all of that. And you? Whatever you do with those girls, she just turns a blind eye to it. When you landed up in the county hospital, she had the cheek to try and hush it up and make me forgive you. Well, never again. It doesn't matter how hard she works on me, I'm not giving in. This is too much, I'm not going to swallow this. You can go off with whoever you like. Pack up your things and go! I've nannied you for too many years, and I've had enough. You've treated me too badly this time! It's obvious from the way you behave that you don't want to stay with me, so let's get a divorce and at least I'll get some peace!'

Mum plonked herself down on the sofa opposite Dad, and hurled an ashtray to the ground. This was followed by a vase, or maybe it was the tea set.

Dad looked at the sitting room floor, carpeted in broken shards, and remembered the scene. Despondently, he went into the kitchen to get a dustpan and brush.

Mum had carried on smashing crockery, swearing and crying. From the sofa, Dad watched. *I've spent all these years working my arse off to make a pile of money for nothing,* he thought. *I've married a shrew.*

'Ai-ya! Have it your own way! If you want to go, you go!' He'd finally said it.

Xue Shengqiang, you're such a fucking big mouth! Dad cursed himself and narrowly avoided treading on a piece of broken glass.

So that was third crazy thing. Dad picked up the bits, and threw the lot into the bin where they landed with a crunch.

He had a pounding headache. *How the fuck did Anqin get to hear about it so quickly?* He did not understand but soon dropped it. It really didn't matter, especially compared to the current problem: the stupid cow had done a runner! He had to get her back. Surely she must accept the baby in the end. Dad was trying to think of everything at once, including where Mum had gone and when she would be back.

Then his phone rang and Duan Zhiming's name lit up on the screen. He answered grumpily and Uncle asked if Zhu Cheng had left yet. Then Dad remembered that he was supposed to be at the factory to meet Aunt Coral.

He wiped the table and cleared up the remaining fragments. Then he walked out into the April day to wait for Aunt Coral.

7

DAD CALLED MUM. The phone rang and rang, but she didn't pick up. That was not unusual. These women, they weren't like men, who always kept their phones on them. They hung from their trouser belts like grenades, or nestled like beating hearts in their breast pockets. It must have been Zhong who complained: 'Women and their phones, they might as well not have them at all! They leave them lying around miles away, stuff them in their bags, and then drop their bags on the sofa or the table. You give them a ring, and, nine times out of ten, they don't hear them! They might as well stick with a pager. Why waste a mobile phone on them?' It was true. But over the years, Dad had got used to it. Besides, he hardly ever phoned Mum. In a piddling little town like Pingle, he never needed to ask where she was or what she was doing, any day of the week or time of day. It was as clear as sesame seeds in a bag of flour.

Mum had worked twenty years in the Grain Bureau, first in the retail section, then in the offices. As an office worker, she had it cushy. She strolled in sometime after ten in the morning, made herself a cup of tea and sat down. Then she took out her knitting, cracked melon seeds between her teeth, read a novel for a bit, or went online ... whatever she felt like. Sometimes, she chatted with the other office workers, about family matters or national affairs. She had known some of them, like Liu Yufen, for years, as they'd all grown up in the neighbourhood. They

were always completely at ease with each other, in as perfect
agreement as lips and tongue, you might say. At twelve noon,
she'd be feeling a bit peckish. She had lunch in the canteen,
which supplied a decent choice of two meat dishes and three
vegetables and a soup, all for just five *yuan*. There was always
plenty of chicken, duck and pork, sometimes with the addition
of some nice fresh river fish. When she'd finished eating, she
just threw down her chopsticks and left her bowl where it was.
There was someone to clear away, of course. She might go out
for an afternoon stroll with a couple of friends, to look at a
pair of shoes perhaps, or take a nap on the sofa in the Union
activities room. Sometime after two o'clock, she went back to
her desks to while away another couple of hours, until it was
time to go home.

At four o'clock, Mum would get into her red Toyota and
make a leisurely trip to the market to buy food for dinner,
then go back home and cook. Sometimes, Dad came home to
eat, sometimes he didn't. Once Mum had cleared away and
washed up, she retired to bed, to watch TV, do a bit of knitting
or idly flick through the pages of a novel. By half past ten, she
was washed and ready for sleep.

It was an enviable lifestyle, and even Dad envied Mum.
One evening, he came back from a dinner with clients, a
disgusting smell of cigarettes, liquor and food clinging to him,
to see Mum reclining on the bed, book in hand, like a classical
beauty asleep under a flowering crab-apple tree. 'Just look at
you, Anqin!' he burst out. 'What a life you lead, eh? Why don't
we trade places?' Mum just smiled, and poked a leg out to give
Dad a kick. 'Sure!' she said. 'No drinking or going out for three
days then! Let's see how you like that!' Dad made a grab for
her foot and plumped down on the bed. He pressed his mouth,
laden with alcohol fumes, against hers, and retorted: 'OK, if
you play no *mahjong* for a week, then I'll lay off the booze!'

That was never going to happen. *Mahjong* was huge in

Mum's life, always had been. At one o'clock every Saturday afternoon, on the dot, without exception. And every now and then, when the occasion offered, she might get in a game during the week too, on Monday or Tuesday evenings, or Wednesday or Thursday afternoons, or Sundays after dinner. A lot of women in our town who were really addicted (not Mum, of course) got a table together every day. The ones who lost everything were wretched, the ones who swept the board crowed with victory, but these women were nothing if not tenacious; they played on with verve, their fleshy arms rising and falling, they sat glued to their seats till their bottoms went numb, as day turned into night, but no one was going to leave the table. And sure enough, as the hours went by, fickle fate ensured that the losers were transformed into winners and the winners into losers. 'Did someone's mobile ring?' 'Not mine!' 'Whose is it?' Not a single woman left the table to answer it.

Oh yes, all the husbands, including Dad, knew the score. They understood why none of their womenfolk answered their mobiles. It was because they were having a little flutter. So they scratched their heads and went back into their restaurant side-room to have a few more glasses with the boys and stroke the little hands of the hostesses, and wait until the 'boss' had finished up. There would be a phone call—'the fire alarm's gone off!' they joked—and they sallied forth to reclaim the high ground. Each one drove off to the *mahjong* hall to collect the 'boss' and, at dead of night, husband and wife returned home.

Dad stood outside the chilli bean paste factory office building, thinking nostalgically about the good times he and Mum had shared, as he waited for her to answer her phone. After twenty or so rings, it was obvious that she was not going to. There was nothing for it but to stuff his phone back in his pocket and go upstairs to join Aunt Coral.

Zeng, the young office manager, must have been quick off

the mark today. Dad had no sooner stepped in through the door to his room than he saw Aunt Coral with a cup of tea in her hands, sipping from it and flipping through a pile of the factory's newly-printed advertising material.

'What do you think, Sis? Are the leaflets OK?' asked Dad. 'We got Zheng, from the Number One Middle School, to write the copy, and people seem to think he's done a good job.'

'They're nice,' said Aunt Coral, putting the flyers back on the coffee table. 'Is Anqin coming for lunch?'

'Ah!' exclaimed Dad as if he had just remembered. 'She never picked up! She must have got separated from her phone again! It doesn't matter, we'll go and eat, we won't wait for her. She'll call us in a bit.'

'But didn't you tell her yesterday that I was coming?' asked Aunt Coral.

'I was late home yesterday. She was asleep so I couldn't talk to her.' Dad sat down. His hand automatically went to his pocket for a cigarette but he stopped himself, embarrassed to smoke in front of Aunt Coral, and pulled it out again.

'Are you and Anqin getting on all right?'

'Ai-ya! We're an old married couple! We're just like all old couples! Besides, you know Anqin!' And Dad burst out laughing.

But Aunt Coral wasn't letting Dad off the hook so easily. 'It's coming up twenty years since you married, isn't it?' she pursued.

Dad counted up on his fingers. She was right, it was New Year's Day, 1988, and Mum had just had her twentieth birthday. It would be twenty years this New Year.

Damn it. 'Right! Twenty years,' admitted Dad with a sigh.

Aunt Coral smiled and took another sip of tea. Dad looked at her. Her eyebrows, drawn together in a slight frown, gave her an air of melancholy. OK, OK, he knew quite well that he was about to poke his nose in where it wasn't wanted. You could ask anyone in Pingle Town and they'd tell you that Coral Xue was a very lucky woman. A girl from an ordinary family, plucked from the Grain Bureau to marry a man with a job on the provincial Party Committee and move to a new home in Yong'An City. 'Fantastic! Of course, she was May Xue's daughter. That woman could always get her way!' In the blink of an eye, Aunt Coral was off to university to do a master's degree, and in another blink of an eye, she was presenting shows at the TV station. The neighbourhood buzzed with the news. 'On TV! There's never been a girl from Pingle Town who made it so good! To be on the television! How very fortunate you are, Mrs Factory Director!' Gran was always being stopped when she went out into the street, and had to listen to the flustered exclamations. Gran would go pink, and smile deprecatingly and dismiss the fuss with a wave of her hand: 'Ai-ya! It's not such a big deal! It really isn't! I've always told her not to get arrogant and self-satisfied. She's got to carry on learning, carry on making progress, and not get above herself!' Of course, all that stopped years back, in 1999. When she turned forty-one, Aunt Coral stepped down. She trained up news anchors, read programme drafts or planned new productions, but she was not seen on TV any more. Luckily, the townsfolk took it all in their stride. 'After all, Coral Xue still works at the TV station,' they said. 'The TV station!' The glory would rub off on the family for generations to come.

'What about you, Sis? How have you been lately?' Dad ventured the only question he dared ask.

Aunt Coral smiled again and put down her cup. Taking her time, she began: 'Shengqiang, there's something I need to talk to you about now I'm back. It's nothing bad. Sooner or later, everyone will find out anyway. I'm just afraid that Mother will make a huge fuss about it. So I'm telling you first, so you're ready for it. I filed for a divorce with your brother-in-law yesterday.'

Dad was so shocked he got a pain in his chest. He felt like he was choking on glutinous rice balls, or had chilli meatball fumes rushing up his nostrils. Without waiting for him to say anything, Aunt Coral went on: 'I've already mentioned it to Zhiming and he agrees—with the way we've been living, it's best to divorce. Then I can have a nice quiet life. I've also told him, if you think I'm still up to it, I'll be back to help with Mother's eightieth celebrations, and give her a good time,' his sister finished, with a wave of her hand and a smile.

Dad suddenly realized where all this had come from, and where it was leading. Naturally, he cussed Uncle first: *You son-of-a-bitch, Duan Zhiming, you well and truly made me look an idiot there!*

Then his thoughts went to Uncle Liu, his brother-in-law, and his stupid pasty face behind those gold-rimmed glasses. *Liu Qukang! Just make sure you don't ever bump into me ever again! In fact, don't ever set foot in Pingle Town again!* And there was some more silent, colourful swearing.

Of course, Dad never swore in front of Aunt Coral. So he said nothing now, and even stopped himself frowning. Finally, with a great deal of effort, he managed: 'So, what do we do about Mother's birthday?'

He felt like boxing his own ears the minute he'd spoken but, luckily, Aunt Coral did not get angry. Clutching her cup, she said: 'I've already talked to Zhiming and we agree that Mother mustn't get wind of it. It's her eightieth birthday, so your brother-in-law will come, and Xingchen and his wife and their child. Everyone will be there.'

Dad said something like: 'So you've told Liu Xingchen about the divorce? What's he going to do?'

He realized he sounded ridiculous. What was Liu Xingchen going to do? He was a young man in his twenties, with a wife and child, a very nice job at the provincial TV station, and a spacious apartment with two bedrooms and two reception rooms. He had his own car too. He must be the envy of other youths of his age. He didn't need to do anything.

And Aunt Coral smiled: 'He's got a home and a family, and he's known about his dad's affair for ages. In fact, he tried twice to persuade him to drop her, but his Dad wouldn't listen, so he just turned a blind eye. So when I told him about the divorce, he was OK about it. 'Mum,' he said. 'You and Dad don't feel anything for each other, you should have got divorced long ago. Divorce is no big deal nowadays. So long as you're both happy, then I support you!'

That, at least, made Dad smirk. So he'd said that, had he? That was one pampered kid, butter wouldn't melt in his mouth. His mum and dad were going to get divorced and all he could do was bleat the sort of thing a woman would come out with! *He got that from his father!* Dad decided. *We wouldn't have talked like that when we were in our twenties!*

By the time Dad was twenty-five or twenty-six, he'd been earning a living at the chilli bean paste factory for nearly ten years. He'd graduated from stirring the vats, of course, and was managing the retail department. 'Shengqiang,' he remembered Gran saying, 'Retail is a tough job. You make sure you do your job properly. You don't get anywhere in this life without a struggle, but it'll reward you and bring you respect. I believe in you, son. You'll make a good career for yourself.'

Some son-of-a-bitch career. Dad had been in the retail department for a month when it dawned on him that Gran was talking through her arse. The fact of the matter was that working in retail was all about drinking: *Drink! Come on, bottoms up! You're all my sworn bros, any problem you just bring it to me and I'll solve it! You want bribes? I'll get them to you. You want hostesses? I'll procure them for you. I'll be your escort girl, and sing and dance and keep you company!* In those years, Dad truly understood the meaning of working 24/7.

He spent his days running around the Pingle area, from one county town to another, wearing out the shoe leather, spoiling more than one bed with vomiting up the alcohol he had been forced to drink, putting on so much weight from too many client dinners that his belly swelled like his sales record, and he looked pregnant. 'You have to give it to him,' they said in the factory, 'that Xue Shengqiang certainly knows what he's doing. And he's a hard worker too.' The acting Director, Zhu Shengquan, began to feel the director's chair being pulled from under him. Even Dad began to believe in the myth of his invincibility: whatever he turned his hand to was a winner. There was nothing he could not achieve. Then there was the thing with 'Wei Wei' and from one day to the next, he was confronted by some very unpleasant truths.

He remembered going home the day after—in those days, they were still living in the old place behind the factory. Mum did not suspect anything, she thought he'd been off on a business visit to Chongning County.

It was nearly noon when he got home, and Mum was in the courtyard hanging out the sheets to air. She was wearing, he remembered, a blue dress with a white pattern on it, and ivory sandals. Her arms were raised, in the act of throwing the sheets over the airing frame, and he saw the fine dark hair against the whiteness of her armpits, and felt a rush of warmth for her. In two strides, he was across the yard and snatching the sheets from her. 'Let me have those, Anqin! I'll do it.' he said.

'Why are you back at this time of day?' Mum was startled. She lifted a hand and stroked his hair. 'Were you out drinking with clients last night? You don't look good! Did you have breakfast? There's still some fried bread sticks on the stove. Have a couple! Why don't you have a nap? Xingxing cried all night. I've just got her to sleep. You have a nap too.'

Mum and Dad, stood side by side, and arranged the sheets on the airer. Dad's nostrils were filled with the lingering fragrance of White Cat Washing Powder. Mum's cheeks were flushed a rosy pink. Dad was in turmoil. He cursed himself for being a fucking animal, reached out and gripped Mum's waist hard. It felt like butter under his hand, as if it might melt at his touch.

'Shengqiang!' Mum, embarrassed, gave him a little push. 'It's the middle of the day! And what about the baby?'

But Dad was not to be put off. He carried Mum off into the house. He pressed his lips to Mum's damp earlobe and, whispering, 'The baby's asleep,' he grabbed Mum's soft round breast.

When Dad thought back on that moment, a dozen or so years later, he still felt a tremor in those balls of his. The east wind blew, the war drums rolled and rain, sweetly-fragranced with apricot blossom, misted over him—and he suddenly discovered his pecker was as dead as a dodo.

The memory still appalled him. For a whole week afterwards, he felt like a walking zombie. Mum, on the other hand, was careful not to mention it. Solicitously, she said: 'Shengqiang, you mustn't work so hard, you must take more care of yourself, drink less and rest more!' When Dad went to the toilet, he furtively took his penis in his hand and said to himself: *This is not on! You look perfectly healthy. I've never done you any harm, have I? I'm still not thirty! I can't have worn my pecker out yet! Did I catch something off that hooker?*

He racked his brains, but the more time he spent thinking about it, the more intractable the problem seemed. All the time, his pecker stubbornly refused to stand up. Finally, he broached the subject with Zhong. 'Do you think I ought to get a doctor to check me over?'

Zhong was eight or nine years older than Dad. He heard Dad out, frowning, and was silent. Then he said: 'Shengqiang, don't get in a state about this. Come with me to Fifteen Yuan Street tonight, right?'

'Fifteen Yuan Street?!' Dad snorted. 'Why would I go there now?'

'You just come with me,' Zhong insisted, and patted Dad on the hand.

So they went. They found a nightclub that had just opened and settled themselves in a dark side-room, lit with glinting spotlights and smelling strongly of new paint. Bottles of beer and bowls of snacks and fruit arrived, the karaoke machine lit up and two hostesses arrived. Dad and Zhong, with a mike in one hand and a girl in the other, sang 'Fields of Hope', then 'Meeting at the Yurt', then 'Sweet Honey', and rounding off of course with the Olympic Anthem.

And it was just like the words said, 'We are Asia, our mountains raise their heads high'. That evening, Dad finally got it up. To tell the truth, Dad never even saw what the girl looked like. He just remembered she had a big arse which he kneaded between the fingers of both hands as they had sex. 'Ai-ya! Ai-ya!' The girl's moans rose and fell, in perfect time with the Olympic Anthem. Dad did it twice that evening, pumping into the girl like a chicken with its head cut off.

Fuck it, that was a diabolically clever idea of Zhong's, thought Dad. He was recovered. He was walking on air. And he knew exactly what he wanted. He walked out of Fifteen Yuan Street and through Pingle Town in moonlight so bright he could see every detail of the street beneath his feet. Back home, he headed straight for Mum's bed, grabbed hold of her and made deliriously happy love to her.

And that's the story of Mum and Dad's young love. *Son-of-a-bitch, after all these years, we can't really have screwed it up now, can we?* Dad looked at Aunt Coral, sitting on his sofa opposite him, and did not dare raise the thing he really wanted to say to her. He thought back on how in love he and Mum had been, and felt the pulses at each temple pounding.

The clock was ticking on and his belly needed attention. It was nearly noon and there was no sign of Mum. They decided on tripe hotpot. Gran always said she didn't like hotpot: 'I've spent my whole life around chilli bean paste. I'd really prefer something a bit lighter. But Aunt Coral loved spicy food. She wouldn't touch even plain boiled *mouli* without ordering two ounces of ground chilli pepper to dip it in. So Uncle suggested: 'Lets go for hotpot, then. We haven't had it for a long while.'

And off they went. Zhu Cheng took Dad and Aunt Coral from the factory, and Uncle drove to Cornucopia Court to pick up Gran, and they met at the South Gate Tripe Hotpot Restaurant, where they ordered the Mandarin Ducks option—a double pot with spicy broth on one side, and mild broth on the other. They arranged themselves around the table, poured glasses of soy milk and opened bottles of beer and then Gran asked, as if it had just occurred to her: 'Where's Anqin?'

There was silence. Then Dad said: 'She had to go to work.'

Gran was just extracting a piece of luncheon meat from the plain broth. She let it drop and laid her chopsticks down on her saucer. 'Shengqiang, you think you can tell me lies because I'm an old woman? What kind of a job does Anqin have, that she can't get off work to take a lunch break? She might never come and see me, but she could surely come and see your big sister now she's back? Is missy having a hissy fit?'

Strictly speaking, Gran got it wrong. Mum was thirty-nine or forty years old by then, and no way could she be considered a 'missy'. All the same, it was clear what she meant. Her quiet words spoken, she picked up her chopsticks again, neatly took out the slice of luncheon meat, dunked it in the dipping sauce, and popped it elegantly into her mouth.

There was not a sound from the others. A bellyful of rude retorts bubbled up in Dad but finally it was Uncle who broke the silence: 'How's your digestion these days, Mother? Would you like a slice of chitterling?'

'Good heavens, no!' Gran said. 'Much too chewy.' She put her chopsticks down and surveyed the dishes on the table. 'Put some shitake dumplings in for me.'

'Of course!' Uncle got to his feet and tipped almost a bowlful of the dumplings into Gran's side of the pot. 'They're soft! Try them, Mother!'

Dad shot him a look, then sipped his beer.

As for Aunt Coral, she sat bolt upright in her chair, and dunked the morsel of tripe she held between her chopsticks into the spicy soup. It was an art, cooking the tripe. Some people said that you should count to eighteen and then the meat was cooked, other people said to count to fifteen. Anyway, Aunt Coral was anxious not to overcook it so it went tough, and watched it with close attention.

'Well, it's a good thing there are no outsiders present,' said Gran finally, with a sigh. 'We can say what we want between ourselves.'

Uncle began, talking eloquently and happily about the arrangements for the birthday. They were well in hand: the fermentation yard was spick and span, the order of proceedings had been drawn up, and Professor Zhu, of the Yong'An City University Chinese department had written a poem in honour of the Mayflower Chilli Bean Paste Factory. Mr Yin, the calligraphy teacher in Cao Jia Alley, had made a fair copy. Eight of the county town's most eminent figures had contributed a birthday couplet each, and the advertising company had constructed a rectangular canvas-covered frame, at least nine metres by four metres, the most imposing that Pingle Town had ever seen. This was in addition to the forty-eight free-standing display boards which the advertising company had erected around the yard, and so on, and so on ... On the great day, thirty-eight banners would be carried from Celestials Bridge all the way to the factory entrance, and so on, and so on ... There would be a goodie bag for each of the guests, containing flyers, jars of chilli bean paste, pens and notebooks, as well as paper tissues printed with a blurb about the factory. Uncle was so excited he got a pair of chopsticks and sketched the scenario on the table. Dad harrumphed to himself: *Gao Tao, you have been a busy boy, haven't you? Your company's really made a killing out of us. The bill for all this will put food on your table for a year!* Even Gran asked: 'Zhiming, how much is all this going to cost?' 'Ai-ya, Mother!' Uncle protested. 'This is such a big occasion, we've got to get it right, the money's not important!' He waved away their objections, and went on: 'Now, the performances ... There's a company from Yong'An City that specialises in spectaculars. Normally, they wouldn't do a small gig like this, but they've agreed just because we're friends. We'll have several singers and other stars, and they do a special *son et lumière* too. We can get Sis to host the show, and that will make it even more special. So don't worry, Mother, I absolutely guarantee that this will the birthday of a lifetime!'

No one was as persuasive as Uncle, Dad had to give him that. Duan Zhiming really was a prize arselicker. Even since he was a little kid, there had been no one to beat him. So, of course, Gran smiled until her face was a mass of wrinkles. 'Shengqiang,' she said. 'You heard your brother. What do you reckon?'

'Very good! Excellent!' Dad pulled himself together, jumped to his feet and slapped the table for emphasis, making the diners at the neighbouring table turn and stare.

A chuckle escaped Aunt Coral, and Gran looked at her. 'Coral,' she said gently, 'I really must thank you for going to all this trouble, I'm sure you have enough on your plate with your own family. I'm really moved that you should have come back for this.'

'Mother, don't talk like that,' said her daughter. 'Zhiming and Shengqiang have done all the hard work. I've only done what a daughter should do.' And she added. 'The important thing is for our mother to have a wonderful day.'

'Yes, I'm going to enjoy it!' Gran exclaimed, as if she could already see the celebrations in her mind's eye. 'But all this spectacle, it's fine, but it's really for people outside the family. The important thing, the thing that will make me really happy, is to have the whole family together. We haven't done that since your father passed on. If he knew, it would make him happy too.'

Not necessarily, Dad figured. If Granddad was here, he'd spend most of the day puffing on cigarettes with old Chen in the fermentation yard, watching as the singers came and went on the stage. 'Duan Xianjun,' he imagined his *shifu* saying, 'you've had a good life, old man!' And Granddad would eject a gob of tobacco and shake his head, what more could he say? 'I've passed on, so you can say what you like. You say I'm happy, then I'm happy. You say I've had a good life, then that's what I've had.'

And, somehow, the conversation turned to Granddad. He'd been gone more than two years, but Gran liked to talk about him from time to time. For instance, she might say to Dad that she was thinking of buying a couple of new outfits. 'Shengqiang, I never thought I'd need any new clothes, I mean, at my age, what would I be doing buying clothes? The ones I've got are good and they've lasted me. If I bought any more, I'd never wear them. But now I'm thinking of your father. If he were still alive, he'd want me to live comfortably, and have good food and good clothes, so I think if I got another couple of outfits, your father would be happy.' Sometimes, eating a mouthful of steamed pork, she would say: 'Do you remember, Shengqiang, how this was your father's favourite dish? I always found it too fatty for me, but when I think of your father I feel I ought to eat a bit more of it, as if I was eating for him.' Other times, she would urge Dad to work hard: 'The factory results are pretty good nowadays, but don't rest on your laurels, Shengqiang. You must work even harder next year. Think of your father. It was his dying wish that the chilli bean paste factory should prosper.' *Father never gave a toss about the chilli bean paste factory!* thought Dad. But he listened obediently. After all, wasn't Gran always good-hearted and reasonable?

Now that she had an audience of the three of them, Gran had started to reminisce. 'Your father and I were destined to be together, don't you think? We wouldn't have got together otherwise, because he was a university student, and I never even finished primary education. Your father was so handsome when he was young. All the girls were after him. We were together all those years, through the ups and the downs, and we had you three and you've all done well for yourselves. He shouldn't have died before his time, and left me all alone, though. Sometimes I sit alone at home and think I really don't want to go on living. It's hard to be parted from him forever. But I know if your father was still here, I know he'd want me to have a good life. So I'll soldier on for a bit longer, not for myself, but for your father.'

Dad had heard all this so often he could recite it by heart. He paid even less attention because he was so on edge. Aunt Coral had things on her mind too. It was only Uncle who made out that he was hearing it for the first time. He leaned towards Gran and said: 'Mother, don't talk like that. You've got to look after yourself, take care of your health, eat well and wear nice clothes. Just remember heaven has blessed you, there are still good times to come.'

Well said, well said. You just carry on talking. Dad concentrated on putting the fish balls into the spicy broth to cook, then fat pieces of beef, then a rack of rabbit, then some cubes of duck's blood, some of the pig's arteries, some leatherjacket fish. The whole lot went in. He was so engrossed that he almost forgot his worries, as he watched the roiling, bubbling mixture and waited to pop another delicacy into his mouth and fill his belly. Then there was a shrill ring came from the phone in his trouser pocket.

It was Mum. Dad was startled when he saw 'Anqin' appear on the screen. He jumped to his feet and hurriedly left the side-room with a muttered: 'I've got to take this call.'

He stood outside on the pavement, as the traffic streamed past. 'Have you sobered up?' asked Mum. 'Why were you calling me?'

She spoke perfectly normally and, faced with an enemy of such cunning, Dad felt he should play his cards close to his chest too. So he hedged, with a disarming: 'Sis came back today. She wanted me to get you over for lunch. Mother and Zhiming are here too. They're all asking about you.'

'Ai-ya!' Mum sighed. 'I just put my phone down on my desk and went to the office next door. I didn't hear it. Have you finished eating? Shall I come now?' She sounded genuinely sorry.

Dad watched as a metallic pink Suzuki Alto nosed its way down the street. He had never seen an Alto that colour before.

'Shengqiang, shall I come now?' Mum repeated softly in his ear.

'Eh?' Dad pulled himself from his reverie. 'It doesn't matter. We've almost finished, there's no need for you rush over now.' He finished in a jumble of words.

What fucking shit are you chatting? He muttered, as another car passed by.

'OK, then will she still be here this evening? We can have dinner together tonight, can't we?' Mum suggested helpfully.

'She's going home this afternoon, I'll get Zhu Cheng to drive her. She's got to baby-sit Diandian tonight.'

'Ai-ya!' Mum sighed in genuine regret. 'OK, so will you be home for dinner tonight? I'm going shopping a bit earlier this afternoon. Shall I do you stewed chitterlings? I'll buy some.'

You really want to do chitterlings for me? Dad sent up a heartfelt thanks to the Goddess of Mercy, even though he couldn't see her because the noonday sun shone like a 120W light bulb in his eyes. 'Fine!' he said. 'Stewed chitterlings are good! Let's have stewed chitterlings!'

They exchanged a few more words, about the evening's dinner, and Mum mentioned that the son of someone at work was getting married that weekend , and they were invited to the wedding banquet. 'I don't know her that well, but we've worked together for a number of years, how much should I put in the red envelope gift?' 'Whatever you think, you decide how much money to put in, I'll leave it to you,' said Dad, all generosity. Then he said that he needed to take the car to Yong'An City for a service tomorrow, and would do a bit of shopping at the same time. Etcetera, etcetera, etcetera.

They chatted happily on, until Dad's belly rumbled and he said: 'I'd better get back to the table, they're still eating. I'll be back for dinner this evening.'

He cut the call and stood in a trance on the pavement, watching the stream of passing cars. It was as if he had woken up from last night's nightmare to find his ferocious, snarling vixen was now a cooing turtle dove. He looked up from the phone and was about to go in when he was suddenly immersed in another reverie, about the time when Mum really had been a cooing turtle dove.

It was in 1987. He'd broken up with Xi Hongzhen and was courting Mum. That made Gran very happy, but Anqin's father, Chen Xiuxiao, was outraged. Dad did not see what happened next with his own eyes, but in a piddling little town like Pingle, the news made its way back to him anyway. Mr Chen created a scandal, chasing his daughter round the County Party Committee Officials' residential compound, brandishing a feather duster, beating her and yelling: 'Have you gone mad? Why do you want to get mixed up with that family? Do you want to be a gutter-snipe? What kind of people do you think they are? How dare you say you want to marry into that family! Don't even think of it! Let me tell you, you're not marrying into any family called Xue while I still have breath left in my body! Every principle I've taught you since you were a child, it's all gone out of the window! Fancy throwing away all that education to marry a bean paste seller!' Or words to that effect.

Dad was a pragmatic young man. When he heard what had happened and was waiting for Mum in their usual place, he thought to himself: *the old man might have put paid to Anqin and me.* But to his surprise, along came Mum. It was a boiling hot day, but she wore a long-sleeved white shirt and dacron trousers, which made her look like the manager of the local Neighbourhood Office. Dad was delighted to see her. He beamed a smile and said: 'Chen Anqin, let's go to a film today.' Mum looked at him: 'Let's go then,' she said. They went to a film, *Hibiscus Town*, starring Liu Xiaoqing. As they came out of the cinema, there was a man selling ice-lollies. 'Let's have ice-lollies,' said Dad, 'Isn't it hot today!'

They walked along licking their lollies, and Dad said: 'What are you wearing a long-sleeved shirt and trousers like that for, on a day like this? You must be roasting!' Mum still said nothing. Suddenly, to Dad's alarm, her eyes reddened. Light dawned at last, and he grabbed her arm and pulled up her sleeve. Her arm was covered in purple bruises, feather duster imprints.

That was the day when Dad made up his mind to marry this girl and take her home. They stood by the wall of the cinema compound and, just like in the films, their lips met in a kiss.

Dad stood outside the restaurant, still tasting the fiery hotpot in his mouth. He felt his anxieties being soothed away. *Whatever!* he thought. *If she doesn't want to talk about this baby, then I'm not going to raise it. If she wants to row about it, then I'll admit I'm wrong. But we definitely shouldn't get a divorce!* As soon as he had made up his mind, his belly told him in no uncertain terms that he was hungry. He pulled himself together and strode back into the restaurant, ready to enjoy some more hotpot with peace of mind.

Too late! As he went into the room, he saw Aunt Coral finishing off her meal with a bowl of sweet potato gruel and Gran organizing the waitresses to pack up the remaining dishes into take-away containers. 'Have you finished your call, Shengqiang?' she asked him. 'You're not having any more to eat, are you? Can you take me home? Your brother's taking Coral to see the fermentation yard.'

I wasn't that long on the phone. How come they've finished eating? Dad wondered. Uncle spun round from the cashier's desk, brandishing the bill for the meal and exclaiming: 'It's not expensive at all! Can you really eat so cheaply in Pingle Town? The whole meal only came to about 200 *yuan*!'

He was declaiming as if he were performing opera, but no one else took any notice. Even Gran stared abstractedly out of the window.

As no one answered him, Uncle shut up too. He put the bill down on the table, and scratched off the wax square with a pair of chopsticks. He had not won a prize, so he folded it and put it in his pocket.

Dad looked at Aunt Coral and she looked back at him. Dad had a bellyful of things to say, besides which, he was starving. Whoever would have thought the meal would end like this?

As they left, Uncle bounded up and took Gran by the arm. Aunt Coral walked next to Dad and told him quietly what had happened in his absence: 'That brother of yours ... Mother only asked him when he was going to get married, and they started rowing again!'

By rights, Dad should have taken Uncle's side, but hunger

had made him bad-tempered. He looked at Uncle's back view and cursed. *Duan Zhiming! You're such a smooth talker, how come a simple question like that stumped you?*

He waved his brother and sister off and, empty-bellied, gave Zhu Cheng a call. Zhu did not pick up so Dad called again. Zhu answered this time.

Dad gave his orders. 'I'll be right there!' said Zhu Cheng hurriedly. Dad knew he must be eating his dinner but that could not be helped. When the boss commands, you have to throw down your chopsticks and leave your steaming bowl of rice on the table. Like servant like master! Dad felt his sagging empty belly and cut the call.

I'll take Mother home and then go and get both of us some chilli dumplings, he decided.

But things are rarely so simple. It was over an hour before Gran had finished chattering and he could leave, by which time his belly was so empty, his legs would hardly hold him up. He slumped into the back seat of the car and stretched out, with a hopeless sigh. In the driver's seat, Zhu Cheng asked: 'Back to the factory, boss?'

'Not yet. Let's go to Xie's chilli dumpling place first. I never had lunch. You have some too.'

Zhu Cheng turned the steering wheel and headed towards the East Gate. The chilli dumplings place was outside the East Gate, almost as far as the Ling Yan Temple. It was a fly-blown shack and when Dad took Zhong there once, Zhong objected: 'Shengqiang, has all that money's turned your head? Why do you want to drive all this way to eat this stuff? Come to my house and I'll cook you noodles. They'll be a lot better than this!'

Zhu Cheng probably did not get it either, but at least he obeyed orders. If Dad ordered him to drive east, there was no way he could drive west. If Dad did not talk, he had to keep his mouth shut too. If Dad said he wanted to smoke, then it was Zhu Cheng's job to find the lighter and pass it to him. Zhu Cheng was so skilled at reading Dad, that Dad only had to lift one buttock cheek for his driver to know a fart was coming. What a demon! Never mind all the hostesses and hookers, not even Jasmine, or Mum, who had known him twenty-odd years, knew Dad that well. *He's a clever man, my driver!* Dad often thought, with feeling. He remembered when Gran had tried to get the elder Mr Zhu, his father, to retire and the old man agreed on one condition: that when Zhu Cheng finished his military service, the family should give him a job with the company. Gran was a fair-minded woman. 'He can drive the factory Santana!' she said. And Zhu Cheng had spent the years keeping his head down and quietly learning his job: he fended off some of the toasts at drinking sessions, handed him the money at the brothel door, and generally put the boss's interests before his own. At home, he pulled the wool over Mum's eyes; outside, he coaxed Dad's other women into behaving themselves, and generally kept the peace between all parties.

'Have you sorted out the business of Jasmine?' asked Dad.

And Zhu Cheng answered: 'An apartment's been rented in a new-build estate. The block has a lift, and the place is fully-furnished. The removal people are moving her in tomorrow.'

Dad nodded. Then he pursued: 'What about a nanny? Has the one you mentioned before agreed?'

'I called her up. I offered her 1,500 *yuan* a month. She was very happy, says she'll go over next week and start helping Jasmine.' Zhu Cheng brought the car to a smooth halt at a red light. 'Boss, I know you said to offer her 2,000,' he said. 'But 1,500 is plenty. You don't need to pay her more than that.'

'I don't mind,' said Dad. 'I'll give you 2,000 every month anyway, and the remainder you can do what you like with.'

'No, no, boss!' Zhu Cheng protested, turning to look at Dad. 'There's no need for that!' But Dad just waved dismissively.

'Ai-ya! No more arguing! I'm in charge here.' Dad said no more, just pressed the window controls to open it and lit a cigarette.

The car moved off and they drove on. Dad took a drag on his cigarette, then blew a smoke ring out, felt his scalp tingle. He conjured up the vision of the chilli dumplings he was about to eat, and a heavenly vision it was too: the dumplings swimming in clear red chilli oil in their dish, the scattering of ivory-coloured sesame seeds on top, with a sprinkling of white sugar to finish off.

Dad sighed. Sometimes he just felt so tired, and then he'd think about handing over the factory in a year or two and enjoying a bit of quiet home life. He'd garden, eat his dinner at home, then go out for an evening stroll. That would be good.

It was a nice thought. But he'd have to get around Gran first. When he went to her apartment, she had said: 'Shengqiang, sit down, there are some things I want to talk over with you.' So Dad sat down. Today's conversation ranged over everything and everyone in the family. No detail of their lives was too small for Gran to delve into. 'Your big brother has worked his socks off since he came back home. You should give him some help so he doesn't exhaust himself. It's very gratifying that your sister wants to help too. She's a good daughter to me. Better than that useless daughter-in-law of mine. How have orders been in the factory this year? You need to keep an eye on the condition of the production areas, because the quality of our product is key, you don't want the quality to go down now that we're so much better known. As for you, less wandering off and hanging around with Zhong and that lot. They have cushy jobs in state-run companies, we run our own business, we've only got ourselves to rely on, we can't fritter our time away like they do. Besides, your friends are all losers. It seems to me that they only invite you out so you can foot the bill, right? How can a grown man like you be so stupid,

Shengqiang? How often have I told you to keep a proper distance from them? These friends of yours are no earthly use to you, and you'll get tarred with the same brush if you don't watch out. If you want friends, why don't you find some who can really help you? Do you understand what I'm saying?' Dad felt like he was at the end of his tether. Apart from the fact that he was starving, it was clear as daylight that the one who had really got on the wrong side of Gran was Zhiming, but he, Dad, got the blame. In desperation, he got out a cigarette, but just as he was about to light it: 'Shengqiang, you're a big boy now, you look after your health! Don't spend so much time drinking and smoking, or sooner or later you'll pay for it! And don't expect me to come running to get you out of another mess. I'm eighty years old! I can't do it anymore. Just grow up!'

I've grown up, haven't I? Dad shoved the cigarette back in his pocket. So this was the song sheet she was singing from today. Ever since he left the house this morning, he had a bellyful of things he wanted to talk to Gran about, but could not. Jasmine and the baby would have to wait until it was born. When he knew if it was a boy or a girl, he could plan his next move. Gran had to be kept in the dark about Aunt Coral's divorce too. As for Mum, he really wanted to find out from Gran what magic potion she had poured into her ear, that time when he fainted in Jasmine's bed. His head ballooned with all these thoughts as he drove Gran home but her words had popped the balloon. There he was, slumped on her sofa, nodding dutifully and enduring more than half an hour of nagging. When he finally made his escape and jumped into the car, all he wanted to do was go and eat dumplings.

That dumpling place ... it was Granddad who first took Dad there. In those days, Dad was still in the house behind the factory, along with Mum, Granddad and Gran, all living in each other's laps. It took him three or four minutes to get to work, and only five to get home, even if he took a detour via

Cao Jia Alley. Sometimes the lack of privacy—he and Mum couldn't even have an argument—drove him mad, and then he used to slink off to a little spot behind the flowerbeds at the entrance to the compound where he could crouch down and smoke a cigarette. One day, Granddad went out just before dinner was served, and passed Dad having his smoke.

It was winter, Dad remembered, and he was well bundled up. Six o'clock and night was drawing in. Quickly stubbing out his cigarette, Dad called after him: 'Where are you off to, Father?' Granddad looked back and saw Dad. 'What are you doing here?' he asked. 'Why aren't you at home?' Dad was embarrassed to say he had come out for a smoke. 'Chilling out!' was all he could think of. Granddad smiled. 'Some chilling out! Come on, I'll take you for some dumplings, you want some?' Dad immediately realized he must have quarrelled with Gran. He got to his feet and emerged from behind the flowerbed. 'Let's go!' he said.

So they went to eat chilli dumplings at pretty Sweetie Xie's place. They got a tricycle cab so it took quite some time. From West Gate to East Gate, they rolled through streets shrouded in darkness, lit by small pools of light from the street lamps. Granddad puffed out white breath and got out a pack of Tianxiaxiu cigarettes. He gave one to Dad and said: 'Have a smoke.'

Dad was startled. Of course, he had been a regular smoker for five or six years, but had never dared smoke in front of his parents and this was the first time Granddad had offered him one.

Screw it, Dad took it and got out his lighter to light his father's. Then he lit his own.

There was hardly anyone at the dumplings place that evening, just a table of workers drinking, eating pig's brawn and making a racket. The fair-complexioned Sweetie Xie brought out two bowls of chilli dumplings. On top, fragrant sesame seeds were sprinkled over the fiery chilli oil. Sugar sweetened the numbing heat of the Sichuan peppers. With each bite, the luscious minced meat mixed with the spicy oil, and the scalding liquid kissed their tongues. They ate a big bowl of dumplings each, then ordered roasted peanuts and washed them down with hot wine. Granddad looked out at the pitch darkness, and heaved a sigh.

'Bring us the bill, Sweetie!' he finally called, and put the money into her delicate hand.

Dad got to his feet and they left. A ten-minute walk brought them to the second ring road where they hailed a tricycle cab and went home.

Feeling as if they had returned from a long journey, they stood in the dark courtyard, looking at their brightly-lit windows a couple of metres apart. 'I'll see you to your door,' said Dad.

'No, no, you get off home. Anqin must be worried. I can see myself home,' said Granddad.

And Dad came to a discouraging conclusion. *We men are like the roiling, rebellious waters of the Yangtse River in angry spate. We can get into earth-shaking fights with our womenfolk, we can tear the house half-down but, when push comes to shove, those surging waters have got to subside and flow meekly into the ocean.*

That day, he and Granddad took time out to go and eat chilli dumplings outside the East Gate. But then they each went back home to their woman. And so things continued for a good many years.

8

TWO DAYS LATER, Jasmine moved into her new place, and
Dad went over for a housewarming meal. The walls had
bright yellow wallpaper, and the windows were framed with
flowered curtains. It was very comfortable. Jasmine cooked all
Dad's favourite dishes and sat at the table looking pretty as a
picture. Dad drank his beer and patted her small hand. He
could not help feeling very blessed. It led him to broach the
subject of the baby's name.

'But we don't have any idea whether it's a boy or a girl,
Shengqiang,' protested Jasmine.

'It doesn't matter, let's choose one of each!' Dad waved
dismissively, emptying his glass and helping himself to some
shredded soy-sauce pork with his chopsticks.

Jasmine did not know how it was done in his family, of course,
but Dad had vivid memories of it. Granddad had chosen Dad's
generation of boys' names with the utmost care, making sure
that they each had high-sounding historical references. He did
not bother about Aunt Coral's name, because she was a girl.

Even Gran had to admit: 'He was very good at creating
subtle meanings, your father was. The names he chose for you
were most unusual. There was nothing tacky about them.'

To be quite truthful, Dad never felt that his name was
that unusual. He would repeat it in full, Xue Shengqiang,
and thought it sounded common as muck. 'Huh! You don't

understand anything!' said Granddad, a cigarette dangling from the corner of his lips, and took Dad into his study.

'Read that aloud, Shengqiang,' Granddad instructed, pointing at the wall.

They were still living in the old house at the back of the factory, and the walls were roughly plastered and whitewashed. As time went by, they had begun to flake unattractively, like a face plastered with too much makeup. It did not bother Granddad, however. He just hung his favourite things all over them. Now he was pointing Dad to a scroll next to a map of the world.

'Read it out, Shengqiang. Do you know all the characters?'

Dad was just a boy, still at lower middle school. He plucked up his courage, studied the scroll and found he could read it: 'Knowing the self is enlightenment....Mastering the self needs strength.'Granddad gave a satisfied sigh. 'Very good! "Zhiming" ...enlightenment! And your name means "self-mastery", Shengqiang!'

Dad relaxed. So his name had a classical allusion!

When it came to the next generation down, Granddad was even more painstaking. 'Don't you think this is a really good name?' he said when I was born. 'It comes from a Li Bai poem. Li Bai! A really famous poet! 'Ecstatic, our thoughts take flight, yearning for clear skies and bright moonlight.' So we'll call your daughter Yixing, Ecstacy.' And he shook his head in wonderment at this elegant solution. 'Very nice. It makes her sound very cultured,' Mum hastened to approve.

Gran was happy too. 'Definitely a cut above the ordinary. She may be a girl but our family is not giving her any of the usual girlie names. They're so tacky. This name is just right. 'Yearning for clear skies and bright moonlight.' That'll give her a great start in life.'

Sometime later though, she changed her mind, and complained to Dad: 'What kind of daft name is that to choose for his granddaughter? I mean, who was Li Bai?! Just a mad poet! Duan Yixing indeed! Fancy naming her after a poem about ecstacy! What is there to be ecstatic about in this life? Calling her "Ecstasy", that's what sent Xingxing crazy, you know! Whyever did your father give her that name? Now it's other people who are ecstatic, at the fools we've made of ourselves!'

Of course, Gran did not grumble in Granddad's hearing. When it came to Liu Xingchen, Aunt Coral's child, he did not bother with suggesting a name. After all, from the moment his daughter married, she belonged to her in-laws and they could do as they liked with her progeny. But privately he muttered to Dad: 'When you think that Coral's in-laws are provincial officials, what kind of a name for a boy is "starry"? Nothing like as good as the names I chose!'

'You're so right,' Dad said, nibbling peanuts and clinking glasses with his father.

But you never know what's around the corner. In the blink of an eye, Granddad had popped his clogs and shot off to the Underworld, and in another blink, Dad was gripping his wine glass and scratching his head and wondering what name to choose for Jasmine's baby. The family had a silly rule that every child born should take Gran and Granddad's surname alternately, first Xue, then Duan. So this baby would take the surname, Xue. If it was a girl, well that would be fine, but a boy would be even better. 'What do you think of "Xue Tenglong", how does that sound?' he suggested. '"Soaring dragon," that has a grand ring to it!'

Jasmine raised her eyebrows, and suppressed a smile. She considered for a moment, then said: 'It's not that it's a bad name, it's just that back home people say you shouldn't have "dragon" or "phoenix" in a child's name because they're supernatural beings, you can't just name a child after them. It's bad luck, it might harm the baby. It's best to give it quite an ordinary name. That way, you don't tempt fate, and the child can grow up safe and sound.'

Dad smiled. This girl might look like a delicate flower, but she had her feet on the ground. He put his arms around her shoulders and smelled the fragrance of her hair. 'Ai-ya!' he exclaimed. 'How could any child of mine suffer bad luck? I think it's a good name! Don't you fret! Have you got everything you need for this place? I've been so busy lately with the old lady's birthday, and my brother's back and my sister too. If you need anything, give Zhu Cheng a ring and he'll buy it for you. I've told him. Whatever you want, you buy it, right?'

'Right. Shengqiang, please don't worry. I can look after myself. You've got your family to look after.' Jasmine looked up and leaned her head against Dad's shoulder. She looked endearingly vulnerable and Dad felt overwhelmed with frustrated desire.

To be perfectly fair, Dad never set out to betray Mum. No one deliberately went looking for trouble in a marriage, did they? But at heart Dad was really, really fond of young Jasmine. She was a simple village girl who'd had a hard childhood, but she made him feel very much at ease. So different from Mum, raised in the County Party Committee residential compound and always looking down her nose at the world. He remembered his future father-in-law scowling at him on the day of the wedding: 'Xue Shengqiang, Anqin is our only child, and she's been the pet of the family. I'm putting her in your hands and you'd better look after her properly. She's always had an easy life and she needs to get her own way. You and she are going to be a new family so grow up and behave like a family man!'

'Such a grown-up girl,' said Dad cupping Jasmine's delicate face between his hands and scrutinizing her. Then he bent to kiss her lips and her perfume rose into his nostrils, sending him into transports of delight.

Dad had lived in Pingle Town for forty-odd years and its streets were more familiar to him that any woman he'd screwed. Summer progressed to autumn, and then winter and then spring, roads and streets were widened today, and narrowed again tomorrow; shops opened for business today and were sold off tomorrow. But nothing could stop Dad sometimes feeling nostalgic for the days of his youth, when he hung out with the gang and got into fights, played three-card poker and snooker and drank beer. He missed his old lovers too.

From South Street to West Street, from East Street to North Street, memories crowded in on him everywhere he went. The West Gate snooker table hall had long since been torn down and a large food stall serving kebab hotpots stood in its place. But every time Dad went there for a beer of an evening, he could not help thinking of young 'Wei Wei'. Fifteen Yuan Street had had a substantial facelift, and glittering nightclubs had opened. Baby Girl had long ago retired from the game, but every time Dad buried his head in the breasts of a migrant worker hooker, it was always her scent he smelt. By the East Gate night market, there was the block where Bai Yongjun's wife, Deng Juan, used to live and, if he strolled down there on a summer's night nowadays, the sweaty smell of the crowds brought back fond memories of the fun they had had together. They never bothered to talk, just rolled on the bed, ripped off each other's trousers, and got stuck in, no holds barred. Then there was Xiao Jingmei, now married to Zhu, the county hospital deputy director of paediatrics, and herself a hospital matron. He remembered being admitted once with an inflamed throat. She came to put him on a drip and, stern-faced, jabbed the needle into the back of his hand. A shiver came over him as he remembered parting her lily-white thighs one day in the nurses' hostel. And Xi Hongzhen, at the North

Gate Local Products factory, who'd taken early retirement last year, so they said, when the site was sold to a privately-run electric bike business. But whenever he passed the shop, he remembered her, playfully pushing him back onto the bed and riding him. She, with her sweet pointed chin and narrow eyes, had been his first proper girlfriend. There were so many, too many to remember.

As far as Dad was concerned, marrying Mum was a milestone in his life, getting together with Jasmine was another, turning forty was yet another. He was not sure when it happened but at some point he made up his mind to turn over a new leaf and become a reformed character. One by one, all his old squeezes went their separate ways and, apart from the odd bit of hanky-panky with a nightclub hostess, he completely gave up playing away. 'Train an army for a thousand days to use it for an hour.' When Dad finally left Jasmine's place that evening and passed the Thousand-Mile Steed Electric Bike Shop on his way home, he could not help heaving a nostalgic sigh.

Now everything had gone horribly wrong: Mum's saccharine smiles shriveled him up, and then Jasmine rejected his advances and lectured him on the dangers of having sex until she was at least four months into her pregnancy, no matter that he was just about ready to shoot his load. He had got nowhere with either of them, and there was nothing in the offing for miles around, and there he was left high and dry, wandering the streets in broad daylight, his pecker desperately craving attention, as pathetic as a wingless bluebottle or an oriole with its vocal chords shot.

But you should never give up hope. In Pingle Town's streets, it was impossible to walk more than two steps without bumping into three acquaintances. And so it was: Dad was standing there dithering when he suddenly caught sight of Liu Yufen coming towards him. Yufen worked with Mum and was an old high school friend of Uncle's, and he often heard her name, but he had not seen her lovely face for at least a couple of months. His face lit up in an admiring smile, and he called out: 'Hi, gorgeous!'

Yufen made quite an impression as she walked down North Street in a peach-pink flowery skirt. She looked round, momentarily startled, then beamed as she recognized Dad: 'Ai-ya! Shengqiang, I haven't seen you for ages!'

'Not for ages!' Dad echoed. 'Have you finished at the office?'

'No, no, I've only just had lunch. I'm out for a stroll.'

Dad looked at her and felt the years had not been kind. That was the thing with women, they suddenly looked old, fat, sallow, faded, their looks blasted away.

Of course he could not say so. 'You're getting more gorgeous by the day,' he lied cheerfully.

'Ai-ya!' Yufen laughed. 'You're the one who's still handsome as ever. Anqin certainly makes sure you're well turned-out!'

The shot went home. As soon as Mum's name came up, Dad lost all desire to sweet-talk her. 'Has Anqin not come out with you?' he enquired like a good husband.

'No,' said Yufen, shaking her head. 'She doesn't like window-shopping these days. 'She goes around glum-faced and silent all the time. Have you two quarrelled?'

Rude old cow! Dad's heart skipped a beat, but he said impassively: 'Ai-ya! We're an old married couple! If we argue every now and then, what's the big worry?'

'Shengqiang,' said Yufen, her smile still firmly fixed in place. 'We've known each other nearly thirty years, and I've shared an office with Anqin for fifteen of those. I know what marriage is about. If I see Anqin looking down, then I feel down too. You two don't understand, some things you've got to hang on to or they're gone. Look at me, all on my own, what kind of a life do you think that is?'

You still make the most of yourself, though, Dad thought. He was stumped for a response, so he just chuckled: 'Yes, right ...'

Just when he was thinking of moving on, the woman wouldn't let him. They stood there, chatting about this and that. Now that she was divorced, she really must be bored to death. At any rate, she showed no signs of running out of things to say. She finished with Mum and started on Gran's birthday party, then asked if Uncle was back and what he was doing with himself here, and so on and so forth.

'I never see hide nor hair of him,' said Dad. 'He's always rushing around!'

Yufen gave a little laugh: 'Well, that's a good thing. It shows he's in demand!'

'Ai-ya! Rubbish. He just runs around like a headless chicken, and doesn't do the stuff he's supposed to do,' said Dad, but his mind was already elsewhere.

Yufen, as if she had guessed what he was thinking about, said: 'Ai-ya! Don't you worry. Your big brother knows exactly what he's doing. Relax.'

As if you know anything! Dad scoffed inwardly. Aloud, he said with a smile: 'I must get back to work now, Yufen. I'm pretty busy with the old lady's birthday celebrations too. Let's arrange something for another day.'

They had been standing there so long they had practically worn a groove in the pavement but Dad finally got away, adjusted his trousers and flagged down a taxi to take him back to the bean paste factory.

The factory was a hive of activity. The noise and bustle soon dispelled Dad's feelings of disappointment. Three days ago, Uncle had brought Aunt Coral to have a look at the fermentation yard and, as they nosed around, someone had the idea (*Duan Zhiming, with a bee in his bonnet again!*) that the factory staff should put on a performance. They would recite to music an ode to the Mayflower Chilli Bean Paste Factory. And it did not end there: Aunt Coral offered to stay on and rehearse the performers. The pair of them swore Dad to secrecy. 'Let's make it a surprise for Mother.' The first day, Dad went along to the yard to watch the spectacle of the office staff, the workmen and the salesmen and women, even two who helped out in the canteen, all volunteering for the auditions and standing on the makeshift stage, declaiming in loud voices and mangled mandarin accents: 'The ancient city of Pingle stood here before the Qin dynasty, surrounded by mountains, watered by clear creeks, inhabited by happy people. And here is the Mayflower Factory, famous for hundreds of miles around.' Dad found the enthusiasm of his workers hard to believe, until Uncle told him that everyone who auditioned successfully, would be awarded a 200 *yuan* bonus. Dad was furious, turned on his heels and left. *Talk about the prodigal son! Throwing money around like this?* That afternoon, Zeng the office manager brought him a chit to sign for the banquet (now dubbed 'the Mayflower Chilli Bean Paste Factory Celebration'). In the blink of an eye, the cost had leapt to 8,000 *yuan*, but Dad signed anyway. It rankled to pay a bunch of frogs to croak, but if it kept the old lady happy. 'Anyone would think they weren't being paid wages!' He grumbled to Zhu Cheng.

'Ai-ya, boss! Let everyone have a bit of fun. This party will make everyone in the factory happy, and in the end it'll make them more productive.'

'Huh,' Dad lit a cigarette. 'Every man jack of them just wants to stuff their faces and live it up royally. The day it makes them more productive, I'll eat my hat!'

'Ai-ya, don't get angry, boss,' said Zhu Cheng.

Don't get angry. Just like Gran had always drilled into him: 'Meet other people's temper tantrums with a plan of your own.' As Dad got out of the taxi and walked into the factory compound, he cheered up. The flowerbeds on either side already had gaily-coloured flags printed with factory advertising planted in them. *Duan Zhiming's done good. He's not just a spendthrift,* he had to admit to himself.

He walked across the fermentation yard on his way to his office. It was almost May and getting warm. The afternoon sun glared down. Aunt Coral was still standing on the stage, shouting at the top of her voice as she drilled the ten who had landed parts, syllable by syllable. Dad went over. 'Don't roast in the sun, Sis, take them into the boardroom to rehearse!'

'We're fine, Shengqiang,' Aunt Coral called back. 'They're not professional, and I don't want to risk them getting stage fright. They need to get used to the stage, that's why we're rehearsing here.' Aunt Coral held a rolled-up notebook in her hand. She had not taken her eyes off the stage.

Dad had no idea about these things and could think of nothing to say. He said: 'Have you been drinking enough? Have you got water? Get Zeng to buy you a couple of cases.'

'We've got some,' said his sister, pointing to a pack of mineral water bottles on the stage.

'Where's Zhiming?' asked Dad, looking around. Normally at this time of day, his brother would be running around like a blue-arsed fly, just in case anyone forgot to give him credit for the event.

'He went out after lunch today, said he had something to do.' Aunt Coral finally turned to look at Dad, and he saw the beads of sweat on her brow.

Dad felt a pang of pity, and an obscure fury at his brother. *You bastard, leaving everything to Sis!*

It was only three days ago that his brother had said to him: 'Shengqiang, I don't want Sis to get too tired, but you know what's going on between her and Liu. I think this'll help take her mind off things. At least she's got family here in Pingle Town and lots of old friends to look after her.' Dad had thought he was quite right and nodded in agreement: 'If Sis wants to stay, that's fine. We've got room for her and she can stay as long as she likes.'

The slimy creep! he thought now. *He's fucked off, leaving Coral here rehearsing the workers in the blazing sunshine!* And Dad, after trying unsuccessfully to persuade them to move to the boardroom, stomped off to his office, cursing his brother.

This time, nothing could damp down the flames of Dad's fury, not even a pause for a cup of tea, and he picked up the phone to call Uncle.

It rang and rang, but no one answered. Dad fumed. He pressed the number again, and again it rang. He hung up, abstractedly pulled a felt-tip pen out of the pen mug and twiddled it irascibly between his fingers. Where on earth could Uncle have got to?

When I don't want to see you, you're forever poking around and getting in the way, but when I need you, you disappear off the face of the earth! Dad thought, making perfect circles with the black felt-tip.

It was not that Dad was really missing Uncle, just that he was pissed off at himself. Then there was that son-of-a-bitch Zhong and his match-making! Him and his stupid poking his nose in where it wasn't wanted. What had got into him? Dad carried on twiddling the felt-tip and frowning: *I only said it while I was drinking! Why on earth is he taking it so seriously!*

But Zhong could get out of that one easily enough: 'Shengqiang, don't blame me. You honestly seemed as if you meant it. How was I supposed to know you didn't? I went straight home and talked to my mother and she had a good think about it. She found a possible match for him, a woman who grew up in our paper mill, a Ms Wang. She's a really nice woman, if she wasn't, I certainly wouldn't be introducing her to your brother. She's thirty-three years old, good-looking, never been married, has a nice temperament, runs her own beauty salon. She's got her own apartment. and a car, and she'd be a great match for Zhiming. You've got to get things moving, otherwise it'll be awkward for my mother, and then she'll give me a beating!'

Dad was stymied. He knew perfectly well that, as far as his mother went, Zhong was just pretending to be a scaredy-cat. He said: 'You're over fifty, Zhong. You're not telling me your mother still beats you?'

'Ai-ya, Shengqiang! Don't mess with me! You just talk to Zhiming and we'll all go out for dinner and they can get to know each other. It's nothing more than that! The woman's agreed, and if he doesn't, it'll be really embarrassing,' Zhong implored him.

Well, as I said, Dad was a kind-hearted man, and the combined effects of Zhong's nagging and seeing his brother roaming around all on his own and behaving more and more eccentrically made him realize he had to do something. So the next day, first thing in the morning, Dad went off to Jasmine's for a quick meal and from there went straight to the factory in search of Uncle.

Dad gave his brother another ring. As Zhong said, good things should not be put off. Since the weekend was coming up, he should get an answer out of his brother before dinner today. He listened to the phone ringing in his ear, just like a pair of feminine hands tugging at his heart strings, and then Uncle picked up.

Uncle gave a cough, which sounded completely fake to Dad, then said gently: 'Shengqiang, have you been calling me? I'm so sorry, I didn't hear it!'

'Ai-ya!' Dad burst out, then sighed: 'Where are you? I've been ringing you for ages!'

'I, umm, I'm at North Gate,' said Uncle.

'North Gate? I've just come from there, but I never saw you. What are you doing there?'

'Oh, something, just something,' Uncle said vaguely. 'What was it you wanted?'

'Ah, well, it's like this, Zhong's invited us to dinner tonight,' Dad said casually. He really didn't know how to broach the subject, even though this was his own brother. He was an enigma. He decided to get him on board before telling him anything more.

'Another meal? I was planning to eat something quick and go back to the hotel and do stuff on the computer, do some work,' Uncle said.

(It occurred to Dad that Uncle had been here almost two weeks, instead of teaching classes. *Education's not up to much, if the teachers can just do a flit when they like!* was his silent conclusion.)

This university-educated brother of his couldn't hold a candle to Dad, who'd knocked around and knew what was what, and couldn't be overruled that easily: 'Ai-ya! Zhiming, you're back after all this time, and Zhong's booked the room at the restaurant! OK, come and eat, and when you've had your meal, you go off and do your work, and we won't go on anywhere else!'

'Just a meal then? No drinking, OK? I really need to work afterwards,' Uncle emphasized.

'Absolutely, just a meal, half past six at the Leaping Fish. And don't be late!' Dad said earnestly. Inwardly, he jeered: *Just a meal? No drinking? That's a new one on me! A lifetime's education in Pingle Town never taught me that!*

Now that he'd successfully primed the intended victim, he got straight back to Zhong: 'I've done it! Half past six at the Leaping Fish, we'll be there!'

'I haven't said a word about a blind date, because if I did he definitely wouldn't come. OK?' he added.

Zhong just said: 'OK! No problem!' After all these years, they knew each other inside out. Well, that was that done. Dad had fixed it for Zhong and got his brother to agree to come out to dinner. Relieved, he put the pen back in its pot and had another sip of tea.

The two West Street youths that everyone knew in the old days were Stutterer Qin and Withered Hand Duan. There was a story about Stutterer Qin: he once turned up at the food market's knife-shaved noodles stall at crack of dawn. 'You want a bowl of noodles?' asked bar owner. 'Yes ... yes ... yes ...' stuttered Qin. The man threw a handful of noodles into the wok with a great sizzling. And Qin finally finished his sentence: 'Yes, but not right now.' The story they told about Withered Hand Duan (Zhiming) was that he went to the cinema one day and saw a very pretty girl sitting next to him. He moved close and let his very small hand rove all over her. The girl got annoyed and grabbed the hand and started to say: 'Why's no one looking after you, little boy ... Ai-ya! But you're a grown man!'

Those two stories may have been urban myths but anyone who had grown up on West Street had heard them a thousand times and, every time they were bored, they brought the stories out one more time. And when it got to the punch line, they would chorus: 'Not till this afternoon!' or 'You're a grown man!' They were a harmless bunch, the Pingle Town folk, with their corny jokes, wheeled out year after year.

Dad used to get angry. No one dared tell the Withered Hand Duan story to his face. That was asking for a thumping. Then Uncle went to university, and did not come back for a couple of months, then half a year, then two years went by without anyone seeing him. And Dad stopped caring. If anyone happened to wheel out the old joke yet again, he would laugh along as well. Just for friendship's sake.

Dad felt there was no harm in the old joke, as he arrived at the Leaping Fish, and sat down in side-room number five next to Zhong, and opposite the willow-eyebrowed Ms Wang Yandan. Uncle had not arrived yet and Yandan was chatting

about this and that, and then she asked: 'Shengqiang, I hope
you won't think me nosy, but is it true that your brother has a
problem with his hand?

This was the crunch, Dad could not avoid the question,
and, anyway, he reckoned that if she was to be his brother's
girlfriend, she ought to know. So he not only admitted it, he
turned it into a joke by telling her the old story about that
roving little hand. 'Even though my brother has one hand
that's on the small side, there's nothing he can't do with it,' he
finished.

Wang Yandan cracked up laughing and seemed reassured.
She sipped her Sichuan 'red-and-white' tea and said:
'Shengqiang, you're too funny. Was Professor Duan really
such a magnet for the girls when he was young?

'Ai-ya! He certainly was. My brother was a handsome young
man. Aren't all boys a magnet for the girls?' Dad looked at
Yandan's complexion, which had a sheen like lustrous satin. *I
suppose if you have your own beauty salon, you can really look
after your face,* he thought.

Yandan gave a tinkling laugh but refused to lob the ball
back. 'Now you're joking, Shengqiang, it may have been like
that in Pingle Town but those of us who grew up in the paper
mill compound led very sheltered lives. We'd run a mile from
boys like that!'

'Of course you would, Yandan,' said Zhong, with a brotherly
air. 'I remember you used to have a little, thread-like voice and
anything could make you cry! But you're fine now, you're a big
girl, you can handle it!'

'You flatterer!' Yandan reproved him gently. 'I'm in my
thirties and an old maid. And why are you calling me 'big'?' At
the mention of 'big', Dad unconsciously found his eyes drawn
to her breasts. He rapidly assessed them. *She's big,* he decided.

Uncle had still not arrived but the conversation in the room
showed no signs of flagging. Dad took his own pulse on the

matter, and felt that it might well work with his brother and this woman. As Zhong had said, she was good-looking, open and pleasant in manner, and quite intelligent, and already well-disposed to Uncle. *I can't believe Duan Zhiming will turn her down,* he concluded.

At that moment, his mobile phone rang. It was Uncle. He'd just parked up and was walking into the restaurant. 'Which room?' he asked Dad.

'I'll come and meet you!' Dad said hastily and got his feet. He shot Zhong a look and went out.

Afterwards, Dad summed up what followed: 'I've met some boorish men in my life, but I can honestly say I've never seen one quite as boorish as Zhiming! Never!' And just to underscore his point, he added: 'So fucking boorish!'

Be that as it may, Uncle cut an elegant figure as he strode in, dressed in a pinstriped blue-grey shirt and beige trousers. It would be hard to find anyone to beat his looks and style. When he saw Dad, he waved his right hand and trotted over.

'I'm sorry, Shengqiang, I'm so sorry to be late,' he said apologetically.

Uncle was heading for their side-room when Dad stopped him. 'Hang on a minute, Zhiming, there's something I need to tell you.'

Uncle stood stock-still and looked at Dad, a worried expression on his face. 'What's up with you now, Shengqiang?' he asked.

Don't you sodding blame it on me! It's damn all to do with me! Dad thought sourly.

All the same, he had to give his brother some sort of an explanation: it was Zhong, or rather his mother, she was so warm-hearted, and Wang Yandan was a remarkable woman, and he (Dad) just hadn't been able to get out of it.... 'Anyway, you just go in and have a meal. We can all get to know each other, and make friends!' he finished.

Dad thought he was being utterly reasonable and persuasive. He had brought the horse to water, how could it possibly not want to drink? To his astonishment, Uncle's face darkened with anger: 'Shengqiang, that's very wrong of you! You should never have done something as important as this without discussing it with me! It's not appropriate, not at all appropriate! I don't think I should stay!'

And he really did turn to leave, until Dad stopped him. The pair of them stood deadlocked, in the doorway of the Leaping Fish, blocking some ugly-looking brutes of customers from getting in or out. 'Zhiming, stay!' said Dad desperately. 'Don't show me up! Come in, please! We can't stand here manhandling each other!'

'Stop pulling me!' said Uncle obdurately. 'I really want to leave. This is not on!'

Dad was almost weeping from chagrin. He felt like shouting: *You weren't so backwards at coming forwards back then with Baby Girl. Aren't you a man anymore?!*

With difficulty, he held his tongue and just at that very moment, Zhong burst from the side-room like a genie from the bottle. 'Ah, you're here, Zhiming, come in, come in, what are you doing standing in the doorway?'

Flanked on either side by Dad and Zhong, Uncle had no escape. Besides, he did not want to make a scene in front of an outsider. So he went inside.

It's going to be OK now, Dad thought. After all, even Duan Zhiming had to be be won over by the delicately pretty Ms Wang. At least, they could have a friendly dinner, even if it did not last longer than that. It was all going to be OK. It would work out.

But it damned well didn't work out, he reflected viciously later.

Uncle took a chair, and the Wang woman's eyes lit up. Duan Zhiming really was very handsome and refined. She greeted him sweetly as 'Professor Duan' and went to pour him a cup of red-and-white tea with her lily-white hands.

But Uncle said brusquely: 'I'll serve myself!', grabbed the teapot off her, filled his cup and tipped it down his throat. He looked as if he was a condemned prisoner eating his last meal.

It must have dawned on Yandan that Uncle felt he was here under duress. Luckily, she was a well-bred young woman, and just smiled and sat down. Turning to Zhong, she said: 'Shall we order some food?'

Surely filling their bellies would lighten the atmosphere. There was a steaming, simmering hotpot of ribs, white fish head, chilli peppers and green Sichuan pepper, to which they gradually added pieces of swamp eel, brains and meatballs, potato and shitake mushrooms, and slices of bamboo shoot. Things got a bit more lively, and everyone found something to chat about.

Dad had to take his hat off to Zhong, who leapt from one topic to another with such acrobatic skill that their table threatened to levitate and spin in the air. He started by talking about Uncle, what a loyal band of bros he'd gathered around him back then. Even he, Zhong, had been drawn into the band, although he was a good bit older. Of course, everyone knew Zhiming had topped the league tables at his university entrance exams, there was no need to go over that again. And now he was a professor in mathematics at Yong'An City University. Yes, mathematics! He certainly had a high IQ, that man! He was often on TV as well, wasn't that right? His career had really taken off! It couldn't have been easy for him, but he had thrown himself into his work! And then there was Wang Yandan. She had been the true star of the paper mill school, one of the highest-scoring pupils in her class. She had all the young men in the school at her feet, but she was having nothing to do with them. She was a dutiful daughter, and when she was twenty and her father got cirrhosis of the liver and spent all his money on treatment, she went out to work instead of finishing vocational college. She worked so hard and now look at her, only in her thirties, with her own large beauty salon, two apartments, and a car of her own, and still pretty, and of unblemished character. A magnificent achievement

Zhong spoke in such glowing terms that Yandan kept exclaiming charmingly: 'Oh please, Zhong, don't exaggerate! Professor Duan will think I'm ridiculous! There's nothing to say about me!' And Dad gulped down a whole bottle of beer and began to wonder if Zhong was planning to divorce his own wife and marry Yandan. Uncle, however, listened carefully, then smiled and put in: 'Quite an achievement indeed, Yandan. All those years of hard work!'

They all imagined that this comment was finally a sign that Uncle was getting interested. 'Not a bit of it,' said Yandan. 'Don't listen to Zhong. I just got on with running my business.'

'So your beauty salon, it must be quite a big business by now,' Uncle probed pleasantly, as if trying to draw one of his students into conversation.

Leave it out, Duan Zhiming! She's a lovely girl, why are you interrogating her? You planning to marry and move in with her? What kind of seduction of technique is this? Dad wondered, suddenly anxious.

But he said nothing and Uncle carried on relentlessly: 'So your salon is on two floors, right? With thirty or so employees? You must be turning over more than a million. Then there's your two apartments, I think Zhong said. What's the location? Hmm, not a bad area. At today's town prices, they must be worth a million and a half, I'd say. Plus your car, what make is it? That's a good one, wouldn't go for less than half a million. Have you got any stock market investments? You've never played the stock market? You're quite right, of course.'

Unsurprisingly, Yandan was bewildered. She looked appealingly at Zhong for help as she answered Uncle's questions. Zhong was in a predicament. He had praised Yandan to the skies, and he could not take it back now. He wondered what devious tricks Uncle was up to. Surely this was not the way that university academics got off with women? No wonder Uncle had been single for so long.

Dad, on the other hand, swore silently and just wanted to bury his face in his bowl of hotpot.

'So, Yandan,' Uncle wound up, straightened up, ladled some pearly white fish soup into a bowl, sprinkled on some chopped spring onion, dipped his spoon in and gave it few stirs, then said reasonably: 'I'm sorry to be so inquisitive at our first meeting, but we're not children any longer, and we have come here in all sincerity to get to know each and make friends, so let's not beat about the bush. Honesty is the best policy.'

'You're quite right, Professor,' said Yandan, 'We really should get to each other better. Ask whatever you want.'

'I do have one more question,' said Uncle, raising a spoonful of soup to his mouth, blowing on it then drinking it. 'It might be a rude question, but I'm an intellectual, so perhaps I'm nitpicking, but now I've thought of it, I'd like to know the answer, I hope you won't take offense.'

'Ai-ya, Zhiming! You've just said it's a rude question, so don't ask it!' Dad finally managed to get out.

'It doesn't matter, honestly,' said Yandan. 'Ask away, Professor. Feel free.'

So then Uncle put the bowl down, put his spoon down too, and placed both hands neatly on the table in front of him. 'This is what I want to ask you, Yandan, you were born and raised in the paper mill, never finished vocational college, and started work in a hairdresser. You don't play the stock markets in any shape or form, and you haven't won any big awards. So

I wonder how, as a woman in your thirties, you've managed to do so well. You've clearly got ability but I can't make the sums add up. I'm curious about where your money came from? I find it hard to believe that your salon has earned you so much.'

Dad swears that he went scarlet to the ears when he heard these words.

There was total silence in the room, broken only by the cheerful bubbling of the fish head in its pot.

Yandan's eyes reddened but, with an effort, she finally managed to hold back the tears. She put her chopsticks down, and took a deep breath. Dad looked at her, and wished heartily that he could disown his eccentric brother. *Son-of-a-bitch, Duan Zhiming! You've got a nerve!*

'I can tell, Professor Duan, that your motives when you came to this meal were far from sincere. I had no idea you were like this, in fact I didn't give it much thought. I just thought we could be friends. Obviously you feel differently, so I will go,' Wang Yandan said, in a voice that quavered slightly. And without further ado, she got to her feet, picked up her bag, and left.

'Yandan! Yandan!' Zhong shouted, then went after her. Then, honest soul that he was, he could not help looking back and delivering a parting shot: 'Zhiming, you may be a top professor and think she's not worthy of you, but there was no need to be so rude!'

With Wang Yandan and Zhong gone, Dad was left in the side-room with Uncle. He said he had his fists clenched rock-hard on his equally hard knees.

Thinking back on that evening, Dad realized this had only happened to him a couple of times in his life. Once when Gran left him in the fermentation yard to stir the chilli bean paste for the first time. Another time when he discovered that Mum had cuckolded him, and again at the meal in Cornucopia

Court, the day they buried Granddad. And today.

Every time it happened, Dad asked himself: *What am I supposed to do? What the fuck am I supposed to do?* Well, he could simply clench his fists, send the table rocking backwards and fling out of the room, leaving someone else to deal with the mess. Or sit it out, and take things as they came, listen and watch, watch the weird antics that these weirdos got up to. In other words, grin and bear it, though of course Dad would refuse to put it like that.

Dad swears that at that moment, he really was halfway to his feet, one fist raised in the air, about to smash Uncle's face into the table, to hell with all the crockery, and shout: *Are you sick in the head, Duan Zhiming? If you really want to undermine me, why go about it this way?'*

He looked at Uncle. He was impeccably dressed and his steel watch glinted on his left wrist, but when he lowered his head, there were flabby wrinkles beginning to form on the back his neck. And with a great effort, he swallowed the words back, took a gulp of cold beer and said: 'Zhiming, it's not just me telling you this, you really went too far today. She's just a young woman, why did you have to drag her through the mud like that?'

Uncle said nothing. He picked up his own beer and drank a mouthful. And sighed.

Dad heard the sadness in that sigh and his heart flipped. 'Zhiming,' he burst out, 'You've been in the academic world all these years, and we know you've set your sights high, and you're determined to do things your own way, but you have to understand that Mother, Sis and I can't help worrying about you. You really ought to settle down, get yourself a wife and start a family.'

Uncle opened his mouth, then shut it again, then opened it, shut it, and finally opened it again: 'Shengqiang, it's not that simple. You're the baby of the family, and you're intelligent and capable, you've stuck by Mother all your life, she adores you, she's always there for you, she's always looked after you through thick and thin. It's different for me. I was only a teenager when they kicked me out, I had to look after myself. You have no idea what a terrible mess I'm in, you really haven't. Don't you think I'd like nothing more than a wife and a family?'

Dad's immediate reaction was, *You do come out with some bizarre things!* He wanted to laugh, but it stuck in his throat, he wanted to get angry, but it all seemed too absurd. Finally, he poured himself another beer and downed half a glass. 'You're being ridiculous, Zhiming!' he protested. 'You reckon I've never had it hard? You went off to university leaving your kid brother behind, stirring the bean paste in the fermentation yard day after day, washing out the vats, getting beatings, is that what you call Mother looking after me?'

It was Mum, as an outsider, who understood the relationship between Dad and Uncle best. 'You see,' she told me, 'they complement each other. Your Dad jumps into everything feet first, without giving it a second thought, and your Uncle, he thinks so much, his head's a labyrinth an ant couldn't find its way out of. They make such a ridiculous drama out of things. All these years, and they've never stopped squabbling!'

Dad had to admit that Mum was quite right. 'I've spent all these years being angry with Zhiming—whatever for?' he said.

It all started in 1983. Before that, they'd been good friends, both cool dudes, hanging out together, even taking it in turns with Baby Girl. Then, in the blink of an eye, his elder brother was off to Yong'An City University to study, bedding roll on his back, thermos in his hand. And he, the kid brother, was left to moulder away, shifting chilli bean paste around the warehouse, getting hit over the head by old Chen for the slightest mistake. *What the hell,* he thought, *maybe I brought it on myself, I wasn't as good as Zhiming so I didn't get into university. I was only good for factory work and getting beaten.*

Dad knuckled down and saw out his apprenticeship hoisting chilli bean paste around, and twenty years or more had trickled by. But today was the first time he had heard this fantastic version of events from Uncle's own mouth.

Uncle drank half a glass of beer too. 'Shengqiang,' he went on, 'You're really telling me that Mother hasn't looked after you? You're the one she looks after the most! Just think ... at home, in the factory, you've got it all! What have I got, or Sis? Nothing! How can you say Mother doesn't look after you?'

Dad was flabbergasted. He could not get a word out. He, Xue Shengqiang, had spent his life keeping watch over the piddling little Mayflower Chilli Bean Paste Factory in piddling little Pingle Town, having the odd drink and screwing the odd girl now and then. Just how had he got the better deal? And how had Zhiming lost out?

He watched Uncle glugging back the rest of the beer, and finally thought of his objection: 'The factory belongs to the family, it's not mine. If you and Sis want to run it, you come home and run it!'

'You reckon?' Uncle picked up another beer to pour himself more, but it was empty. He took the bottle in front of Dad and filled his glass, then went on: 'When Qin got pregnant back then, I got on my knees to Mother and begged her to let me off university, I'd work in the factory and earn money. I wanted to marry Qin, and have our baby. You know what Mother said?'

Dad had never heard this before. He stared at Uncle, and saw his eyes redden. He also saw the fine web of wrinkles around them.

One thing was certain, Gran would have spoken softly, she always said shouting did not make you right. It was never easy, bringing up her children, one stubborn, another hopelessly romantic, the third too quick with his fists, and she had to be fair to each of them. She had said to Uncle that day: 'Zhiming, you're not even twenty yet, right? You want to get married and raise a family? Work in the factory? I'm going to be honest with you: in your situation, you can't go thinking about things like that.' She pointed to Uncle's left hand. 'You should understand things by now. Ever since you were a little boy, we've been the laughing stock of the town. You still want to work in the factory? It'll be Shengqiang who takes that job on. Your future lies in studying. You've got to leave and go to the city, it's the only way for you not to have people laughing at you, for our whole family to earn people's respect.' Gran had paused and looked at Uncle: 'You and Qin are too young,' she said with a sigh. 'You don't know what a hole you're digging yourself into. I've been there, I've made the same mistake, all young people do. Well, what's done is done and I'm not going to tell you off any more, it doesn't take a sledgehammer to crack a nut, but I don't want to hear another word about this. Let this be a lesson to you. I'll sort it out for you, just this once, but don't let it happen again. You keep your mind on your books and get good grades. If you don't get into university this year, then you can try again next year. If you don't get in next year, then you try the year after. That's the only way for you, do you understand me? There's no other way.'

Dad was certain about one thing at least: his brother was a good student. This all happened years ago, but Uncle wouldn't have forgotten a single word Gran said. To be honest, Dad couldn't remember exactly how it happened but he seemed to have got the blame for Qin's pregnancy himself, he remembered getting beatings from Gran, Granddad and Qin's father, he remembered cursing and swearing and spitting with rage… but what the hell. What happened to Uncle, and what he did, had completely faded from his memory. He had the impression that Uncle had shut himself away in his room, reading, doing practice exam papers, revising for his university entrance exams.

It was never the same for Zhiming, he thought sadly. He got into fights and played the field with girls, but he still revised for his exams, and came out tops.

Dad sat on his chair listening to Uncle talking. Damn it to hell, he was in such an acute state of anxiety, he was gasping for a smoke. The burner under the fish-head hotpot had long since gone out, and the oil on the stew had floated to the top, sealing the half-eaten fish head and the chilli peppers underneath. Dad was desperate. He got out a cigarette, lit up and took a deep drag. Then he puffed out the smoke and it hung pale in the air of the room. Through the haze, he could see Uncle and his reddened eyes. His mouth was opening and shutting and he was saying things, about himself, about Gran, about his hand, about his old flame Qin, saying they were still close, saying how lonely and hard-up he had been all these years.

'I really envy you,' Uncle was saying, 'I always have done. You were the closest to Father, and Mother always protected you. This is a substantial family business, and it all belongs to you. The factory is yours and, as for the inheritance, you're sure to get the lion's share. I'm not talking about money, it's more a matter of feelings, isn't it? Just look at me, I always felt got at. Every time Mother had a go at Father, she said my withered hand was his fault.' He waved his hand in the air. 'All that was really directed at me. She was doing it so I could hear. She wanted me to understand that I was deformed. I could never be like you, Shengqiang, I could never do what I wanted. I always had to be the sensible, obedient one, get good marks at schools, and make them happy, otherwise I had nothing. Look at you, you got bad marks in school but Mother said nothing, you get into trouble now and Mother fixes it for you. You have a fancy life-style and you can spend all you like, right? You get a mistress and Mother persuades Anqin not to make a fuss, while I've been an impoverished teacher all my working life and have only myself to rely on. And I still can't sort out my love life. Don't you think I want to? Qin, to me, was…' His eyes were bright red and he sniffed. 'I've felt guilty for what happened to her ever since then. I wouldn't have the face to go and marry anyone else. Can't you see that Mother was to blame? If it wasn't for her…. And what attitude does she take now? She acts angry with me for not marrying, as if it was the worst crime in the world! Shengqiang, I know I went a bit too far with Yandan this evening, and I know you and Zhong had good intentions,' Uncle lifted his right hand to rub his eyes, then picked up his glass and had another swig. 'But I'm not letting anyone arrange a marriage for me. Qin and I …' He could not go on, just put the glass down and wiped his eyes.

Dad did not know if he was alarmed or shocked. Uncle's words reached his ears like prayers intoned on the mountain of the Immortals. He missed a lot of the detail but was determined to grasp the one key point. So this was what it was about. All his brother's grievances and oddities down the years were down to this one thing!

All of a sudden, anxieties gnawed away at him like thousands of ants. Uncle's eyes had gone as flaming red as chilli oil. He picked up a paper serviette from the table and handed it to him.

Dad was overwhelmed with bitter regrets, though not about Zhong and Yandan. That was just tough tittie. He did not care two hoots about them. *What a plonker I've been,* he cursed himself.

Of all the things he regretted, buying the two bags of Sichuan peppers for Uncle, and handing them over, like a ticking time bomb, in the foyer of the Golden Leaves Hotel, came top of the list.

He wanted to say: *Zhiming, I'm so sorry, I should never have bought you the Sichuan peppers. What happened with Qin is all in the past. She's fine now, you've no need to feel guilty.* And he wanted to say: *How could you have kept the lid on all of this, all these years, and never talked to anyone? You're angry with Mother—well, talk to me about it. Tell me what you want. I'm in charge now, I'll support you. Don't be angry any more, it's over and done with. You should be living a good life now. After all, you're a top professor, you've really made it!* He also wanted to say: *I was a fool, I should never have involved you in today's meal, it was my mistake.* And: *Don't be angry with Mother. She may have said those things, but she was really protecting you. She's so proud of you now. She never stops telling me. Every time she talks about you, she's all smiles.*

But Dad said nothing at all, just sat there wreathed in smoke and listened to Uncle talk. Dad smoked one cigarette after another until he nearly set the room's smoke alarms off. Finally, Uncle ran out of steam and stopped.

'Have something to drink, Zhiming,' said Dad and got another bottle of beer out of the pack at his feet. He opened it and filled Uncle's glass to the brim, then filled his own.

Uncle had talked himself dry, and drank thirstily. Dad emptied his own glass, and then re-filled both.

9

Dad had come a long way since he was a kid. At the start, when his cucumber was beginning to grow a stem, whenever he met the South Street youths who were always honing their fighting skills, it would shake him up a bit and he would think how cool they were. But in just a few years, he'd got that out of his system and bumped into the North Street businessmen from out of town, at the noodle shop. They were smartly dressed, and could afford two dollops of meat sauce on their noodles. *They've got money!* He said to himself. Then when he started work, and had money for meat sauce, and for smokes, and even for girls, he started to admire the sons and daughters of the East Street officials: he watched the black Red Flag limousines as they drove in and out of the county government buildings, the county hospital, the retirement home for cadres and the County Party Committee residential compounds. 'They've all got telephones, you know!' Zhong told him. Soon afterwards, he and Mum became an item and he was going in and out himself, to the home of his future father-in-law, Chen Xiuxiao. So that was how the official class lived.

Dad came to know all the nooks and crannies of Pingle Town, and all the local tittle-tattle, like the back of his hand. And this was the situation in 1995, the year in which Dad turned thirty: he was assistant to the director of the chilli bean paste factory, in actual fact, second-in-command. The acting director, Zhu Shengquan would be retiring in a few years. By that time, Dad had acquired enough connections to get things done, directly or the back door. He had friends— captains of industry to a man—in high places, and when they spoke, they were listened to. Around town, Dad cut an impressive figure: he was tall, good-looking, with no trace of a pot-belly yet, and known as a generous friend. All the girls were after him. At home, his daughter was at primary school, that was one milestone achieved, and he had a slender, fair-skinned wife who impressed both with her easy conversation and her culinary skills. The solid backing of her official father was a bonus. Every one of his friends envied him. That Xue Shengqiang certainly knows how to pick a woman, they said.

Then there was one springtime in Pingle Town, when the city was covered in a mass of flaming red azalea blossom, and love was in the air and Dad, walking down the street, felt a breeze brushing his face and lust stirring in his loins.

The fact that something was up came out bit by bit. First, Zhong asked him over drinks: 'Are things still good with Anqin?' 'Fine!' said Dad, then added: 'It's like this, if she has time on her hands, she takes herself to the beauty salon, for a hair-do and a facial, she likes that.' Then there were a few times when he was eating with his bros in a restaurant, and someone would say something like: 'You better watch out, Shengqiang!' 'Watch out for what?' Dad asked. There was no answer and Dad forgot all about it. But after a bit, even he began to feel something was not quite right, though he could not put a finger on it. It was just a vague feeling he had, that when Mum talked to him, or they ate together, even when they were having sex, there was something a bit odd going on. *Son-of-a-bitch, maybe she's discovered I've been screwing some girl! But I was only messing around!* Dad scratched his head and wondered. He decided to wait and keep an eye on things. Best not to show his hand too soon, and put his foot in it. A couple of weeks passed and Gran called him over to her place: 'Shengqiang, have you and Anqin been having problems lately?'

Dad's heart dropped into his boots. *Anqin! That woman's a menace! She never said a word to me and she's gone straight to Mother and denounced me!*

Dad was going to deny everything to his last breath, but to his surprise, Gran, a woman of the world after all, came out with something quite different. Sitting bolt upright in her armchair opposite Dad, she said quietly: 'People are saying that Chen Anqing is having an affair.' She was watching him carefully as she spoke.

'Mother! What rubbish! Anqin would never have the balls to do that!'

'Well, that's what I've heard,' said Gran. 'And the person who said it has told me exactly who it is too. Otherwise I wouldn't have dared say anything to you. If you don't believe me, you go home and ask her.'

This is rock-solid proof that the unpleasantness between Mum and Gran started then. 'Your Gran is a spiteful woman,' Mum told me. 'She's always got something nasty up her sleeve. That business was between me and your father. Why did she have to go sticking her nose in? But she was determined I wasn't going to be let off the hook this time!'

But there was something Mum had forgotten. Amongst the people who put in a good word for her—Zhong was one, Aunt Coral was another—there was Gran. Dad's eyes were bloodshot and he had yelled himself hoarse, but in the end it was they who pulled him back from the brink. Gran, secretly distressed at the state her son was in, began patiently to work on him: 'Shengqiang, you're going to learn from this sad mess. You see, I was right all along, when I said you'll never understand what people feel in their heart of hearts. So you should be careful not to put noses out of joint by acting cocky and smug. Pride comes before a fall and when people see you're about to take a fall, they give a silent cheer. So just you keep a low profile in all things, that's the proper way for a man to behave.'

So Dad learnt his lesson. After that, if someone started saying: 'Xue Shengqiang, your factory's doing so well!' he would exclaim: 'Ai-ya! I'm a factory worker, just a high-up one. I spend my time escorting the clients here there and everywhere, I'm exhausted, there's no money in it!' When people said: 'How grown-up your daughter's getting, Shengqiang!' he would answer: 'Ai-ya! She's still a silly kid at heart, just grown a bit taller! Her school results are terrible!' When the neighbours saw Mum coming home laden with shopping bags, and called to him: 'You get good dinners, Mr Xue!' he would respond: 'Dinner? Oh, we just eat bits of this and that, left-overs, you know!' When he was out drinking with his bros and they got rowdy and said things like: 'Such a virtuous wife you've got, and such a pretty mistress! You certainly know how to pick them! You've got the best of both worlds!' Dad would heave a sigh and say: 'Oh, I just got dragged into it. What could I do? I'm tired of it all!'

No one was taken in, but it was only Zhong who confronted him: 'Listen, bro, when did you learn to act so hypocritical? Cut it out, at least with me!'

Of course, Zhong was his very closest, long-time friend, Dad wasn't in any doubt about that. Zhong hadn't even been particularly angry with him about the dinner fiasco. The very next morning Dad got on the phone to him. Zhong picked up and said a cheerful 'Good morning!' then started turning the air blue with 'son-of-a-bitch' and 'arsehole' and much more besides. Well, what could Dad do but offer a string of grovelling apologies? But Zhong said: 'Why are you saying sorry to me? It's your brother who should apologize. It was he who behaved so badly and put Ms Wang in such a fury. Then when I got home last night, I got it in the neck from my mother. What was

I supposed to say?'

'Ai-ya! Zhong!' Somehow Dad was relieved that Zhong wasn't blaming him. He tried to appease his friend: 'You know what my brother's like, he's done so much studying, it's addled his brain! Don't let it get to you! He's not a bad man, he's just an old stick-in-the-mud!'

'Old stick-in-the-mud?' Zhong sounded even more disgruntled. 'He was a slick operator when he took that kickback off Gao Tao. Let me tell you, Shengqiang, you don't need to put in a good word for him, or apologize on his behalf. This business has nothing to do with you, stop worrying about it. It's him I'm angry with, and as for me and you, forget it, it's nothing to do with us!'

It would be fair to say that Zhong's words made Dad choke on ash. He was appalled at this piece of information: *That Duan Zhiming!*

But he couldn't put the boot in, because Zhong was an outsider. So he made excuses: 'Ai-ya! He's so busy and works so hard. Taking a kickback, helping someone make money, and making a bit for himself, none of that's easy. I know he behaved badly but he's my big brother, what can I do about it? And you said it: my brother is your brother too, we're all one family. Don't be angry with him. I'll drop by your mother's and give her a nice present by way of an apology. Satisfaction guaranteed!'

Zhong laughed despite himself. Dad heard a 'tsk', at the other end of the line: 'Shengqiang! You really can talk the hind legs off a donkey! Well, we'll see. We'll see!'

'Hey, I'll come any time. You let me know when, and I'll be right there!' Dad was determined to settle things.

Well, that was that. Dad cut the call, went to clean his teeth, and joined Mum for breakfast. 'Shengqiang, do you remember how drunk you got last night? Your brother had to bring you home, aren't you ashamed of yourself?' she said to him.

But Dad was not upset. He picked up a fried dough stick, took a bite and said: 'Ai-ya! Can't I get drunk once in a while?'

'Once in a while?' snorted Mum.

They carried on with their breakfast, talking about the usual stuff that couples do at breakfast time: tonight's dinner, tomorrow's lunch, we must make time to have another meal with Duan Zhiming and Coral. Dad watched as Mum took his empty bowl from him and went to the kitchen to refill it with rice porridge. He could not help feeling sorry for her. *She's a wonderful woman,* he thought. *She hasn't once mentioned the business with Jasmine. She's great, I'm damned lucky to have a wife like this!*

When Mum came out of the kitchen and put down in front of him a bowl full of velvety smooth, white rice porridge, he found himself saying: 'When Mother's birthday is over, let's go on holiday somewhere. Where would you like to go? Hong Kong and Macao? Or Singapore and Malaysia? We'll buy you something nice.'

Mum chortled: 'Shengqiang, have you hit the jackpot? How come you're so happy today? First, you smile at your porridge, and now you're talking about taking me on a foreign holiday!'

Dad gulped down half his bowlful. "Huh!' What's wrong with me being happy?' Then, as the silky smooth porridge warmed and filled his hungry belly, it occurred to him that other people were not so fortunate. 'When we're at dinner the day after tomorrow, don't mention Sis's divorce to her.'

'Ai-ya! How many times have you said that? Of course I won't mention it, you've made it quite clear to me!'

'And don't mention it to Mother either!' Dad repeated.

So that was how the morning started. Dad ran through in his mind what he needed to do, effortlessly ticking them off and putting them neatly in order. He could count on the fingers of one hand the number of days till Gran's birthday banquet. He threw down his bowl and chopsticks and picked up the phone. He decided to go to the factory and make his presence felt, with a bit of praise here, and a bit of criticism there.

Mum still loved him. Later she said to me, with a heavy sigh: 'Your Dad, he's an honest man, he really is. Don't make him out to be some sort of monster. He's a good man at heart. Once he accepts someone as a friend, he sticks with them through thick and thin, and then he gets taken for a ride!'

Well, husband and wife often have a different view of things, and Dad wasn't worried about being taken for a ride. As he took a taxi to the factory, he thought again about the kickback Uncle had taken. In the past, he would have had a real go at him, but after last night's heart-to-heart, he felt differently. *Hey! My brother's doing OK! He's learnt to take kickbacks. He's learnt to do business!* He slapped his knee. *Right! Gao Tao thought he was dealing with someone with more money than sense! He took my brother for a fool, and thought he could make money out of him! Huh!*

Dad had always said that money was made to be spent. Spending the chilli bean paste factory's money to get what you wanted out of life, that was a recipe for happiness.

Mother mustn't get to know, was Dad's final thought, as he paid the driver and got out of the taxi.

People usually assumed that, as far as the factory was concerned, Dad had had it handed it to him on a plate. But they got it quite wrong. When it came down to it, Dad had had to crawl his way up the beanstalk to get to the top. And the fact that he had acquired all those useful contacts in Pingle Town was largely down to his generous, equable nature.

And that was all down to Gran's upbringing.

He, Uncle and Aunt Coral had all grown up in hard times. In 1968 and 1969, Granddad was sent to work in the mines and Gran endured many Red Guard struggle sessions. They often went to bed ravenously hungry, with nothing but saliva to fill their bellies. At least the midday meal was solid boiled rice, but the evening one was rice gruel with sweet potato peelings or turnip slices. For the gruel, just a handful of rice was boiled up with water in a pot the size of a washbowl and when Gran said it was ready, they lined up to serve themselves. First, Uncle carefully dipped the aluminium ladle in and slowly circled the bottom of the pot with it, before bringing it to the side of the pot, and gently raising it. When he reached the rim of the pot, he would pause to let the rice water drain from the ladle and then transfer his helping of sweet potato and rice to his bowl and carry it to the table to eat. Then it was Dad's turn. He did it with gusto, sank the ladle in, lifted it out and sloshed the watery contents into his bowl. Another go with the ladle and another splosh, and he carried the bowl to the table, drinking from it as he went. Aunt Coral's turn was last. Always genteel, she sank the ladle in as if she were lowering a bucket into the well—it must never quite touch the bottom of the pot. Ever so diffidently, she would bring up one scant ladleful, tip it slowly so that the contents ran down the side of her bowl, turn and walk away.

'Have some more, Coral!' urged Gran. 'You haven't got nearly enough!'

'Give it to Zhiming and Shengqiang,' said Aunt Coral. 'They're boys, they get hungry.'

They all sat around the table and Dad slurped down two bowlfuls of the rice water. But that only filled him up till he went for a pee, then he was starving all over again. 'I'm hungry!' he complained to Gran. He was just a little boy back then, and didn't understand what his mother was going through.

She sighed. 'I can't help that. Go to sleep. There'll be breakfast tomorrow.'

Dad was frantic with hunger. 'Why does big brother get much more than me?' he whined. 'And why does he get first helping?'

His siblings said nothing. His mother, her face like a thundercloud, led him into the bedroom and administered the ruler to his palm of his hand. 'Shengqiang,' she said, 'Do you know why I'm beating you today? Your sister knows how to behave properly, why don't you follow her lead? Everyone in the family has to help each other, we've got to stick together. Every household in Pingle Town has a down on us just now, you know that. They spit when they see us! But instead of defending the family, you're trying to do your brother out of his dinner! He's your own brother! Do you understand? Just imagine if I, or your father, or your sister, tried to do you out of your dinner! Is that the way for a family to behave?'

Dad was only just three. Most of what his mother said went over his head but the palm of his hand burned like fire, and the pain helped him to remember the lesson. He remembered right into adulthood: The family sticks together.

It was probably the first truth Gran taught him.

For instance, he walked into the chilli bean paste factory now to see Zeng the office manager in the downstairs office, settling up with Mr Zhou who had mounted the celebration banners: one celebrating the Mayflower Factory and eight long scrolls mounted on silk. Total, 560 *yuan*. 'Mr Zhou,' said Zeng, 'Wouldn't it be neighbourly to round it down?' 'Good heavens no!' Zhou waved the suggestion away. 'Have you seen the materials I've used, and the amount of work I've put into it? And I've delivered it you myself. I can't take a cent less!' Zeng caught sight of the minibus cab waiting behind Zhou and wavered: 'All right, ten *yuan* less, we'll pay you 550.' As they haggled, Dad came up and broke in: 'Zeng, give him the money, all of it! He's done a lot of work, what do you think you're doing, bargaining!'

Zhou was all smiles at the arrival of the boss, and counted his fee. Dad and Zeng set off upstairs with the scrolls.

'My brother not here yet?' asked Dad. He imagined that

Uncle had been as drunk as he was last night.

'Not yet,' said Zeng. 'He called to say he'd be in later. He had something to do first.'

'And my sister? Has she started rehearsals yet?'

'She said after yesterday's rehearsal, they could practice on their own today. She's taking a day off and she'll be in at the weekend to see the dress rehearsal.'

'Of course,' Dad nodded. 'She needs a break, she's been working hard these two days.'

Having done the roll call, and finding himself at a loose end, Dad told Zeng to go and make him some tea and began to unroll each of the scrolls on the side table so he could take a look. Powered by their artist's fee in its red envelope, the calligraphers had let their brushes blossom and Gran had been immortalized in high-flown phrases and propitious-sounding good wishes: 'May you have rosy-cheeked good health', 'May you have endless good fortune,' and even 'Your virtue and modesty are lauded world-wide.' It all put Dad in a very good mood. Uncle's idea had been a brainwave. There was no one to beat these old gents, you didn't get to their age in China without learning how to pile on the flattery. One of them, his father-in-law, Chen Xiuxiao, had written a verse:

> Long life to our distinguished Madame May,
> As we celebrate her eightieth birthday
> Long life to the Mayflower Factory,
> Where the fragrant vats embrace the stalk of longevity.

Dad read it, then read it again: 'It's all flattery, of course, but my father-in-law puts it exquisitely. Better than anyone else.'

He drank his Hua Mao Peak tea, admired the scrolls, and stubbed out two cigarette butts in the ashtray. A fresh spring breeze wafted through the room, and the air was filled with bird song and the scent of flowers. *Mother's going enjoy those birthday celebrations so much!* he thought.

Just at that moment, Gran called. This time, Dad was delighted to hear from her. 'Mother,' he began, 'you just wait till your birthday, my brother's really done you proud!'

To his surprise, Gran did not even say 'hello'. 'Shengqiang,' she said coldly, 'Come over to my house right now. I have something to ask you.'

Dad knew this tone of voice only too well. Something had seriously upset the old lady, that was clear. He searched his conscience as he plodded down the stairs and thought back over recent events. *Surely it can't be Sis? Or Jasmine? Gran's not gifted with second sight!* In a cold sweat, he said a hasty goodbye to Zeng and left.

He stepped into Cornucopia Court, past a riot of pear blossom in the flowerbeds. It occurred to him that since Jasmine had moved out and Uncle had started bustling around getting things ready for the banquet, he had not been here much. But he imagined that the old lady was the same as always, spending each afternoon sitting on the sofa, a silk cardigan round her shoulders, reading the newspaper, or a magazine or watching TV. She was in the habit of saying: 'And why shouldn't I get some peace, after a lifetime of ups and downs. Don't come bothering me unless you have something to discuss, let me have a quiet life.' She was also in the habit of saying: 'I'm a poor lonely old woman. My husband's passed on, the children have gone. They don't even bother to call me.'

Anyway, Dad stood downstairs and smoked a cigarette right down to the end, then ground the butt out under his heel and plodded up.

Gran did indeed look just the same as always. She sat on the sofa in a petrol green silk blouse with a crocheted gilet over it, but put down the newspaper she was reading as he came in and got to her feet and went into the kitchen. 'Ah, Shengqiang, you're here.'

'Uh-huh,' said Dad and sat down. The sofa sank beneath his weight. 'Anything interesting in the newspaper, Mother?'

Gran came out holding a cup of tea between both hands. She carefully put it down on the low table in front of Dad and sat down again in her usual armchair: 'Nothing. There's just something I want to ask you.'

Dad's heart began to race, just as if he was scraping the number off a lottery ticket. 'Ask away.'

'Did you and Zhiming have dinner with a woman on Friday evening?'

Dad thought he had foreseen every eventuality, but this question dumbfounded him. He did a quick reckoning on his fingers. *Fuck it, the dinner was only yesterday evening and the news had reached his mother's ears already.*

'Who told you, Mother?'

'Never mind who. Did this happen or not?' Gran asked again, with polite persistence.

Son-of-a-bitch, some piece of shit's been shooting his mouth off, Dad thought. Aloud, he said: 'Well yes, we did have a quick meal with her.'

'Ai!' Gran sighed. 'Shengqiang, you're a grown-up man now, and your brother too. How could you both be so reckless?'

Dad felt Gran was making a mountain out of a molehill. 'It was just a meal. What's wrong?'

'Don't treat me like a fool, Shengqiang,' Gran sat up straight in her chair. 'It wasn't just a meal, was it? You were setting up Zhiming with a date, isn't that right? Did you make any enquiries about this woman or did you just go along with it? Never mind the girl and her background, whatever were you thinking of letting that Mrs Xiao introduce her to your brother, a top university professor? Just consider their relative positions! How could you make such a mess of things?'

Dad could not get a word in edgeways, as Gran continued: 'That Mrs Xiao is a North Street slut, everyone knows that.

As a young girl, she was a hussy, and now that she's older, you really don't want to get on the wrong side of her. Whatever made you go near her? Now Zhiming won't look at the girl she introduced to him (and why would any son of mine look at a girl she introduced, anyway?) and it's properly put her nose out of joint. Do you have any idea what terrible things she's been saying?'

Of course Dad knew all about Zhong's mother, Mrs Xiao from North Street. As a girl, she certainly stuck out from the crowd, she was the first to walk the streets of Pingle Town wearing a flared skirt. When Gao Yang (Gao Tao's little sister) died and left Zhong a widower, it was that woman who sent the Gaos packing when they demanded their share of their late daughter's assets. And that woman who, as a widow in her sixties, made sure that her son and his next wife were properly tied to her apron strings. Obviously, it was she who had told Gran about the dinner.

He sighed inwardly. He and Zhong always boasted that they were not afraid of their wives, but could they say the same about this feisty pair of mothers they had? Gran's words clogged Dad's nostrils like ash he dared not wipe away. Finally he said: 'You're right, mother. I should have thought.'

'Yes, you should. I know you meant well, but really, Shengqiang, just use your brains next time! You're old enough to know better. Surely you don't need your mother's guidance in something as trifling as this?'

Gran's tirade had punctured Dad's good mood. He looked down at the two jasmine flowers floating in his tea, and nodded.

Well, at least his mother was not like that hussy, Mrs Xiao. In fact, she was sweet reason. Now that she had said her piece, she changed the subject, and asked how Uncle was getting on.

'Tell me, Shengqiang, has your brother said anything about a girlfriend to you? I didn't dare ask him myself, but I'm really worried.'

Dad suddenly remembered talking to Uncle at the Leaping Fish last night, when they were at the tipsy stage. In fact, he thought it was he who had raised the subject. 'I know how you feel, Zhiming, but you really can't go on like this, as a lonely bachelor. Is there really no one you fancy? Just tell me, whatever you want, I'm your little brother, I'll back you all the way! To hell with what Mother says, I'll fix it for you!'

And Uncle had finally opened up: 'Don't worry, Shengqiang, I'm working on it myself. In fact, my trip home this time is something to do with this. But I can't tell you just yet. When the time is right, I'll bring her home and introduce you all.'

Dad felt he'd been making a fuss about things that were none of his business. *Thank heavens for that,* he thought drunkenly. *He's found himself a woman! What an idiot I was, worrying about it for no reason.*

Of course, today he was sober again and perfectly aware that he should not mention anything of this to Gran. 'I'm sure that Zhiming's sorting it out himself, and there's no need for us to worry.'

Gran had been leaning back in her armchair. Now she sat bolt upright and remonstrated: 'Shengqiang! Are you too well-fed to remember what hunger pangs feel like? It's all very well for you to talk. You've settled down and you've got a nice family, but your brother is in his forties, a lonely bachelor. In a close family like ours, if he's not happy, then we can't be either. You're obviously prepared to let things drift because they don't affect you personally. Well, if you're not worried, I am!'

Dad could hardly believe his ears. *How can Zhiming say that Mother protects me but never protects him? One of us must be hallucinating!*

He lifted his cup to his lips and silently sipped. The water in the kettle must have been boiled the night before. The tea had not infused properly and left a raw taste in his mouth.

He was silent. Gran had nothing further to say either. The pair of them sat facing each other, neither enjoying the other's company, neither willing to be the first to leave.

'Shall I top you up with hot water?' Gran finally asked.

'No need.'

Gran sighed, and said more gently: 'Shengqiang, I know things haven't been easy for you either. I don't normally say this but we all know that you have the hardest job in the family. Your sister's married into another family, and your big brother is always travelling, so it's all down to you. We're such a big clan and such a big family business, and everything depends on you.'

With difficulty, Dad resisted the urge to fall on his knees and kowtow his thanks. Finally, he said very earnestly: 'No need to say things like that, Mother. I'm just doing what's right and proper.'

Gran nodded. 'I've given a lot of thought to your brother's situation, and I'm not blaming him, I have some responsibility there too. Oh dear, I always saw him as a clever, mature man who could sort things out for himself, so I kept quiet but now it's come to this.'

'Don't blame yourself,' said Dad. 'Fate plays a hand in match-making too.'

Gran shook her head. 'You're over-simplifying it. This has nothing to do with fate. Zhiming is a high-flyer and he's set his sights high. It won't be easy to find a match for him. Forget about the Xiaos of this world, I've racked my brains and, even among the people that I know, I can't think of anyone suitable for him.'

That was true. *I don't know who Zhiming would go for either,* thought Dad. *He tells me he can't give Qin up, and at the same time he's seeing someone else. Extraordinary! She must be an amazing woman!* There seemed to be nothing more to say about that. But Gran still had plenty more to say about other things. She rambled on about hard times long ago, and the good life they lived now, the next-door neighbour's sweet little grandson, her own domestic headaches, other gossip from the Court's residents and the neighbouring streets, old Mr Zhang had lost his carrying pole, the Lis were really putting on airs these days, and so on and so forth.

Dad, on the sofa, felt it was getting softer and he was sinking deeper into it the longer he sat there. He realized it was a very long time since he had been as relaxed as this, since before he fainted in Jasmine's bed, and Uncle and Aunt Coral came back to Pingle Town. It felt good relaxing in Gran's house, as two hours slipped by, or three, and she talked about her stuff, and he let it wash over him. Neither of them got in each other's way. They just got on with their own lives nowadays.

Dad sighed inwardly. *Let's get this birthday bash over quickly and pack the Immortals off back to Heaven's Gate, and the spider demons back to their Silken Cave, then I can get some peace and quiet,* he thought as he leaned back comfortably and listened to Gran. He almost nodded off, but instead got up and went to kitchen to top up his teacup with boiling water.

Even though he'd taken a pasting from his mother, Dad was in high spirits as he walked home. He had a couple of ideas and got out his mobile to make some calls.

The first was to Uncle. It rang and rang, but Uncle did not pick up. *Surely he's not busy at the factory?* He wondered. Then he called Aunt Coral, and she picked up straightaway.

'Are you taking it easy today, Coral? Anqin says we're having dinner together tomorrow evening, did she tell you? So what have you got lined up for today? If you've got nothing on, why don't you come and eat with us? You'll be bored on your own ... Oh, you're meeting old school friends? Right, right. Well, you go and eat with them, enjoy!'

Then he called Jasmine. She did not answer the first time and Dad was about to try again when she called him back.

She did not sound very happy. 'What's up? Who's been bugging you?' Dad laughed. ' ... Oh, you're not feeling well? A cold? There's a lot of it about, you look after yourself. I've got to spend the weekend with the family. You'll have to care of yourself, I'm sorry, but next week when the party's over, I'll come and spend time with you ... So eat whatever you feel like, buy whatever you want, OK?' And Dad cut the call.

Then he called Mum. She must have been in the market, judging by the amount of noise in the background. Her first question was: 'Do you fancy duck's blood soup tonight?' 'Sure, sure,' said Dad amiably. 'Besides, I fancy staying home tonight ... Ai-ya! It's not true I like going out every night, sometimes I like staying home with you, wifey! ... Hey, what's wrong with calling you "wifey", why does that mean I've got a screw loose? ... OK, OK, I'll see you later, see you later.'

Finally, he thought he would give Zhong a ring. Gran had not laid it on the line, but her meaning was clear: one way or another, that woman Xiao had to have the lid put on her ravings as quickly as possible. 'Hey, bro ... where are you? I've just left Mother's house ... . Son-of-a-bitch, tell me about it! Mine certainly gave me an earful! What? About trying to find my brother a girlfriend! Mother heard that Zhiming snubbed Wang and she was livid. She said I shouldn't have meddled, said I should come over and apologize to your mother straightaway! ... Really! What a cock-up! Ai-ya! Yes, yes! It's really not our business, you and me, but old folk are much more proper about these things. Forget it, tomorrow I'll be over to see your mum, right? ... Really! OK, see you tomorrow morning then.'

Then he called Zhu Cheng. He picked up after the first ring. 'Hey, Zhu Cheng? You answered quickly today! Waiting for orders from the boss lady, were you? ... Ha ha! Yes, yes, yes. I need you to do something for me. Isn't your wife involved in importing health products? My wife said they did her a lot of good, last time she took some. Can you get some more for me? I'm going to see someone tomorrow morning on North Street. Spend between 1,000 and 2,000 *yuan*, OK? ... It's for an old person, so ... stuff like spirulina, protein powder, royal jelly, that sort of thing ... you get the idea. Then come and pick me up tomorrow morning and give me the stuff. About nine o'clock. I'll call you when I'm ready.'

By the time he finished, he was nearly home. When he thought about what Gran had said, he thought she was absolutely right, he had to sort out everything in this shambolic clan, including all their squabbles and back-biting. Son-of-a-bitch, he was tired of it! Apart from himself, was there anyone else who could sort it out, really, truly, sort it out?

Dad got home in the same high spirits with which he had gone out, ate his dinner, watched TV and had a shower.

He walked to the bedroom, to see Mum sitting cross-legged on the bed, rubbing some scented cream into her thighs, her face illuminated a rosy-pink by the bedside light. The last of the gloom of recent days vanished. Fired up, he took a couple of strides and pounced on her fragrant white body. He was going to kill the enemy good and proper this time. The long pent-up bullets spattered forth. 'Fuck your mother!' he yelled, with renewed energy.

Afterwards, he stretched out and slept. Mum got up to answer the phone, then came back and sat for a long time on the edge of the bed. Dad slept on, oblivious.

The next day, however, was to spring some unpleasant surprises on Dad. There was only one way to describe what happened: catastrophic.

The first thing was that when he got up, Mum was gone. There was half a potful of rice porridge on the cooker and, on the table, a bowl of stir-fried pork and pickled green beans.

Dad assumed that she had gone to do the shopping since they were having guests tonight. He sat there alone, eating his breakfast and called Zhu Cheng. No one answered. Thinking Zhu Cheng had not heard it ring, he cut the call and waited for his driver to call back. He finished his breakfast and tried again. Still no answer. As he waited, he looked outside. It was drizzling. Half an hour passed and it was nearly 10 o'clock. Still not a squeak from Zhu Cheng.

Son-of-a-bitch! That Zhu Cheng is getting worse and worse! He's really gone too far this time. If Dad left it any later to get to the Zhongs, he'd have to stay for lunch. Besides, he had nothing to take. He rifled through all the cupboards, pulling out other people's gifts of tea, milk powder, dried wild mushrooms and such like, and put them all in a bag. Cursing Zhu Cheng, he made his way downstairs. The rain made it difficult to get a taxi and his feet were complaining by the time one finally came along. Supressing his annoyance, he flagged it down, opened the door and hopped inside. His trouser cuffs, he saw, were covered in mud.

He groaned aloud. The driver asked: 'Where to?'

'The old paper factory residential compound, past North Street Seven Immortals Bridge. You know where I mean? By the way, do you have any paper tissues on you?' Dad asked.

He rubbed the mud off his trouser cuffs, paid the driver and walked off, the bag of presents in his hand. After all these trials and tribulations, he was finally to the Zhongs' house and rang the doorbell.

It was Mrs Xiao herself, in a red silk jacket, who opened the door. Her hair was tightly permed and puffed into a bouffant on her head, which made her look like a scientist in an atom bomb blast. Her smile was so broad, it seamed her face with wrinkles, he noticed. She welcomed Dad and invited him in: 'Ai-ya! Come in, Mr Xue. What an honour to have a visit from the big boss!'

'Don't called me "big boss", Xiao! Shengqiang will do fine!' Dad unconsciously raised his voice, in case she was hard of hearing.

Zhong came out of the bedroom and greeted him. 'Make our guest a cup of tea, quickly!' ordered his mother.

Watching Zhong scuttle into the kitchen almost made Dad smile. He put his presents down and sat on the sofa. 'I haven't seen you for ages. How are you, Mrs Xiao?'

'Fine, fine!' Mrs Xiao beamed, her smile positively unctuous.

Dad decided to get his visit over with as soon as possible and get out of there. He got straight to the point, apologizing profusely for the business about Uncle.

To his astonishment, Mrs Xiao exclaimed: 'Ai-ya! Yes, I got myself so worked up worrying about him, I didn't stop to ask. Now we know that Zhiming already has a girlfriend, we're not at all worried!'

Dad glanced at Zhong, who was coming out of the kitchen holding a cup of tea in both hands. 'So my brother's got a girlfriend?' he asked, doing his best to keep his surprise out of his voice.

'Oh yes! Yesterday evening, I was coming back from playing *mahjong* and I saw him as I passed the houses on Chun'An Gardens. A woman was showing him out, a beautiful, tall, slim girl. Quite a looker!'

Zhong looked meaningfully at Dad. Dad knew only too well what that meant, he and Zhong had been friends for a long time. It was the same sort of look Zhong gave him they were playing *mahjong* in a foursome and he could see the idiot playing before Dad had a winning hand. *You still think your brother is such an old stick-in-the-mud?* was what Zhong obviously wanted to say.

Fucking son-of-a-bitch! This news was a bombshell. Dad's already short fuse threatened to blow. He sat on the Zhongs' sofa, facing mother and son. What through his mind was: *Chun'An Gardens—that's where I got Jasmine her new apartment!*

That wasn't the only thing that happened. Dad left the Zhongs and, as he walked along North Street, wondered whether to get out his phone and give Uncle a call. He was still wondering when he got to the old Local Products Factory.

This, as we know, was where his first girlfriend, Xi Hongzhen, used to work. Dad liked her, and wanted to marry her, it was Gran who was dead set against it: 'Are you out of your mind, Shengqiang? Never mind that she's two years older than you, she's so short! Why would I want a daughter-in-law like that? Now take a look at Chen Anqin, she's got everything going for her. The daughter of a County Party Committee official, a good girl, well-brought up. Do you think she would so much as look at you if she wasn't friends with your sister? I've only got your best interests at heart, you do understand, don't you?' Gran was so angry about Hongzhen that she was off her food for two days. Granddad played peacemaker and had a word with his son: 'Shengqiang, just let it go, don't be angry with your mother, hasn't she got enough to worry about without this? You do what she wants, and go and see the girl.' Dad was no more than nineteen years old back then, and yelled at Granddad: 'Do what she wants? When did anyone do what I want?'

Granddad gave him such a clap on the side of the head that the sound ricocheted off the ceiling. That was over twenty years ago and Dad's cheek muscles still ached at the memory.

I'm not running scared, he thought now, and he steeled himself and pressed Uncle's number.

Uncle answered on the second ring: 'What's up, Shengqiang?' Dad felt emboldened. His brother's affected tones indicated a guilty conscience, he was sure. 'Where are you?' he demanded.

'Where am I?' Uncle hesitated. 'Why do you want to know?'

'Where are you? I've got something to ask you,' Dad repeated into the phone.

Uncle must have heard from Dad's voice that something was amiss. He said nothing. There was a rustling sound at the end of the line, as if he was talking to someone else.

'Shengqiang, your brother's at our house. Come home. He's got something to tell you.'

It was Mum, speaking ever so gently, as if anxious to put the handbrake on Dad's temper. *Son-of-a-bitch, why bring Anqin into this? You want her to tell me what's what?* He thought.

Dad went home. His home was on West Street, three traffic lights beyond Cornucopia Court. It was a journey he had done millions of times. Inside the compound, third block on the right, sixth floor.

As he plodded upstairs, he remembered Gran's words. 'Shengqiang,' she was always saying, 'You're always flying off the handle, but it gets people's backs up. I've told you before, and I'll tell you again, it's no trouble to lower your voice. Take a step back and give people a bit of space.'

At his front door, he really did take a step back. Then he got out his key and let himself in.

Uncle and Mum were in the sitting-room. They both jumped to their feet the minute the door opened, as if welcoming their leader.

'Sit down, Shengqiang,' said Uncle.

'Come and sit down,' said Mum, with a broad smile.

Anqin, Anqin! You're so devious. Why am I surprised you've suddenly been acting as everything's fine for the last few days! What joke are you about to spring on me now? Dad thought coldly. He felt a distinct chill inside his trousers too.

He sat down and waited for them to make him some tea. But no one made him tea. They just watched him in what seemed like mute embarrassment.

Finally, Dad could bear it no longer: 'So what have you got

to tell me? Spit it out! Not much shocks me at my age! I've seen it all! Nothing freaking scares me!'

Inwardly, he thought viciously, *Lets just see you introduce Jasmine to Mother as your new girlfriend, brother!*

It was Uncle who spoke first: 'Calm down, Shengqiang. I have something to tell you about Jasmine.' Mum sat on the other sofa, her eyes on him.

'Go ahead.' Dad got a cigarette out, lit up and took a puff and waited to hear what nonsense his brother was going to come out with now.

'I've been worried all along about the business with Jasmine, and so has Anqin. In fact, she asked me to help. Don't blame us, Shengqiang, we've only got your interests at heart. So, yesterday I went to see Jasmine and we talked the whole business about the baby through very carefully. Shengqiang, you're a grown man, you can see reason. I thought yesterday, this baby must not be born. If it is, how are you going to make it OK, with Mother, or Anqin? The baby won't have a proper name or status, and it'll only make mischief for itself and everyone else. Do you follow me?'

Dad dragged on his cigarette over and over as Uncle carried on quacking away.

'So I went to see Jasmine and told her what we feel. I think it would be better for her too. I mean, look at your situation, she'll be an unmarried mother. And one day she'll want to get married and start a family, and she won't be able to.'

Even though he knew now he'd got the wrong end of the stick about Uncle's visit to Jasmine, Dad seethed with rage. He put out his cigarette and looked up.

'I'm the family head here! Just keep your nose out of my business!' he raged. 'Whatever you went and told Jasmine, I'm telling you I'm going to have that baby and anyone who tries to stop me can just like it or lump it, because I'm having my way!'

'Shengqiang!' This was Mum. Uncle couldn't get any words out. 'Just get off your high horse, will you? You talk such nonsense, what kind of "family head" do you think you are?'

'Anqin.' Uncle stretched out a hand to calm her, but Mum leapt to her feet.

'Xue Shengqiang!' She marched up to him, opened her mouth wide and spat a gob of spittle at him. 'Family head, huh! You make a fine family head. Shall I tell you what you really are? You're just a fathead! Do you think this baby is really yours? Of course it's not! You're going to have that baby, are you? In your dreams! You fathead!'

Mum had not shouted at Dad for a very long time. She always prided herself on coming from a cultured family. No screeching like a fishwife for her. But this was too much. She was so angry that Dad could hardly make out what she was saying.

Dad was still sitting on the sofa. He wanted another cigarette, but could not remember which pocket he had put the pack in.

'Anqin,' Uncle got up and tugged Mum's sleeve.

'Zhiming!' she turned to look at him. 'Look at the stupid son-of-a-bitch! And you said I shouldn't tell him, you said, spare him the cruellest cut. But if I don't give it to him straight today, he'll be a fathead for the rest of his life!'

Talk about iron hand in velvet glove. Mum turned to look at the 'fathead' and repeated what Uncle had told her, enunciating the words very clearly: 'Listen to me, Shengqiang. That lover of yours is a little slag. She's been two-timing you with Zhu Cheng right from the start. The baby is Zhu Cheng's. Your brother asked her and Zhu Cheng, and it's clear as daylight, there's absolutely no doubt about it. They've fooled you good and proper, you dumb idiot!'

The whole of Dad's life flashed before his eyes, every little bit of it, every smile and every tear. And that woman's seductive poses, and emotional deceits.

It was a toxic moment. Then he thought of Gran. He thought back to the time when, in 1996, or maybe 1995, around then anyway, when he and Gran and Zhu Cheng went to see the pear blossom in Pear Blossom Gully. He knew perfectly well that Gran didn't want to see pear blossom. Firstly, she was upset about him. She could see that one thing after another was going wrong for him: his wife, his daughter, there was trouble from all quarters. It was going to drive him over the edge. Secondly, she was angry with herself. When he first got to know Anqin, she had praised the girl to the skies, it was Anqin this, Anqin that, she was so desperate for Dad to marry her. Now she wanted to give herself a good slap for that. Well, it was too late for recriminations. They should get out in the fresh air for a bit of distraction.

Gran sat in the back seat of the Santana and took Dad's hand. Then she said: 'Shengqiang, the ancients never tried to lay down the law in the matter of love affairs. Try to stand back from it, look at it dispassionately and don't get bogged down in the small details. People are always like this, and the closer people are to you, the more easily they can hurt you, and the more you have to mind your back. Of course, you shouldn't go out to hurt people, but you should always be sure to protect yourself. No one is true to you the way your family is true to you, no one. And since you can never trust outsiders, you shouldn't waste your energy getting angry with them, right?'

Mother and son sat, hand in hand, and thought of other people's cruelty and their own regrets. *Yes, Mother does protect me*, thought Dad.

10

A S A GENERAL RULE, Dad avoided talking about Mum to
any girl he was screwing. Of course, all of them knew the
score: he had a woman at home and he shared a bed with her.
Dad referred to her as 'her indoors'.

When he got to know Jasmine, and first invited her out to
dinner, she asked: 'Mr Xue, what animal year were you born
in?' '66, the year of the horse,' Dad said. 'And what about your
wife?' she asked next.

Hah! She gets straight to the point! Dad thought to himself.
'She was born in 1967,' he told her. 'Year of the sheep.'

'You're very well matched,' Jasmine gave a little smile, and
took a sip of her ginseng and abalone soup.

'Well matched!' Dad yelped as if someone had trodden on
his corns. 'She drives me mad the whole time! You youngsters
don't understand, there's nothing I can do about it. When
you're in your thirties or forties, you can't get divorced just
like that, even if your relationship's completely broken down!'

He finished speaking and saw that Jasmine was looking
down at the table. Yes! Things were looking good. He drank
some Asahi beer and said nothing.

This was how Zhong summed up the three rules for laying
a woman: you bad-mouthed your wife, flashed some money
around, and told a few jokes. It was crudely put but true. Dad
did all of these things and fixed things up with Jasmine Zhong.
The two of them became an item, and had been together two

years. At particularly lovey-dovey moments, or when a public holiday loomed and Dad had to go home, Jasmine would needle him with comments like: 'I've heard your wife likes her *mahjong...*' or, 'What about your wife? Giving you a hard time, is she?'

At those moments, Dad would feel he was being put to the test. But he would keep his nerve, twitch his nose, clear his throat, and give a little frown. 'Ai-ya, that woman! Don't talk about her!'

As time passed, it did not matter whether he was with Jasmine or any other girl, Dad even convinced himself that his relationship with Mum had broken down, and they were not getting along at all.

This, however, was far from the truth. Finally, his conscience pricked him and he thought: *Anqin's all right in her own way! I'm going to stick with her!*

What he meant was that 'a friend in need is a friend indeed'.

He had played the field for so long and now he was finally in deep doodoo, blatantly cuckolded by his mistress and his own driver. But Mum was not going to hit a man who was down, or make harsh remarks along the lines of: 'You certainly know how to choose them, Shengqiang!' The opposite was true, quite the opposite, Mum had had a cultured upbringing and had always behaved accordingly. All those TV soaps and novels hadn't been a waste of time either. She was tenderly solicitous towards Dad, like a spring breeze and a gentle rain nurturing his frosted aubergines.

First thing in the morning, she would ask him: 'Shengqiang, what would you like for breakfast, rice balls or noodle soup? Here, start with a cup of honey water!'

During her lunch break, she phoned and asked: 'How did your morning go, Shengqiang? Is the stage up yet? Any problems? It's like a furnace today, don't spend too much time out in the sun and drink plenty of water! Have a nap in your office after lunch!'

When he got home in the evening, his dinner awaited him, the table groaning under dishes of food. By the standards of the 1970s, they ate as if it was New Year every day. There was chilli bean paste fish, chicken fried with *matsutake* mushrooms, pork fried with bitter melon, wax gourd and spare rib soup, stewed duck and soy beef, a different selection every day. As Dad grimly tucked in, Mum suggested, without being asked: 'A little wine, Shengqiang?'

'No, no,' said Dad, taking a mouthful of white rice, plain-boiled but fluffy and fragrant.

Having eaten her food, he felt he had to apologize again: 'Anqin, I'm so sorry about the way I behaved! And you're being so kind. From now on, I'll do whatever you say!'

Mum took a look at my foolish Dad, and said: 'Shengqiang, we've said all that needs to be said. Let's not talk about it anymore.'

'That girl Jasmine did a fine thing!' Mum had to admit later.

It was true, too. Just the evening before, husband and wife had sat peaceably on the sofa, hand in hand, having a heart-to-heart.

Mum had come to the conclusion that the baby Jasmine carried in her belly was a ticking time-bomb. Just the thought made her break out in a cold sweat. After all she'd put up with these twenty years, she felt really fed up. They just could not divorce because of Jasmine's pregnancy. In fact, she and Shengqiang were both thinking along the same lines there. The day after their big row, when Shengqiang sobered up, he regretted what he had said. While Anqin sat sighing at her office desk, wondering how to get out of this mess.

'What are all these heavy sighs about?' asked Yufen, who sat opposite her.

Yufen was a good friend and Mum could not hide the truth from her. 'That thing you told me,' she said, 'it was true.

Yesterday I went home and asked Shengqiang and he confirmed it. I was so angry I told him I wanted a divorce. Ai, what am I going to do now? The old lady's still in the picture, and if we divorce now, everything I've done will be wasted effort. All this hard work for twenty years, and I haven't benefitted by a single cent yet. If we divorce now, that little slag will have won.'

Yufen rolled her eyes. 'Don't you worry about it. Let's you and me talk it through. Now, how about you ask Zhiming to smooth things over between you, why not?'

'Do you think he would?' asked Mum doubtfully.

'Don't you think he'd be only too happy to, with things as they are?' said Yufen encouragingly. 'If he puts in a good word for you now, then you'll put in a good word for him when the time comes. You give him a ring, he's family after all, there's nothing to worry about!'

So Mum called Uncle and asked him to buy Jasmine off. There was nothing that couldn't be fixed if you tried hard enough. When push came to shove, Mum did not want a divorce, heaven knows, she really did not. 'That stupid girl's shot herself in the foot! So much the better for our family!' she concluded.

Of course, she could not put it in those terms to Dad. She looked down and squeezed the palms of her hands together. Then she carefully said her piece.

As he listened, Dad thought: *I've been such a son-of-a-bitch! Anqin has been with me all these years, and she still doesn't want a divorce, she wants me back! I don't deserve such a marvellous wife!*

Dad was putty in Mum's hands by now. She wanted to give him a spanking, but ever so affectionately; he wanted to be spanked, and submitted to it cheerfully. How could they not thank Jasmine for what she had done for them? They were so grateful!

When it was all finished, they went back to eating their

dinner. Dad said another heart-felt sorry, and Mum picked out a choice morsel of steamed pork for him, with her chopsticks, as a small token of how much he meant to her, and they both felt that a cloud had lifted and the sun had broken through.

Dad had not been out with Zhong and his other bros for two or three days, however, and they were not happy. 'Have you been off somewhere making money?' they demanded. 'Why haven't you been out for a drink with us? Landed in the clink, did you?'

'I've just been on the wagon for a couple of days,' said Dad evasively.

These bums could never imagine Dad turning over a new leaf, so they concluded that 'Anqin's taken that prawn of a husband of hers in hand finally!'

Dad did not care what they said. It was different with family. That afternoon, as the sun blazed down, Dad and Uncle sat in his office drinking tea, and talking about everything that had gone on. Dad said what a good woman Mum was: 'It's all thanks to Anqin, and to you too, brother, that we've weathered the storm. They'd have gone on taking me for a ride otherwise. Those two! Just a few days ago, I was still furious with whichever idiot blabbermouth it was who told Anqin, and made us fight. And now look. Fucking hell, I really was nearly taken for a ride!'

Uncle said nothing. He sipped his tea and studied the tealeaves floating on the surface, as if the person Dad was calling names was not him at all.

In any case, Dad was paying no attention. He dragged hard on his cigarette, coating his lungs with yet another layer of tar.

Finally he burst out: 'Zhiming, what have you done about them?'

Uncle leaned back in his armchair and put down his cup. He looked at Dad: 'I've told you, forget it, I'll sort it.'

Dad took the cigarette from between his lips and stubbed it out in the ash-tray. But it still rankled: 'Fucking hell! OK, I'll leave it be for the moment, but when Mother's party's over, I'll sort the pair of them out! Son-of-a-bitch, I'll send them packing, or my name's not Xue Shengqiang!'

'Shengqiang,' Uncle hurriedly straightened up in his chair, and said earnestly: 'Don't do anything rash, whatever you do. There's a lot at stake, I've told you that. For starters, Zhu Cheng's father has been with our family for years and years, and Jasmine was not going out with you openly. If you make a big fuss about it, think what will happen. You don't gain anything, in fact, it will reflect badly on the whole family. Just calm down and leave it to me, I'll deal with Jasmine, and Zhu Cheng, and I promise you I'll come to a suitable arrangement.'

Dad said nothing. He lit another cigarette. There was a lot more bad language on the tip of his tongue, but he also knew quite well that if Gran ever got to hear about the baby, it would be very bad news indeed for him.

What the hell, he inhaled savagely. All that smoke was going to have to find its way out somehow. Still, right now, all he could do was, as Gran put it, 'step back and let nature take its course.'

He stood with his back against his office window, with the eucalyptus tree leaves glittering white in the sunshine outside, and said to Uncle: 'We don't have to talk about this mess I'm in all the time. What about you? What about the thing you talked to me about? This birthday party of Mother's will soon be over, you've had long enough to fix it, haven't you?'

Uncle was drumming his fingers on his knee: 'Shengqiang, you're still worrying about me, please drop it.'

'Ai-ya,' Dad said. 'How can I not be worried? It's the family's biggest problem at the moment. Two days ago when I went to see Mother, she kept asking me about it.'

Uncle looked anxious. 'You didn't tell her?'

'Of course not!' Dad waved dismissively. 'I said nothing at all. You can talk to her as soon as you think it's OK. But Mother's really worried, you know.'

Uncle sighed. 'I'm pretty worried myself, it's really tricky, but it'll soon be OK, very soon.'

Looking at his brother's eyebrows knitted in a frown, Dad could not help smiling. 'Zhiming, far be it from me to interfere, but you do do things in a funny way! You're looking for a wife, not doing a lab experiment! When you see one you like, just get a move on!'

'It's not as simple as all that, Shengqiang,' said Uncle with another sigh. 'She's not a young woman anymore, she comes with baggage. I'm worried that Mother won't approve. Will you back me up?'

Dad's interest was piqued. *Does that mean he's found someone his own age! That's a bit of a problem!* he thought. Of course he did not say that. 'Don't worry. I already told you, from now on, I'll do whatever it takes! It doesn't matter what Mother says, whatever you want, we'll make sure it happens. Pay no attention to her. Besides, we all know she's an old woman. She's been wanting another daughter-in-law all these years, she's bound to be fine about it. Stop pussy-footing around and bring her over to be introduced, right?'

He wasn't putting it on, he really was itching to see this woman. He had only ever met one of Uncle's serious girlfriends, and that was Qin, the woman who sold Sichuan pepper. Back then, she was in the third year of Pingle Town Number One Upper Middle School, in the humanities stream, while Uncle was doing science. Dad kept hearing about her. Apparently she was a stunner. At the flag-raising ceremony, it was always she who presided on the platform. When they did exercises at break-time, she stood at the front of the whole third year group and led them. Little pipsqueaks like Dad who were still in the lower middle school used to gawp at this goddess. She was even prettier than the girls on TV! Apart from a few boys who liked to live dangerously and went for firecrackers like Liu Yufen, everyone else acknowledged that, amongst the girls at Pingle Town Number One Middle School, she was the flower of them all.

One day after school, Dad went looking for Uncle and his bros at the sports field ping-pong tables, and there was Qin. He could still remember the blouse she was wearing, it was pale yellow, almost white, and she wore her hair in a ponytail. It gleamed like silk. Dad scampered over to them, but when he saw Qin, he ground to a sudden halt. He could not get a word out. Qin beamed an easy smile at him: 'Is this your little brother, Zhiming? He looks just like you!'

Uncle was standing at one of the tables, ping-pong bat in hand. He looked round and told Dad: 'Say hello to the lady.'

Looking at Uncle that day, with the spring breeze brushing his face, and a spring in his step, swinging his bat and beating three or four opponents in a row, Dad could not help but be impressed. *He's one in a million, my brother!* He thought.

But Zhiming and Qin were still at school in those days, and even if they were going out together, they always behaved very properly. Dad did not remember ever seeing them holding hands in public. They would walk along, Qin with her satchel over her shoulder, three fists apart, sometimes five. That low-life Zhong would jeer at Uncle: 'Zhiming, where are all those tricks you learnt from the Baby Girl and the others? Have you gone soft in the head?'

Uncle was not angry, he just looked mildly at Zhong and said: 'I don't think this one is like them, do you?'

Dad was about fifteen years old, so it was 1982 or 1983. He was still wet behind the ears but he understood well enough that Uncle really cared for Qin. He was very fond of her himself. *My future sister-in-law's a real stunner!*

Fine thoughts, fine words. But in the end, Uncle and Qin

turned out to be as star-crossed as Romeo and Juliet. Dad gave a heart-felt sigh and thought: *This time, it's going to work out for him!* 'Whatever she says, don't worry, Zhiming. I'll back you to the hilt this time!' he told his brother.

The day was drawing in when Dad left the chilli bean paste factory, now festooned with lanterns and banners, and pottered off home to dine alone with Mum. Uncle said he had something on this evening. Aunt Coral had rehearsed the singers for the last time and was nowhere to be seen. It was really hot, and he started to sweat after just a couple of steps. He felt drained. *They've worn me out, those scumbags Zhu Cheng and Jasmine, making me so angry, he thought. I'll take some medicine as soon as I get home. I wonder if there's any still left over from when I last saw the doc.*

He thought a couple of cigarettes might make him feel better, and fumbled in his pocket, but the soft pack was almost flat in his hand. There was just one left. He lit up, crumpled the pack and threw it away, and headed over to Zhou's kiosk at Celestials Bridge to buy more.

And who should he bump into there but Chen Xiuliang, his old *shifu*? The old man stood near the kiosk, looking relaxed in a white vest and silver-grey shirt over his trousers.

'Shengqiang!' he greeted Dad cheerfully, clutching a pack of White Hibiscus in one hand.

'*Shifu*! Have you finished the cigarettes I bought you? If so, I'll get them to bring you two more cartons tomorrow.'

'No, no!' the old man waved the offer away and pulled the pack open. 'I've still got some left, look! Ai-ya! The truth is, my taste-buds aren't what they were, and that's why sometimes I fancy a smoke like White Hibiscus!'

'Then I'll have one of your White Hibiscus too!' Dad said with a laugh.

'Sure!' Chen was delighted. He pulled one out of the pack

and handed it to Dad. They stood outside Zhou's kiosk and lit up. Old Zhou looked out and laughed: 'What a pair! What's the world coming to when two company heads come here and smoke White Hibiscus?'

'My pupil's a company head, I'm not!' Chen told him, patting Dad on the shoulder.

Life was good. As they smoked, the White Hibiscus taste filled their mouths and got up their nostrils too. They watched the milling crowds in the park opposite and Chen said: 'Your mother's birthday banquet is pretty soon, isn't it?'

'Yup! This Saturday. You're coming, *shifu*, aren't you? There will be lots of entertainment and gifts.'

'No, no, I'm off on a family visit to Chongning County. I fixed it ages ago!'

'Ai-ya! Whatever do you want to do that for? The entertainment will be great! They've got some real stars coming to sing!' Dad was lobbying hard.

But he knew, when push came to shove, that if Chen said he didn't want to come, that was that. He was a stubborn old man with a will of his own. Sure enough, Dad had a few more goes but Chen would not budge.

'Then come tomorrow,' Dad said finally. 'It's the dress rehearsal, just family. And come and have a meal with us afterwards!'

'All the family?' asked Chen.

'Yup! My brother's here and my sister's come back too.'

'So Coral's back,' said Chen, stubbing out his cigarette on the ground then stamping on it. 'Then I'll come. I can help out!'

'Ai-ya! What are you going to help with? Just bring your eyes to see and your mouth to eat with!'

By the time they'd finished their cigarettes and exchanged a few more words, Dad felt a lot better. Then Chen went off, leaving Dad to buy his soft pack cigarettes.

So there he is, getting his money out, and his phone starts beeping away in the other pocket. That song again, *A Pretty Sprig of Jasmine*. Dad thrust a one-hundred *yuan* note at Zhou, the kiosk holder, and answered the call.

To his horror, it was Aunt Coral's husband.

'Shengqiang!' Uncle Liu greeted him in his usual unctuous tones.

'Yes!' Dad almost addressed him as 'brother-in-law' although that seemed inappropriate now. 'What can I do for you?'

Dad took the change Zhou gave him, and stuffed it in his trouser pocket. Then he turned away, cursing Uncle Liu with single-minded venom, *You son-of-a-bitch! You're up to no good, trying to contact me now, I know it! Well, spit it out. As soon as you're done, I'm heading right home for my dinner.*

'I'm back in town, Shengqiang,' he heard Uncle Liu say. 'I'm at the North Gate. Have you got time to see me? There's something I want to talk to you about.'

It was obviously something to do with Aunt Coral. And that being the case, Dad couldn't duck out of it, even though poor Mum had prepared a great spread for dinner, and poor Dad was so tired that all he wanted to do was go home and pop a couple of his pills. As he changed tack and headed off to see Uncle Liu, he grumbled to himself that this clan was just too big, he couldn't handle it all. Like Gran said, being head of the family was really, really difficult.

Dad found Uncle Liu sitting in a teahouse, with what looked a girl's leather handbag beside him. As soon as he saw him, Dad understood: he was wearing a sloppy old shirt, and he had neglected to shave. His face was covered in grubby-looking patches of stubble which made him look mildewed. Uncle Liu leapt to his feet as soon as he saw Dad, almost knocking over the tea cup on the table top, and hailed him with a big smile: 'Shengqiang! Over here!'

What does he want to talk about! Dad swore silently and plonked himself down. *No doubt he's having second thoughts and wants to get back with Sis. Forget it! It's far too late for that, you son-of-a-bitch!*

But Uncle Liu was still piling on the bonhomie: 'Shengqiang, I hope my wife hasn't outstayed her welcome, she's been with you such a long time!'

Dad's temper had been on a short fuse for some days. *So, Liu Qukang, you've jumped out of the frying pan into the fire this time.* 'What did I tell you last time we talked? Just behave yourself! My sister has never let you down in any way, so tell me how it's got to this point?' he demanded.

Uncle Liu went pale, then flushed, quite a pretty pink colour. 'How it's got to this point, Shengqiang? Honestly, I really wish it hadn't!'

'Then what are you going to do about it?' asked Dad, tired of pussyfooting around.

'You really have to make your sister see sense,' Uncle Liu said. 'We're too old to divorce at our age! Your sister's signed the divorce papers and left them with me to sign, but I haven't done it yet. I really don't want a divorce, but she won't see me. Please, Shengqiang, put in a good word for me. A divorce won't do either of us any good. Surely nothing's so bad it can't be sorted by discussing it?'

It was very strange, listening to his brother-in-law, Dad felt a weight drop from his shoulders. 'Liu Qukang,' he said, 'I'm not blaming you, but my sister's made up her mind. You must have driven her stir-crazy for her to get so angry. She's a very sweet-natured woman!'

'Right, right,' Uncle Liu bobbed his head. 'It wasn't a big deal at the start, you know, I don't know why she got so determined. She suddenly said she wanted a divorce and then things got like this, with no warning at all!'

No warning at all?! Dad was tempted to give him a couple of slaps around the face. *You son-of-a-bitch, renting an apartment and installing your mistress in it, wasn't that a warning?* In the normal course of events, he would have said that, and told him a few more home truths too. But he was not unreasonable, and he wanted everyone in the family to be happy. He couldn't help putting himself in Uncle Liu's shoes, and thinking what a mess he himself had made of things, and of Mum's generosity.

So he controlled his temper and said: 'OK, I'll help you out this one time, but let me be quite clear, this is the very last time! If you get up to any more tricks, I'll hang you out to dry!'

'Ai-ya! Shengqiang,' Uncle Liu rubbed his forehead. 'I absolutely take your point. I won't ever put a foot wrong again! With your sister gone, home isn't home anymore! Xingchen has been on at me day after day, telling me I've driven his mother away and there's no one to look after the baby. My life's not worth living anymore!'

Dad said nothing. He wanted to ask more, but there was nothing to ask. He thought of giving him a few words of comfort, but really, the man had got what he deserved. He looked at the briefcase on the chair next to Uncle Liu, and tried to think. At that moment, the waitress suddenly remembered to come over and ask what tea he wanted to drink. 'Nothing!' said Dad brusquely! 'We've finished. I'm off.'

He got up and left, without even asking Uncle Liu if he'd had dinner, or wanted a drink, or how he was going to amuse himself after dinner. 'Shengqiang!' Uncle Liu called after him. 'You won't forget, will you?'

Outside the teahouse, Dad saw Uncle Liu's Citroen parked at the roadside. He felt another surge of fury. But he'd given his word and took out his phone to call Aunt Coral. *You lot come trotting back to Pingle Town, like a stick-load of candied haws! As if I haven't got enough troubles!*

He waited for Aunt Coral to answer the phone, grumbling

away to himself, his belly rumbling with hunger. He did not know that he would thank Uncle Liu for all this in the end. 'Dammit, it took me a while to work it out,' he said later. 'If it hadn't been for my brother-in-law coming back, I would have been a fathead for the rest of my life!'

Well, even the Immortals couldn't know that. The Pingle townsfolk had a jingle:

A beggar that everyone hates
Takes a hoe out of the city gate
In the field he digs for yams
Hits buried treasure instead
And ends up with a wife and a home.

It all goes to show, you never can tell.

But as Dad hurried to the Golden Leaves Hotel in search of Aunt Coral, he had not yet worked all this out. Aunt Coral was in her room reading. She invited Dad in and said: 'What are you doing here, Shengqiang? Is something up?'

Dad had his words all prepared but, face to face with his sister, he was tongue-tied. He went to the toilet, then said he wanted to eat, and Aunt Coral phoned Room Service for a bowl of beef noodles. They sat there waiting for the order to arrive, and waited and waited. When it did not come, Dad finally opened his mouth:

'I know I shouldn't be raising this with you, Sis, but Liu's come to me about it, so here goes ...'

Aunt Coral put down the book she had in her hand: 'That's a clever move, coming to you for help!'

Dad did not know what to say. He was flagging, and the fact he was starving didn't help either. Finally he said: 'Actually, it was only a couple of days ago that Anqin told me she wanted a divorce too.' Or words to that effect.

'Really? Now what's with you two?'

Dad stumbled through the story of the shenanigans with Mum. He had wanted to tell his sister for a while, but had never found the right time. Now he got it out as quickly as he could. It was different from telling Uncle, his feelings poured out as he told her about Mum, Jasmine and the baby. In the middle of all this, Room Service arrived with the noodles, but he was so engrossed that he ignored his food. 'So you see, Sis,' he finished, 'At first I thought you two getting divorced was a good idea, but after what Anqin and I have been through, I feel differently. It's not easy for a couple to stay together but if they can, it's for the best. Plus, Liu came and begged for my help. So, even though I don't like doing this, I've come as a go-between. Can't you think again? After all, the divorce papers are not signed yet. Once they are, there's no turning back. You've been married for decades. What do you think?'

His sister did not know whether to laugh or cry. *He's grown so mature,* was the thought that passed through her mind. *Who would have thought it, a golden oriole's song issuing from the mouth of a hippopotamus?*

'Eat up your noodles,' she said.

Suddenly remembering his food, Dad pulled himself together and began to shovel it down. As he ate, he waited for Aunt Coral's response.

Aunt Coral watched him ravenously devouring the noodles, and noticed a couple of genuine white hairs sprouting from his crown. 'You need to eat more, don't get so hungry,' she advised him.

It was a casual comment, but it somehow made Dad think of the old days when they were really hungry. He laughed: 'Sis, I can't eat any more! Look at the size of my belly!'

They both looked, and had a good laugh. Finally, Aunt Coral said: 'About Liu, there's no need for you to put in a good word for him, we're divorcing and that's that.'

'Why?' Dad had not expected his sister to be so adamant.

'You see,' she began, clasping her hands around her knees, 'we haven't had feelings for each other for a very long time.

It's been like that from the start, but now, with this business of Mother's, we definitely can't go on. If we stay together until she dies and the three of us inherit, he'll benefit hugely, won't he? I'm not bothered about the rest of it, like him taking my money to keep his girlfriend, that's my lookout. But I won't have him taking what I inherit from Mother.'

Dad was staggered. This was the first he had heard of a legacy. In complete confusion, he put his bowl down on the writing desk and said: 'What are you talking about, Sis? I don't understand a word you're saying. What do you mean, "We inherit"? What's she got to leave us?'

Aunt Coral looked at him. This kid brother of hers really had no idea. Her tone softened: 'Things her father left her. Mother always said it would run to seven figures, and she would leave it to the three of us.'

Seven figures? Dad did a quick calculation on his fingers. Incredible! When had the clan ever had this much money? And how the hell had he never heard a whisper of it? 'How's that possible? And I never knew? Is it all in the factory?'

'No, this is other money,' Aunt Coral explained. 'Mother probably never told you because you were just a kid. The Xue family used to own half of West Street next to the factory once. Then the buildings were taken into public ownership, but our grandfather secretly stashed away some antiques, and they're still valuable. That's why there's so much money.'

Dad's mouth dropped open, it was like listening to a fairytale. His head was buzzing. The issue was not the money, he'd had plenty of that for a good while now, it was the fact that Gran had never once mentioned something so important to him!

'You and Zhiming both knew this?' Dad asked, and suddenly remembered that the word 'inheritance' had come up that day when he and his brother were at the Leaping Fish restaurant.

'Yes,' Aunt Coral nodded. 'It was Zhiming who told me. He said,' and she hesitated a moment, 'he said Anqin had told him.'

Aunt Coral's face was porcelain white in the glare of the lights in her hotel room. She had not aged a bit, and Dad was reminded of her days as a newscaster, when he used to sit and watch her on TV: America was about to go to war today, people would starve to death in Africa tomorrow, it would rain the next day, the sun would come out the day after. These events seemed to have nothing to do with titchy little Pingle Town but watching her gave Dad a warm glow, and he always sat glued to the screen.

What he was hearing from Aunt Coral now was a very different kind of news. There was a lump in his throat and it was not just phlegm.

He had lost all interest in talking about Aunt Coral's divorce, and she packed him off home. 'Have an early night, Shengqiang, you need the rest. Tomorrow's the dress rehearsal and there's tons to do. Stop worrying about things, get a good rest, right?'

'Right,' said Dad, and walked away. He was aware of painful twinges in his chest. He called Uncle but there was no reply. Then he remembered him saying he had someone to see, and called Zhong instead.

Zhong answered the phone at the first ring, and said cheerfully: 'So you've been let out, Shengqiang, you young prawn! I thought you'd been given a life sentence!'

Dad was walking down the steps of the Golden Leaves Hotel. The sound of that familiar voice made him want to say, *Hey, old boy, I've been made a fool of again! My mother's been hoarding a stash of money behind my back!* And there was another thing he wanted to say, *Son-of-a-bitch, Zhong, is Anqin being so nice to me because of that money? My brother and sister could do with a bit extra, but I'm not short of money, I'm rolling in it! Surely that woman wouldn't...?* And he wanted to say too, *Honestly, I can't work it out. I've been a proper idiot this time! Come out drinking with me!* But he did not dare say any of this aloud. Gran had drilled it into him: 'Mind your tongue, Shengqiang. You've got to know what things can be said and what can't be said, think about it. Never talk to outsiders about family business. You've always got to be on your guard!'

Instead he said: 'Zhong, that doctor you mentioned, the one Yao found, I think I need to see her. I've had a bit of discomfort in the chest the last couple of days.'

He heard a yelp at the other end of the line. Zhong was really concerned about Dad: 'Ai-ya! What's up, Shengqiang? You get straight home and rest, straight home, you hear me? You've got to be careful, heart disease is serious. And don't forget your medicine!'

'Yes, right, I'm on my way now. Don't shout.' Dad went on down, taking the steps one at a time. His head felt as if it was pounding in time with his steps.

'Why are you trying to tough it out?' demanded Zhong. 'Fancy not letting me tell anyone about something as important as this! Does Anqin know yet? You must tell her! I'm going to call her straightaway, and tell her to take good care of you for the next couple of days, and on Monday we'll go to Yong'An and see the doctor!'

'Ai-ya! Ai-ya!' The mention of Mum made Dad increasingly desperate. 'Don't you go telling Anqin, whatever you do, especially not the next day or two!'

'What's the matter?' Zhong was getting angry too. 'It's only your mother's birthday! You can't be wishing her long life and kick the bucket yourself!'

In spite of the brutal words, Dad knew his heart was in the

right place, and tried to mollify him: 'It's not the birthday. Something's happened between Anqin and me.'

'What thing? It's about Jasmine, isn't it? Ai-ya, Shengqiang, I didn't want to say this but you've really got it wrong this time.' Zhong was clearly getting into his stride.

But Dad was tired, dead tired. He had no more energy for chatting and just said: 'I can't tell you over the phone. Why don't you come to the factory tomorrow? We're doing the dress rehearsal, Mother will be there and the rest of the family, we can have a meal. There'll be too many people on Saturday and we won't be able to talk.'

'Sure!' Zhong sounded brisk. 'I'll come and lend a hand. Now you listen to me and take a good rest. Don't go running around doing stuff!'

Dad walked along North Street in the dark to the crossroads. His bleak mood deepened. In the old days, he knew every shop front, every lamppost, inside out. At the crossroads, he turned right along West Street. There used to be a private tutor school on this street. That was before Liberation. It was called the Min Yang Academy. Granddad used to teach there. Then it became the Pingle Town Number Two Primary School, and every afternoon, parents streamed up to its gates to collect their offspring. Just past the school was Celestials Bridge and, over the bridge, the chilli bean paste factory. After that, came Caos' Alley (there was a back entrance to the compound where the family used to live, which opened onto the alley). Diagonally opposite from Caos' Alley was Cornucopia Park and, heading out of town over the newly built Second Ring Road, was where Dad and Mum now lived.

Of course, there had been times when Dad did not want to go home but the solution was simple. He just went out drinking with his bros, or to Jasmine's place (or, if push came to shove, to Gran's). *How have I got into this mess?* He asked himself as he walked down West Street. Things could hardly be worse, and he felt painfully depressed. He dragged himself up six flights of stairs and was home.

His first thought was to go and get his pills, until he heard Mum on the phone in the sitting-room. The door squeaked as he pushed it open and she said into the phone: 'I can't talk about it now, tomorrow, OK?' And she cut the call. Dad said nothing, just took his shoes off. Mum came over: 'How come you're so late, Shengqiang? Did something keep you again? Have you had dinner? I've had mine but if you haven't, I'll warm something up for you.'

Dad paid no attention, just asked: 'Who were you talking to on the phone?'

Mum's expression did not change, but she paused for a fraction of a second, then said: 'Yufen.'

'You do get on well, you two. You don't get enough time to chat in the office, you have to carry on chatting in the evening.' Dad went to the dining table and surveyed today's left-overs. He picked up a morsel of pig's tail between finger and thumb and popped it in his mouth.

'Shengqiang! Wash your hands!' Mum squealed anxiously.

Obediently, Dad went to wash his hands. Mum re-heated his dinner and they sat down together. He ate, Mum watched him eat. 'You eat some, Anqin,' said Dad.

'I've had mine.'

Dad started with two mouthfuls of rice. When his mouth was empty, he said: 'My brother-in-law got in touch, and asked me to work on Coral, so I went to see her.'

'Uh-huh,' Mum said, then asked with every appearance of concern: 'What did she say?'

Dad shook his head, crunching on a morsel of stewed pig's tail, then said: 'Sis has made up her mind. There's nothing I can do.'

'Ai!' Mum sighed. 'Coral's a stubborn woman. Getting divorced at her age? The pair of them should sort it out and stick together.'

Dad looked at her and reached out with his chopsticks for some fish-fragrant aubergine. The conversation turned to Uncle: 'Did you hear Zhiming's found himself a woman? I asked him today, and he said there were still a few snags she had to sort out.'

'Really?' Mum looked astonished, as if it was the first she had heard of it. 'What kind of snags?'

'He didn't say much. He was being very mysterious. He just said he'd bring her along and introduce her when the time was right. Ai-ya, I don't think it matters who she is. My brother's getting on in years, he just needs to sort it.'

'Yes, right.' Mum was about to say something more, when Dad exploded. He did sell fiery chilli bean paste, after all. Throwing his chopsticks down, he said: 'Anqin! Coral told me that Mother has an inheritance and that it was you who told Zhiming and her about it! When did this happen? How come I didn't know about it? Why did you run and tell them and not me?'

'Ai-ya!' Mum was struck dumb. In the lamplight, her throat worked as if she had a fish-bone stuck in it. Finally, she pulled herself together: 'When your mother told me, she said you were so slapdash with money, that you'd spend it as soon as you got wind of it. So she just told me. How your brother and sister got wind of it, I really have no idea. Honestly, Shengqiang, it wasn't me who told them! You know I'm never in touch with them!' She looked stricken, even more shocked than Dad.

Dad ate the heart-warming food and looked at her. *Hell, it's just money,* he thought to himself. *I should cut her some slack, after all, I haven't been exactly virtuous myself. We're an old married couple, why pick a quarrel now?*

Afterwards, he was sorry he had let it drop. He went over and over it in his mind: *It was that day, wasn't it? The stupid cow knew perfectly well but she never told me. I was such an idiot I just stuffed a pair of socks in my mouth and never asked her. Everyone went behind my back and made a fool of me! Son-of-a-bitch!*

That may have been Dad's view, but Mum had another take on it. She pulled a wry face and sighed to me: 'I knew it was going to turn out like this, I told him at the start. Ai! You can say what you like but I'm not to blame! It was all your uncle's fault. OK, he wanted a girlfriend but why did he go and set the cat among the pigeons like that? There are plenty of women that would have suited him! Why did he have to go and choose her? I wanted to tell your Dad, but how could I? It's not my business after all, I'm an outsider, I can't just go saying anything I like, now can I?'

'As for that money!' she went on. 'What a difficult bunch your family are! Your Gran is ridiculous, and she never liked me. She really thought that I was so desperate for her crappy bit of money that I wouldn't dare to divorce your Dad! But I had a good think about it and decided not to. It was all because of you. If I divorced, where would I get the money for your hospital fees? So it was all because of you! Let me tell you, the Xue clan can't hold a candle to the Chens! Look at your maternal grandfather and grandmother! Every one of us Chens is highly educated and accomplished, always courteous and reasonable. But the Xues, they just have to hear about some piddling inheritance and they're rushing off to butter up the old lady. It's ridiculous! And they honestly thought I was like them!'

This was being wise after the event, so we can ignore it. That evening Mum and Dad finished their dinner, and washed and got ready for bed just like on a normal day. They had different things on their minds, how busy they were going to be with Gran's birthday celebrations at the weekend, about everyone in this great clan, about the farcical events of the last few weeks. Dad reached out for Mum's hand under the bed covers and squeezed it, and said: 'When all this fuss and bother is over, we ought to take a weekend and go and see Xingxing in the hospital, see if she's any better.' That prompted Mum to say, in a voice that hardened as she spoke: 'A few days ago, Xingxing's teacher called me to say that she's a bit better. She can write a diary now. And now we're on the subject, there's something I want to say: your mother is cruel to Xingxing. She's a kid, she just got ill, and your mother has turned her back on her.' *Ai-ya! They're impossible, the pair of them,* thought Dad. He pretended he was only half-listening: 'She's an old woman. Try and forgive her!'

And after that exchange, they both fell asleep. Outside the window, a full moon shone down and an easterly breeze blew, and there was absolute stillness.

The day of the dress rehearsal dawned. Dad drove the Audi himself to Cornucopia Court to pick up Gran. The old lady took her sweet time coming down the stairs. She looked very nice, in an ivory silk blouse, its collar embroidered with two orchid sprays, topped with a lightweight jacket in dark red, cut long and slim, very striking. Underneath, she wore a pair of tailored trousers with a fine silvery stripe and, on her feet, brand-new shiny leather shoes.

Dad, the one member of the family not intimidated by Gran, smiled and exclaimed: 'Good heavens, Mother! Are you having a birthday or going off to get married? And this isn't even the day itself! What are you going to be wearing tomorrow?'

Gran reddened at his loud vulgarity. She looked around her to make sure none of the neighbours were nearby, then tugged at his arm and admonished him: 'Shengqiang! Don't make such a song and dance! I'm not wearing anything special. I've just thrown on any old clothes and you start jabbering on!'

'Ai-ya!' Dad chuckled as he bent and helped his mother into the car. Gran settled herself and asked: 'Where's Zhu Cheng? How come you're driving?'

'I don't want him driving!' Dad started the engine. 'I told him to go home. I'm going to get myself another driver.'

'You can't do that!' exclaimed Gran in alarm, from the back seat. 'Shengqiang, how can you take a big decision like that without consulting me? When Zhu Cheng first came to work for us, it was because I agreed it with his father Zhu Shengquan, and you're letting him go without discussing it with me? That's no way to act!'

It would have been better if she'd said nothing. As it was, Dad could not stop himself answering back: 'What is there to discuss? He's just a driver. And by the way, Mother, I've just heard that you've got a considerable private fortune put away, you told Anqin about it, and Sis and my brother. It was only me you didn't tell. Why didn't you discuss that with me too?'

Gran was never slow on the uptake. She understood immediately that there was an ill wind blowing today. She gave a laugh: 'Who told you about this?'

'Sis,' Dad sounded gloomy as he turned the steering wheel. 'Is it true, Mother? Where have you been hoarding such a lot of money? I don't believe you told them and you didn't tell me. I don't believe it.'

Gran looked fondly at the back of her son's head, round and sleekly black, and snorted with laughter. 'Shengqiang, why are you in such a sulk? You just said you didn't believe it!'

Dad could not help turning to look at Gran. 'So is it true or not? And how come Sis says she and Zhiming and Anqin all know about it?'

'She's got a big mouth, that wife of yours!' Gran shook her head. 'Think about it, you certainly gave me a problem when you had a turn in the apartment upstairs, and ended up in hospital. It looked really bad! So embarrassing! Anqin came running over to see me and how was I supposed to explain it away? It was mortifying! I'm eighty years old, I shouldn't be wiping your bum still!'

'So I thought about the kind of person Anqin is,' said Gran, sounding as pleased with herself as if she had won the jackpot. 'She puts on airs about her County Party Committee family, but she's just an ordinary Pingle Town woman, petty bourgeois through and through. Just think back to when you got married. She was going to have you, come what may, obviously because she was convinced we had money. So, right, I talked to her and I told her we had funds squirrelled away, running into seven figures at least, and if she waited until my birthday was over, then I would give the money out. I told her, I'm an old woman, I don't need it. I just want my children to behave decently, and I'm giving my money to whoever puts on the best show. I certainly hope you and Shengqiang will keep up appearances, I said. Of course, you're going to have your rows, but I don't want you to divorce. We're all family, we mustn't be the laughing stock of the town.'

Dad's hands quivered in shock and he almost hit the horn by mistake. He stopped outside the chilli bean paste factory and waited to turn in through the entrance. He looked at his mother. She was as cheerful as if she had just eaten sweet steamed pork, and he could not think what to say. When push came to shove, she was his mother, and protective of her son. She had dreamed up this fantastic lie, just in order to stop her son being divorced, to calm her daughter-in-law down, and to salvage her family's reputation!

'Mother,' Dad said, full of remorse, as he drove through the gates, his hands on the same steering wheel that Zhu Cheng had had his hands on, 'I've given you a hell of a time over this business. I'll never do it again.'

'Don't mention it!' Gran was all generosity. 'It's all water under the bridge! Let's have a happy time!'

And there was plenty to be happy about. It was a warm April day. The sun shone down from a sky dotted with wispy clouds and there was blossom everywhere. Brightly-coloured banners and flags fluttered in the breeze. Gran looked at the scene through the car window and beamed: 'You've done a wonderful job, wonderful, really wonderful!'

The younger generation really had no idea how devastating it had been, decades ago, when she took her old father's arm and led him out of the gates. Then, they were ruined and dispossessed but finally their luck had turned and she could bring her son back in again. She got out of the car and everyone crowded around to greet her. They were all smiles now, no one dared say a bad word about her. She walked into the fermentation yard, transformed beyond recognition, and stepped onto the stage, bedecked with scarlet satin and complete with a backcloth painted with a flowery landscape like a traditional watercolour. It was inscribed with the words: 'In celebration of one hundred years of the Mayflower Chilli Bean Paste Factory'. Gran glued her hand to Dad's.

'Mother, let's go and sit in the boardroom until the others arrive,' said Dad.

Gran composed herself, and followed Dad to the boardroom. Zeng, the office manager, bustled over, eagerly proffering two cups of tea. 'How are you, madam? Good morning, Mr Xue!'

'Yes, yes, good morning!' Dad waved him out of the room and sipped his tea comfortably. 'You wait and see, Mother, it's going to be a brilliant programme. Coral and Zhiming have really put a lot of work into it!'

The minutes ticked by, and people began to arrive: the lighting men, the tuners, the dancers, the calligraphers, the martial artists, the poetry reciters, the stand-up comics and the clapper-talk comics. Old Chen Xiuliang and Zhong and

Aunt Coral came into the boardroom. Surprisingly, Uncle Liu, Aunt Coral's no-good, soon-to-be-ex, came trotting along behind her. Dad looked at him, but Uncle Liu paid no attention and busied himself fetching Aunt Coral a cup of tea, as if he had forgotten about the favour Dad had done him.

That was fine by Dad. Nothing surprised him anymore, certainly not Liu blowing hot and cold. Everyone was greeting each other and chatting, sitting down to cups of tea, cracking sunflower seeds between their teeth and snacking on fruit. It was as rowdy as a tea party. Just as soon as Uncle arrived, the show could begin.

They waited and waited, increasingly bored. Still no Uncle. 'Where's Zhiming got to?' said Aunt Coral. 'Why's he not here yet?'

Before Dad could answer, Gran said cheerfully: 'He called me this morning, and said he had a surprise in store for me today. Maybe he's gone to get it ready.'

Dad reckoned he had worked it out. *That brother of mine knows how to organize things. He's quite right to introduce his girlfriend today, then she can be at the big bash tomorrow!*

Thinking about the bash reminded him that the birthday scrolls were still lying rolled up in the office upstairs. He called the office manager in. 'Bring them down, and the old lady can enjoy them,' he said. 'Let's make her happy and hang them right away.'

Much later, when he thought back to what happened next, Dad still did not really understand. He slapped his thigh and told me angrily: 'She looked if she'd seen a damned ghost! You can never tell what's going through your Gran's head!'

Everyone exclaimed enthusiastically as they perused the scrolls one by one. They got to Chen Xiuxiao's. 'It's good!' 'It's … er … interesting!' 'It's beautifully written!' Dad looked proud. He gave the scroll a little shake and said to Chen Xiuliang: '*Shifu*, this is my father-in-law's work.'

The older generation in Pingle Town all knew that old Chen and Mum's father were cousins, although one had prospered and the other was poor and they saw little of each other. Still, they were family, and the old man stubbed out his cigarette and went over to admire the scroll. It read:

Long life to our distinguished Madame May,
As we celebrate her eightieth birthday
Long life to the Mayflower Factory,
Where the fragrant vats embrace the stalk of longevity.

'Shengqiang, the old man's certainly got some talent!' said Zhong. 'He's gone to considerable trouble over this. Very interesting!'

Dad agreed and looked at Gran, expecting similar words of appreciation. But something seemed to be amiss. His mother had gone pale.

Gran was, in fact, not just pale but white as a sheet. She leapt to her feet, making them jump out of their skins.

'What's up, Mother?' Dad exclaimed.

Gran said nothing, just pushed her chair back and rushed from the room.

Dad looked at Aunt Coral, Aunt Coral looked at Dad, and Uncle Liu looked around the room. Zhong, as an outsider, did not know where to look. 'Mother!' Dad shouted after her departing figure, but before he could follow her, he felt a restraining hand on his arm.

It was Aunt Coral. She held onto him and shouted at Chen: 'Go on then! What are you waiting for?' The old man leapt to his feet and was off.

Dad had never heard Aunt Coral be so brusque with anyone, and it gave him such a fright he felt as if he'd been kicked in the ribs. 'What's up, Sis?' he demanded.

'Mind your own business. Let Chen go,' said Aunt Coral, reading the scroll again.

'What's the matter?' Dad re-read it too but could see no

reason to get upset.

'Yes! What it's all about, Coral?' asked Uncle Liu.

'Aunt Coral ignored him and turned to Dad: 'Shengqiang, we can't use this scroll, you put it away. If your father-in-law asks, just make up some excuse.'

There were no flies on Dad. He knew Gran was angry and he was going to stick to his guns until he found out why. He gripped Aunt Coral's arm. But Zhong said: 'Listen to your sister, Shengqiang. The most important thing it to keep your mother happy. After all, it's her eightieth birthday.'

There were four of them left in the room, and it was two (Zhong and Aunt Lily) against one. Dad didn't count that brother-in-law of his, who was just a waste of space. Dad was desperately anxious; he had no idea where Gran had gone or why. Then he thought of Uncle Duan. 'Where's my brother? Let's see what he says!'

Talk of the devil, no more than a few seconds later, and while they were all still waiting for Chen to bring Gran back, Uncle Duan slipped into the boardroom, leading a woman with him. He looked carefully around and asked: 'Where's Mother? Isn't she here yet?'

There was a stunned silence. Just at this moment, the last thing on anyone's mind was getting Gran back. Dad's eyes, in particular, were riveted on his brother's companion. Discomfited by his stare, she ventured: 'Hello, Shengqiang.'

Dad was lost for words. *Oh, brother, this time you've gone too far!* he said to himself.

In the end, it was Zhong who stepped into the breach and, clearing his throat circumspectly, said: 'What are you doing here, Qin?'

It was Qin, who ran the Sichuan pepper shop (at least she had until a few days ago). And here she was in the Mayflower Factory boardroom.

Qin said nothing, just looked at Uncle Duan. He took her

hand. 'We're going to get married,' he said. 'I've brought her to introduce her to you.'

Introduce her! Dad still could not think of anything to say, except possibly, *You've certainly picked an odd moment to drop that bombshell!*

'I should have told you before,' Uncle Duan said quietly as if he could read Dad's thoughts. 'Only Qin's divorce was still going through. We didn't want to make things any more complicated so we've kept quiet about it all this time.'

'So Zhiming,' this was Aunt Coral. 'When you called to say you'd made up your mind and you were coming back to Pingle Town to take back what was rightfully yours, this was what you were talking about?'

'Yes,' said Uncle Duan, squeezing Qin's hand tightly, but with a degree of confidence. He looked across at Dad: 'Mother covered things up when you messed up big time and ended up in hospital, Shengqiang. How can she object now? Qin and I were torn apart but we've never stopped loving each other, but now we're determined to be together. She can't possibly disapprove, can she?'

Don't bring me into this, thought Dad. He blamed himself for saying he'd back Uncle up, come what may, and now, he wanted nothing more than to go and bury his head in the sand of Clearwater Creek. 'I just fainted and had a little spell in hospital. And how did you find out about that anyway?' he demanded. 'I can't believe you were so upset it brought you running back home!'

To properly get to the bottom of all this, I needed to ask every one of the people involved, without missing anyone out.

I started with Mum. She looked aggrieved: 'I told Yufen about it, but I swore her to silence. How could I know she'd go and blab? I didn't want my husband's disgraceful behaviour getting out. Who told her to go spreading it around?'

Yufen protested. 'Well I couldn't possibly know that Qin had this up her sleeve! I mean, we've been friends for years! She never said a word to me about having a fling with Zhiming. I told her about Shengqiang, and she turns round and tells Zhiming everything. I can't stop their bedroom gossip!'

To be truthful, this was a bit more than gossip. This was betrayal, both Dad going behind Mum's back, and Uncle Duan doing the same with another man's wife. Uncle Duan had had to stay away from home for two years just to keep the lid on it.

The day Qin leaked the news about Dad, Qin's husband was out on deliveries. Uncle Duan drove over and picked her up and took her to the White Hibiscus Hotel on the edge of town. As they lay back exhausted from their lovemaking, Qin remembered: 'Hey, Zhiming,' she said. 'Something's happened with your brother.'

'What's happened?'

Qin gave him a colourful version of the story, even though she'd only heard it third-hand. Dad was just really unlucky, she'd told him. He'd installed his mistress in the apartment right over his mother's head and when he fainted in her bed, there was only his mother to rescue him. Mum had rushed off the hospital in a fury, all ready to tear the lovebirds limb from limb, but Gran had intervened. She dug out a huge stash of money, her private savings, and showed it to Mum. 'Don't make a fuss, and just let me have my eightieth birthday,' she told her, 'and I'll divide this up between all of you.'

Uncle Duan had been too embarrassed to show his feelings in front of his girlfriend, but back home, he really let fly.

'Your Gran let Shengqiang get away with murder!' he said with barely-controlled fury. 'Your Dad's had it good all those years, she's given him everything, and what's she done for me? Qin and I really loved each other, the only thing was she got pregnant before we could marry. And see what she did to us.

And now look at Shengqiang! It must have been so hard for your Mum to put up with it, look what a shambles he made of things, and your Gran was going to let him get away with it! And what about all the money she's going to throw at him? Not that it's the money that counts, it's our feelings! What have I got? Sweet nothing! I'm in my forties, I've spent all these years in a mouldy old apartment on campus, earning peanuts, I have to moonlight to make a living. I've never married, I've got no one at home, there's not even a bite of cold supper waiting for me at night! All my life I've had to put up with this crap, and all for nothing! I don't want a fight, mind you. It's nothing to do with the money. It's my feelings that are hurt!'

Aunt Coral was worried about him. 'Your uncle's a proud man,' she said, 'he was in such a state he phoned me and told me the whole story. He was all for going to have it out with Gran, but I said, 'What are you making a fuss about? Mother will leave her money and the family factory to whomever she wants. No one in this family has ever got the better of Mother.' He was furious with your Dad, but I said, 'He's not had an easy time of it either, he's put up with Mother all these years. No one else would have.'

'Besides,' Aunt Coral's voice softened. 'There's one thing I really admire your Dad for. He's a real good-time guy. No one's going to stop him having his fun, and to hell with the consequences.'

Just now, things were beginning to get out of hand. There was uproar in the boardroom. All six of them was talking at once, airing old grievances and arguing furiously. Uncle Duan was saying that he was going to marry Qin. Qin was choking back sobs as she tried to talk. Zhong was urging the pair of them not to make hasty decisions, after all it was Gran's eightieth and they really shouldn't upset her. 'Zhiming,' Aunt Coral said judiciously, 'You've put up with it so long, surely you can wait another couple of days. If Qin goes home now, then in a couple of days' time, you can raise it with Mother and we'll all back you up.'

'No way, Sis!' exclaimed Uncle Duan. 'This has gone on for so many years, why should I beg for her blessing when I want to get married? Why do you think I picked today to bring Qin to introduce to you all? It's because it's Mother's eightieth and we can celebrate as a whole family!' He gripped Qin's shoulders. 'I talked to Shengqiang about this a few days ago, and he said he'd back me up. So I told Qin to finalize the divorce as quick as she could while you were all here so I could bring her to meet you all. I did this with the best of intentions, and if Mother's angry about it, well, that's her lookout.'

Dad suddenly realized he'd been made the fall guy. *Never in my fucking wildest dreams did I think you were talking about Qin!* he thought. He swallowed his fury, however: 'Zhiming, it's not that I don't support you, in fact I'm delighted you're going to get married, but you really should wait until the birthday celebrations are over. Please don't put a spanner in the works now!'

'Shengqiang!' exclaimed Uncle Duan rudely, totally unaware of the effort it had cost his brother to get those few words out. 'That's the pot calling the kettle black! Haven't you done enough to upset Mother? Zhong! Sis! Liu! Be honest! Who's done most to upset Mother, Shengqiang or me?'

Just then, Uncle Liu, getting the wrong end of the stick as usual, jumped in with: 'Too right! Spare a thought for your big brother, Shengqiang! He's over forty, he should be able to get married if he wants. They're both single, so why would your mother possibly object?'

'Liu Qukang!' shouted Aunt Coral. 'This has nothing to do with you!'

'Why doesn't it?' her soon-to-be-ex-husband was

disgruntled. 'Aren't I part of the family?'

'No, you are not!' said Aunt Coral. Even in front of Zhong, the 'outsider', she did not bother to hide her contempt for him. 'Our divorce is almost finalized, you have nothing to say in this!'

'Coral Xue!' the old rogue wasn't giving up that easily. 'I have every right to speak until the day we're divorced. It was you who invited me to your mother's birthday and asked me to pretend nothing had happened. So I can't speak? Well, if you don't want me to speak, I'm off right now!'

'Go, then! Go!' Aunt Coral pointed towards the boardroom door. 'Off you go right now! And don't delude yourself that I'm scared of you because my mother's here. She's a reasonable woman. You've been keeping a mistress, and you think she won't let me get a divorce?'

'What?' exclaimed Zhong. 'What are you talking about, Coral? Has that man had the nerve to keep a mistress? How long for? Shengqiang, did you know this? Why didn't you tell me?'

What's it got to do with you? Arselicker! thought Dad to himself, glaring at Zhong but not daring to say it out loud. Besides, he was too tired to talk. The room was swimming before his eyes. He was worried about where Gran had gone and even more worried she might come back to this uproar. He wanted Uncle Duan and Qin out, he wanted to keep Uncle Liu here. He only had one pair of hands, but he was going to make sure Gran had a good birthday party, even if it killed him. Suddenly, he felt a lightning jolt to his heart. Pain tore through him with an intensity that made him tremble.

Son-of-a-bitch! I forgot my pills last night. The thought flashed through his mind.

Gran had taken refuge by the flowerbed behind the bamboo

thicket next to the fermentation yard, and was sadly wiping her eyes and thinking how harshly life had treated her, when she heard a rustling. Someone was coming.

It was old Chen Xiuliang, of course. Who else but he would know that Gran would hide here? He put his hand on her shoulder. 'May,' he said, 'don't take it so hard. My cousin's a silly old fart, just ignore him.'

'He's not a silly old fart! You saw what a good couplet he wrote, he doesn't miss a trick!' As soon as Gran opened her mouth, she was spitting with fury. 'Xiulang, I've always treated you with respect. What happened between us, we went into it with our eyes open. Then it was over and we drew a line under it. You tell me, how could your cousin have known about it, and written it into the couplet? How could he show me up in front of all my children? How could he be so evil?'

'Ai-ya!' said Xiulang with a sigh. 'It was all my fault, we were drinking once and I had too much and I told him. It was all such a long time ago. I mean, we're old, and you're a widow, and Coral's grown up and has children and a grandchild of her own. What does it matter now? What was he thinking of?'

Anyway, that's enough of that. Gran had always upheld the decencies and lived her life accordingly. 'Don't you go writing that down!' she instructed me. 'That scroll's going to be the death of me!' There was no one in the family would have dare⸍ make a squeak in response to such a declaration, no one, t⸍ is, except Dad. Only he was thick-skinned enough to ⸍ his hands together in a gesture of old-fashioned respe⸍ say: 'Mother, who would dare be the death of yo⸍ our esteemed elderly ancestor! May you live for te⸍ years!'

Gran laughed out loud at the thought. O⸍ children, Shengqiang had always been clo⸍ wiped her tears, and she and Chen Xiuliar⸍ past times. Suddenly, terrified cries were ⸍

block. 'Mr Xue! What's happened to Mr Xue?' 'Shengqiang!'

'There's been an accident!' Gran had weathered enough storms in her life to know when something was seriously wrong. An icy fear clutched at her heart, she got to her feet and hurried out of the thicket. All the factory staff were clustered in the fermentation yard. Uncle Duan, Uncle Liu and Zhong were coming out of the office block and across the compound, carrying Dad between them, with Aunt Coral following behind. She pushed people out of the way, commanded: 'Give him a bit of space, let him breathe!' Everyone was as white as a sheet, not just Dad. 'Zhiming! You can't tell me you didn't know!' Zhong was saying to Uncle Duan, 'I told you! You knew he had heart trouble, that syndrome, whatever they call it, it's dangerous. Why did you make him angry?'

Uncle Duan looked awkward, then said: 'I didn't want to make him angry. Someone call the doctor, quick, has anyone called the doctor?'

The bookkeeper, the office manager, everyone crowded around, genuinely concerned for Dad, even those who normally got the rough edge of his tongue. There were too many of them, all standing in Gran's way, for her to notice Qin among them. Gran was unsteady on her feet, and felt a little dizzy too.

Chen Xiuliang took her arm. 'Go on, quick! Go and see him!'

Now they were really concerned about Dad: Uncle Duan called for an ambulance, Zhong asked the office manager for a wet towel and propped Dad's head up. And Aunt Coral, her eyes reddened, her lips quivering like leaves on a tree, said: 'How did Shengqiang get like this? He always looked fine!'

'What do you mean, fine?' Zhong hissed. 'He's been like his for a long time, his last birthday he had a turn. I had a at him until he went to the doctor, and the doctor said it s heart disease. I wanted him to have an operation but he wouldn't. I told him to lay off the cigarettes, the booze and the women, and he wouldn't do that either, and he refused to let me tell you about it. What a prawn, drinking and smoking himself into an early grave, but he wouldn't listen to me!'

'It's going to be fine,' said Gran, parting the crowds as if she were in a maize field, and wading through. She glanced at her youngest. 'Just hang on, Shengqiang, till the doctor gets here! Just hang on!'

You think Dad was really unconscious? Not a bit of it. He was wide-awake, he could hear everyone squawking away, and it was pissing him off.

Can't you pipe down a bit? You're giving me a headache, was what he wanted to say but no words came out.

Gran, Uncle Duan, Aunt Coral, Uncle Liu, Zhong and old Chen Xiuliang were packed so tight around him that he felt as he was being squeezed between handfuls of chopsticks.

Ghosts from the past passed before his eyes with a flurry and a whoosh. He was a child, he was growing up, he had his first job, he was screwing Baby Girl, he was marrying Mum, he was a father, he wanted a divorce, then suddenly his daughter was going off the rails and dropping out of school, he was starting to rake in the money, rake it in big time, and screwing one girl after another, so many he couldn't keep count of them.

I've been so bad, he thought dismally. *I'm really sorry, everyone, I really am.*

Dad was convinced he was going to die. But as the blood clogged, his mind became crystal clear. For just a few moments, he foamed at the mouth, and saw many things: all the creatures of the earth and the air, the whys and wherefores of people's lives down the ages flashed before his eyes. The Pingle Town folk had always been the same, for centuries, for millennia. Plus ça change, as they say. His blood may have been bunged up, but these truths trickled out.

Over the next few years, this is more or less how it will pan out: Zhong will continue as Dad's assiduous drinking partner until, two years on, his wife Yao gets pregnant. A life sentence is handed down and Zhong just has to knuckle under meekly. Dad is annoyed, but has to accept that the drinking days, for these two, are over. He'll have to go out with Gao Tao and his other bros instead. He lets Zhu Cheng go but then Gran puts her foot down and insists that they have a reputation to keep up and she made a promise to Zhu Cheng's father that they can't go back on. So Zhu comes back as his driver, looking hangdog. Dad is angry at first, but gets over it. After all, they're both men, they understand each other. As for Jasmine, Dad will meet her one more time. Soon she will be leaving the apartment he rented for her, so he decides to take her out to dinner. Jasmine's eyes redden as she sits down and she says: 'I'm so sorry, Shengqiang, I had to say it was yours, I thought at least that way the child would have someone to look after it.' Dad, looking at her shrunken belly, feels sorry and not a little guilty. He pulls out his wallet and gives her a stash of notes. Then there is Aunt Coral, who will go ahead with her divorce. Gran is furious, and keeps moaning: 'What did I ever do to deserve a daughter like that? I always said she was the most obedient out of all of you and now look, she's giving me no peace, married to such a fine man and insisting she wants a divorce. I'm so furious, she'll be the death of me!' Of course no one will be the death of Gran, as everyone knows perfectly well, and Aunt Coral, once divorced, puts her resentment behind her, makes it up with Gran and comes back to visit every couple of weeks. Gran enjoys the visits and gradually stops grumbling. It is Uncle Duan who's the most resourceful: silver-tongued as ever, he skilfully works on his mother until she finally gives a nod of agreement to the marriage. He and Qin hold a lavish wedding banquet arranged by Dad in the grand surroundings of the Prince's Mansion Hotel, with everyone in town in attendance. Uncle Duan is so busy totting up the contents of the red envelope gifts, he has no time to complain that the occasion is tacky. Dad's *shifu*, Chen Xiuliang, introduces the only note of sadness. The old man has just smoked too many cigarettes; they consume his lungs, then his liver, then his stomach, and his heart. He wastes away day by day until he is thin as a rake, and all the tonics and treatment Dad buys him can't bring him back, and before New Year three years later, he will pass away. Dad is inconsolable, and Gran takes the opportunity to lecture him about his own lifestyle and this time he listens and cuts down on his smoking and drinking.

As for Dad, he just has to take life as it comes. After he loses his Jasmine, he doesn't go looking for anyone else, and is in low spirits for about six months. He realizes he needs to take care of himself and gets a pacemaker fitted. But, when all's said and done, you can't put a wildfire out for good and, by springtime the next year, as the sap is rising, lust blossoms again. Rather to his surprise, his new squeeze is Wang Yandan, the woman Zhong tried to introduce to his brother Zhiming. They turn out to be really well suited, soul mates in fact. Finally he has been tamed. He no longer plays around with other women, and even the brothels of Fifteen Yuan Street rarely see him. In the factory, he trains up two young marketing managers, and no longer has to play the escort hostess himself. As for Gran, Dad is never so presumptuous as to laugh, even to himself, at the way she hoaxed them over the 'inheritance'. *Unbelievable! Certain greedy people fell for it, hook, line and sinker!* In general, in the family, he senses without quite knowing why, that things have settled down. Mum knows all about his affair with Wang Yandan but says not a word. She goes to work, she plays *mahjong*, she reads her novels, she visits her father like a dutiful daughter, and when she wants to go shopping, she uses

Dad's credit card. No one gossips about them because, after all, she is the only woman in Pingle Town who is fortunate enough to have found a husband as rich and generous as Dad.

But all this is some time in the future. Right now, in the present, Dad needs to wake up so that everyone can stop dripping snot and tears all over him.

And so he wakes up, and mutters: 'Ai-ya! ...'

There are flustered cries of: 'Shengqiang! Shengqiang's come round!'

'Ai-ya, keep your voices down,' his voice, clearer now, gathers strength. 'There's nothing wrong with me, don't shout, everything's fine. Let's just get Mother's eightieth over with....'

TRANSLATOR'S ACKNOWLEDGMENTS

A TRANSLATION IS never an unassisted birth. In this case, there were several midwives who each played a key role at different stages and to whom I owe enormous thanks. First I am grateful to Ou Ning, literature and arts activist extraordinaire, who introduced me to Yan Ge and published my translation of Chapter One in his ground-breaking magazine Chutzpah. Second, my thanks go to Roh-Suan Tung, who brought *The Chilli Bean Paste Clan* to life as a book, and to PEN Translates, who part-funded the translation. And third, my thanks go to the author herself. Yan Ge went above and beyond the call of duty in examining and discussing the English text with me. *The Chilli Bean Paste Clan* is deeply rooted in the culture and language of a small Sichuan town, and at the most basic level, I needed to be sure I had understood the dialect (her explanations were exemplary). Then there were the interactions between the protagonists. This family is a veritable maelstrom of conflictual emotions and seething resentments. Take, for example, Dad's love-hate relationship with his brother and his mother. We had lengthy discussions about whether my English had captured the degrees of animosity with sufficient subtlety! Yan Ge's writing is highly allusive, and that quality could not be lost in translation. One area in which we almost (but not quite) came to blows was in translating Dad's colourful obscenities. Simply sprinkling the text with the F word was not enough. (The number of F words in the English is actually exactly the same as in the original Chinese, I neither added nor took away.) The key word here is 'colourful'. Frequently, English swearing can sound quite pale, so I had to dig deep into thesauri to find a sufficient variety of rude words to express Dad's frustrations and fury. Author-translator discussions like this can get quite bruising, but I can say with perfect sincerity that I feel very privileged to have worked with an author whose knowledge of English is so good and who so painstakingly tried to ensure that I got things right. Any remaining inadequacies in the translation are, of course, my own responsibility.

NICKY HARMAN, 2018

Lightning Source UK Ltd.
Milton Keynes UK
UKHW04f2203161018
330635UK00002B/29/P